I Won't Be a Nun

Michaela Francis

Matador
9 Priory Business Park,
Wistow Road, Kibworth Beauchamp,
Leicestershire. LE8 0RX
Tel: 0116 279 2299
Email: books@troubador.co.uk
Web: www.troubador.co.uk/matador
Twitter: @matadorbooks

ISBN 978 1838593 278

British Library Cataloguing in Publication Data.
A catalogue record for this book is available from the British Library.

Printed and bound in Great Britain by 4edge Limited
Typeset in 11pt Minion Pro by Troubador Publishing Ltd, Leicester, UK

Matador is an imprint of Troubador Publishing Ltd

Contents

1

The story begins

Standing at the traffic lights on a cold November morning, Sonia held back her tears, feeling lost because she had had no idea that what had happened in her relationship would create the feelings that she was experiencing. She began to walk across the road as the green man appeared on the traffic light display. Her focus was to just walk with her head down, aware of the traffic light beeping sound alerting blind people that it was safe to begin walking. She was not concerned if the cars approaching had come to a stop. She could feel her emotions become more apparent as the crowd of people on the opposite side of the road drew closer. Sonia walked as she watched the different footwear approaching, manoeuvring, avoiding collision. The people approaching her appeared to be more motivated and determined to find a gap with haste as they shoved past to get to where they were going. Some looked tense, clenching themselves with hands in their pockets, pressing their arms tight to their sides as they bore the cold. This didn't prevent one or two slightly banging against her as they shuffled past. Sonia just wanted to get away, to find solitude.

Sonia lifted her head and also began to manoeuvre, seeking a gap between people, avoiding touching anyone as she stepped off the island between the two roads. She moved swiftly towards the pathway with no final destination in mind as the traffic light display counted down, 04, 03, and 02 flashing in white. She manoeuvred diagonally to get free as quickly as possible. As Sonia approached a girl walking opposite her, they mirrored each other's movements just before she reached the curb, Sonia felt frustrated and had to stop. As she sighed, having to change direction to pass, she gazed into the girl's eyes, causing her feelings to become overwhelming, lifting from her stomach and building a pressure on her chest. Her eyes welled up as her face felt like curling inwards. A feeling of numbness on her cheeks and lips became more apparent as the feeling began to creep up around her nose.

It was like her face was becoming paralysed. There was nothing that she could do to stop this feeling and the sensation of helplessness made it worse for her.

She could not let go of the image of her ex-partner Gregory as she gazed down at the path, holding back her tears. She couldn't relate to the reason why she felt emotionally this way because this wasn't how she felt before their meeting. Sonia was quite content being single, enjoying her life as she discovered this beautiful, vibrant new city.

As Sonia reached the footpath, she decided to walk down the less congested pathway to the left so that she could compose herself and take her thoughts to finding a distraction. The distraction was a shoe shop with a bright red, high-heeled pair of shoes. The red shoes were standing on the display at an angle amongst all the other different styles. They had a six-inch pure heel, finished in a sultry red gloss reflecting the bright lights from the ceiling as they sat on a white veneer surrounding for the shop display.

She found herself staring at the shoes with a blank mind until she noticed her reflection in the shop window. She had a moment of connecting with herself, realising how tired she was while noticing her pale complexion as she needed to eat, feeling weak in energy. She could see her breath exhale as it blended with the cold air, reflecting on the shop's glass front window. The day seemed to have passed quickly and she had not eaten because of the sick feeling within. Leaving the shop front, she began walking again, confused, until she reached Regent's Park. She stopped and stood with a gaze, staring at the golden brown leaves lying on the ground that had fallen from the trees all along the pathway in front of her. There were leaves strewn across the path as she walked on them in her flat shoes. Her shoes had seen better days as one was showing a gaping hole along the ridge of her left foot. She could feel her tights, wet and cold, but this didn't faze her. She had so much on her mind that this was the least important issue to sort out.

The sun pierced the grey clouds and a rainbow formed in the distance as the misty rain swirled with the light breeze. This brought a glimmer of hope to her. Sonia felt that her thoughts were being listened to as she kept asking God for help. She stood staring at the rainbow as it filtered into the clouds.

Reaching into her handbag, she pulled out a packet of tissues. Opening the wrapper, Sonia carefully took a single tissue and patted her eyes carefully as they began to weep. She tried to avoid her eye mascara. As she tapped lightly with the tissue to dry around her eyes, she began to wonder why this had happened. She began to blend more with herself as her conscious mind shifted inwards as she processed images and memories of Gregory. Sonia just wanted to be held. She just wanted to feel appreciated and to be acknowledged, to feel wanted.

The feeling of loneliness drew closer as she reached into her left-hand side coat pocket to take out her mobile phone. She knew that there were no messages as she entered her passcode. All that she wanted was to receive a text from Gregory. Sonia was resisting contacting him because she didn't want to give in while feeling lost and confused. But she very much wanted to. This made her more frustrated and she began to feel alone and unwanted.

The rainbow began to disappear as the cold damp air started to draw closer and the sun faded into the twilight sky. As Sonia walked, not knowing where she was going, the street lights began to switch on, appearing red as they heated, reaching their full illumination, then calming to an orange glow.

The evening seemed to disappear quickly as she walked and walked but avoided eating as the feeling remained in her stomach. Sonia felt miserable and very down within herself. She didn't want to reach out to her friends so she remained contemplating her life on her own.

It was a year since they had seen each other. They had parted ways because circumstances were beyond their control and this created frustration for both parties, resulting in stress within their relationship. Their union was something very special and they both knew this, causing them both to miss each other constantly during the year apart as it passed.

London was their chosen destination to settle down and start a life together. This didn't happen due to the breakup, but both managed to move to London the year they were apart to find themselves meeting once again.

Sonia was an independent, strong-minded woman who knew what she wanted and wouldn't be taken for a fool.

However, when it came to relationships she tended to daydream and try to make situations happen rather than allow them to develop naturally. Sonia was a real thinker; she would analyse everything and worry terribly, causing inner frustration and emotional chaos. Time was on her mind as she had reached her mid-thirties and wanted to have a family.

2

Prior to their meeting

It was just on the off chance that Sonia text Gregory to say hello. Sonia was not busy in work and she was scrolling through her contact list when Gregory's name appeared. Sonia glanced at it and thought to herself, *Nah, I won't message him*, but her curiosity got the better of her, so she began to write a message. She wondered if he had met anybody else as she was writing to him. *Hi Gregory, I hope you are well and happy out!* ☺ *I'm in London.*

Gregory was just finishing up at work and was about to start the engine of his car to begin his journey home. He took his phone that was sitting on the passenger seat and read the message, wondering whether or not to reply, but he knew Sonia could see that he had read the message. A few minutes passed as he sat staring at the message, so he replied, *Hi Sonia, I'm great.*

How are you? Gregory saw that she appeared online, and Sonia replied in an instant. *I'm great too. Just in London, walking after work.* Gregory wasn't aware that Sonia had moved to London until she had messaged him and this made him curious. He replied, *When did you move over or are you visiting?* Sonia replied, *Let's meet and we can talk. Just about to see a client.* Gregory knew then that she was living in London. He began to wonder if Sonia had met someone.

They both agreed to meet again after sending several messages between them. The meeting point was at Oxford Circus Tube Station at 3pm the following Saturday. It was now Monday evening.

Gregory started his engine and began driving home, thinking about Sonia. He thought about the times they had spent together and the places and countries that they had visited. Several times during the week as Saturday drew closer, Gregory was puzzled with thoughts of why he should or should not meet her again. He scanned through photos that he had saved on his phone, jogging up memories of the times they had spent together.

He was fighting his heart with his mind. His heart was curious as he only wanted the best for her, he still hadn't let go as his love for her was still very much evident, but he also missed the fun times. His mind, on the other hand, was against it as he didn't want to go through all the drama again.

He decided he would attend anyway as he had nothing to lose in doing so. Curiosity was eating away at him, plus the fact he couldn't stop thinking about her. Gregory was single and remained this way as he just didn't feel like dating. The idea of starting all over again and getting to know someone else didn't appeal to him at all.

Saturday arrived and it was 2.55pm. Gregory stood leaning against one of the building's entrance doors as crowds of people jostled past each other to enter or exit the Underground at

Oxford Circus. The Underground had one entrance that was near to where he was standing and an exit around the corner. Some of the people who had gathered were also waiting to cross the road. It was quite congested where he was standing but he enjoyed people watching.

Nothing about Sonia had changed. She was never on time and this was no exception. She left Gregory standing for forty-five minutes in the cold. He stood with his back against the wall as he admired the architecture of the buildings opposite. He gazed at his watch as he began to wonder if she was coming at all. Standing still, feeling the cold penetrate his clothes, he could feel his legs twitch and ache. The only satisfaction he had was the warm air rushing out of the tube station from time to time.

Gregory took his phone from his pocket and text Sonia *Hello* as he was tired of waiting and contemplating leaving. He sent the text as he was going to leave without contacting her, but he began to feel something wasn't right. He knew that she was fighting her own feelings and that she was tinkering about in her mind with the idea of whether or not she wanted to meet. She replied to his text some minutes later. *Be there in 10, I'm just around the corner!* He waited another forty minutes, getting more and more frustrated as he kept looking at his phone to see if he had received anything. As he looked one more time, he received another text from her. *Where are you?* Looking at his phone, he was pretty annoyed and wondered what the hell he was doing waiting. As he began to reply she arrived, sneaking up beside him and standing still. He looked up and turned to his right to see her smile.

He was feeling awkward but relieved that she had come and wondered whether or not they should hug. He moved forward and embraced her anyway. Sonia stood rigid as though more concerned that he might knock the hat she was wearing off her head. She was wearing an elegant winter vintage flower felt cloche bucket-style red hat. They held each other for a moment and Sonia pulled Gregory closer just as Gregory was beginning to pull away, pressing her head alongside his. He felt her warmth through the heavy coat he was wearing and smelled the perfume that he recognised. Gregory had bought this type of perfume for Sonia months before they broke up. They moved apart, both slightly confused, and stood looking at each other. They peered into one another's eyes in silence. Gregory felt drawn to Sonia and he had an urge to kiss her.

Sonia began to chat and the feeling Gregory had was strange; he felt it grow more and more. He was getting warm inside and it felt like he was beginning to sweat a little. It was like his skin was on fire around his stomach, chest and arms.

Sonia asked, "What shall we do?"Gregory said, "I am hungry and would like to get something to eat before I die."Sonia pulled her phone from her pocket and said, "Okay, grumpy," as she smiled, entered her passcode, clicked on an app and began looking for restaurants nearby. As she was doing this she began to walk and talk, flicking through different restaurants around the area as they appeared on her phone.

Gregory just followed behind, trying to keep up, avoiding the large number of people walking. Sonia would push through the crowds but Gregory was more mannered and would wait. This was nothing unusual for him; he had experienced this many times before with her. Sonia would move swiftly when she wanted something but would let everyone wait for her if she wasn't too interested. She didn't like crowds of people so it was in her interest to get onto a street where there were less of them.

Not much had been agreed with regards to where to eat but Sonia began to dial a number and speak to the person who had answered her call. She requested a table for two and said they would be there in fifteen minutes. After the call Sonia said, "All done, I'm marvellous," and smiled. Gregory just smirked and

Sonia pottered on feeling all wonderful about herself as she put her phone in her pocket and pulled on her gloves. She then mentioned that she had a discount card and that she had to phone and reserve a table to get the discount. This was new to Gregory so he just followed, feeling the cold on his face as the night drew in. He asked how the card worked but Sonia didn't hear him so he just remained quiet and followed, pushing his hands further into his pockets, trying to keep warm. At this stage he was getting tired. He needed to eat something.

Gregory started to think about the time they had spent together as they wandered through the streets. It was like they had never parted. This surprised him as he had felt that he had moved on from her. He was also very content being single – well, that's what he had thought. Gregory had broken up with Sonia the year prior and ceased to contact her. He felt it was best for her to move on. It hurt him more than he expected when he broke up with her but he couldn't continue with the way things were. Sonia had the point of view that she was there for the long haul in the relationship and would have continued being committed. *I guess she wasn't the one receiving the abuse all the time,* Gregory thought.

They were walking for quite some time as Sonia got lost. She began to follow her phone's map app. They appeared to have crossed over the same street twice as Gregory noticed shops and cars he had seen minutes before. He just followed, hoping that she would find the restaurant soon. They eventually found the restaurant. The walk brought back memories for Gregory; in the past, Sonia would brag about her navigation skills but would at times walk in circles. Gregory could never figure it out as Sonia knew her left and rights, but navigation on a mobile map was a painful experience for Gregory at times as she would get confused, especially if it was cold and wet. It was worse if Gregory was hungry, which was normally the case. Sonia was fussy about eating out so he always left it up to her to decide. It was better this way as when Gregory selected a venue, Sonia would want to leave after sitting down and looking at the menu or simply because she didn't like the décor.

They finally reached the venue and settled. The evening flowed in a beautiful way in a pizza restaurant, laughing and discussing over a bottle of wine. They talked about where they were in their lives and what had happened over the year that had passed. Sonia had mentioned several countries that she had visited and venues that she had been to in London. It appeared that Sonia was out a lot and enjoying her single life. Gregory didn't travel but focussed on his work and savings.

As the night drew to a close Gregory became more aware of the time. It was 10.30pm and he had to leave to make his way back to his living space. He was living in a house in Clapham South, South London. He would have to get two trains on the Underground network. He also had to prepare some tender quotations for his work, to be completed for a Monday morning deadline. This is when the realisation began.

3

About Gregory

GREGORY WAS ALSO INDEPENDENT IN NATURE AND A few years more mature in age than Sonia. He could be quite stubborn at times. He tended to be a little eccentric, but Sonia and he were very similar in their ways. They both complemented each other, but could also push one another's buttons to get what they wanted.

This became more apparent as they grew closer in their relationship over the four and a half years before the breakup. They discovered each other's traits as they struggled with circumstances beyond their control. This made the relationship very interesting for both parties as they enjoyed each other's company at the best of times.

Gregory began working for his father at the age of eighteen. As a child, from around the age of five, Gregory could remember his father saying to him, "Some day this business will be yours." This continued for years as Gregory attended primary school and secondary level education.

I guess he was brainwashed into looking forward to working for his father. He also wanted to get to know his father as he didn't see much of him as a child. It was important to him to try to build a relationship with his father. Gregory wanted his father to acknowledge him as he didn't receive much attention as a child.

Gregory's parents separated when he was four. It wasn't possible to divorce in Ireland back in those days. His parents continued to live in the family home, his father residing in the master bedroom and his mum in the guest room. His father came home late from work and left early in the mornings. Gregory would miss seeing his father as he would be sleeping. Gregory didn't see much of his father during the week and the weekends were no different.

When he left school at the age of eighteen, Gregory began working in his father's business. He enjoyed his work, starting by cleaning up after the senior engineers and making tea. He was a very quick learner and began installing equipment himself after a year. Two years later, he began managing the installation team of ten engineers. He was very much devoted to making sure he did everything right to impress his father. Gregory took pride in his work to achieve a high standard of quality.

Unfortunately, his father didn't notice and it didn't improve their relationship. As his father continued to see company profits in his accounts department, he stayed pretty much away and focussed on himself and his own hobbies.

Gregory continued to grow within the business and soon started in sales. This is where Gregory shone. He tripled the company's size in five years and developed strong relationships with clients. Unfortunately, his father was interested in another business venture and would spend the company profits on new equipment to build his own interests. When Gregory or his sales team won a project, there was no finance to purchase the equipment needed to begin the installation. This was a major frustration for Gregory.

There was a constant battle between himself and his father as he was told that there was no money in the company and that things were bad with the cash flow, yet a new expensive piece of equipment would arrive by courier for his father the following day. This caused friction between Gregory and his father but his dad didn't care much.

His dad showed up less and less as the company grew. Gregory began to run the business and take the responsibility of making decisions for the future.

His dad focussed upon himself and his own interests yet again. The company cash flow was always an issue, especially when his father wanted something for himself.

It wasn't easy working for his dad, but he continued to build the business as that was the aim. His father began to say to him when they would meet for the odd board meeting, "Eventually the company will be yours when I retire." Gregory was always told, "In a certain year I will retire and this will be yours." It was a motivation for Gregory to build the business and be proud of his accomplishments. His father never mentioned an exact date that this change would happen.

Gregory spent twenty-four years working for his dad while listening to the same old stories and whims. It was all just promises and nothing was fulfilled. He was never told what year his father was going to retire but as the years passed by, Gregory began to get fed up.

(Gregory was born in the Combe Hospital in central Dublin, Ireland. His mum had always told him that it was a long labour. I guess Gregory knew what he was going to endure in life and chose to hang out a little bit longer in the comfort of his mother's womb.)

His eldest sister, Linda, had taken care of Gregory as his mum Rita had had a nervous breakdown when he was four years old. This put a lot of pressure on Linda, who was seven years old. Linda persevered, trying to reduce her mother's stress as she discovered the challenges of bringing up a hyperactive young boy. Gregory was a child who was into exploring everything. He had to investigate anything he could lay his hands on. This led to him finding it difficult to understand the word 'no'.

The reason for his mother having a nervous breakdown was the difficulties in the relationship between herself and Gregory's father, Bernard. His father was a difficult man. He had no patience at all, always more focussed on himself and his life. His father had a short fuse and his temper would emerge at times when Gregory would play. Gregory would play with his toys like any normal child, on the carpet in the front sitting room. He would have all his cars in a row or scattered across the floor, pretending to repair them after an imaginary accident scene. His father would say to him often, when he was at home on the nights that Gregory would see him, while he would be getting off the couch to go to the bathroom, "I'll count to five and if they aren't tidied before I get to five, I will dance on them." The bathroom was on the first floor to the rear of the house. Gregory, being the testing child that he was, wouldn't budge. I guess Gregory was testing his independence and his father's relationship with him. He would sit back on the floor and stare at his father to see what he would do. It was short-lived, but he felt that he was getting the attention from his father that he missed so dearly. Once his father had counted, "Five, four, three, two, one," he would dance on the toys, smashing them into pieces, and Gregory would scream, bursting into tears as he felt the anger and emotion build around his chest. His father would then proceed to walk up the stairs to the toilet, leaving Gregory devastated. He would then return from the bathroom and sit on the couch, where he would continue to watch *Star Trek* or a John Wayne film.

The same pattern would continue from time to time but his father came home less and less as he grew older. Gregory lived with his mum and two sisters and he would spend time with his mum until bedtime each night hoping to see his father before bed. Sometimes he could be waiting for over a week before he would see his father.

On occasion, his dad would purchase new toys for Gregory to try and make up; this was his way of showing his love and affection. He didn't know how to show love or affection at all in person. Bernard was very difficult around people as he didn't know how to mix; his way of mixing with people would be to talk about gadgets as he was very technically minded. He would always need to have the latest technical gizmo to play with. I guess he was trying to fill an empty void within him, to feel happy. This was short-lived because when he got the item he lusted for, he was already looking for something new. Nothing excited Gregory's father much. His happiness was to sit and watch movies, zone out. He tried in his own way to blend with his children on occasion. He once put up a traffic light in the back garden for his three children to play with. He managed to get himself a real traffic light which changed between the colours green, orange and red once plugged into the 240-volt mains supply. He erected a pole in the garden and installed a catenary wire to the garden shed. This is where he plugged in the 240-volt connection.

The children had many days of playfulness, driving around the garden and imagining they were in a car, bus or truck, or simply on a bicycle, pretending that they had a puncture or were in a crash. These were the usual things children would do playing. This was one of the good memories for Gregory. He couldn't really remember much of his childhood due to the stressful times he chose to forget.

Gregory had two sisters; Linda was the eldest and Carla in the middle. Gregory was the youngest child. He was the baby, as his sisters would call him. His mum had a miscarriage prior to having Gregory, which added to the reasons for her nervous breakdown. His brother, who had passed before Gregory, his mum had called the baby David. Gregory only became aware that his mum had had a miscarriage when she told him when he was in his late twenties. Gregory's mum was very private about the difficulties she had endured since marrying his father.

The first house they lived in as children was a terraced house with three bedrooms on the north side of Dublin. As you walked in the front door, the stairs were on the left-hand side. On the right-hand side there was the sitting room, which led into the kitchen-cum-dining room with a window and the back door.

At the top of the stairs there was a bathroom and two bedrooms at the rear of the house, one bedroom on each side of the bathroom. The master bedroom was at the front of the house. Gregory had his own bedroom and his two sisters shared.

The children played in the back garden, which was square in shape with a path around the edge and grass in the centre. There were some flower beds with roses planted and clipped to the surrounding walls. The garden shed was attached to the back wall to the right in which his father would leave his painting supplies and tools. There was also a bird cage. This was a large cage containing several budgies. It was very therapeutic listening to the birds chirping from time to time.

Gregory began to become more frustrated and angry due to having very little connection with his father. This created a challenge for Gregory as he felt he was the reason for his parents breaking up. He began to think that it was his fault. He didn't understand what was happening at this young age of four until he was a teenager, therefore he took it personally.

His sister Linda focussed on bringing Gregory up and this helped her. It helped by taking her mind off things that were difficult in the home. It was a distraction. Gregory was a challenge at times; so much so for his parents that the family would go on holidays each year and leave Gregory at his grandmother's. Being the eldest child, Linda had more of an understanding regarding the family dynamics and what was going on, but this also made it more difficult for her. She became very independent and focussed at a young age.Gregory's parents and sisters would travel to the Canary Islands each year. This was very difficult for Gregory as he felt abandoned and rejected. It also led to him feeling that he was adopted and not part of the family. His grandmother and great-grandmother on his mum's side of the family lived together. His granny Pauline was pretty much anti-male, so she was particularly strict and said things that were hurtful when he was left in the caring hands of his grandmother and great-grandmother. Winifred was his great-grandmother, she was like a mother to him.

Winifred felt so sorry for Gregory that she would keep him busy all day playing games; she taught him how to play chess, dominos and snap. They had fun together. It was a ritual each day, doing the same things: having breakfast, cleaning up, walking to the shops and cooking lunch in between playing games. Winifred would also cook dinner every day as Pauline would lie on the couch for most of the day. In fact, she practically went from the couch in the sitting room to the bathroom to bed and back again each day. Pauline watched all the soaps on television.

The love connection between Winifred and Gregory was something very special. She even gave him her own toy bear that she had slept with as a child for him to sleep with. The bear had a strange smell. It had one eye, no fur and a texture that felt like skin. It also had a wobbly head that could have fallen off at any time, but it remained attached by the heavy stitching. The teddy was browny green in colour.

The grandparents' house was dim with brown wooden furniture and had a musky smell. Gregory rebelled each time he was told that he would be staying at his granny's house. He knew it was a time when the rest of the family would be going away.

His parents would put their packed suitcases in the boot of the car the night before the holiday as Gregory and his sisters were sleeping. He was only told that he was staying with the grannies and that the others were going away on holiday while driving to his grandparents' home. I guess his anger became more and more acute the more he was treated the way he was. He would always challenge the situation but they still left without him. Pauline would hold Gregory tightly as the rest of the family drove away to the airport. Gregory would be screaming at the top of his voice and wriggling as much as possible to get away but he was not strong enough to break free from Pauline's hold. Winifred would take him inside and give him a fresh glass of milk and biscuits to try to calm him down. She would from time to time approach Gregory and place her hand on his head, standing silently as she looked at him. Gregory could feel sadness when she would do this. He would stop eating and look back into Winifred's eyes as his tears would dry up.

Gregory found it difficult to deal with his emotions and he began to suppress them, resulting in him becoming angry and frustrated. He would challenge his parents and try to control situations so that he didn't get hurt. This resulted in more tension and outbursts.

When Gregory was four years old, going on five, his father bought the children sweets on a day when the family went for a drive. This was a rare occasion before his parents' breakup. One of the sweets was in the shape of a whistle and it worked. In fact, it gave a high-pitched piercing sound when one would blow through it. His sisters ate theirs and Gregory kept his for the journey back in the car and repeatedly blew it as he sat behind his father while he was driving. Gregory had behaved on the outing to ensure that he got the same treatment as his sisters and the goodies that came with it. He waited until the journey home before he kicked off. After several times of hard constant blowing through the whistle and being shouted at to stop, with threats that his father would take it away, Gregory continued, blowing, laughing, blowing again and laughing in hysterics.

Lo and behold, he was told to stop again but didn't, so the car was swerved to the side of the country road and his father unbuckled his seat belt, leaned over his seat and grabbed the sweet from Gregory's mouth as he was blowing hard. Bernard flung it out of the window as he began to drive off again.

Gregory always sat between his two sisters in the back seat. They never wore seat belts in those days. Sometimes, when Gregory was tired, he would lie and sleep in the back window; he could squeeze there between the back seat window shelf and window. I guess the heat of the sunshine helped him drift into sleep.

On another occasion, his mother was driving with him to the shops early one morning. Gregory didn't want to go but was forced into the car, leaving his sisters behind in the house. He rebelled, wanting to stay with them, so he continued to shout in the back of the car. His mum warned him several times to stop or she would drop him off somewhere on the street. Gregory didn't listen. She pulled over in a housing estate in Dublin and put him standing on the footpath. She drove away, leaving him there screaming as he cried with fear, not knowing what to do. A woman from one of the houses saw what had happened and came out to comfort Gregory, inviting him into her home. She calmed him down and gave him cookies and milk. They were handmade cookies with chocolate inside. Gregory sat in the kitchen and the woman stood at the sitting room window, watching as Gregory's mum frantically drove up and down the street when she returned to collect Gregory, looking out for him. The woman waited until Gregory's mum stopped at the position where she had dumped her son out of the car and as she stood, confused. There were no mobile phones in those days to call for help.

The woman in the house proceeded to open her front door and walk towards Gregory's mother as she was standing with her hands on her head, crying. There was an intense discussion with raised voices as the woman voiced her disgust towards Gregory's mum. Gregory was relieved that his mum had returned and proceeded to eat the cookies and drink the milk. He didn't hear the conversation but he knew it was serious. The woman allowed her to collect Gregory and they drove home. Nothing was mentioned to his sisters when they returned. Gregory's mum held Gregory tightly and promised never to repeat that again as she kissed his head. Gregory didn't know how to feel as his emotions had become difficult to understand most of the time. He was just relieved to be home and loved again. To feel held in her grasp was enough for him to process; he couldn't deal with too much as it was frustrating for him.

At this young age of five, Gregory couldn't comprehend what was going on so he began to go inwards with his feelings, suppressing them further. He developed an empathy towards others as he didn't like anyone being treated badly in any shape or form. He hated to see someone sad. He began to feel other children's sadness and anger. He had an understanding that made him feel comfortable around them.

Gregory began to mix with other children in school, defending those who would be bullied or who would appear to be sad or angry. He would make it his priority to console them with conversation and try to make them feel better. This gave Gregory an identity and he felt needed. His anger contributed towards this as he was physical, so much so that the bigger kids started to back off. He was no stranger to the principal's office and received the cane across his hands and had his bottom swiped every couple of days. He definitely had a visit to the principal's office once or twice a week. All of this contributed to Gregory becoming more and more independent and not relying on others. He also began to realise that the principal was venting his own frustrations on the children when disciplining them. It was his way to vent his anger with whatever personal stuff was going on in his life. Gregory became more and more sensitive to his feelings as he got older. He could feel how other people felt within themselves but he didn't understand the process and what it meant. This developed more and more as Gregory had more personal encounters with relationships.

Pauline, his granny, was married to his grandfather, Patrick. Everyone would call him by the name Paddy. Paddy was a builder and he was the first to build housing estates in Dublin, and he also built petrol station garages all over Ireland. He was very successful.

Unfortunately the relationship between Pauline and Paddy was difficult due to him living with not only his wife but also her mother, Gregory's great-grandmother Winifred. Their three children also lived there, two sons and Gregory's mother.

Paddy was a certified carpenter and specialised in roofing. He was a hard grafter and didn't get home until late and would leave early in the morning for work. As Gregory grew older, he began to take an interest in his grandfather's knowledge, visiting his home with his mum every second weekend.

Gregory's grandfather moved out of his family home when Gregory was a young boy and lived in Dún Laoghaire, south Dublin, on the coast road. Gregory and his mum used to visit often.

Gregory's grandfather's house had a beautiful view of the sea and a Martello tower. From time to time, Gregory would sit and watch people swimming during cold, rainy winter days. His grandfather taught Gregory carpentry and vehicle mechanics as he was a motoring enthusiast, especially with his sports cars. His grandfather cherished his car, which was a Jensen Interceptor. It was dark green in colour and Gregory would help with the maintenance when he would visit. Gregory's grandfather also had a vintage Aston Martin, which he drove once a year to make sure the wheels turned and it hadn't locked up. This car was covered at all times in the garage and was raised slightly to take the weight off the suspension. Gregory would assist his grandfather by handing tools to him during projects. He didn't really get to do or touch much more than that. However, by doing this Gregory began to learn the different names of the tools and what they were used for. More importantly, he learnt how to use them and how to fix things.

His grandfather's influence helped Gregory discover his natural ability to work with his hands. As Gregory got older, he could do most DIY jobs. He learnt carpentry, plumbing, tiling, electrics and all types of building works.

His grandfather owned several homes throughout Dublin. Unfortunately, his mother used this to her advantage to cause issues with Gregory's father. She would move herself and the children between houses on and off so that his father didn't know where they were staying. This was done to prevent Gregory's father from seeing them. Gregory was always told by his mum that his dad didn't want to see them and that he didn't care about or love them. This prevented Gregory and his father having any type of relationship.

When Gregory took his communion, he was seven years old. His father attended late. He had more important things to do, apparently. He went to work that morning and the church service started at 11am.

He arrived outside the church after the service with a large box of toys as the photography was taking place, organised by the principal of the school for the year book. I guess he was trying to buy his son with gifts, but yet again he didn't show any affection. One of the toys was a dartboard, which was immediately seized by his mum. Another toy was a bow and arrow set. This was what Gregory feasted his eyes on as he grabbed it from the box and held tightly until he got home. His mum continuously warned Gregory not to fire the arrows at anyone or it would be confiscated and destroyed.

It was a surreal feeling meeting his father yet again for a short period and then being at home without him. Gregory often wondered what his father was doing at any time of the day and when they would meet again.

Some days had passed and yet again, there was no sign of a phone call from his father. Gregory could feel the frustration building within him as the days passed and he didn't understand why he was feeling this way. He became angry, asking his mum, "Where is Daddy?" He would be answered with the same answers from his mother: "Your father doesn't care", "He is more concerned with your cousins than his own children" etc. On one occasion, this fuelled Gregory's anger so he went and got the bow and arrow and sneaked into the kitchen, watching his mum wash the dishes. He carefully placed the arrow on the string of the bow, pulling it back slowly so as not to be heard as it stretched to the limit. Aiming, he let go, hitting his mother's head with a wallop. She dropped a pot in the sink while she was washing it and went crazy, opening the top drawer on the kitchen unit. This is when Gregory was introduced to the wooden spoon. She chased Gregory as he laughed until he was cornered; she whipped his bottom with impact. It hurt and stung shortly after, it hurt really badly, but Gregory shouted, "That didn't hurt!" His mother lashed out again and this time Gregory fell to the ground screaming with pain. Shortly afterwards, as he began to stop crying, he went to his bedroom and just stayed there for the remainder of the day. His mum went back to finishing the dishes and continuing her chores.

Gregory began to suppress his emotions more each time that he had confrontation with his mother. He didn't know how to be within himself; his defence was to react and fight back with anger.

His mother had wooden spoons hidden everywhere. In fact, there were many planted around the house, so they were within easy reach from any spot in the house if Gregory caused a scene. On some of them, his mum had drawn a face on the back with a black marker. A happy face was drawn on some and this made Gregory react more when he saw them.

Gregory would search the house from time to time to remove the wooden spoons prior to causing any stress in the future. He would break them in half and leave them where he found them. It became a game, but he always lost to the painful wallops he got. He was hit so hard on three different occasions that he was nearly hospitalised between the ages of four and five. Around this time, his great-grandmother Winifred came to stay because she was so concerned and she took Gregory to her home for a week or two.

From time to time, Gregory would hear his parents or grandparents speak about a memory that often came up in conversation. It was of when the family went to Dublin Zoo.

Gregory had been focussed on chasing the ducks up and down the outside of the railings of the enclosure that was protecting the ducks. He eventually found a way through the railings and had wandered off into the distance before he was missed by his family. Gregory was four. Once the family had located him, after searching everywhere, his parents were amused at the way he blended with the ducks and at how they all followed him in a row as he walked. He was wearing denim dungarees and red wellington boots. This was when Gregory began to connect with nature. His father would always comment on this memory as it was one rare time that the family had an outing together. His father also had a photograph of Gregory with the ducks in a row behind him.

There was a time when Gregory's parents tried to come together and rebuild their relationship. His father's business was successful, so he and his mum began to build a new house near Dublin Airport. It was out in the countryside. There was just fields and fields of sheep and cattle. This brought an excitement to the whole family and an inner happiness for Gregory as he thought that he would spend more time with his father. This all happened when Gregory was at the age of five and six, as the house took a year to build. He would travel from Finglas, on the north side of Dublin, with the family as a treat to see the new house as it was being built. He also spent time with the builders as they taught him how to catch field mice and rats on occasion. The builders would get a paint tin, a length of straw and a piece of meat. They would pierce the meat with the length of straw, then half fill the tin can with water and balance the piece of straw across the top of the can with the meat in the centre over the water. On some mornings there would be a mouse or rat floating in the water. The builders were from Northern Ireland and they enjoyed playing games with Gregory. They would explain how to mix cement and allow Gregory to watch as they built the external walls. Gregory found this to be fun. These trips also gave Gregory's parents time to speak with the project manager about changes to the build.

As the walls began to reach the first floor, the excitement grew as Gregory could imagine the size of his new bedroom. Well, he could imagine the shape of it, at least. The house was built in approximately one year and the family moved in. It was a strange feeling as the distance in the relationship between him and his father was still there. The same routine continued. His father would return home late when Gregory was in bed and leave early in the morning before he got up. It was a surprise when his father was there on some Saturdays, but he slept in the master bedroom while his mum stayed in the guest bedroom. Gregory was too young to understand this. He just wanted to spend time with his father and he would try to stay awake at night and get up early in the morning, but he didn't succeed.

His father would say to him all the time that "When you are older you can come and work for me, and when you are the right age you can take over the business". I guess this was drilled into the little boy's head so that he began to want this more and more. Gregory and his sisters were always promised that they would go to Disney World in Florida, The United States. This was a promise made by their father for many years, but nothing happened. Their father would go on holidays with his sister and her family, their first cousins, all the time to great places, including Disney World several times. This was difficult for Gregory and his sisters. Their mum would get so angry and say not-so-nice things about their father, which made Gregory want to be with him more and more.

Gregory began to spend more time outdoors, walking through the fields alone. This helped his mum make the decision to buy him a dog. One day after school, Gregory got to the car outside the school gates to see a box sitting on the back seat of the car. He couldn't see into the box from the window, but as soon as he popped the seat forward to squeeze into the car, he could see a puppy. It was black and white with blue eyes. It was a Border Collie sheepdog. Gregory couldn't believe his eyes and got really excited as his mum said, "That's your dog, Gregory, you have to take care of him and feed him. That's your job. If you don't, we will return him". Gregory just replied, "Yes, yes, yes," in excitement. This was one of his happiest moments.

Gregory decided to name him Tamango. This dog helped Gregory discover more about himself. He would only discover the truth in time as he spent time alone with his dog. The relationship became so deep that he and the dog went everywhere together. The dog would sleep at the end of his bed. He walked on Gregory's left-hand side and paced himself at the exact speed that Gregory walked. As soon as Gregory stopped walking or running, once in a stagnant position for a few minutes, Tamango would sit on his feet and lean against his legs. He would also lean his head against Gregory's thigh and look up into his eyes for a few seconds. When his mum would load the children into the car on a school day, Tamango would sit on the driveway and wait all day until Gregory returned.

Gregory began to show signs that he couldn't cope in school as things began to become too much for him. He lost large patches of his hair, leaving bald spots, and this created problems as he was bullied, and he started to miss school as his mum kept him home. He had a nervous breakdown and missed over seven months of school. He was between ten and eleven years old. He developed alopecia. The difficulty was that he was becoming overwhelmed with emotion as he began adolescence. He found it difficult to spell. He was dyslexic but in those days, the school thought he had learning disabilities, so it was recommended that he would attend a special school.

This wasn't the case as Gregory was very intelligent and had photographic memory, but his mum placed him in a special school for learning disabilities on the south side of Dublin. He had to get two buses in the morning, one into Dublin city and then one to the school. This meant an early start for him and he arrived home in the evening on the 5.30pm bus. Tomango would wait at the side of the road at the bus stop from the time he left until the time he arrived home. The local community knew when Gregory was at school and the days that he did not attend because of the dog. Some years later, his dog became ill and Gregory began to see colour around Tamango at times and he also could see the sickness build. Gregory began to have strong feelings and an inner knowing about his dog. It was like he could understand the dog's feelings. His dog had cancer and died the same year that Gregory was suffering from within.

The cause of his nervous breakdown was when his mother and father decided to part. The children were moved yet again to a new house, their mother's new home. His mum had moved to the south side of Dublin. This all happened between the ages of nine and twelve. The stress was too much for Gregory. Moving to the south side made it easier for Gregory as he didn't have to get up for buses so early in the morning. In fact, he could either cycle to school, walk or get a bus.

While he was living on the south side of Dublin and his father in the countryside on the north side of Dublin, a good hour and a half journey away, Gregory would miss seeing his father and wanted to see him more.

Once Gregory started secondary school, his mum allowed him to visit his father on weekends. Gregory would travel straight from school to his father's house on a Friday and return to school on the bus the following Monday morning. The adjustment of starting a new school was not too difficult because Gregory knew that he could visit his father on weekends, giving him an incentive to get through the week. He just wanted to have a relationship with his father.

4

About Sonia

Sonia was born in County Kerry in a place called Killarney, situated in rural Ireland. Her parents lived in a small village, where she grew up with four brothers. There was an instant connection between Sonia and her father. He was an electrician when she was born. She was the first of the children and much loved by her father. Her life was traditional, being born into a small community. Sonia was brought up surrounded by gossip. The importance of the children being on their best behaviour was paramount for her mother. Having manners and self-discipline was more important than how the family functioned behind closed doors. It was all about what the neighbours and community thought of them.

Her father had many choices regarding his career before the children were born, but his love for his partner would determine his destiny. His partner would use this to her advantage and control him by using her emotions to get what she wanted. He could have become a Garda (policeman) in Ireland but the relationship stirred him from this. He became a taxi driver.

The reason was because he would have had to complete training in Dublin to become a Garda and his girlfriend made him change his mind as she didn't want him to go. She was afraid that he would meet someone else as the distance travelling back and forth would have become an issue. In her fear, she thought that this would have parted them. He cherished the ground she walked on and he was very well brought up by his parents, and she knew not to lose him. He was a 'steal', as they would say in the village. Sonia was brought up to believe that good men were hard to find in small communities from listening to the daily gossip growing up. She would listen to the comments passed about neighbours from time to time between her mum and her grandmother or friends who had dropped in. Family and friends would just arrive and knock on the back door. It was very seldom the front doorbell would ring. When it did, it was someone lost, a salesman or the local priest visiting.

Growing up for Sonia was mainly being surrounded by relatives, as most aunties and uncles lived nearby. The country life would start with a family breakfast, normally a big fry-up consisting of bacon, sausages, beans, potatoes and eggs with black and white pudding. To soak it all up, several slices of fresh bread and butter would also be consumed.

Her father would eat quite a lot of food for breakfast so that he wouldn't have to worry about lunch. On occasions he would have a cake sometime in the afternoon if he was feeling peckish; his favourite was the chocolate éclair. Her father was a gentle person and always wanted the best for everyone. He was well known in the community and would do many jobs for the locals to help them out. Some actually took advantage of his skills and never paid for his services. He was a man who could put his hands to anything. In fact, he could do almost any trade – well, except plastering. This he didn't have the time or the experience to improve. He would read a book and get the job done.

Religion was very important in the rural community that Sonia grew up in. She went to a Catholic school from the age of four right up to her leaving certificate at the age of seventeen. She only really mixed with the other children from the local community. This started a curiosity within to get away from the life she was surrounded by and get to know more about other places to visit around the world. Sonia was an innocent young woman who was determined to shine in her career and make her father proud.

Sonia left school and started college to become a nurse. This was the case for most living in this area as a hospital was nearby and this meant that she could apply for a job. During her first college year, Sonia moved onto the campus and she began to change her appearance. She started to wear makeup and bought dresses instead of wearing trousers. She also started work in the local chip shop to earn some money so that she could socialise. Sonia always missed home and particularly she missed her father. She would return home every second weekend to catch up on washing her clothes and eat some proper food. Living on campus, she didn't have a healthy diet; also, socialising and often waking with hangovers didn't help. Sonia changed her hair colour from a natural brown to blonde overnight. She began to become more aware of the attention she received as she changed her image. She missed her father so much and that feeling, the feeling of being wanted and appreciated, made her feel lonely. Sonia's relationship with her mum was different. Her mum showed resentment towards her due to the attention and time her father dedicated to Sonia. Jealousy developed gradually within her mum, creating a negative distance between herself and Sonia. Her mum would shout at her and be nasty when her father wasn't present. She would purposely wash her daughter's clothes in the washing machine at higher temperatures than recommended, destroying them. Sonia would never let her mum wash her clothes, but her mum would go into her room from time to time when she would be out with her father on errands and bundle her clothes in the washing machine. Sonia was very proud of her clothes as she bought nice dresses that were expensive. To annoy Sonia, her mum would hang her dresses on the clothes line so that when they drove around the back of the house to park the car after an errand they would be hanging in full view, looking tatty and creased. In fact, on some occasions her clothes had shrunk or would have holes in them.

No matter how Sonia showed affection towards her mum, it wasn't enough. Her mum would be nasty. Sonia was kind-hearted and always bought her mum nice birthday and Christmas presents. She always had a gift for her parents when she visited home on weekends from college. Sonia began to avoid her mum as much as possible and spent time with her father. She would go in his car and visit neighbours while her father did some odd jobs and Sonia would sit and drink tea while chatting with the neighbour or client, or she would assist by getting tools or stuff from the car if needed for her father.

Sonia met a guy she liked just before she graduated. He had his own car, which was a bonus as public transport was difficult. There was only the public bus service that ran seldom throughout the day. The relationship grew but she soon began to become distant with him because she felt herself react to situations like her mum would. The relationship lasted eight months but it was more a convenience to her because of his car. His name was Paul and he wanted more with Sonia. He was very keen and even spoke about marriage. Sonia didn't feel attracted to him and soon she ended the relationship because he was so overpowering that it began to freak her out. It reminded her too much of her mother. His anger became more acute as she became more distant from him.

Sonia joined St John Ambulance as a volunteer and she attended many music venues and VIP events. It was through this experience that she met Brian. Brian was a search and rescue pilot. They spent so much time together, hiking, going to events. It was when he took her up in the helicopter that she began to fall for him, with the rush and the excitement and the caring feeling she received from him as he constantly asked via the headphones if she was okay. The reassurance began to melt her heart. When they landed, Brian asked if she was hungry and Sonia said that she was starving. He asked her if she would like to go and have a bite to eat with him and she said yes. This was the beginning of the relationship with Brian. He was a guy who found it difficult to express his emotions. He was a little awkward in himself and didn't know when to hug her or kiss her. He so much wanted to kiss Sonia but kept holding himself back. He had the opportunity many times but he would look for a distraction and talk. Sonia so much wanted to kiss and hug him because she knew she wanted more. Sonia needed the attention and was a girl who required a lot of love. Brian eventually conceded and moved closer to kiss Sonia as he opened the car door for her after an evening meal out. Brian had a house that he owned – well, he was paying off the mortgage. He invited Sonia out the following Friday night and this is when they spent their first night together. The relationship moved very quickly as Sonia moved in with him a month later. They spent so much time together as she was there all the time in his home. It was just easier for Brian not to be driving her back and forth from her family home. Six months later, he proposed to her and they were engaged. Sonia was so excited. The wedding planning began and she was even talking about falling pregnant. Everything was surreal but it didn't last long. Sonia began to feel strange around Brian after he returned from weekends away with his work. She began to feel something wasn't right. It took her months to build the courage to ask if there was another woman. Brian denied it and got very angry. This was the first time that Sonia witnessed Brian showing his temper and making her feel terrible. Sonia was very annoyed with herself for questioning him and therefore went out of her way to make him feel happy. She would buy him small gifts of clothes and cook meals for him all the time. Her inner feeling didn't go away. This concerned her. Sonia arranged to meet a friend of hers on a night out as she had lost contact with her friends during the period that she was with Brian. It was after several drinks that her friend told her that Brian was seeing another woman and that everyone knew but Sonia. Sonia broke down, crying with shock, finding it hard to function normally as her body shivered. All she could do was drink more alcohol. Her world was turned upside down. The more she drank, the worse she got, becoming hysterical. Her friend eventually called her father and he came to collect Sonia. Sonia returned the engagement ring to Brian the next day and spent many days and nights staying in her bedroom. Sonia just wanted to run as far away as possible. She decided to travel so borrowed money from her bank and travelled the world for a year. During the time away, Sonia developed her independence and built up her self-esteem. Sonia travelled with a male friend from school who she had known for a number of years. He had talked about travelling for many years and as soon as Sonia said that she would go with him, it was booked.

Sonia returned back to Ireland after the trip over a year later feeling like a different person. She had returned home to debt with the bank and knew that she would have to pay the money back. Sonia had the professional qualifications and therefore proceeded to apply for work. It wasn't long before she was offered a job after several interviews. Her new job was in Dublin, Ireland.

Sonia wasn't the easiest girl to love; she had developed the ability to overthink things due to feeling less than confident about herself and this created stress. She began to overreact if she wasn't getting the attention she needed and would become insecure every once in a while. These feelings and thoughts gradually began to increase more and more as she tried to date and socialise. Sonia would need plenty of attention from her partner or whoever she was in the company of. This included her friends, as she became competitive for their attention. Sonia would take up all of your time as she would want you to herself, and she would need plenty of reassurance to remove herself from her overthinking mind as it created doubts and fears. Sonia wasn't capable of fully trusting another. She would have no problem pushing a person away as she would defend her corner even if she was wrong. She would also push a person away as she could feel that they may be close to hurting her. This would be her defence mechanism, making her feel that she was in control and protecting herself from being hurt. Unfortunately, it would hurt her more as her overthinking mind would take control. She would get so demanding that you'd be tempted to walk away, it would get so hard that you'd think about giving up, and it would get so complicated that you wouldn't want to deal with her anymore. To love a girl like Sonia, you would get to see her at her worst and most vulnerable. This you would need to be strong enough to handle as she would do things that you would not be able to comprehend and she would defend herself until a conflict occurred. She would need you to be patient, observing her, while every now and again she would point out how you made her feel. She would push your boundaries to breaking point and slowly pull you back closer to her as you felt miserable.

She would wait until she felt you push her away as you felt that you needed space.

A relationship with Sonia would not be easy, but if she loved you, you would forget the heartbreak from time to time and enjoy the passion and intensity as each day progressed.

5

The same evening after Sonia and Gregory met in London

SONIA TEXT GREGORY THAT EVENING WHEN THEY parted to go their own ways home. *I had a lovely evening and it felt surreal, as though we never parted.* This put a smile on Gregory's face as he exited the tube station and connected back to his mobile network. He replied back to Sonia, *I would love to meet up again soon.* Sonia replied, *Let's meet Friday after work as I'm free then.* He replied, *Great, see you then.* The date was arranged; he had no idea where and what time but the fact of meeting was enough for now.

The week leading up to them meeting again was interesting as there was an excitement. Gregory felt really good and was full of joy. He was thinking of Sonia quite often and wanted to text, but he held off. Sonia, on the other hand, although also thinking about the meeting, was also contemplating the time when they broke up. I guess she hadn't got over the hurt and anger that she had experienced. From time to time she wondered what she was doing meeting him again.

Wednesday morning had arrived and Gregory text Sonia, *I'm looking forward to Friday* ☺. Sonia replied, *What are we doing?* Gregory replied, *We can go for a meal.* It just happened so quickly. Sonia entered 'Restaurants' in her search browser, finding two restaurants with good reviews. Because she was coeliac, it was best that Sonia looked at the menus at each. One was a Thai restaurant and the other an Indian. They both agreed on the Thai restaurant but it was booked out on the Friday evening, so the Indian it was.

It was 3pm on Friday afternoon, therefore Sonia left work early to drive down to South Clapham from the centre of London. The traffic normally got busy around 4pm, so she decided to try and beat it so that she could relax a bit before meeting Gregory. Sonia stopped at a garage to get some fuel and text Gregory at 3.35pm. *On my way, be there before 16.30.*

Gregory had planned his day to make sure he was ready for her arrival. It had passed 4.30pm so Gregory was waiting. Another thirty minutes passed and he waited a little longer. He gave up with a sigh as he looked once again at the time on his phone and text: *Where are you?* He received a text fifteen minutes later: *I'm outside.* He jumped from the couch and moved swiftly to the front door. He opened the door and Sonia stood in a red dress, black leggings and a pair of long black boots, covered in a black fur coat. She had bright red lipstick on and smiled, showing some lipstick smudged on her upper front teeth. Gregory decided not to say anything about the lipstick but commented on her outfit. He said, "You look very nice," and Sonia replied, "Okay." Gregory raised his arms for a hug and they embraced. Sonia held Gregory tightly as they hugged one another. She pulled him closer as he tried to break away from the hug, but he surrendered and remained standing there, embraced. They moved away from each other and stared into each other's eyes in silence. As Gregory withdrew he could smell the perfume that he had bought Sonia. He remembered it was Nina Ricci Original. Sonia then said in an instance, "I'm here, let's go," with a cheeky smile. Gregory went back inside, grabbed his coat, switched the alarm on and closed the door behind him, locking the five-lever master lock. As they walked towards the main road, Gregory placed his keys in his pocket and zipped it closed. They began to talk about how hungry they both were.

Gregory asked Sonia, "What did you eat today?" Sonia ignored his question, so he asked again.

Sonia replied the second time, saying, "I ate earlier."

Gregory replied, "What?"

Sonia then said, "I only had an apple and a few nuts to eat since morning."

Gregory replied, "That's not enough to live on, you need to look after yourself."

Sonia replied, "I was busy and I couldn't take a break at work." Gregory became concerned but remained quiet as he could feel that Sonia was getting frustrated with the conversation.

Shortly afterwards, a taxi came around the bend in the road in front of them. Gregory flagged it down. Sonia said, "Great." It only took around twenty minutes until they arrived at the Indian restaurant. Sonia began talking in the taxi about when she had moved to London from Ireland. She spoke about the delay she had in receiving the invitation for her job and all the security clearance she had to complete. Gregory sat, listening to her. He would glance at her from time to time as he was watching out the front window of the car. Gregory could feel her frustration, but the end result was that she got the job and she had been working for the same company since she moved over to London. Gregory moved his right hand closer to her left leg and placed it open, facing upwards. Sonia looked down and moved her left hand onto his. They intertwined fingers and relaxed in quietness. Sonia quivered a little as she felt good inside with a little excitement. All Gregory was thinking about at this time was food. He was hungry and starting to get agitated as his energy was fading.

They arrived at the restaurant and were seated beside the window. The view was onto a side street with a public house located on the corner. Several people were outside drinking while smoking. It was a cold November evening. As they were seated, Sonia put her fur coat on the back of her chair. It flowed onto the floor. Sonia sat quickly as the waitress tried to take her coat and Sonia ignored her, asking, "Do you have a wine menu?" Both Sonia and Gregory were handed a food menu and told the specials for the evening. The waitress also handed Sonia the drinks menu. Sonia immediately handed it to Gregory. She said, "You pick a white wine; I feel like white wine tonight. You always pick a good wine."

Gregory scanned the wine list while Sonia looked at the food menu. He decided on a red wine and discussed it with Sonia. Both agreed so they ordered the wine.

As Sonia was saying how tired she was, the waitress came over with the bottle of wine and showed them both the label. The waitress began to open the bottle and asked who would like to taste it. Gregory immediately waved his hand in the direction of Sonia. The waitress poured a small amount into Sonia's glass and stood patiently. Sonia picked it up and swirled it as if she knew what she was doing, took a smell and then drank some. She sat with a blank look on her face and proceeded to say, "Yes, that's a nice wine." Gregory smirked and looked at his menu quickly as he didn't want Sonia to see his reaction. "Gregory, you always picked a nice wine," said Sonia as she gestured towards him to taste. Gregory sampled the wine from Sonia's glass and agreed it was nice. The waitress poured the wine into both glasses and proceeded to place the bottle on the table.

There was an elderly couple being seated next to them while they both drank some wine. Sonia said 'cheers' while they looked into each other's eyes.

The elderly couple just sat and stared around the room. There was very little conversation and the gentleman spent quite a lot of his time staring at the décor on the ceiling. Gregory pointed this out to Sonia and he said, "Why would people remain in a relationship if they can't even have a conversation when they go for a meal?"

Sonia looked over in silence. This reminded her of how they got on so well together. She drank some more wine. She then said, "You never noticed my hair; I had it done today."

Gregory said, "It's the same, but the blonde looks very natural with the curly bits." Sonia took another sip of her wine and sighed, looking at the menu.

The waitress arrived at the table and asked, "Are you ready to order?" Sonia ordered the chicken korma with plain rice. Gregory ordered the same.

As they were waiting for the main course there was a young boy running up and down the stairs. The restaurant had a private party on the floor above. The young boy was just entertaining himself. He kept coming down to where Sonia and Gregory were sitting and standing behind Sonia. He would stare out the window at the people standing outside the pub on the opposite side of the street. The main course arrived and was placed on the table as the little boy came and went. Sonia and Gregory continued to eat and ordered a second bottle of wine. The evening was going really well and then Sonia began to speak about their breakup. She showed tears and wiped her eyes several times, allowing her hair to fall in front of her face to try to hide them. She got up from her chair without speaking and went to the bathroom in a hurry. Gregory continued to finish his meal and had some more wine. He was in a good mood and felt very relaxed in Sonia's company. Sonia returned a while later and said she had lost her appetite, placing her knife and fork together on her plate. She had only eaten about a third of her meal. Gregory had finished his meal by this time; nothing came between Gregory and his food.

The waiter in the restaurant came over, asked if they were finished and proceeded to remove the plates. He asked if they would like a dessert menu. Sonia said, "Yes, we will look, thank you." Gregory asked Sonia if she was okay. Sonia replied, "I guess I still haven't got over everything that happened, and I still have feelings." Gregory said that he also felt the same. Sonia had two drinks from her glass as she looked out the window at all the people outside the pub. She remained quiet as the waiter arrived with the dessert menu. Sonia decided that they would both share a dessert and ordered a cheesecake. The waiter arrived and placed the dessert in the middle with two side plates, placing one in front of each of them. Sonia drank some more and so did Gregory. They ordered a third bottle of wine and continued to eat the dessert. The conversation got serious and Sonia asked Gregory why he broke up with her and told him that she was devastated. Sonia ate the upper part of the cheesecake, avoiding the biscuit base. She said that she always thought that he was the one. She said that from the time they first met, she knew. As they talked, they consumed most of the third bottle. Gregory was explaining why he had broken up with Sonia when she said out of the blue, "I feel tired." Once she had said this, her head tilted forward and her face landed on the plate in front of her, with her body leaning on the table. Gregory watched as it happened, as if everything was in slow motion. She had fallen into a deep sleep. Sonia's face was covered by her hair and her hands were down by her side.

The elderly couple on the opposite table went into a flurry of conversation as they watched Sonia. Gregory lifted his glass and had a drink after he tried to speak to Sonia and wake her. He placed his left hand on her head as he leaned forward, tapping it and saying 'Sonia' a few times. She didn't move. He sat back into his chair and continued to drink, contemplating how he was going to get her out of the restaurant. He requested the bill with a hand gesture to the waitress as he looked at Sonia's head still resting on the table. The manager came over and asked if everything was okay and if he needed help. Gregory replied, "I can manage," as he smiled with embarrassment.

He paid the bill and the staff opened the double doors at the entrance to the restaurant as they knew this was going to be a mission. Gregory proceeded to put Sonia's coat on, pulling it up onto her shoulders from around the chair. He moved the table with the waiter, holding her head, and began to lift her onto his right shoulder. The chair remained attached to her as he lifted; it was held attached to her by her coat. One staff member came over and helped by pulling the chair out from under her coat gently. The elderly couple watched in amazement as Gregory stumbled towards the door with Sonia resting on his shoulder, holding her handbag in his left hand.

He managed to bang her head against the wall as he tried to avoid tables and chairs making his way out through the double doors as he left the restaurant. Once outside, the manager waved for a taxi that was approaching. He opened the door for Gregory as it pulled up. Gregory bent down, holding Sonia's back as he moved her forward. He flung Sonia inside the car, being as careful as he could. As she landed on her back she woke up, laughed and slurred her words. Gregory had no idea what she said but was relieved he had got her out of the restaurant.

Sonia had a hotel booked for the night but he couldn't get the name from her. She was to stay somewhere on the way back to Gregory's but he had no idea where. The reservation was on her phone and she had a pin code to open it. He decided to take her to his place. He gave the taxi driver the address as he watched Sonia try to sleep. All the way during the car journey he was talking to Sonia, telling her to stay awake and breathe. She slurred her words and pushed him away, laughing. They arrived at Gregory's address so he paid the driver. He pulled Sonia out of the car, assisting her as much as he could while she stumbled to stand straight. Drunk as she was, she managed to stand in her high heels. As he held her they kissed while the car pulled away, leaving them standing on the road. Sonia pulled him closer and they kissed again. Gregory pushed his tongue into her mouth and she slammed her teeth onto it, grasping it. She did it with great force as it was instinct. Gregory moaned as he froze with his eyes open and she released. He pulled back away from her and Sonia laughed out aloud. She said, "Don't stick your tongue in my mouth," slurring her words and laughing. They walked as Gregory felt his tongue with his right hand, checking for blood, looking at his fingers under the street lighting. He was a little surprised to say the least but glad she hadn't bitten his tongue off.

They arrived in Gregory's place and he told Sonia to go up the stairs and enter the second room on the left. She went as he got two glasses of water from the plastic natural water bottle in the kitchen. When he entered the room Sonia was fast asleep, fully clothed in her coat, lying on her back across the bed. He removed her boots, coat, tights and dress, leaving her underwear on. This was a struggle as she was out cold, fast asleep.

He lifted her up and pulled back the duvet, lay her down and covered her. He removed his clothes and lay beside her. It wasn't long before he also fell asleep.

6

The next morning

Sonia began to move in her sleep. Unaware that she was cuddled up with Gregory, she lay on her left side with her head just below his shoulder, resting on his chest. Her right leg was sitting in between his legs as he slept on his back. His head was facing in the opposite direction to her. Sonia began to move her pelvis, thrusting gently towards his hip area as she was becoming aroused in a dream. Her right hand was resting on Gregory's chest and she began to move it while she was starting to awaken. Gregory was out cold. Sonia opened her eyes and was pleasantly surprised that she was with him as she couldn't remember leaving the restaurant. Sonia moved her hand slowly down his body, caressing him until she touched his penis as she slid her hand under the elastic of his boxer shorts. She gently stroked it, finally resting his testicles in the palm of her right hand. Here she held them. As they reacted to the heat of her hand, Gregory moved slightly as his penis began to become erect. Sonia moved her hand gently along the shaft and grasped it as she caressed him. Gregory opened his eyes with delight, turning his head in her direction. They both stared into each other's eyes as she smiled. Swiftly, he turned towards her, moving her onto her back with his left leg placed between her legs. She moved her left hand, resting it on his left bottom cheek and giving it a squeeze. With his penis still erect, she could feel him press against her. He put his hands on both sides of her head, leaning on his elbows, holding her head as he moved her hair away from her face with his fingers. Staring into her eyes, he moved his mouth slowly towards her lips and kissed her, closing his eyes. The feeling of warmth caressed his lips as Sonia's felt moist. This was because she had curled her lips just before he kissed her. As he kissed, his penis secreted some fluid and he became more excited. He moved his left hand down towards her right thigh and gently moved it up towards her right breast, touching only with his fingers. As he touched the bottom of her bra, he slid his fingers under the wire and grabbed her left breast. Sonia squirmed, adjusting her body as she felt aroused and excited. Gregory moved his left thigh against her underwear, pressing her private area. He could feel the heat from between her legs as he leaned against her.

Caressing her breast, he pinched her nipple, making Sonia lift her pelvis towards his thigh as she moved forward. She began to rub herself against him. He then moved his mouth from kissing her lips to her left breast as he licked her nipple, retracting as she stared at him. She could feel the cool breeze as he did this and she became more turned on. Pushing him off her to her left side, she arched her back and removed her bra with both her hands. Gregory took her panties from around her hips and gently began pulling them down. Sonia quickly grabbed his hands and said, "I'm not prepared."

Gregory replied, "I don't care, I want you." He moved up alongside her and kissed her lips again. She grabbed his head and kissed him like she hadn't seen him in years. The energy became intense as both got excited. A wet patch began to show on her panties as he touched her through them, gently caressing with his fingers. He quickly slid his hand under her underwear making her wet. Sonia adjusted herself as she felt a quiver down her body. He kissed her once more and then grabbed her underwear, pulling it down and off as she raised her feet. He did notice as he moved his head between her legs that she had short hair growing around her private area. This didn't stir him but intrigued him to taste her. He moved his tongue from the base of her opening to her clitoris. There he moved his tongue gradually until he could feel it become erect. This enabled him to put his focus there as it became moister as the fluids ran from his mouth. He moved his right hand between her legs and positioned his finger under his tongue, inserting it inside her. Sonia moved her pelvis upwards and Gregory inserted his tongue with his finger inside her. He massaged the upper part of her vagina from inside and played with her clitoris using his tongue. Sonia moaned as she became more aroused. Her body was starting to feel lighter and she felt tingly between her legs. As Gregory ran his right hand along her inner thigh she got excited. Gregory removed his finger from inside her and continued with his tongue. Sonia moved her right hand down and began to play with herself. Gregory jumped off the bed, pulled open his upper drawer in the bedside table and began to open a condom. As he rolled it on his penis, Sonia smiled and played with herself quicker. He grabbed both her feet, lifted and pulled her legs towards him and placed the tip of his penis with his hand stimulating her vaginal opening. Sonia pushed herself towards him as he pulled away. He then inserted the head of his penis only and took his right hand, moving it up and down, rubbing against her vagina wall. Sonia started to get frustrated and grabbed his erect penis. She put it inside her, pulled him towards her at the same time, twisting him as she pushed Gregory backwards onto his back. Then she pulled herself up onto Gregory's waist. She began to manoeuvre herself up and down intensely, feeling him inside her. She could feel herself building up an orgasm as her body got tingly all over. Gregory took control and pushed her back down on her side and took her leg over his right shoulder, penetrating her from the side. She ejaculated and he could see the fluid surround his penis, shrouded by the condom. He penetrated deeper within her as he lifted her body, pulling it closer to his. She became limp as she felt another orgasm. He began to slow down and this drove Sonia crazy. She was building up to cum again but the sensation was becoming intense. Gregory just continued at a slow pace. Sonia screamed as she came; her body shook as she tried to relax. Gregory removed his penis and put his tongue between her legs. Sonia reacted by slamming her legs against his head and trying to push him away with her hands. Shortly after, she relaxed and her legs fell away from his head. Sonia came again and Gregory rolled over to the side to gasp for air as it was incredibly hot. Sonia sat up and took his penis in her hand, rolling the condom off. She took his penis in her mouth and caressed his testicles. As she stroked his testicles Gregory ejaculated before Sonia could remove her mouth. She remained steady. Sonia moved away and swallowed his semen. She wiped her mouth with her arm and snuggled up against him, watching his penis dribble more fluid onto his thigh. As this happened, she put her finger under and rubbed it on his leg. Gregory pulled the duvet up over them both and they held each other as they fell back asleep.

A few hours had passed and Gregory begin to stir in the bed. He opened his eyes and turned to look at Sonia sleeping. He saw how he fell in love with her the first time. He stared at her and felt he was looking at her in a different way; not just looking at her, but he felt a connection, a connection of unconditional love. He felt very content. Sonia opened her eyes and pulled the duvet over her head when she saw him looking at her.

She felt hungover and started to question in her mind what she was doing there. She couldn't remember the end of the previous evening and when they made love, she was still drunk. Her mind was spinning with information and throbbing at the same time. Gregory cuddled up beside her and slid his arm under the duvet as he went to hold her. Sonia moved away and said that she was confused. She asked why she was there in his bed. Gregory moved onto his back and in his mind, he thought, *Here we go again.* It wasn't the first time that Sonia had got weird about something. In fact, he thought at times that she was bipolar. Gregory began to tell her what happened in the restaurant and Sonia laughed. She laughed about the older couple talking when Sonia faceplanted the plate on the table. Gregory had made a joke that it was their first date and that his partner was so uninterested in the conversation that she fell asleep. He then told her about her biting his tongue. Sonia denied she had done it until Gregory stuck it out to show her. Her reply was, "Don't stick it in my mouth then."

Gregory decided to shower as Sonia remained in a weird mood. While he was gone, Sonia took her phone and checked in with all her friends, not telling them where she was but just checking that the girls were still meeting later that night to go out. She kept her life private and never shared it with Gregory. Gregory returned shortly with a towel wrapped around him and he began to dry himself in front of her. He felt very relaxed and didn't pay any heed to getting dressed in front of her. Sonia at this stage had the TV on with music playing while she scanned apps on her phone. He told her that the bathroom was free but there was no budging her. He had finished getting dressed and was beginning to get frustrated because she was just ignoring his gestures to get up and go somewhere for breakfast.

Eventually he just said, "Okay, I am going to the coffee shop."

Sonia then moved and said, "I'll shower. I'll only be a minute," putting her phone on the bedside table. Nothing was ever a minute with Sonia so Gregory lay on the bed and started to watch a television programme.

Sonia returned dressed some time later with wet hair, and stood in front of the television as she took out a portable hairdryer from her handbag. She reached for the plug socket beside the television and switched it on while Gregory was trying to watch and listen to his programme. Gregory tried to get her attention by calling her but to no avail; the hairdryer was too loud so he just let it go. Gregory knew that if he had done this to Sonia, she would have gone mad. She finished drying her hair while she was scrolling through her phone. Once happy, checking it with her fingers, she unplugged the cable and threw the hairdryer on top of her handbag. Then she grabbed and began putting on her fur coat, standing looking at Gregory as he was trying to watch his programme.

"Are you ready? I am ready," she said with a smile. Gregory took the remote and pressed the on/off button to switch off the television and he jumped up and began walking towards her. He went to kiss her but she pulled back. This startled Gregory as he wasn't expecting it at all. He just said, "Okay," and walked past her, and proceeded to get his coat off the chair and make his way downstairs. He opened the front door and waited for Sonia to walk outside. He switched on the alarm system and closed the front door, locking it as Sonia waited. Sonia followed behind Gregory as he walked past her at the gate to the footpath. As they walked along the footpath, Sonia walked on his left-hand side. She always had to walk on his left-hand side.

As they walked, Gregory was deep in thought. He was thinking about how great a night it had been, but he had no idea what was wrong. Sonia knew he wasn't happy and began to talk about an event that she had to attend the following week with some VIP guests. Gregory wasn't exactly interested but pretended that it would be very exciting for her. They reached the coffee shop where there was a small table along the wall. It was the only table left so they both sat down. Sonia immediately scanned the room and noticed a man slurping as he put a spoonful of soup into his mouth. She got agitated and couldn't focus on the menu. Gregory was ready to order as he was starving.

Sonia jumped up from her seat and said, "I can't stay here." He looked at her and then looked at the man and Sonia said, "Exactly." Gregory just put the menu down with a sigh, slightly pissed off, and stood up to put his coat on. Sonia made her way towards the door and he followed. He reached past her and caught the door handle, pushing it outwards for her. Sonia just continued as Gregory followed.

As soon as they got outside, Sonia said, "I couldn't stay with that disgusting noise."

Gregory replied, "Where now? I am starving and weak with the hunger." Sonia pulled her phone out of her handbag and began to search for coffee shops nearby on her browser.

Gregory stood looking down the street as Sonia looked at her phone. She replied, "There is one just around the corner." She switched on her map app and began to walk. She turned and said, "Come on." Gregory walked behind her, knowing the café, and watched as she got confused with the map.

She started to say that she was the best at following maps and that she walked everywhere in London. Gregory said nothing. Eventually she realised that she was walking down the street the wrong way. She burst out, "Shite, we are to go on the other side." She turned with a smile and walked past Gregory in the opposite direction. He turned and just followed, saying nothing, shaking his head. She knew he was quiet so she began to ask him questions. Her first question was "Why haven't you moved on?" Then a pause. "Did you meet anyone?" Then she said, "I don't want to know the answer to that question."

Gregory replied, "No, I haven't met anyone as I thought you were the one." Sonia got tearful and tried to hide it, but she couldn't. She stopped walking and covered her face with her left hand, holding her phone in her right hand. Gregory walked up to her and he held her shoulders with both hands. She began to shake and tears ran down her face. She pulled away, put her phone in her pocket and reached into her handbag. Searching through it, she eventually found her tissues and proceeded to take one out of the wrapper. She dabbed each eye. She then said, "Let's go," taking her phone back out of her pocket and entering the pin code. Gregory decided to say nothing and walked yet again behind her as she sniffled down the street, looking at her phone for directions. They eventually found the café and Sonia walked in. Gregory followed behind her as she let the door fling towards him, Sonia just barged in leaving it swing behind her. She walked straight to a table and sat before the waitress could assist.

The waitress came over and said, "Sorry, this table is reserved."

Sonia replied, "Can we sit there?" as she pointed to another table beside the window.

The waitress said, "Yes."

Grabbing her handbag, Sonia slumped over to the table as if it was a bigger task than it was. Gregory had already sat down as he was closer and began to read the menu that was on the table. Sonia got to the table, plonked her bag on the window ledge and grabbed the menu, saying that she was hungry and tired.

Gregory looked at her and noticed her mascara was smudged on her right eye. He pointed at his own eye and said, "You have black here on your right eye." Sonia rubbed her left eye with her hand and Gregory smiled. "Nope, that's the left eye."

She rubbed her right eye and said, "Now?"

He replied, "It's gone." Sonia put both her arms on the table, stretching towards Gregory with her hands facing down. Gregory placed his menu down and took her hands with his and looked into her eyes.

Sonia stared and said, "What are you going to eat?"

Gregory replied, "Porridge with honey and some pancakes."

Sonia replied, "I'll have porridge too."

The waitress came over and Sonia pulled her hands away, taking up her menu. The waitress asked Sonia, "What would you like?"

Sonia replied, "Coffee, white Americano, and porridge with honey, the gluten-free option, please."

Gregory said, "Make it two but one normal porridge, and I'll have pancakes also, with berries and cream."

The waitress said, "Good choice," smiled and said, "Thank you." She walked to the till and entered the order.

Sonia stood up and excused herself to go to the bathroom, taking her handbag. Some time had passed and the waitress brought over the coffee. She also placed the cutlery on the table. Sonia eventually appeared through the door at the top of the stairs leading from the rest rooms. As she walked towards the table, Gregory noticed that she had bloodshot eyes. He knew that she had been crying but said nothing.

She sat and began to pour milk into her coffee and said, "What will we do today?"

Gregory replied, "I'm easy but need to get back before ten tonight." He then said, "How about a movie?"

The waitress appeared with the porridge and placed a bowl in front of them both with Gregory's pancakes. Sonia began to look up movies and cinema locations on her phone. There was one not too far from them so she booked the movie but couldn't reserve seats. As they ate there was little conversation, but Sonia kept looking at Gregory. She just picked at her porridge as she had lost her appetite. He was too engrossed in his food to even notice. When he finished, he ordered another coffee. Sonia also requested one. They both finished eating and the waitress cleared the table, leaving new mugs of coffee with them. Sonia said that she had enjoyed the evening and was feeling tired as she yawned. They finished their coffee and Gregory asked for the bill. The amount came to £15.45 and Gregory presented his card. The waitress went and fetched the card machine from the cash register desk and returned, pressing the necessary buttons to enter the amount as she looked at the bill. She then handed the machine to Gregory and he placed his card in the bottom slot. He pressed the 'yes' button and entered his pin when the machine prompted him. He then pressed 'enter' to finish the transaction while saying, "That breakfast was lovely." He then handed the card machine back to the waitress and she smiled while watching the paper receipt print.

As soon as it finished, she ripped it away, handed him his card and receipt and said, "Thank you, have a nice day."

Gregory replied, "You too."

Sonia just carried on getting her coat and bag sorted. Gregory jumped up and grabbed his coat, putting it on as he walked to the door. Sonia followed as he held it open for her. As soon as he exited, Sonia said, "This way," and pointed in the direction with one glove on. They jumped onto a tube and made their way to Baker Street. Once off the Tube, they both walked in silence towards the cinema.

Sonia entered the cinema through the double glass doors leading to the stairs and Gregory followed. There was an old ticket office booth to the right as they entered, which was unmanned and mainly for display, beside a lift. Sonia began descending the stairs to the basement while Gregory took his time glancing at the posters displayed on the walls to his left. The stairs turned to the right and finished with a reception area and a bar with two cash registers. There was a seating area for clients to sit and drink while waiting for their movie to start.

Sonia requested the wine menu from the male bar tender behind the counter and she handed it to Gregory. Gregory decided on a South African bottle of white and ordered. Sonia also requested two seats right up the front. This wouldn't have been Gregory's choice. Sonia chose two seats on the left-hand side, pointing on the LCD cash register screen. The man printed the tickets and handed them to Sonia. He then proceeded to request payment for the wine and Gregory handed him his card. All transactions were completed, so Sonia proceeded to cinema screen number one. As far as Gregory could see, there were three cinema rooms. As they entered theirs, he could see the room was small with about thirty seats and it looked very comfortable. Sonia found the seats and she sat at the aisle. Gregory sat to her right. Sonia poured the wine into his plastic glass and handed it to him. She then poured her own. Both took a sip and said it was fine. Soon after, the lights went out and the trailers began before the movie. Gregory and Sonia just relaxed and drank some wine. Over thirty minutes had passed before the movie started after the trailers.

It wasn't long into the movie when Sonia fell asleep but she managed to hold her glass without spilling any wine. Gregory found this amusing as the movie was boring to him. Every now and again Sonia would make a snorting noise and grunt, and this brought a giggle up within him. He watched the movie and poured himself another glass of wine as Sonia slept. Just minutes before the movie finished, Sonia woke and announced that the movie was good, that she had enjoyed it. Gregory just peered at her in the dim lighting. She jumped up and began getting ready to exit, gulping her wine, putting her coat on and leaving the plastic glass under her seat. Gregory followed suit and did the same.

As they exited the cinema, Gregory looked at his watch and said that he would need to go and get a Tube. Sonia appeared sad and said that she needed to go also. She had decided to leave her car parked at Gregory's and would collect it another day. Sonia very seldom used her car as she would walk or use public transport to get to most places she needed to visit.

She hadn't far to walk but Gregory had to travel on two tubes back to his house. Sonia mentioned that she was going out with her friends but didn't say which night. It was a work get-together. Gregory didn't show much interest. Sonia noticed this.

They said their goodbyes and Sonia grabbed him for a hug. He didn't resist but felt uncomfortable. He turned away and began to walk towards the Tube station. Sonia walked in the other direction. He turned and looked at her from behind. She was walking slowly. Sonia didn't turn to look back at him. He proceeded and entered down the stairs to the Tube station. He passed the machines using his card and descended on the escalator to the platform. All he could think about was Sonia and how the same situation occurred each time. When they were out drinking, all was great, but as soon as they were sober Sonia would be weird. Weird in that she would become distant and shut down in a way from communicating. He was thinking of how well they would get on together. Then the train arrived, slowing down as it came to a halt. The doors opened and he walked over to a free seat beside another man. The man looked drunk as he was glaring at everyone. The Tube was warm and didn't smell too good as some people were eating fast food. Gregory just stared at the posters along the carriage and kept thinking about the night before. He struggled to keep his eyes open as he felt tired with the heat in the carriage and the fact that he was still hungover. He managed to stay awake and catch the second train at Stockwell Tube Station.

The train finally arrived at his station and he loped, walking to the escalator to take him up to ground level. It was a busy night; a queue formed at the base of the escalator. He jumped in line, stood onto the escalator to the right-hand side and waited patiently until it reached the top. He had a short walk of about fifteen minutes to his house and he walked thinking all about the whole situation. Along the walk, his phone beeped with a message from Sonia: *Thank you for a lovely evening and for today* ☺ *Sorry for being upset.* Gregory replied, *You're welcome, sleep well.* She replied, *You too.*

Gregory reached his house and sat on his bed, taking off his shoes. As he undressed, his mind couldn't rest for thinking about Sonia and why they had all the drama. He lay on his bed and he could smell Sonia on the sheets as he was thinking.

7

Memories Gregory began to reminisce on

As his mind was racing as he lay in his bed, he remembered on a few occasions the drama of booking into hotels with Sonia. One particular event was this.

They both arrived at a four-star hotel and entered the foyer, walking to the check-in desk. Sonia was dressed in a dress and had her sunglasses on. When they reached the check-in desk, the receptionist asked if they were staying at the hotel. Gregory said, "Yes, Fitzpatrick." He knew the procedure so he put his passport and credit card on the desk.

The receptionist proceeded to book them in and Sonia said, "Can we have a quiet room, please?"

The woman replied, "The hotel is fully booked but I will do

my best." Room 101 was given. She pointed to the lift, explained which floor the room was on and mentioned breakfast times, then proceeded to say, "Enjoy your stay with us." Both Gregory and Sonia pulled their suitcases to the lift. On the first floor, they reached the room and Gregory opened the door with the key card. It was an old-style room with light browns and a reddish colour design. Gregory removed the blanket draped across the base of the bed which was design feature and commented on how dirty it was. He also removed the pillows in the same colour and threw them onto the chair near the window. Sonia checked out the bathroom to make sure there was a bath and that it was up to her standards.

Gregory put his suitcase against the wall and closed the curtains. He said he was going to shower as they had travelled for a few hours. He stripped off, folded his suit on hangers and walked to the bathroom, leaving his underwear on the floor.

As he was showering, the lights went out with a clunk and he was left in complete darkness. He heard the door to the room slam after some fidgeting at the door. He called out but there was no answer. He reached out and felt around the bathroom and managed to switch off the shower once he had rinsed the shampoo off himself. Carefully climbing out of the bath and pushing the shower curtain to one side, he found the towel rack at shoulder level and dried himself. As it was dark he couldn't see anything. The bedroom was no different as he had closed the curtains. The blackout curtains completely darkened the room. He left the bathroom after fumbling around to find the handle, using the countertop as guidance.

He felt around the room, using his hand along the wall to find his suitcase, but it was gone. He couldn't find his underwear either as Sonia had thrown it onto one of the chairs in the room. He made his way to the curtains and opened them slightly to allow the street lights to shine into the room. It didn't make much difference, but it helped. He found his way back to the bathroom and put a towel around himself. He sat on the bed looking at his underwear on the chair.

About thirty minutes passed before the door to the room opened with Sonia standing there. "I got a better room and moved the cases up to it." Smiling, she thought she was great but Gregory wasn't amused. She put the card in the socket and the lights came on. "I left your clothes there," she said as she pointed to the underwear.

Gregory said, "Yes, my underwear is here, but my clothes are gone."

Sonia said, "Oh, I'll get your case." She let the door close and went for his suitcase.

This was an occurrence that Gregory had experienced on a few occasions with changing hotel rooms.

As he began to drift into sleep, he started to think again and remembered this memory.

This memory was of a night out when Sonia had got drunk. She was so drunk that she had grabbed all her glasses of beer when the bar closed and guarded them, surrounding them with her arms on the table. Moving one hand, she pointed to his one glass and said in a slurred voice, "This is yours," then, as she held hers on the table, "Mine, all mine," laughing to herself. Sonia had three glasses to finish.

The glass she pointed at was Gregory's empty glass that he had finished up to an hour previously.

This was only the start of the night but the pub was closing; they had been drinking most of the day with friends and they had another venue to attend. But they didn't make it. Yet again they were booked into a hotel for that night.

Both Sonia and Gregory were requested by one of the bouncers in the bar to leave the premises as it was closing time. It was taking Sonia an eternity to drink her drinks and Gregory was long finished. She wouldn't share hers as she sat quietly staring into space. Sonia, in an instant, took her two drinks, stood up and wandered over to a bar stool. She plonked herself down and Gregory followed. They sat on two bar stools as the waiters began clearing the tables. Once Sonia saw the waiters spraying the tables and wiping them, she moved. The bouncer came over after he saw that they had both sat down again and he said that they could go nearer the door and sit for ten minutes. Sonia stood up and wobbled over to the seats near the entrance, leaving her drinks behind. Gregory took her two drinks over to her as she watched closely that he didn't drink any. They sat for a few minutes until one of the waiters came over and asked Sonia to leave as the pub was closed. She turned and proceeded to tell everyone that they worked for her and that it was her bar and to go away. The bouncer laughed and said to Gregory, "Please make your way out the door." Gregory nodded and took Sonia's hand, asking her to come. He got off his seat and Sonia looked pretty annoyed with him.

He said, "I'm leaving. Stay if you like."

She replied, "I will."Gregory walked to the door and Sonia stumbled off her stool, holding her coat, and followed behind. He pushed open the double doors and Sonia fell out the door behind him. She collapsed onto her knees with her arms stretched out both sides of her in the air. Gregory turned and laughed, extending his right hand to help her up. At this stage he was pissed off with her but managed to get the attention of a taxi. As the taxi stopped, he opened the back door and swiftly helped her in. He climbed in behind and she was out cold in minutes as the car drove down the road. The driver was quiet until they arrived at the hotel. "That will be £12.40, please."

Gregory handed him £15 and said, "Keep the change." He jumped out and pulled Sonia towards him across the black leather seat and lifted her up, placing her on his right shoulder.

He had to hold down her short dress with his left hand so that her bum wasn't flashing to everyone as he walked or stumbled with difficulty. In this particular hotel, the entrance door was at one end and the reception desk at the other. The lift was to the left of the reception desk and the guest seating area was in the centre of the foyer. He had to walk this distance as other patrons were sitting having a drink. He was struggling as Sonia wasn't light. She was nearly his height of 5' 11" and he was sweating. As he walked, she would wake periodically and slap his bottom, laughing, then return to resting again. He approached the lift and pushed the button while everyone was staring at him, including the hotel staff at the reception desk. Standing there, he realised maybe the lift wouldn't be a good idea as it would be too hot inside and Sonia might vomit, so he made his way to the double doors leading to the stairs. He presented his hotel door key card to open the door and entered the stairwell. He put the door card in his front pocket. There were four flights of stairs to climb and as he approached the last level of stairs his legs were getting tired. At the top of the stairs on the landing, he entered a corridor through a set of double doors and walked down another corridor to the next set of double doors. He stopped and leaned against the wall, holding Sonia, as he was exhausted. There wasn't a peep from her; she was out cold. He walked again until he reached their bedroom door. While standing at the room door he managed to get the key card from his front right pocket, balancing Sonia on his right shoulder while leaning against the wall. The door lock opened as he pushed the key card into the slot and he pushed his way inside, inserting the card to switch the lights on. He stumbled over to the bed and placed her on it with a flip, thrusting her in the air slightly. She landed gracefully and remained asleep lying on her back. Gregory went to the bathroom as he had been bursting to use the toilet since being in the pub. He brushed his teeth, finished in the bathroom and proceeded to the bedroom. He removed his clothes to his boxer shorts and climbed into bed. At this stage, Sonia climbed onto the floor as she was too hot and disorientated. Gregory climbed under the bed covers and switched off the lights, leaving her on the floor, fully dressed with her coat on, smiling as he closed his eyes. He too fell asleep but this was short-lived as he woke to a rattling noise about an hour and a half later.

He couldn't figure out what the noise was but soon realised that there were several mice munching on their chocolate on the chair in the room. Sonia had put the chocolate that she had bought earlier on the chair while she was getting ready to go out.He couldn't see any movement as his eyes adjusted to the room, watching from the bed. Each time he moved, the noise stopped for a few minutes, to start again when he was quiet. He was exhausted and realised that Sonia would scream something terrible if she woke so he didn't stir. He smiled yet again and left her on the floor, thinking about how he would tell her in the morning. Sonia was completely relaxed and fast asleep so he didn't want to disturb her now. He fell asleep again to wake around 6am with Sonia sitting on the bed talking to herself, saying that she had slept on the floor and was all confused. She took her coat off, letting it fall to the floor, and removed her clothes in the same fashion. She climbed under the duvet and snuggled up to Gregory, saying she was cold. Gregory pretended he was asleep as Sonia cuddled into him, breathing heavily as the hangover had begun. At this stage the mice had gone and the room was bright as the sun entered through the curtains. The curtains didn't have the blackout material so the light shone through them. Sonia and Gregory slept cuddled up to one another.

Gregory had set the alarm clock for 10.30am as breakfast finished at 11am. The alarm activated and Gregory pulled away from Sonia to switch the alarm off, returning to cuddle and hug into Sonia. There was a slight groan from Sonia and Gregory laughed as he pressed his left-hand index finger on her right cheek. He did it a second time. Sonia lifted her head and said, "What's so funny? It's really hot. I need water." Gregory smiled and told her that there were mice eating her chocolate while she slept on the floor. Sonia turned over and thrust her bottom against him and lay her head down. She didn't believe him and requested another ten minutes just to sleep. Gregory continued to tell her about the munching sounds from the mice on the chair.

This got Sonia's attention. She turned to face him and said, "You left me on the floor."

Gregory laughed and said, "You wouldn't get into bed last night." He flicked the blankets off him and proceeded to get up. He stood at the edge of the bed and said, "Are you coming for breakfast?"

There was no reply so he entered the bathroom, leaving Sonia to think while she lay there.

Gregory finally went into a deep sleep after this memory.

8

Waking feeling exhausted

GREGORY WOKE UP AFTER HAVING A NIGHT OF WAKING in between sleeping and twisting and turning as his mind wouldn't relax. This was unusual for Gregory as he would normally just put his head to the pillow and float away into a deep sleep. While lying facing the ceiling, he thought it would be nice to go away on holiday with Sonia. He picked up his phone and the display showed that it was 8.33am. He began to type the message and send it regardless of the time. *Good morning Sonia, how would you feel about going to Thailand or somewhere else together? Xx.* Surprisingly, Sonia text back immediately with a reply. *Yes, I'd love that. When? X.* Gregory text, *Can we meet this afternoon?* Sonia said, *Yes, 15.00 @ Oxford Circus Tube Station. X*

Gregory replied, *Looking forward to it. X.* Gregory put his phone down and lay thinking of places to go but fell back asleep as his eyes felt really heavy, to wake later at 12.15pm. He jumped up with shock after looking at the time on his phone and proceeded to the bathroom to shave, shower and get ready to meet Sonia later that afternoon. He was very aware that she had to go away on a trip for work for several months and wondered when they could book the trip together. He decided to wait until he saw her rather than to overthink. He got himself ready and ate breakfast, some porridge with honey with a cup of coffee. He even managed to put on a clothes wash in the washing machine and hang it all up on the drying rack before leaving to meet her. Gregory was organised like this as he enjoyed his own company.

It was 2.15pm and Gregory got his coat, scarf and gloves on as he made his way to the Tube station. He had two trains to catch, the Northern Line to Stockwell and then the Victoria Line to Oxford Circus. The travel time was about forty minutes. He locked the five-lever lock on his front door and began the walk to the Tube station. He was excited to discuss travel plans with Sonia but he also reminded himself why they broke up previously. He sat on the Tube reminiscing about the time that they had had together, both good and bad.

Sonia was a very independent girl, confident in her abilities, but she lacked self-esteem. She didn't have confidence in her own self-worth or self-respect. This was an issue in their relationship prior to them getting back together as Sonia would have to keep in contact with all her exes and have a string of admirers to make her feel better about herself.

During their relationship previously, Sonia went to Saudi Arabia, to a place called Jeddah, to gain experience in her profession. While she was there for several months, there were many parties that Sonia had attended. In the beginning, Gregory and Sonia would Skype every night when they would chat for hours. The communication reduced over time as she made new friends and attended many of the expat parties. There were some nights Gregory wouldn't hear from her until the next afternoon and he became suspicious. Sometimes he didn't hear from her for up to two days. He was correct in his intuitions because Sonia was seeing a Saudi guy while abroad. He questioned Sonia during a Skype call and at first she denied it, but she admitted it later in the conversation. This gutted Gregory, therefore he couldn't communicate with her anymore.

At first Sonia had told stories, like she stayed in a friend's bed and there was no Wi-Fi, but the stories kept changing and Gregory could remember word for word every conversation. He had caught her out several times and got very frustrated because she had lied to him. He found this to be so hurtful because it reminded him of his father and the way his father continued to promise things to him as a child and not fulfil the promises. Gregory just didn't like to be lied to. He would have preferred her to be upfront as this was playing with his emotions. It took a while for Gregory to work out that at the parties, she was seeing maybe two guys at the same time. Sonia was very clever because she knew that for the parties that she attended, one of the guys she was seeing wouldn't be allowed in, or get an invitation, because he was a citizen of the country. This enabled her to see another Irish guy too. Gregory totally removed himself from contacting Sonia as he worked out that the stories continuously changed. Sonia had forgotten what she had told him previously so she would keep trying to change the topic of conversation.

Several months had passed and Sonia had returned home from Saudi Arabia to go back home to County Kerry. While she was home with her family, she text Gregory to see how he was. They began texting again to arrange a meet-up. That's when they began to date again in Dublin. Sonia would drive to Dublin on the Weekends to see Gregory and they would stay in several hotels as they selected the cheapest one for that particular weekend. It was very stressful because neither of them had the money to throw away on hotels but they really needed to see each other.

9

Meeting at 3pm, Oxford Circus Tube Station

GREGORY ARRIVED AT 2.45PM AT THE EXIT TO THE TUBE station. He stood on the pavement and text Sonia. *I have arrived. X.* Sonia replied, *I'm on Regent Street, be there in 5 mins.* Gregory waited patiently and Sonia arrived on time. She had gone to a shop to buy underwear but couldn't find anything that she liked. She wasn't in the best of moods so Gregory said that he would help her find something. He was good at picking out clothing as he had a good eye for things and he liked sexy underwear. His afternoon felt like it had started off well. Sonia was tired as she had also not slept the night before. She was also frustrated that she hadn't found underwear that she liked.

They arrived at a department store on Oxford Circus and Gregory walked around the underwear section with Sonia. Immediately he began to take items from the display hangers, handing them to Sonia. She would then say, "Do you think…?" as she stared at the garment. Then she would proceed to search for her size. Gregory had found several items in minutes and Sonia felt relieved. Sonia went to try on the underwear in the changing room while Gregory wandered and found the sex toy section of the shop in the basement area. Gregory wasn't long looking around before Sonia came to stand beside him. She smiled, rubbed her nose playfully against his while grabbing his crotch area, and she then walked away. Gregory jumped with shock as he felt a rush of heat through his body. He smiled but quickly looked around the shop to see if anyone had noticed. Sonia made her way to the till area to pay for her items that she liked and fitted correctly. She didn't want Gregory to see what she had decided upon as he walked to stand beside her, all giddy. Sonia paid the assistant and the items were placed in a bag. They left the shop in each other's arms.

Sonia became quiet and Gregory knew something was up with her. He asked if she was okay and she said she was fine but remained quiet. After several minutes, Sonia asked, "Where is this going?"

Gregory replied, "Really, can you not just enjoy the moment together without dragging the situation down?"

Sonia sighed and said, "Okay," as they continued to walk.

Gregory asked, "Where are we going?"

Sonia replied, "To get food and chat about the holiday you asked me about."

Gregory just followed alongside her, not feeling great as he knew there was more to come regarding Sonia's insecurity. Gregory just remained silent as he could feel the turmoil that Sonia was showing with her body language due to her over thinking. Sonia walked straight to a restaurant that she had been to before. She entered through the main door and waited at the waiting area to be seated. Gregory just followed. When the waitress came over and asked if it was for two, showing two fingers in the air, Sonia nodded and she followed the waitress quickly to a table. Sonia removed her coat, placing it beside her as she sat on the comfortable padded wall seat, leaving the hard wooden chair for Gregory to sit on. Gregory noticed but didn't complain. He just took his coat off and placed it on the back of his chair with his gloves and scarf beside Sonia. He sat quietly looking at the menu placed on the table.

Sonia sighed and said, "I'd like a glass of white wine."

Gregory replied, "I'm not drinking today." Sonia looked at the menu again to choose what type of wine to drink by the glass. She would have ordered a bottle if Gregory was going to share as it worked out cheaper. The waiter came over and Sonia asked which wine he would recommend. He pointed at the Italian wine and said that it was a light wine infused with pear. Sonia asked for a taste of the wine so the waiter acknowledged and walked to the bar.

Sonia stared at Gregory and asked, "Are you okay?"

Gregory replied, "Yes I'm fine, but you're not, what's up?"

Sonia said that she was thinking a lot. Gregory sat back in his chair. Sonia then said, "I was happy going out and enjoyed my independence. Now there is no excitement and I would love my own house that I could call home and to have a family."

Gregory had heard this so many times that it made him become tense. He explained again, "Sonia, I am saving for a mortgage so that I can get a house."

Sonia replied, "Whatever."Gregory felt his entire body recoil away from Sonia as she said this. It was his body's reaction as a defence mechanism. The waiter arrived back at the table. He placed an empty glass on the table in front of Sonia and opened the bottle top, pouring a sample to taste. Sonia reached out and lifted the glass, swirling it as she raised her hand, peering at the liquid. Gregory looked in surprise and said to himself, *Really?* as he felt a little uncomfortable. She sipped the wine and took a moment to say, "You try," as she handed the glass to Gregory.

Gregory took the glass and drank some. Immediately he said, "That's nice, you should have that one."

Sonia replied, "Are you sure you won't have some?" Gregory shook his head and requested a lemonade. The waiter took the wine bottle and poured a fresh glass of wine for Sonia and returned with a bottle of lemonade with ice and a slice of lemon for Gregory.

The waiter asked, "Are you ready to order?"

Sonia said, "Yes, I'll have the sea bass with potato and spinach." Gregory ordered the fillet steak cooked medium to well with pepper sauce and fries. The waiter proceeded to the kitchen as Gregory and Sonia lifted their glasses and said 'cheers'. Sonia would be offended if they didn't say cheers while looking into each other's eyes. She believed it would put an omen upon them sexually if they didn't.

Gregory asked Sonia, "Where would you like to go for a short trip away and also a place to get some sun later in the year?"

Sonia smiled and replied, "Edinburgh." They both talked about going to Edinburgh as the food arrived at the table. Sonia asked, "Would you like to go there?" Gregory just put a piece of steak in his mouth and began to chew. He thought for a moment and agreed by nodding his head.

When he finished chewing he had a drink of lemonade and said, "Yes, let's look shortly and book for the weekend after next." Sonia picked up her phone and checked her calendar. She confirmed that she was free that weekend. While Sonia was checking, Gregory noticed several messages and missed calls on the upper left-hand side of her display as her phone vibrated. Sonia closed the apps by swiping quickly. A message appeared as Sonia was showing Gregory an image of Edinburgh; quickly she swiped this one away also. Gregory felt a little weird inside when this happened and he sat back in his seat and took a breath. He began to eat again.

Sonia said, "You've gone a bit quiet and funny."

Gregory replied, "I'm good, just thinking of Edinburgh." Gregory could feel that something wasn't right but tried to remain neutral and chose not to ask. Sonia jumped up from her chair and left the table, holding her phone in her left hand, walking towards the toilet. She tried to hide the fact that she had her phone, as she moved it in front of her while her back was facing Gregory. Gregory noticed this behaviour and continued to eat. A strange feeling came over him as his energy felt like it moved downwards from his head and he felt sick in his stomach area. He continued to eat and pondered on why she would be hiding her phone and placing it on silent.

Sonia returned from the toilet and sat in a giddy humour, asking if Gregory would share a dessert. As he replied Sonia placed her mobile into her handbag, which was sitting on the seat to the right side of her. Sonia hadn't eaten much from her main course but picked at her food in deep thought.

Gregory had just finished his meal and asked, "Are you okay?"

Sonia replied, "My tummy feels funny."

Gregory asked if she would like something else and Sonia said no. After a few minutes passed, Gregory said, "Would you like a brandy?"

Sonia replied, "Yes."

Gregory decided to have one too. Sonia immediately called the waiter over and requested two double brandy. The waiter asked which brand and Sonia replied, "Hennessy, please."

The waiter replied, "I will bring it shortly." He also asked if they had both finished their meals and they replied, "Yes." He cleared the table.

Sonia smiled again and sat back in her seat looking at Gregory. Then she asked him, "What's happening?"

Gregory replied, "What do you mean?"

Sonia replied, "With us, life?"

Gregory adjusted himself in his seat and replied, "You keep trying to control everything and I can't relax when you do this. I would like to feel and make decisions myself."

Sonia sighed and reached for her mobile phone in her bag. She appeared to have tears forming from her eyes as Gregory watched her. He didn't comment but asked what dessert she would like to share. Sonia turned to her left to notice the waiter arriving with the brandy glasses. The waiter placed the glasses on the table and gave both Sonia and Gregory a dessert menu. Sonia glanced and said, "Eton Mess, I'll share that."

Gregory said, "Okay." As he replied, Sonia began to check her messages and she smiled, looking at her phone. Gregory felt sick again in his stomach. He reached for his glass, raised it and said, "Here's to a trip to Edinburgh."

Sonia lifted her glass in between looking on her phone and said, "Yes, here's to Edinburgh." Shortly after sipping the brandy, Sonia showed Gregory an image of the main street in Edinburgh.

Gregory said, "That looks really nice."

Sonia said, "Yes, I was there before."

Gregory drank some more brandy and he felt more relaxed. He asked Sonia, "Who are you texting?"

Sonia replied, "What do you mean?"

Gregory said, "I know it's another guy."

Sonia said, "Nope." She opened her phone and selected a text thread with a girlfriend of hers and said, "It's Ruth that I am texting." Gregory felt sick again in the stomach and really uncomfortable. He excused himself and went to the gents' toilet. As he walked towards the toilet, he was thinking that there was another guy that Sonia was texting and that she was hiding this from him. He knew that something wasn't right. While Gregory was in the bathroom, he decided to believe Sonia and not ask her again.

When he returned to the table, Sonia said, "I found a hotel and it's really nice."

Gregory said, "Okay, can we book it?"

Sonia said, "Yes, it's booked."

Gregory smiled and said, "That was quick."

Sonia replied, "I love to travel." She then asked, "Where shall we go for the sun?"

Gregory pulled his phone from his right-hand side front jean pocket. "I'll have a look," he said. As soon as he entered 'sun holidays' on his search engine, an image of the Maldives appeared on his screen. Straight away he selected the image and said, "Check this out." The image showed a timber-built structure on stilts standing in the sea. The colours were beautiful on the image.

Sonia said, "The Maldives, I've always wanted to go there."

Gregory typed in the search engine 'flights London to the Maldives'. As soon as the costs appeared, he said, "I can't afford that."

Sonia said, "Me too." They both began searching for other destinations, Sonia asked Gregory if he would like another brandy.

Gregory replied, "Yes." Sonia left the table and asked the waiter for two more drinks while she made her way to the toilet. The brandy was having an effect on Gregory; as he was looking at his phone, he felt a little light-headed, therefore he placed his phone on the table and glanced around the restaurant. He sat gazing at a picture on the wall. The picture had a human skull with a black bird standing on it. He loved the picture, therefore he stood up and walked closer to read the sale value. It was £3,500. Gregory looked at the image again and returned to his seat. As he sat, Sonia appeared and smiled at Gregory as she walked towards him. Gregory watched her walk over.

Sonia squeezed between the tables to sit as Gregory said, "What do you think of that picture?"

Sonia said, "It's freaky."

Gregory told her the price and she replied, "It wouldn't be in my house." After she said this Sonia went quiet again.

Gregory noticed and asked again, "What's wrong?"

Sonia replied, "I'd love a house I can call home. I want a family." Sonia started to cry. The tears rolled down her face. As she wiped her eyes, more tears appeared. Gregory handed his table napkin to Sonia and she wiped her eyes. Gregory sat quietly, feeling uncomfortable, while Sonia composed herself and then sat quietly. It wasn't long before she got up and returned to the bathroom. This time she remained there for at least twenty minutes.

Gregory began to get frustrated as he sat waiting. Several times the waiter passed and asked if everything was okay. Each time Gregory would reply, "Yes, everything is okay," but feeling tenser each time as it was embarrassing for him. Sonia returned to the table and took a large gulp of brandy then placed her glass on the table. She appeared agitated as she picked at her chin. The waiter returned with the second brandy and Sonia looked away so that he wouldn't see that she was crying.

Sonia started to comment when the waiter left the table about how Gregory didn't have to worry but she had to because she was getting older. Gregory said that he would love a child and to get married but they needed to find a proper place to live and then start a family. Sonia remained quiet again. Gregory reached across the table with both hands open, facing upwards as he waited for Sonia to place hers within his.

She did this and Gregory said, "I love you. It will all work out but you have to be patient and stop trying to control how I feel. You keep telling me how I am feeling when most of the time you're wrong, then you get me frustrated and you get frustrated, then the communication breaks down and you get annoyed, you blame me for everything. I can't handle this."

Sonia replied, "I'm sorry I make you feel this way but I am not any younger."

Gregory replied, "It's not my fault you chose the path you did. I came into the equation later in your life but I seem to have to put up with you blaming me for your past decisions. Sonia, I am trying my best but sometimes it feels like I am not good enough for you." Tears were still running down Sonia's face and from time to time she would wipe them with the napkin. She took another drink from her glass and sighed. Gregory said, "I love you and I am one hundred percent with you."

Sonia squeezed his hands as she held them tightly. Gregory felt a heat rush through his body and he felt himself becoming turned on sexually. Gregory very much wanted to have a child and settle down with Sonia, but past events kept raising their ugly heads as Gregory would remember them. His worry was that Sonia didn't know when to stop drinking and then the anger would surface and she would cause a scene. This was very embarrassing for Gregory as he hated to be the centre of attention, especially in these circumstances. As the night drew closer, Sonia and Gregory had had quite a lot to drink, especially the two double brandy they had both consumed. Sonia began to get a little aggressive and started to put Gregory down. She said things like, "If you loved me you would cuddle more and show me more attention." Then as Gregory moved closer or try to give Sonia a kiss, she moved away or twisted her head in the opposite direction. Gregory then retracted and remained quiet. Sonia then got agitated and drank more.

Gregory never gave into the drama or games that were played to gain attention and this caused Sonia to rebel in another way. Sonia felt a heaviness around her and a sick feeling in her stomach, which made her more agitated. The alcohol didn't help.

She said to Gregory that her past boyfriends would really take care of her. She compared intimate details and questioned why Gregory didn't do what the other guys did. Gregory felt really uncomfortable and wanted to leave. The love connection that he had for Sonia was something special and he only wished that she would stop doing this when she didn't get her own way. Sonia had never lived with another guy, so all her experience was from short-term relationships, one-night stands, or returning to the same exes for a night or weekend away.

Sonia began to reflect on the past every time she got drunk. She would discuss their past breakup and how it had affected her but never the reason why they broke up in the first place. The more she would talk like this the more the anger would surface, and at times she would push Gregory away and say not so nice things. This would make Gregory close up emotionally and he would distance himself from her. He would excuse himself and go to the bathroom and contemplate leaving without her, or he would take out his phone in her company and lose himself scrolling through apps. As soon as Sonia would realise Gregory was not happy with her, she would grab him and kiss him. At this stage he would lose interest. He would just want to get her home. This in itself would create a feeling that Sonia didn't like: rejection. Sonia had always had an issue with rejection, especially when it involved a male.

The fact that she really loved Gregory made it more difficult for Sonia as her pattern of behaviour that would normally work with others didn't affect Gregory. He didn't bite when she threw her toys from the pram; he would observe Sonia and not react, therefore her emotions would accelerate. He hated to see Sonia like this and he tried every time to console her. The worst part was getting her out of the pub or venue they were in once alcoholic consumption was involved. It would be a mission as Sonia didn't know when she had reached her limit and then the drama would begin. Gregory would sober up quite quickly once she had kicked off and he would have to escort her home. She would always have to stop several times while walking home and tell Gregory to go on his way and that she would be the finest. This would annoy Gregory because he cared so much for Sonia; it hurt something terrible. Gregory would feel so much empathy for Sonia and he would do everything for her, but in her eyes it wasn't enough. Nothing that Gregory did for her was good enough. Sonia would find fault in anything he would organise or do. Over time, this situation would gradually chip away at him, making him feel less of a person.

Sonia had half a glass of brandy left to drink and Gregory had finished his. Sonia wanted more but Gregory said no to this and requested that they begin their journey home. Sonia looked at Gregory and said, "I'll stay, you go on your way," slurring her words.

Gregory felt a pain in his heart and replied, "Please Sonia, I love you and I would like to go now."

Sonia stood up and walked towards the toilet. On her way she stopped and spoke to the waiter. Gregory watched but remained seated and felt that the night was going to turn into another mission to get Sonia home. A few minutes later Sonia emerged from the toilet corridor and walked towards the table. She stopped at the bar and the waiter gave her another glass. Gregory wasn't impressed at all but he sat quietly.

Sonia sat and said, "I'll have this, you be on your way, now!"

Gregory replied, "Come on, Sonia, have some respect for me, will you please?"

Sonia laughed and drank some of her brandy. At this stage she had two glasses in front of her. She said, "You broke my heart."

Gregory replied, "Sonia, you pushed me away and you are doing the same as you have done every time you get drunk. The pattern seems to be repeating itself. You told me you had changed over the year we were apart and that you had travelled and discovered that you wanted to settle down and have a family."

Sonia remained quiet, then she slurred, "You walked away."

Gregory said, "Sonia, you're not listening and you won't remember yet again tomorrow."

Sonia replied, "Whatever." She felt angry and was in fear of losing Gregory again. Her method to draw him closer was to push him away to the edge of breaking point and then draw him closer again. Sonia liked to be in control but Gregory was too laid-back and would just agree when Sonia started becoming intense. Sonia would feel a build-up of energy around her heart, a pressure. She would also feel a heaviness around her shoulders and her stomach would feel sick. As soon as this would begin to build during the frustration, she would feel her temperament becoming defensive. Sonia would then forget what she had discussed previously and her stories would change, making Gregory challenge her once he noticed this. Sonia would become more defensive and the stories would continue. Gregory had issues with people that lie. He would get very frustrated as it reminded him of his father and the way his father promised the sun, moon and stars but nothing happened. Gregory was a very honest, truthful guy and he only expected the same from his partner, but this wasn't the case.Gregory stood up and began to put his coat on. Sonia watched him and said, "Where are you going?"

Gregory replied, "I'm going home."

Sonia replied, "Best of luck."

This fuelled the fire, so Gregory zipped his coat and began to walk out. As he reached the door and began to open it, Sonia called, "Wait." Gregory felt relieved in one way but wanted to just get away also. He was drained inside and felt emotionally destroyed. Sonia lifted her glass of brandy and knocked it back in one gulp. She proceeded to follow it with the second glass. Then she stood with a wobble, holding the table while she laughed and struggled to put on her coat.

Gregory walked over and tried to help Sonia, to be pushed away again as she shoved against him. He said, "Okay," and stood back away from her. Gregory walked, embarrassed, towards the door, feeling pretty useless. He opened the door as Sonia walked behind and he held it open for her. She just walked past him as she adjusted her bag on her shoulder. As Sonia walked, she lost her footing as she caught her high heel on a paving slab. Sonia dropped to her knees and Gregory tried to catch her.

Unfortunately he wasn't quick enough and she said, "Leave me," in an angry voice. Gregory continued to try to help her up as he grabbed her arm and Sonia pushed him away as she stood up again. She reacted with, "That was your fault; you should have been holding me."

Gregory, at this stage, wasn't impressed and had already walked in front of Sonia. He felt that he wasn't appreciated and was confused as Sonia wanted him to hold her but pushed him away. There was silence between them for about fifty metres as they walked.

Sonia then said, "Why are you walking ahead?"

Gregory replied, "You told me several times to go."

Sonia remained quiet and walked some more. She went deep into thought and became emotional. She started to cry but kept her head facing the ground, remaining quiet as she stumbled along trying to walk in a straight line. The high-heeled shoes didn't help at all. As she walked, she began to think about her life. She began to get a pain in her chest area and a pressure around her heart. She thought of how nice it would be to be married and have children of her own. This made her feel more emotional and she stopped walking. She turned and faced a building entrance. Gregory was walking ahead of her and would turn to check that she was still behind periodically. Gregory turned and saw Sonia standing facing the building and he knew she was crying. He turned and walked straight to her with no hesitation and held her tightly. Sonia placed her head on his left shoulder and he moved his face to the side of her head. Sonia's hair completely smothered his face and he could smell her perfume and her natural skin smell. He pulled back slightly, lifted Sonia's chin with his left hand and kissed her on the lips. Sonia became light-headed as their mouths touched. Her lips were moist and her mouth opened as she wanted more. Gregory pulled her closer to him and their bodies became warm as Sonia pressed up against Gregory's groin. Sonia moved her face alongside his and put his earlobe in her mouth and said, "I want you."

Gregory moved his head back so that he could face Sonia and he began kissing her again. After a passionate kiss, Gregory said, "Let's go home and continue this."

Sonia said, "Yes."

Gregory was relieved that she was going to go home with no more hesitation and at the same time feeling deflated. They were near the Tube station and had two trains to catch before they could get off to make their way to Gregory's place. Gregory and Sonia walked hand in hand. Sonia would stumble from time to time and laugh. Gregory was in full concentration as they descended the steps into the Tube station. As they reached the control barrier, Sonia grabbed her bag from her shoulder and began to rummage around. She stood frustrated and plonked her bag on the top of the machine, blocking the passage for passengers wanting to continue on their journey. Sonia continued searching in her handbag, oblivious to her surroundings. It took a while and Gregory remained calm, watching Sonia pull all sorts of stuff from her handbag. At one moment she commented to herself, "I was looking for that," then she said aloud, "Found it," smiling as she looked up to a group of unhappy people staring at her blocking the machine. Sonia just swiped her card and soldiered on towards the escalator. Gregory had to wait and get back into the queue and swipe his card to follow. Sonia waited at the top of the escalator and they took each other's hands as Gregory stood on it first. He turned to face Sonia as she followed and they embraced in a short kiss. Gregory then turned and faced the direction of the escalator. Sonia moved closer and hugged into him. Gregory just stared at all the advertisements as they passed. Sonia remained snuggled into him until they reached the bottom.

They both disembarked and proceeded in the direction of the Victoria Line. There were many waiting already on the platform so Gregory said, "Let's walk to the end." Sonia just grunted at this moment. The heat was starting to make her feel sleepy and drunk. Gregory could feel she was beginning to slow down as she walked and he became concerned. He continuously talked to Sonia to keep her alert but she was fading. She was more relaxed within herself as the anger dissipated but Gregory was still feeling the after-effects on his system. Sonia managed to get a seat on the train near the doors and she leaned up against the glass partition and closed her eyes. Gregory stood in front of her and watched her as she drifted off. He was very much in love with her and this showed as he fixed her hair as it fell forward, covering her face. He gently moved her head back slightly and slid his fingers under her hair, moving it back from her face to behind her ear. He smiled, watching her head vibrate leaning against the glass partition as she tried to get comfortable. Gregory touched Sonia on her shoulder when their stop was approaching and Sonia just jumped up and stood beside him. As the train began to come to a stop, Sonia cuddled into Gregory and closed her eyes. Gregory had to talk to Sonia and insist that she opened her eyes and get ready to get off. Sonia just moaned quietly.

The train stopped and the doors opened. Gregory had his arm around Sonia and he walked her to the Northern Line platform. As they walked to the platform a train was already pulling up. The doors opened and Gregory walked Sonia to a seat. This time he sat beside her. Sonia immediately leaned to her left, placed her head on his shoulder and closed her eyes. Gregory placed his right hand on her leg and she placed her left hand on his. Gregory was also starting to get tired but he knew he had to remain awake. Eventually they arrived at their stop and this time Gregory had to wake Sonia up. She lifted her head and looked dazed. He said, "We are here now." Sonia smiled and closed her eyes. Gregory poked her and said, "Come on, Sonia, time to get off." Sonia didn't move. Gregory took his left hand and twisted his body, lifting her head and saying, "Wakey wakey." Sonia grunted and opened her eyes. She jumped up again and grabbed the handrail. The train came to a stop and the doors opened. Sonia proceeded to exit on her own and manoeuvred out the door, just about keeping her balance. She managed not to fall on the ground but staggered to the platform seating area. There she waited for Gregory, who came behind, laughing. Sonia wasn't impressed and she gently boxed him in the stomach area.

Gregory said, "Wait till I get you home."

Sonia replied, "Uhh, I'm scared."

Gregory embraced her and kissed her lips once again as they faced each other. Sonia began to kiss him back with passion and she was exhaling as her mouth touched his. He could feel how moist her lips were and that she was feeling aroused. Gregory was also becoming aroused and was very conscious of having an erection. He knew he had to walk some distance and this wouldn't be comfortable. He could also feel a moist spot forming on his boxer shorts. Gregory placed his two hands each side of Sonia's face and he kissed her lips, holding that position for a few seconds. When he released her, Sonia felt dizzy.

As she stood looking and grinning at him, she took her right hand and grabbed his crotch. She said, "Now then, I want you to show me the way home." Gregory jumped with surprise and composed himself. He wrapped his left arm around Sonia and began to walk with her to the escalator. As they arrived at the escalator, Gregory let Sonia walk on first. Gregory followed and Sonia turned to face him. In an instance she grabbed Gregory's head and placed it between her breasts and laughed. Gregory pushed her back gently with caution, still holding her, and said, "Sonia," with embarrassment. Sonia turned to face the direction of the escalator, laughing to herself. Gregory cuddled her from behind and Sonia held both his hands on her belly area.

They had a short walk to Gregory's house when they exited the station. Once they arrived Gregory opened the five-lever lock and then the upper lock, opening the door. He switched on the light and turned off the alarm system. Sonia took off her high-heeled shoes and walked up to Gregory's bedroom. Gregory made his way into the kitchen, got two pint glasses and filled them with natural mineral water. He then proceeded to the hallway, turned on the alarm to the night setting, double-locked the front door, switched off the lights and proceeded upstairs. When he reached the landing, he could see through the hinged part of the door that Sonia was on the bed, lying on her back with her feet on the floor, asleep. Gregory walked into the room, placed the glasses of water on the bedside table and walked back into the landing area to switch off the lights. He took off his coat, scarf and jumper and placed them in his wardrobe. He closed the curtains and walked over to Sonia, put his legs each side of hers, learned forward and pulled her up towards him. He leaned her to one side as he pulled her arm out of the sleeve and then repeated the same for her other arm. Eventually he removed her coat . It was a difficult manoeuvre as Sonia's head dropped onto his right shoulder. He managed to get her coat off and he placed her back down on the bed. He folded up her coat as best he could and threw it onto the chair beside the wardrobe. He then turned and gently placed his hands up her dress and took hold of her tights. He lifted her up slightly as he pulled her tights and knickers down her thighs to her feet. He took her right foot out of the tights first and her knickers followed. Then he removed her left side. He threw the tights, with knickers attached, over towards the chair but missed. He was building up a sweat as it wasn't an easy task. He was also very aroused, his penis erect and secreting fluid. He lifted Sonia up again by pulling her towards him, placing one hand behind her as a support and using the other to unzip her dress. Once he managed this, he lifted her up again and pulled the dress over her head. Holding her upright, he proceeded to remove her bra. He was never good at this and struggled to unlatch the clips. As he was doing this Sonia awakened as she felt cold. When she realised what was happening, she reached forward and grabbed Gregory's belt buckle and fiddled a bit until it unfastened. Once she achieved this, she opened his jean button and proceeded to pull apart his fly buttons one by one. She slid her hand between his belly and boxer shorts, grabbing his penis. Gregory jumped. Sonia said, "Wow, you are wet."

Gregory replied, "I know, but your hand is freezing." Gregory managed to release her bra and he pushed her back down on the bed. He placed his hands on both sides of her body as she lay smiling and he placed his mouth over her right nipple. He sucked gently and caressed her breast with his right hand, holding it while he licked it. Sonia exhaled, and thrusted her body towards him. She reached both sides of Gregory with both hands and took his jeans, pulling them down. She then used her feet to guide his jeans to his ankles. Sonia raised her hands both sides of Gregory's head and pulled him closer to kiss him. Gregory bent his elbows and lowered himself until they embraced in a kiss. Once their lips touched, Sonia took Gregory's penis and guided it towards her vagina. She rubbed it gently against her vagina, inserted just a small amount and then used it to caress herself a little more. Gregory thrusted forward as this aroused him, but Sonia stopped him. She then moved her hand along his penis and caressed him. Gregory kissed Sonia and groaned as she teased him. He moved his lips towards her right ear and placed her earlobe between his lips, gently caressing it. This excited Sonia and she placed him inside her.

"Gently," she said. "I'm sensitive." Gregory positioned himself and slowly moved forward and back until she became moist. He removed his penis, smothered his hand with saliva, rubbed his penis and then inserted it again. This time he inserted himself all he could. Sonia groaned. Gregory remained in this position and kissed her. Sonia moved her hips as she felt very aroused. Gregory moved his head down to her left breast and licked around the areola, under her breast and slowly up to the nipple. As he was doing this, his right hand was pinching her right nipple. He then began thrusting in and out with a slow rhythm so that Sonia could feel him inside her. As Sonia could feel him, he removed his penis and proceeded to take off his jeans and boxer shorts from around his ankles. Sonia became frustrated and as soon as he managed to remove his clothes, he took her body and twisted it to the side. He then climbed onto the bed with her body on its side. Then he slid his left leg between both of hers, lifted her left leg and inserted himself. With her left leg on his left shoulder, he moved closer and inserted himself so that he could penetrate more. While doing this, he grabbed her breast with his right hand, leaning on her as he pinched her nipple. Sonia went crazy, especially as he picked up pace and penetrated her more deeply. To annoy her, he then stopped and licked her vagina until she nearly climaxed, then inserted himself again. He did this several times in different positions and eventually she climaxed. He enjoyed teasing her. Sonia knew what she wanted and he knew how to deliver. On this occasion, they both managed to climax together and this brought them closer in an embrace. Sonia reached over Gregory as he lay exhausted on his back and she pulled the duvet over them both. It wasn't long before they fell asleep in each other's arms.

10

Gregory feeling uneasy

THE NEXT MORNING GREGORY WOKE WITH HIS ARM UNDER Sonia. It was feeling painful as the blood was drained from it. He asked Sonia if he could have his arm back. Sonia moved and he shuffled as he dragged his arm away from Sonia but couldn't lift it. The sensation was painful at first but the blood re-entered with a burning sensation as he got full feeling back in a few minutes. Sonia continued to sleep as Gregory stared at the ceiling. He felt bored and restless so he got up. He went downstairs to the hallway, switched off the alarm and entered the kitchen. After he made himself a cup of coffee, he sat on the kitchen counter stool and peered out the back window. As he looked out the window he began to think about his childhood. The following memory began to surface as Gregory sat in silence.

Gregory loved playing football as a young adult. He would kick a ball with his friends in the back garden of his father's house when living in the countryside. From time to time, the ball would accidentally go over the perimeter fence, which had trees planted against it. The next-door neighbour was a horrible little man. He was a married man who worked in the airport, in air traffic control. He had a wife and two young children, a boy and a girl. If he was home and any of Gregory's balls entered his garden, he would find it and puncture it then throw it back over the trees into Gregory's father's garden. Gregory would buy some expensive leather balls and these would often get destroyed by his neighbour. This was very frustrating for him as a young boy, especially during the beginning of his teenage years.

Gregory was around the age of thirteen when it happened again during a day of playing with his friends. The ball went over on a late Saturday afternoon. It didn't return straight away as his neighbour was having a party with his friends. The ball was returned later that evening as it was getting dark; it was thrown back over the trees and landed in Gregory's father's garden. Yet again it was punctured. Gregory was playing with a rugby ball with his friends when the ball was returned. He immediately stormed into his father's house, cursing to himself as he was extremely agitated after he realised it was punctured. He walked straight to the bathroom down the hallway with rage but he needed to use the toilet. Gregory's sisters had previously been in the bathroom doing their waxing and there was a disgusting smell of burnt hair. He noticed they had left a large container of baby powder on the sink unit. Gregory smiled to himself as he conjured up a plan. He finished in the bathroom and took the container out to his friends. Gregory discussed his intention with his friends and they agreed they would love to participate. Nobody on the road liked the neighbour.

Later that evening, Gregory and his friends dressed in dark clothes and met at the front wall of his father's house. They walked to the neighbour's entrance gate and peered in, scanning the front garden. The external lights were switched on so they knew that they had to wait until the neighbour had gone to bed. They found a position in the ditch at the front of the house and it had a perfect view of the garden and surrounding area. The driveway was composed of loose stone and had flower beds on each side. The car was parked beside the master bedroom's front window as the house was a bungalow. The master bedroom was located on the front left-hand side and opposite the gate.

It was at least 11pm when the neighbour's house lights went out. Gregory and his friends were getting bored and pretty tired, and were feeling the cold. There was a frost in the air and when Gregory got up in a standing position he could feel his bottom was damp. He began passing through the overgrowth, crossing the road, and his friends followed. They all stopped at the driveway pillar, making sure that the dog wasn't outside. The neighbour had a small Jack Russell dog that would sleep at the open front porch during the day. The neighbour's car was parked just beyond the master bedroom, outside the main entrance door. It was positioned centrally on the stone driveway.

All was good, so they began moving slowly towards the car along the grass verge as it curved towards the house. When they reached the loose stone driveway, his friends stood waiting as Gregory squeezed around a flower bed to avoid a sensor light detecting him. The sensor light flicked on while Gregory was stepping over a rose bush. The 300-watt halogen light illuminated everything. It was blinding to their eyes as they moved quickly, watching the house for any movement. It took a few minutes for Gregory to refocus because each time he closed his eyes and opened them again, he could see a white image obstructing his view. A few minutes had passed and the sensor light went out. Still blinded, Gregory had the image of the white light obstructing his view as he began to step carefully around the plants. He was mindful not to leave any footprints, so he walked on the clumps of flowers until he reached the flower bed edge. He began walking slowly and with great caution on the driveway stones, one foot after the other until he reached the front windscreen of the car. Slowly, he turned and smiled at his friends as they stood at the grass verge watching.

Gregory pulled the can of baby powder from inside his jacket. He had it pinned against his stomach with his jacket zipped closed. The container was too large to fit in a pocket. As he turned the lid nozzle to the open position, he began to pour the contents into the bonnet grill. This was where the air inlet ventilation was located on the bonnet; he was on the driver's side of the car. He shook the can a few times as the contents would clog, and continued to do this until the can was emptied. Once finished emptying the contents, Gregory put the container back into his jacket and wiped the bonnet with his hands so that no residue was left. He glanced at the house, then he began to retreat, walking through the flower bed and onto the stones carefully until he reached the grass verge. He then ran, laughing, as they all made their way along the grass, through the gate pillars and over to the ditch.

This is where all three sat patiently until the following morning. They knew his neighbour was a religious man, and Mass was at 11am that Sunday morning. He would usually depart at around 10.15am. It was a long night waiting in the cold but the boys talked and talked. The morning finally arrived as it began to get brighter. The three boys had fallen asleep and woke to the noise of the family closing the front door and the dog barking as they walked on the stones towards the car. The two children were placed in the back of the car. In those days they didn't wear car seat belts. The neighbour's wife climbed into the front passenger seat and the father got into the driver's seat. The engine turned over the first time but didn't start. On the second attempt, the exhaust spluttered some smoke and the engine ran. Gregory and his friends could hear the engine get revved up as the neighbour wanted to warm the car inside as quickly as possible and to clear the windscreen of ice. The neighbour switched on the car's heating to full output to clear the windscreen while revving the engine. Suddenly the air intake exhaled the baby powder within the car. The engine stopped revving and the driver's door opened as Gregory's neighbour jumped out. Gregory and his friends were in stitches laughing. The neighbour was white with dust from head to toe, exiting the car as if it was on fire. Gregory and his friends were trying to stay quiet but couldn't stop laughing. They had to get away as soon as possible as the neighbour's wife began to remove the children from the car. Gregory and his friends climbed through the other side of the ditch and backtracked to their homes from around the fields. They all got home without being seen and went to bed.

Later that afternoon, the hall doorbell rang and Gregory could hear a male voice speaking to his mum. He pulled back the curtains to see a police car parked in the driveway. Panic began to resonate in Gregory's body and he knew he had to dispose of the empty can of baby powder he had under his jacket. His jacket was in his bedroom on a chair. He removed the container from his jacket, hiding it behind all the clutter in his wardrobe. As Gregory left his bedroom and entered the hallway, he heard his mum saying, "Thank you, officer," and the hall door closing. Gregory walked down the corridor to meet his mum as she closed the door. When she saw him, she immediately said he looked tired. He replied that he didn't sleep well. She then told him that the policeman wanted to know who lived in the house and asked if he was here last night. She had told him that Gregory was in bed. Gregory was relieved. No more investigation took place.

Gregory, while sitting on the kitchen stool, became more aware of his surroundings and he thought of Sonia in bed. He was in a total dream state and wondered how his friends were doing in life now as he didn't have any connection with them anymore. He missed the fun they had had. He placed his mug in the kitchen sink after rinsing it under water and made his way back to the bedroom. As he was walking up the stairs, he felt tired and dizzy. The alcohol was still in his system. He entered the bedroom to see Sonia on her mobile. When he entered, she put her phone down beside her on her left-hand side as she was lying on her back and she turned in his direction, curling her left leg out over the duvet, revealing her naked body. Gregory stripped off his tee-shirt and boxer shorts and climbed in beside her. Sonia gently moved to cuddle him. They kissed and Sonia lay her head on his chest. As she lay quietly, she played with the hairs on his chest. She manoeuvred her fingers through the hairs as she examined the length of them. She then moved her left leg under the cover, onto Gregory's, and moved her face up towards his. Gregory had his eyes closed. He opened one eye, lifting his head slightly and turning it towards hers. Sonia kissed his lips and gently grabbed his upper lip with her teeth. She then licked the top of his nose around his nostrils and laughed.

Gregory said, "Really, your breath stinks of garlic."

Sonia smiled and jumped on top of him, pressing down on his penis. She replied, "I see you're awake." Sonia leaned forward and kissed Gregory, then quickly jumped up and walked into the en-suite bathroom. She closed the door and Gregory could hear the sound from the shower and the extractor fan hum as he closed his eyes and turned over. He had fallen asleep by the time Sonia emerged from the bathroom. She continued to get dressed and Gregory began to awaken again.

Sonia said, "Good morning, sleepy."

Gregory replied with a delayed 'good morning' as he was in a daze.

Sonia said, "I have to go to the hairdressers today so I'll go shortly." She was talking to Gregory as she was drying her hair with a towel. She was quite vigorous, drying frantically and talking at the same time. Gregory sat up in the bed as he watched Sonia. He didn't have a hairdryer so Sonia needed to dry her hair as best she could before leaving. Gregory jumped up out of bed and picked his boxer shorts from the floor. He pulled them on and fell back in a sitting position on the bed. He proceeded to put on his tee-shirt. As he was getting dressed Sonia's phone vibrated on the bed under the covers. Gregory turned his head to acknowledge that it was her phone and not his. Sonia looked in the same direction and continued to dry her hair. Gregory walked over to Sonia, hugged her and kissed her as she dropped the towel on the floor, placing her arms on each side of him. He walked into the bathroom and closed the door.

As soon as Gregory had closed the door, Sonia walked over to the bed, lifted the blankets and picked up her phone. She entered her pin code and accessed the app for messages. It was from a guy she had had a one-night stand with several months ago. His name was Andrew. The text read, *Hiya, want to meet up? I'm in London.* Sonia smiled as she read the message and continued to check her phone as there were a few messages from different guys. Paul was the last guy who she was seeing from time to time before getting back with Gregory. Paul was in finance. He was a serious type of guy and Sonia enjoyed having fun, although she enjoyed their evenings out as he would take her to fancy restaurants. Sonia liked all the drama of mixing with influential people as she tried to fit in. She barely managed with her wages from one month to the next. Sonia scrolled back to Andrews's text and replied, *Would love that.* She closed the phone and placed it back on the bedside table as she heard the shower finish.

Just before Gregory came back into the bedroom, Sonia made her way down to the kitchen. While in the kitchen, she filled the kettle and switched it on to boil. She proceeded to get a mug for herself and added some coffee, one and a half spoonfuls, and a little milk. Sonia stood gazing out of the bi-folding door, staring at nothing in particular, thinking about meeting Andrew in London. The kettle boiled and Gregory walked in as Sonia was pouring the water into her mug.

Gregory said, "Ah yeah, take care of yourself."

Sonia continued pouring until her mug was full and put the kettle back on the base plate, then turned and said, "Would you like a coffee?"

Gregory replied, "I'll get it, don't worry."

Sonia proceeded to the dining room and sat in the chair near the bi-folding door. She sat looking into the garden and spotted a robin on a branch. As she watched the robin, it flew to the grass area and rummaged around as there was some bird food that had fallen from the bird feeder that Gregory had hanging in the tree. Gregory would enjoy watching the birds from his comfortable chair near the door. Sonia sat and drank her coffee.

Gregory walked over after re-boiling the kettle and making his coffee. He said to Sonia, "Do you remember last night?"

Sonia replied, "Why?"

Gregory said, "Do you?"

Sonia said, "Yes."

He then said, "Do you remember being drunk?"

Sonia said, "You're going to tell me anyway, aren't you?"

Gregory said, "I am just curious if you remember how you treated me."

Sonia took a mouthful from her coffee and thought for a moment. "Was I bad?"

Gregory said, "Yes. I know you want to settle down and have a family but I wonder sometimes, the way you are when you get drunk. There is a lack of respect towards me. You know I love the ground you walk on but I wonder why you do what you do when drunk."

Sonia replied, "I'm still angry that you left me."

Gregory replied, "Can you live day by day and allow the relationship to develop in a natural way? That was over a year ago. The way you treat me makes me question everything."

Sonia jumped up from her chair, walked to the kitchen and put her mug in the sink. She said, "I have to go," and walked back upstairs.

Gregory said quietly to himself, "Great," feeling bad. This isn't the way he wanted her to react but he knew she would think about the precious night once alone and question her actions. Gregory followed Sonia up to the bedroom and walked over to her. Sonia was on her phone and she placed it in her pocket as he approached. He held her and said, "I love you, nobody else! I haven't loved anyone else since being with you, from the time I met you."

Sonia said, "Yep." He kissed her on the lips and she replied, "I love you, too." Then she said, "I have to go."

Gregory released her from the embrace and she grabbed her coat and walked out of the bedroom, down the stairs to the hall door. Gregory followed. When she opened the door, Gregory grabbed her right arm gently and twisted her body in his direction as he embraced her again. Sonia pulled him closer. He could feel the love connection as they both stood together. Sonia looked into his eyes and kissed his lips.

Gregory said, "I'll see you in a few days. Don't think about last night, we will work on this together, I am with you one hundred percent."

Sonia replied, "Me too." She pulled herself away and made her way down the road towards the Tube station.

Gregory closed the door after watching her walk down the street. He noticed that she went straight onto her phone after she thought that he had gone inside and closed the door. Gregory felt that strange feeling in his stomach again, the same feeling he had felt the night before. He felt sick and wondered why he was feeling this way. He was completely baffled. He was feeling tired again, therefore he made his way up to his bedroom. He stripped off his clothes and climbed into bed. As he lay thinking about the night before, he could smell Sonia on the duvet. He lay there and closed his eyes as he imagined her there with him. It wasn't long before the sick feeling in his stomach began again. Gregory began to try to relax more and he felt himself drift in and out of sleep. As he was drifting, he began to see images of Sonia naked. The images began to become more lucid, as if he was with her. This wasn't the case; he noticed another male but couldn't see the guy's face. When he tried to see the person's face, he awoke again. Gregory lay staring at the ceiling, wondering why he had dreamt what he had. He reached for his phone, entered the messaging app, clicked on Sonia and typed, *Miss you already. X.* He saw that the message was sent but wasn't opened by Sonia. Sonia was also active on the app. He lay patiently waiting for a reply but no reply was received. He put the phone by his side and lay on his back again, staring at the ceiling. He drifted off back to sleep again and the same dream surfaced, but this time Sonia was walking with her back facing him along a forest pathway. The path that she was walking on had trees both sides in a continuous straight line. He followed behind her to a cliff. As Gregory looked over the cliff, he saw a waterfall at the base with a river. Gregory stood behind Sonia. No matter how he tried to get her attention, she wouldn't turn towards him. Shortly after trying to get her attention, the ground from beneath him collapsed and he fell towards the river below. Sonia wasn't there anymore. As soon as he hit the water he woke again suddenly.

He lay feeling shocked and frustrated as the strange sick feeling came over him yet again. He felt like he was left alone; the feeling of abandonment became more apparent. He felt lonely and it reminded him of his childhood. He reached for his phone, entered his pin code and opened the message app. A sadness came over him as there was no reply from Sonia. Gregory felt disorientated and confused. He kept thinking of the night before and how Sonia had changed after having her second drink. It brought back memories of previous experiences when they had first dated, the times before they had broken up previously. He kept thinking that it must be the alcohol making him feel strange in his stomach but as the hours passed, he still felt the same. He tried to sleep again but all he managed to do was toss and turn. He would drift off, only to find himself waking with Sonia on his mind. He couldn't remember what he was dreaming about, but he knew Sonia was the main focus. He text Sonia again. *Are you okay?* Shortly after, Sonia checked her message and replied, *Yes, why?* Gregory replied, *I've had a strange feeling since you left.* Sonia replied, *Why do you think that is?* Gregory replied, *No idea.*

Gregory got tired texting, so he called her mobile. The phone rang and rang until her message minder began with Sonia's voice asking to leave a message after the beep. Gregory looked at his phone and pressed the red icon to hang up. He tried to call her again but there was no reply, with the same voice message answering again. He thought this was strange as she was just texting him as he called her. He felt the sick feeling again in his stomach and this made him think that something was happening behind his back. He began to get agitated so he got out of bed. Putting on his tracksuit, he went down to the kitchen where he turned on the television as a distraction. It wasn't long after flicking through channels that he started to think about the whole situation again. A movie had started and he sat and watched it but his mind wouldn't settle. He kept looking at his phone even though he knew it would chirp if a message was received. He decided to call Sonia again and there was no answer. When he checked his phone, he could see that she was active. He began to get very frustrated and he wasn't happy with the situation. Sonia would normally answer her phone. He began to feel strange within himself, it wasn't her character.

He decided that he would try to forget about it and go for a walk and get some groceries. Gregory went to his bedroom and changed his clothes, getting dressed in a pair of jeans and a jumper over his tee-shirt. He went down to the hallway, put on his shoes and coat and switched on the alarm system. He opened the door and locked it, checking as he pushed against it to make sure it was secure, before walking away. As he walked up the street towards the shops, his phone chirped. He pulled his phone from his right-hand side coat pocket and entered his pin code. He opened the message app and it was Sonia. *Hi, my battery went dead so I gave it behind the bar to get charged.* Gregory found this strange as Sonia was supposed to be getting her hair cut. Gregory text back, *Where are you?*

Sonia replied, *I'm with friends in London.* Gregory just replied, *OK* and he closed his phone, placing it back in his pocket. His phone chirped shortly after this and several times later. Gregory went about his business buying his groceries so that he could have some dinner for the evening. He selected a ribeye steak. Gregory enjoyed a steak. He wasn't feeling in the best of moods and he didn't want to talk to anyone. He felt like he wanted to be alone. He paid for his supplies and left the shop to walk home. As he walked, he decided to wait until he could speak to Sonia in person to find out what was going on. He arrived home, entered the house and put all the groceries away. He turned on the television and flicked through the channels to find something to watch. A programme about ancient civilisations came on and he decided to watch this. He switched on the gas hob over the oven and took a frying pan from the cupboard to the right side of the sink. He placed the pan on the hob and got the ribeye steak from the fridge. He brushed a light amount of sunflower oil on both sides of the steak and placed it in the pan with some salt. It sizzled as it settled with the heat. Gregory turned on the extractor fan with the down lights and he stood watching the steak as it began to change colour. All he could think about was Sonia and he began to question in his mind if she was with another guy. This made him feel sick in his stomach again.

He continued to watch the steak as it cooked its way upwards. He wouldn't turn the steak until it cooked beyond the halfway mark. As soon as it reached this level, he turned the steak to seal it, turned off the gas and placed a glass lid over the pan. He left this for about ten minutes so that it became moist again. Gregory also cooked garden green peas during the ten-minute wait. This was his favourite meal. Unfortunately, he didn't feel like eating it once it was all cooked and served up on a plate. He sat it on the countertop and began to wash the pan and cutlery that he had used preparing the meal. He wiped the stove clean and took the plate with the steak and walked to the dining room table. He sat and looked at the food, cut a small piece of meat and chewed. He just didn't feel like eating. He placed the knife and fork on the plate and stared at the television. He felt a cool breeze around his head so he sat up and focussed on this. He looked up to the ceiling then looked at the windows and door to see if they were open. The windows and door were closed. The cool feeling was on the left side of his face and he was very aware of this. He felt warm but the cool feeling remained.

Shortly after, his phone rang. 'Sonia' appeared on the display and Gregory answered his phone.

"Hello." He remained silent as he could hear a very noisy pub in the background.

When Sonia said, "Hiya," she laughed.

Gregory said, "I thought you were getting your hair cut today."

Sonia replied, "No, that's next weekend." Gregory felt confused and remained silent. Sonia said, "You are acting a little strange."

Just as she said this, a male voice said in the background, "Sonia, your drink is on the table." Gregory then asked Sonia who she was with.

Sonia said, "Just the girls from work."

Gregory then said, "Who is the guy?"

Sonia remained quiet for a moment, then said, "He is one of the administrators; he is married and joined us for a drink." As soon as Sonia said this, Gregory felt sick again. He then wished her a good night and she said the same in return, but she questioned why he was acting strange. Gregory just said he was tired and they both said good night again. When Gregory pressed the red icon to hang up the call, he thought to himself that all the events over the weekend didn't make sense. He knew that Sonia was with a guy and questioned whether there were other girls there also. Gregory was not feeling himself at all. He was beginning to feel down within himself. Gregory would normally be happy and have a clear conscience and he would rarely judge another person. He was very much a go-with-the-flow kind of guy. This situation, however, started to cause dysfunction within his normal thinking process, therefore he became less enthusiastic to do anything. He felt that he just wanted to sleep but Sonia was very much on his mind. He made himself a cup of tea and sat looking at his phone. He checked through his apps and felt alone as he just scanned through them. He felt that he needed to talk to Sonia when they next met but a date hadn't been arranged.

Gregory went up to his bedroom after his tea to prepare his work clothes for the next day. Once finished, he went to the dining room and turned off the television. He proceeded to the kitchen and switched off the lights, walked into the hallway and turned on the night setting for the alarm system, and knocked off the lights as he walked up the stairs. As he walked up the stairs, he had the cold feeling once again around his face. Shortly after, he received a text message from Sonia: *I miss you.* Gregory read the message but didn't reply. He closed the app and set the alarm clock for the next morning and switched his phone to aeroplane mode. He was beginning to realise that he was being lied to and this really affected him as it reminded him again about the promises his father used to make as a child, all promises but nothing would come to fruition. Gregory prepared for bed; he brushed his teeth, used the toilet and switched off the bathroom light. He walked to the bed and had an image of Sonia in his mind's eye, lying in his bed as if she was there with him. This image was a quick flash but it made Gregory wonder where she was as he looked at his watch. It was 22.12pm and he thought she would be very drunk at this time if she had been out since leaving him this morning.

He was feeling very down within himself and began to think about when they first dated. He remembered that when he had met Sonia, she was dating a guy named Peter. Gregory wasn't aware of this until a friend of his told him some weeks later, as he and Sonia started to see each other on a regular basis. Once Gregory found out this information, he immediately confronted Sonia and she denied it at first. Gregory pursued to find out the truth and eventually Sonia admitted that it was true, but that she had finished meeting Peter two weeks prior to when she and Gregory started seeing each other.

After this information recycled through his mind again, he began to think that she was seeing another guy now. This rattled Gregory and he began to wonder what he did for her to do this. He thought all kinds of things. *Why would she do this to me?*

Is there something that she needs to do, maybe fill a void from past trauma? Why does she need this attention from males? Does she feel I am not good enough? Gregory climbed into bed with all this processing going through his mind. He was very much awake and didn't feel tired at all. He switched off the main light as he lay in bed with the bedside light on to the right of him. He stared at the ceiling and wondered if he should text her back. He decided to do so, therefore took his phone from the bedside table and opened the messaging app. He replied, *I love you very much.* He waited to see if she would see it but a few minutes passed and there was no indication that she had read it on the display. Gregory switched his phone onto aeroplane mode and switched off the light. He lay on his side looking towards the door before closing his eyes. It wasn't long before he fell asleep but he woke up again at 1.11am. Gregory picked up his phone to check the time on the display. He also opened the messaging app, removing aeroplane mode, and saw that Sonia had read the message at 12.25am. He wondered where she was at that time. He switched his phone to aeroplane mode again and fell back to sleep.

11

The uncertainty continued

THE NEXT MORNING, GREGORY WOKE TO THE ALARM ON his mobile phone. He had had a terrible sleep as he had tossed and turned around in the bed, constantly waking in between. He switched off aeroplane mode and left the phone on the bedside table. He got up out of bed and walked to the bathroom to shave and shower, feeling heavy and groggy. Once he had finished, he got dressed and made his way to the kitchen. Walking down the stairs, he checked his phone. There were no further texts received. Gregory felt sick yet again as he went to make porridge. He sat on the kitchen counter stool while his porridge was cooking in the microwave oven and he thought about Sonia and the events of the whole weekend. Shortly after thinking a little, he was distracted by the microwave chime, as the timer finished. He got up, prepared the porridge by adding some honey and he ate while thinking of Sonia. Sonia, he realised, was all he had thought about that weekend. This was beginning to frustrate him. He wasn't himself at all. He put his bowl in the sink when he had finished and didn't wash it. Gregory was a very tidy guy and this wasn't his character at all. He just grabbed his jacket and locked up the house, leaving for work.

As he sat in his car, while putting on his safety belt he saw a white feather float past his windscreen. He clicked the belt buckle in place and watched as the feather floated away. Shortly after, he started the engine. He looked at the clock in his car; it read 06.35. He looked in his left-hand side mirror and pulled out from behind a car with caution as he couldn't see straight ahead. His vision was blocked by the car in front. Once out of the parking space he began his journey towards his work. Gregory wasn't in a good mood and felt pretty much deflated. He felt rejected by Sonia, but everything he was thinking had no evidence, therefore he couldn't back it up. He just needed to know the truth so that he could get back to normal, whatever normal was, but he felt unorganised and lost within himself. He kept looking at his phone all morning and wondering why he hadn't received a text from Sonia. Sonia would normally text every morning the following: *Good Morning XxX*. But nothing this morning. He looked at his phone periodically during the morning until 11.17am, when Sonia text, *Good Morning*. Gregory felt sick again and replied, *How are you?* Sonia replied, *I'm good and you?* Gregory replied, *I'm great, at work, what are you doing?* Sonia replied, *I just woke up*. Gregory replied, *Okay, Ill chat later X*. Sonia text back, *OK*. The phone remained silent for about twenty minutes until Gregory received a text: *Are you okay?* Gregory replied, *Yes, all okay*.

He focussed on his work and at lunchtime he decided to call Sonia. He walked over to a park bench and sat. He took his phone from his pocket, entered his pin code and pushed the green telephone icon beside her name. The phone began to call. It rang once, twice, and then she answered, "Hello," in a sleepy voice.

Gregory said, "Hey, how are you?"

Sonia replied, "I'm tired."

Gregory said, "I thought you were getting your hair cut yesterday."

Sonia said, "No."

Gregory said, "That's why you left me early, wasn't it? You said it when you had a shower."

Sonia said, "I mixed up my weekends." Gregory stayed quiet. Sonia then said, "I met some work friends and we stayed out late."

Gregory said, "Were you just with one guy?"

Sonia replied in an instant, "No."

Gregory said, "I feel you were and I feel sick now in my stomach. I haven't stopped thinking about the events of the whole weekend and everything that happened."

Sonia said, "What are you talking about?"

Gregory said, "Sonia, you know what I'm talking about. Something isn't right and I can feel it."

Sonia said, "Whatever."

Gregory felt angry after this reply, therefore he said, "I'll talk later. Have a nice afternoon."

Sonia said, "Don't be like that."

Gregory said, "Like what? You're like a dark horse lately. I know nothing about where you go; you haven't invited me to meet your friends but you have met mine. Something isn't right and I feel sick with it."

Sonia said, "I came home last night, Gregory."

Gregory replied, "No worries. I have to go now, take care."

Sonia was about to speak when Gregory hung up. Gregory felt like he was being lied too and this frustrated him. He could think of all the times before that he was lied to by people and he always knew, there was always something inside that he knew, a feeling of sorts. This time it was different as he had a very strong emotional connection with Sonia, so it was more difficult to understand.

Shortly after, Sonia text, *Why did you hang up on me?* Gregory read the text but didn't reply. He left the park to walk to the shops. He needed to get some food and try to unwind a little. As Gregory walked towards the shops, Sonia called his mobile.

He answered, "Hello," as he cleared his throat.

Sonia said, "Gregory, you hung up on me and I haven't done anything wrong, what's happening?"

Gregory replied, "You lied to me and I know this, you knew you were meeting friends or a guy yesterday and you told me you had a hair appointment."

Sonia said, "That's not true."

Gregory said, "Sonia, please don't lie to me, it's killing me inside."

The line went quiet and Sonia said, "Yes, I was meeting friends. It was organised weeks ago."

Gregory said, "Okay, thank you for being honest, but it was with a guy only and not friends, true?"

Sonia said, "It was a group of us meeting but myself and one showed up."

Gregory said, "Really?" in a frustrated voice.

Sonia said, "Yes."

Gregory said, "Was he an ex?"

Sonia went quiet again and eventually replied, "Yes."

Gregory hung up the phone with disgust, disappointment, anger and frustration. He felt betrayed and rejected at the same time. He felt his world had come to a stop. He could feel his whole body exert an energy and a sick feeling became more apparent in his stomach. He felt weak and dizzy around his head.

He arrived outside the shop and entered totally confused. He could feel his heart flutter from time to time and a pressure in his chest area. He wondered what Sonia thought she was doing. He thought to himself, *If you love someone you don't do this to the person you love.* Gregory picked up a sandwich – ham and cheese. He didn't want anything too filling as he wasn't feeling hungry. He knew he had to eat something. He felt sick and had low self-esteem. He didn't seem to care about anything anymore. Gregory felt that with the stress that he was feeling, he needed to sort everything out right at that moment. He needed answers and the thoughts going through his head were really starting to annoy him. He didn't realise that faith and being patient would result in finding out the answers, but this would be at the right and perfect time.

12

Sonia after her day/night out with Andrew

AFTER SONIA CALLED GREGORY AND HE HUNG UP THE phone on her, Sonia felt sick also in the stomach area. She wondered why Gregory was acting the way he was. In Sonia's mind she hadn't done anything wrong. This wasn't the case as she had told Gregory a lie that she was getting her hair cut when she knew she was meeting Andrew for lunch. When Sonia was out with Andrew the day and night before, she was feeling sick also because Gregory had text her several times and she couldn't text him back because Andrew was in her company. The time she called Gregory was when she excused herself to go to the bathroom. She had called Gregory on her way back to Andrew but stood at the entrance door to the pub so that he wouldn't hear the conversation. Sonia enjoyed the attention but never thought that Gregory would have called her. Gregory wouldn't normally text that much or call her, so this affected her as she felt that he would realise what was going on. Sonia was so much in love with Gregory that she wanted to get married to him and have his children. She didn't realise that this would cause issues and make Gregory question everything.

Sonia lay in bed and wondered how to sort the problem out. She began to think of excuses and felt tired and sick in her stomach. Her phone chirped and she hoped it was Gregory. It wasn't. Andrew text, *Hey my little Irish, meet at 3pm at my hotel.* Sonia knew where he was staying because they had discussed it the night before. Sonia read the text and got excited. She thought of Gregory and felt sick again, but the excitement to meet Andrew again was all she thought about. She knew she wouldn't see Gregory until the weekend so she text Andrew back: *See you at 3pm.* Sonia jumped out of bed and went for a shower. While showering she could only think of Gregory and how angry he was and the fact that he had hung up on her. He broke up with her before and she wondered if it would happen again. Instead of being loyal to Gregory, she pursued the meeting with Andrew. While in the shower, Sonia shaved her legs and pampered her body. She washed her hair and added conditioner. She left the conditioner in her hair as she proceeded to sit on the toilet and file her toenails. She filed her fingernails while wearing a dressing gown. She sat filing and thought of the last Saturday night with Gregory. She couldn't remember being drunk and abusive.

It wasn't long that she was enjoying her pampering time for when Andrew text. *I bought some expensive massage oil, would you like a back rub?* Sonia read the message and felt excited. *Of course,* she replied. *Great,* said Andrew. Sonia knew where the meeting was going to end up. Andrew also knew that he was going to sleep with her again. Sonia text, *I'm just getting ready.* Andrew replied, *See you soon.* Sonia finished getting ready and left her apartment at 2.15pm.

She arrived at the hotel at exactly 3pm in the foyer. She text Andrew, *What's your room number?* Andrew replied, *Room 101.* Sonia said, *I'm here,* as she made her way to the lift in the lobby area. She pressed the button for the lift and waited patiently. The lift arrived and the doors opened. Sonia entered and pressed button '1'. The doors closed and the lift began to ascend. Sonia felt excited and she could feel a sensation between her legs, an excitement that made her tingly inside. The feeling of the sick stomach dissipated a little but it was still there; it was more a nervous feeling that had crept in. The lift stopped and Sonia waited for the door to open. As she exited the lift, she looked both ways up and down the corridor to see Andrew standing at his door. He was wearing a white hotel robe and holding a bottle of body oil in his hand with a smile on his face. Sonia also smiled as she walked towards him.

They kissed on the lips and Andrew said, "Come in." Sonia pushed past him playfully while he closed the door. He asked for her coat. Sonia removed it as she checked out the robe he was wearing. He took her coat and hung it on the back of the bedroom door. He walked up behind Sonia as she was standing looking out of the window and placed his hands on both sides of her hips while he positioned his head to the right of hers. He pressed his body against hers and kissed her on the neck below her ear.

He whispered, "Take off your dress." Sonia turned to face him and began to kiss him. They embraced and Andrew felt her back to find the zip on her dress. He located it and began to pull it down; it was stiff so it took a few jerks as he pulled it down and eventually the dress became loose. He reached with both his hands to the base of her neck as he slid the dress off her shoulders, allowing it to drop to the floor. Sonia was wearing some new underwear that Gregory had selected a few days before in the underwear shop. Andrew used his fingers on both hands to glide down her spine to the base of her back. He gently moved his right hand back towards the bra clasps and released her bra. Sonia pulled the dressing gown tie from around Andrew and dropped her right hand to hold his penis. She placed her hand under his testicles and then moved up along the shaft.

"Happy to see me," she said in a quiet voice. Andrew kissed her then bent down and pulled her knickers down below her knees. He released them as they fell to the floor. Sonia wiggled her body to help and she stepped out of them. Sonia was naked and Gregory still had his gown on. She pulled away from him and walked to the bed. She pulled back the duvet cover and sheet and lay naked on her back. Andrew dropped his dressing gown on the floor as he walked towards her. He also climbed onto the bed. He lifted up her right leg and licked the base of her foot. Sonia shivered as he proceeded to lick her toes and then place her big toe in his mouth. Sonia squirmed a little as he sucked it. He gently moved his right hand down the back of her leg towards her bottom. He focussed on caressing the back of her thigh. This made Sonia become aroused and she placed her own hand on her private area. She began to caress herself and Andrew moved his tongue down her leg to her hand. He attempted to push Sonia's fingers away with his tongue while he supported her from under the knee with her leg bent over, resting on his right hand.

Sonia got giddy and said, "I'm really sensitive." Andrew tried again and she moved her fingers, allowing him to squeeze his tongue between her fingers. Andrew moved his tongue along the outside of her vagina from the base and entered from the top. He could feel her clitoris erect and he concentrated there for a few minutes. He caressed by adding and decreasing pressure in that area and then he moved down inside. This made Sonia groan. Sonia said, "I want you inside me." Andrew lifted his head and crawled onto her, positioning his legs between hers. Sonia took his penis in her right hand and inserted it inside her. Andrew pushed hard. Sonia gasped and said, "Go easy, I'm sensitive," as she groaned. Andrew didn't listen and he penetrated hard. Sonia grabbed both sides of the sheets with her hands. She groaned but it was starting to become too much for her. Andrew kept penetrating hard and he was starting to get hot. Sweat was dripping from his head and Sonia was starting to get frustrated. She said, "Slow down, it hurts."

Andrew stopped and said, "Change over." Sonia lifted her body when Andrew withdrew his penis and turned onto her front while raising herself into the crawling position. Andrew placed his right hand down to her vagina and felt her with his fingers. He took his penis and entered her from behind as he held her hips. He penetrated again with haste and this made Sonia gasp. She reached back with her left hand and tried to push Andrew back a little, but this didn't work. Andrew began to increase speed as he got more excited.

Sonia said, "I can really feel you, oh God, I can really feel you."

Andrew said, "Do you like it?"

Sonia replied, "Please cum." Andrew slowed a little and eventually he withdrew and came on her back. Sonia pulled away and said, "I can't believe you did that without a condom."

Andrew said, "What's the issue?"

Sonia replied, "I've no idea who you have been with."

Andrew replied, "Sonia, I haven't been sleeping around."

Sonia jumped up and made her way to the bathroom. Andrew lay on his back, trying to get his breath back. He lay there until Sonia returned. When she came back into the room and lay beside him, she said, "That was a lot." He laughed. Sonia said, "I'm hungry, can we order to the room?"

Andrew said, "Why not?"

Sonia climbed out of the bed, walked to the writing desk and took the menu back to Andrew. She pulled the duvet up over her and began to read the menu. She said, "I'll have the vegetarian stir fry and a glass of white."

Andrew said, "Okay, I'll order." He proceeded to pick up the phone and dial 01. The receptionist answered and he said, "I'd like to place an order, Room 101."

The receptionist said, "What would you like?"

"I would like the Hawaiian pizza, the vegetarian stir fry and two glasses of house white, please."

The receptionist repeated the order and said it would take at least 50 minutes.

Andrew said, "Thank you." He placed the phone back and turned towards Sonia.

Sonia moved her head towards him, kissed his lips and said, "I enjoyed that, I'm still horny."

Andrew said, "Go again?"

Sonia said, "Yes please, but with a condom."

Andrew and Sonia had sex again and shortly after, there was a knock on the door. Andrew jumped up and put the dressing gown on while Sonia covered herself with the duvet. He turned and asked if she was covered then opened the door. A young waitress entered with a large silver tray and placed it on the circular table near the window. Andrew said thank you and the waitress left the room. As soon as the door closed, Sonia jumped from the bed and sat on the chair, removing the covers off the food. She placed cutlery in front of Andrew and took her own.

Sonia said, "Bon appétit."

Andrew said, "Enjoy."

They both ate and remained in silence. Sonia began to think about Gregory and what he was doing. She started to feel guilty about what she was doing but enjoyed the excitement and the attention that she got from Andrew. She was beginning to feel sore from the penetration and wondered where she had put her phone. Andrew started to look at his watch and said to Sonia, "God, I have to be up early tomorrow to catch a flight."

Sonia felt sick again in her stomach and said, "Okay, I have to go soon anyway and prepare for work tomorrow. I'm feeling tired anyway." Sonia felt used and she didn't like this feeling at all. It was like Andrew was now trying to get her to leave. He had got what he wanted and he was satisfied. This made Sonia feel angry inside and she began to get agitated.

Andrew noticed and said, "Are you okay?"

Sonia replied, "Yes, just tired. I had better go." The atmosphere changed and it became awkward for them both. Sonia didn't eat her food but just picked at it. Andrew had had about four slices of pizza and continued to eat. Sonia got off the chair and lifted her knickers, bra and dress from the floor. She proceeded to the bathroom and got dressed there. As she was dressing herself, she began to think about Gregory and started to get emotional. She managed to get the zip up on her dress as she was determined not to ask Andrew for help. She felt sick and just wanted to get out of the room. She wiped her eyes and looked at herself in the mirror. She looked tired and felt sore. She opened the door and Andrew had finished his pizza and was drinking his wine. Sonia walked over and took her glass, downing the whole glass in one go. She put the glass back on the table and took her coat off the door hook. She proceeded to put it on and buttoned it up.

Once finished she said, "I'm going now." Andrew stood up and walked over. They just embraced and Sonia opened the door and walked out. Andrew stood at the door in his gown as Sonia pressed the lift button and waited for the lift. Andrew remained at the door until Sonia entered. The doors opened and Sonia entered while looking at Andrew, saying, "Thank you."

Andrew said, "Mind yourself."

Sonia reached for her phone while in the lift and noticed Gregory had been trying to reach her for most of the day. There were several messages and calls on her phone. Sonia felt sick again and began to feel miserable. She was feeling used and empty inside. She felt that she was disconnected from herself and was light-headed from drinking the wine so quickly. The fact that she hadn't eaten didn't help. As she was standing in the lift, she felt her knickers become wet. This made her become annoyed with herself as she would have preferred if she had been with Gregory. She began thinking about pregnancy and how it must feel.

As soon as she left the hotel for the street, she called Gregory. Gregory answered.

"Are you okay?"

Sonia said, "Yes. I had fallen asleep and just came outside to get food."

Gregory said, "Thank God, I was worried about you. I felt really weird all day. Make sure you eat and I'd love to see you Friday."

Sonia was happy again and said, "Yes, I'd like that."

Gregory said, "Would you like to see a movie?"

Sonia replied, "Yes, that's great, I'm looking forward." Sonia started to feel pressure on her chest and an ache around her heart. She felt sick and empty inside. She was walking towards the Tube station but decided to walk back to her flat as she didn't want to be around people. As Sonia walked, she was aware of the noise her high heels made, step after step. The *click, click* noise echoed around the buildings. Sonia felt cold but her conscious mind was thinking about Gregory and how he was such a lovely person, the fact that he was always there for her regardless of the situation. He was very caring and did everything for Sonia but she wanted more. Sonia felt frustrated and questioned why she wasn't married with kids of her own at the age she was. All her friends either had children or were having them. They all had homes of their own and were married. The other girls who were single partied and enjoyed the company of men. Sonia had talked with Gregory about her friends dating different men and how they got nice watches as gifts and holidays away. Gregory would always ask if they were happy. This always annoyed Sonia as she thought they were happy.

While Sonia walked along the street, she questioned why she slept with Andrew. This annoyed her and she began to worry that she was going to lose Gregory now if he found out. Sonia knew that she wouldn't hear from Andrew for some time and she felt less connected with herself. She began to feel her feet getting sore as she walked along the pavement. She kept looking down to make sure that she didn't trip on the uneven surface in her high heels. Sonia started to feel helpless as she began to feel like her life was wasted, and she started to feel that Gregory would find out about the encounter she had had and he would leave her. This brought tears to her eyes as she bore the cold. She decided to call Gregory because she knew just how to get him on her side again. She stopped at the entrance to the Tube station and pressed the call button on her phone. The phone rang twice and Gregory answered.

"Hi, how are you?"

Sonia replied, "I'm good, I was thinking of how nice it's going to be to get away next weekend."

Gregory said, "Yes, I am looking forward to it."

Sonia asked Gregory what he was doing.

He replied, "I went to work today and didn't hear from you at all. I was wondering what you were up to. I am home now, making dinner."

Sonia said that she had slept most of the day and didn't feel like connecting with anyone.

Gregory said, "I have days like that too, it's nice just to unwind."

Sonia felt good talking to Gregory and she told him that she loved him and missed him. She also said that she enjoyed the passion between them and giggled on the phone.

Gregory felt good when she said this but he still had a strange feeling in his stomach. He said to Sonia, "It's really weird but when I'm talking to you lately, I feel weird."

Sonia said, "Oh, why would that be?"

Gregory replied, "I don't know, I feel sick sometimes."

Sonia then said, "Ah, so I make you feel sick, that's really nice."

Gregory replied, "No, I don't mean that. I do miss you and I can't wait to see you."

Sonia decided to say that she was just walking back from the shops and would have a bath in a few minutes.

Gregory felt he was being pushed away again and the sick feeling became worse. He just acknowledged her by saying, "Okay, have a lovely bath and I'll chat when you want to. Have a lovely night."

Sonia replied, "You too. I love you."

Gregory said, "I love you too."

Sonia hung up the phone and proceeded into the Tube station as she felt sore from the penetration with Andrew being rough during sex. She felt worse as she kept thinking that Gregory would find out the truth. She was concerned that he felt sick while speaking to her and it wasn't the first time that this had happened. She decided that she would buy him a small gift before they met again at the weekend.

While sitting on the train, Sonia felt dizzy again because she hadn't eaten much and after drinking the wine quickly on pretty much an empty stomach. She closed her eyes and dozed off into a deep sleep. She slept while clasping her handbag with both arms and laid her head to the left side. She woke when a gentleman brushed off her knee while stumbling to get to a seat. Sonia realised that she had missed her stop. She jumped up just as the doors were about to close disembarking onto the platform. Sonia felt sick, dizzy and sore. She walked towards the stairs and crossed over platforms. As she stood waiting for the train, the display showed 'Train approaching, stand back behind the yellow line'. Sonia looked at her phone and deleted all the past texts between Andrew and herself as the train came to a stop. She began to feel miserable, lonely and used again, and just wanted a hug. She wanted to feel that someone appreciated her and this she struggled with. The sex with Andrew was intense but she was missing the affection, the feeling of being loved. She began to remember the last Saturday night and what had happened and how she was with Gregory. This made her feel worse. She didn't understand why she got to be like this with him. The frustration of wanting a family became more apparent as she passed several stops on the train. Sonia knew that her frustration was causing the issue. The fact that she had slept with Andrew didn't help either, but she felt she would get away with it. Sonia was always one step ahead – well, she thought she was.

Sonia just wanted to get home and go to bed. She walked from the Tube station, making her way straight home. She got herself ready for bed and switched off her mobile after communicating with Gregory. It didn't take Sonia long to fall asleep but she woke several times during the night. Her restless sleep was due to worry. Sonia was stressed that Gregory would find out that she had been with another guy.

13

Gregory's evening after work and the week up to meeting Sonia

GREGORY ARRIVED HOME FROM WORK. HE WAS concerned because he hadn't heard from Sonia for most of the day. He wondered if something was wrong and the events over the previous weekend didn't help with his thoughts. He felt something was up with Sonia due to the distance between them. He could feel she was avoiding him and he still had an anxious feeling in his stomach. He was worried for Sonia but was also confused as to why she didn't text him all day. Sonia would normally text in between sleeping or while she would be resting. Gregory decided not to contact Sonia as he felt it was best to leave her alone. He also thought that she was embarrassed over the events of the previous weekend.

Gregory had his clothes washing to do as it had got out of control and he wanted to clean his house. It had been a while since he had had time to get his house in order. He put his washing in the washing machine, cleaned the bathrooms, hoovered the ground floor and hung up the washing after the machine finished. He decided to hoover upstairs another evening as he was beginning to get tired. He found cleaning the house very therapeutically relaxing. He thought about Sonia a lot and wondered several times what she was doing. He also thought about Edinburgh and what he would like to do while there. Several times he looked up places to visit using his search engine and he found Mary King's Close Underground Tour. This was of interest to Gregory and he decided that he would book it the next day once he had spoken to Sonia.

Gregory completed his tasks for the evening and retired for the night. As he lay in bed, he missed Sonia and the connection between them. He wondered again why she hadn't text him. Just as he was thinking about his phone, it vibrated with a ping noise, indicating a text had arrived. It was Sonia. Gregory read the text and called Sonia straight away. After the call they wished each other a good night, expressing their love for one another. Gregory went to sleep after their communication and he dreamt of Sonia having a bath with scented candles burning around her. He slept the whole night as he was exhausted.

The following few days passed quickly with more frequent communication between Sonia and Gregory via telephone. Sonia spent the next few days taking time alone, contemplating her life and her actions. She wasn't eating properly and still felt sick. Every now and again she would call Gregory with an issue at her work for Gregory to give his input. Regardless of his input, Sonia would get annoyed and defend what she felt herself, making Gregory feel that his opinion was less important. This made Gregory feel that he couldn't get anything right and this frustrated him. He wondered why she did this but also realised it was her seeking attention again. Sonia was very clever and pretended that she didn't know what to do in some situations, which would normally involve other co-workers. She would ask advice to make Gregory feel good. When he would give a solution to a problem with his opinion, sometimes Gregory even surprised himself. He would give the scenario of events that he felt would take place and most times Sonia would report back days or weeks later saying, "You were right." Sonia would say this out of context, confusing Gregory as they would be talking about a completely different topic. Gregory would then ask, "What was right?" Sonia would then take forever to explain and Gregory would intervene in the conversation so that he understood what was being said. This frustrated Sonia as she would say, "I'm trying to tell you." Gregory would say, "I need to understand as it was said a few weeks ago." During the explanation, Sonia would sometimes not finish and say to Gregory, "It's not important, you know anyway, there is no point, it's not important." Gregory would find this very annoying as he enjoyed a good conversation, especially when he was being told he was right about something. Sonia wouldn't finish the conversation and Gregory would feel not good within himself yet again. He would become quiet and Sonia would say that she had to go and leave the telephone conversation because she was needed in work. They would finish the conversation quickly with Sonia saying, "Okay, chat later. I love you." Gregory would say, "Love you, too."

Sonia began to feel that life wasn't worth living. She contemplated her life and what she had achieved. She had clothes, a job and a bank account. With two days off work, she locked herself in her bedroom and curled up in her bed. She hadn't eaten and felt sick in her stomach. She switched on her mobile music app, keeping away from everybody and listening to her music, bursting into tears constantly. She kept having these negative thoughts about her life and what she hadn't achieved and was wanting to cry all the time. She even held back her tears in a major effort to try to compose herself but the music would trigger her emotions again as she listened to the lyrics of some songs. She knew that she was broken and found this difficult to confront. Sonia had dealt with depression before but this time was different. She began to feel that she was getting too old to have children and that if she finished her relationship with Gregory, she wouldn't have time to find another man who she would be comfortable enough with to have children with.

The panic became physical as her emotions built up with her thoughts. She began to think about her time with Andrew and the fear of Gregory finding out. She started to pick her skin and feel for any abnormalities that she could focus on. Any bumps on her skin, especially around her face or chest, she picked until she bled. Then she would feel around again while listening to her music and pick again. Sonia was very tired and hungry but also extremely agitated, feeling nauseous, helpless, unwanted, angry and worthless. Eventually she fell asleep with her earphones in her ears, curled up with all her pillows.

It was Wednesday evening after work when Sonia began to feel the effects of being with Andrew and the way he had just ignored her and returned back home. Sonia had enjoyed the excitement of being wanted and the sexual rush, but it was short-lived as the feelings of loneliness, guilt and shame began to filter into her system. Sonia just wanted to be alone because she didn't want Gregory to see her. She knew that he would sense something wasn't right and that he would fish for the truth. This made Sonia feel worse and her panic and anxiety began to grow more and more as she knew they were meeting on Friday. She woke at 3.30am on Thursday morning, feeling sick. Her stomach was sore and she felt as though her head was going to explode. She took her mobile from beside her and removed the earphones. The battery level was at sixteen percent so she entered her pin to access the phone. There were no texts so she placed the phone on her dressing room table and plugged in the charger. After this she went to the bathroom and switched on the light. Looking at herself in the mirror, she noticed the marks on her face from picking. She turned and used the toilet before going back to bed. As she lay under her duvet, she began to contemplate not meeting Gregory the next day. She thought that she would say that she wasn't feeling well. As she was thinking of different excuses, she drifted off to sleep again. The next time she woke was when she moved in her sleep to get comfortable. It was 11.12am and the sun was shining through her blinds. She opened her eyes and felt heavy around her head but the pain in her stomach was gone. She sat up in her bed, leaning against her pillows that she had placed between herself and the wall. Her head felt very dizzy and she had blurred vision. After rubbing her eyes a few times, she got out of bed, walked over to fetch her phone and removed the charger. She climbed back into bed and opened her apps. Sonia spent several hours watching videos, checking the news and replying to old messages on her phone.

It was 1.43pm and Sonia decided to text Gregory. *Hiya, what are you up to?* Gregory received the text but waited until he was free to reply. He was with a work colleague and felt that it would be rude to start texting while they were in a deep conversation. Several minutes had passed before Gregory was free to text. He replied, *Busy in work. How are you, stranger?* Sonia read the text as soon as it arrived and she sighed. Her reply was, *I'm in bed, not feeling too good, resting.* Gregory became concerned and replied, *Do you need anything? I can drop over later.* Sonia immediately replied, *I'm the finest, I'll be good by tomorrow.* Gregory replied, *Rest and I'll see you tomorrow. Can't wait.* Sonia replied, *Me too!* When she sent the message, Sonia began to feel sick again and nervous. The pain in her stomach returned and she felt dizzy.

Gregory also felt his stomach turn and a cool feeling on his left arm. He was intrigued by the cold feeling on his arm. As he sat for a moment, he thought to himself that Sonia was avoiding him. He felt strange but continued with his work. It wasn't long before closing time approached. He jumped out of his office chair at 5.30pm and put on his coat, said goodbye to his work colleagues and walked to his car. Gregory started his car and the radio switched on, playing 'Say Something' by Christina Aguilera. Gregory was concentrating on his driving when the lyrics caught his attention. He began to think about Sonia again and the events of the last week. He knew that next week they would be going to Edinburgh and he remembered that he had to book flights. Sonia was off work on Friday morning so he decided to search for flights later that evening when he got home. He also needed to call Sonia to discuss the tour that he was excited about. Gregory was feeling enthusiastic about going to Edinburgh but he couldn't figure out why he was feeling strange when he thought about Sonia. He listened to the radio and began thinking about what he wanted to eat for dinner. It wasn't long before he reached his house and parked the car after driving up and down the street several times to find a parking space. He opened the front door and went straight through to the kitchen after switching off the alarm system. He took his mobile out of his coat pocket and checked for messages. There were none. He felt this was strange as Sonia would normally text more often but then he remembered that she wasn't feeling well. He prepared beans on toast as he didn't feel like cooking a proper dinner. He ate and decided to call Sonia. Just as he began to open the telephone app his phone rang. It was Sonia.

Gregory answered, "Hey, how are you feeling?"

Sonia replied, "I'm okay, what are you up to?"

Gregory replied, "Just home and had beans on toast."

Sonia said, "You need to eat properly."

Gregory said, "I don't feel like cooking tonight. I want to book flights and there is a tour I'd like to go on called the Mary something or other about the history of Edinburgh."

Sonia interrupted and said, "Mary King's Close Tour. It's really good. I've done it before."

Gregory went silent for a moment as he wanted to experience this with Sonia and he felt that because she had already gone there was no point in going again. He felt a little disappointed.

Sonia noticed that Gregory had gone quiet and she said, "I'd love to go with you."

Gregory replied, "I'll book it for 11am on the Saturday. Also we can fly early on Friday morning as I have agreed to take the day off also."

Sonia said, "Great." They both went quiet for a moment until Sonia said, "I can't wait to see you tomorrow."

Gregory said, "Me too. I miss you. I've noticed that you haven't been yourself."

Sonia swallowed and replied, "I have been thinking about life and where this is all going."

Gregory said, "I'm sorry I've asked now."

Sonia said, "Whatever."

The conversation felt awkward and Gregory said, "I can't wait to see you tomorrow. Do you want to stay at mine after?"

Sonia said, "Okay, but I have my time of the month."

Gregory replied, "No worries. Can we meet at, say, 7pm at Selfridges as I need to buy a new coat?"

Sonia said, "See you then, love you."

Gregory said, "I love you too. Good night and sweet dreams."

Sonia replied, "I'm not going to bed just yet."

Gregory said, "When you do."

Sonia said good night and hung up the call. Sonia sat on her bed and sighed because she was worried that Gregory would find out about her being with Andrew. She had noticed that he was aware that she was distant and she decided to connect with him more often so that he wouldn't suspect anything. Sonia ran herself a bath and lay in it for some hours, letting water out and re-heating it from time to time. She had scented candles placed around her with music playing via her phone to a Bluetooth speaker. Sonia felt more relaxed but continued to question her life. She thought about Andrew, especially the way he made her feel great until they parted company; they both felt awkward. Sonia began to think about Gregory and how he was always there for her when she was down, but she felt agitated because she wanted more from him. She wanted to have a family and a life with him. Sonia picked up her phone and text Gregory: *I love you.* Gregory replied, *Love you too.* Sonia left the bathroom once she had dried herself and put on her pyjamas. She climbed into bed and fell asleep quickly, holding onto one of her pillows. Gregory also went to bed shortly after receiving the text, but he was still feeling anxious yet excited about meeting Sonia the next evening. He also slept well that night.

The next morning, Sonia woke to her alarm at 6.15am. She jumped from bed and proceeded to the bathroom to have a shower, dropping her pyjamas on the floor. She was very tired and was feeling heavy as she struggled to wake up. Once in the shower she felt better as the hot water massaged her head, the water running down her face, which was tilted forward as she stood in the same position, not moving. She washed her hair and conditioned it, then switched off the electric shower. She dried herself and left a towel wrapped around her head as she began to get dressed. She picked a red dress for that day as she knew Gregory liked the colour red. She threw her makeup into her handbag as she saw that she was running late and needed to leave shortly to make it on time to start work. She dried her hair by rubbing the towel a few times around her head and put on her coat. She flicked her hair and gave it a shake with both hands so it would position itself down her back and away from her face. She buttoned up her coat, grabbed her handbag, placed her phone in her pocket after removing it from the charger and left her flat. Sonia walked quickly as she was conscious of the time. She needed to be at work for 7.30am.

Sonia would always order a coffee from a coffee shop via her mobile app and this particular morning was no different, regardless of her being late. Sonia needed to have her coffee. She ordered the coffee and proceeded swiftly towards the coffee shop. Once she arrived, she entered and walked to the collection point to find her coffee waiting with her name printed across the side. She grabbed it and removed the lid to add one sugar while stirring with a wooden stir stick. She popped the lid back on, pressed down firmly and took a taste to ensure that it was to her satisfaction. Once convinced, she proceeded out of the coffee shop and walked on, holding her coffee in her right hand with her bag draped over her right shoulder. Sonia was enjoying her walk as the sun was rising in the distance. She continued to sip from her coffee cup from time to time, feeling the warmth around her cold lips as her face felt the chill of the early morning dew. On her way she walked past a pastry shop and decided to return after work to purchase a cake for Gregory. She knew that it would change the atmosphere if she gave him a cake when they met up later that evening. Gregory had a sweet tooth and he loved carrot cake or cheesecake.

Sonia entered the main entrance to her work, scanned her ID card to enter her floor in the lift and proceeded to her locker to place her bag and apply makeup to her face. As she was applying her makeup, Sonia noticed how tired she looked as she gazed at herself in the mirror. The mirror was a free-standing one she had bought and erected on the shelf of her locker. She had a slightly sunken look in her appearance. She touched the tiny wrinkles forming. She quickly applied her foundation and blended it to achieve the best natural look that she could manage in a rush. She closed her locker with a bang, turning the dial on her lock to ensure that it was secure. Sonia flicked her hair and made her way to the manager's office to report in for her shift. Sonia spent most of her day being nervous about meeting Gregory as she was worried that he would probe for information relating to the weekend prior. Her anxiety was building up as the day drew close to the end of her shift in work. It was 6.30pm and Sonia disappeared from her floor to get her makeup bag. She was late finishing work as she got delayed with a client. She proceeded to the toilet and threw her makeup bag on the sink while she gazed at herself in the mirror. She touched up her face and added mascara to her eyelashes and eyeliner to the eyelids. To finish, she applied a bright red lipstick and overlapped her lips to spread the colour evenly.

Sonia stood back slightly, looking at herself. Once happy, she clasped her bag and headed back to her locker to get her coat. She buttoned up her coat and while walking, she reached into her bag and sprayed perfume around her neck and wrists. Sonia pulled her phone from her bag and looked at the time. It was 6.52pm and she knew she had at least thirty minutes' walk. She swiped her card to exit and entered the street. It was already dark with a slight rain drizzle swirling around as the breeze would whisk it to and fro, reflecting the car lights and street lights as Sonia walked briskly. Sonia held her phone and rummaged around in her handbag to find her headphones. She had the wired type of headphones and when she finally felt them in her bag, she pulled to find her scarf, charger cable and an old banana skin attached. Sonia flicked the banana skin to the pavement with disgust as if it wasn't hers and proceeded to untangle the headphones from the charger cable. She was beginning to feel frustrated and this was apparent as she just threw the cables back into her bag. She held her phone and text Gregory: *I'm running late, see you at Selfridges, 20 mins.* It was 7.10pm and she was starting to feel herself sweat a little under her arms. Sonia had deodorant in her handbag and knew that she would need to apply it once she arrived to meet Gregory. She continued walking in the rain as it intensified, adjusting her scarf around her neck and fixing the top button of her coat. Sonia pulled her umbrella from her handbag and opened it. Her umbrella had seen better days; the upper canopy had come loose from its fixings in three places, therefore would flop and flap as she walked. It barely covered her head, but she was content having it. She was just concerned to keep her hair dry.

Some twenty minutes had passed and Sonia arrived at the department store. She entered through the main entrance door and stood in the entrance area shaking her umbrella dry all over the floor before sticking it back into her handbag. She took her phone and called Gregory.

Gregory answered, "Hiya."

Sonia said, "Where are you?"

Gregory said, "Men's department."

Sonia replied, "On my way, I'm here now."

She walked to the escalator and checked the sign. The men's department was on the first floor. Sonia walked onto the escalator and looked left and right to try to see where Gregory was as she passed the ceiling level of the ground floor. As the escalator began to level out, she saw Gregory standing behind a mannequin, peeking over its shoulder and smiling. Sonia walked over to him and they hugged and kissed on the lips.

Sonia said, "You're an idiot," and laughed.

Gregory said, "Check this coat out." Sonia looked and looked, touching the fabric, saying nothing. Gregory knew she didn't like it. He said, "I guess you don't like it."

Sonia said, "You can do better. Come." Gregory followed Sonia and she walked up and down each section until she saw a coat she liked. She took it off the hanger and said, "This one."

Gregory immediately said, "Never, are you joking?" He took it from Sonia and looked at it, holding it in front of him. It was a dark blue duffle coat with eight large buttons, four on each side of the chest, and a hood. Gregory didn't wear hoods and wouldn't be seen in one. He handed it straight back to Sonia and said, "Really?"

Sonia smiled and placed it back on the hanger as Gregory continued to check out more options. Sonia followed but had lost interest and was checking her phone. She looked at a few messages that she had received from a few guys she knew and one of the girls in work. She glanced through the messages and decided to read them later as she didn't want Gregory asking who was texting her.

Gregory found a coat he liked so he found his size and tried it on. It was a one hundred percent polyester outer, three-quarter length black coat that was very smart. Gregory showed Sonia and she also liked it. Gregory bought it and they decided to go for some food.

This time, Gregory had organised earlier a booking at a nice restaurant for 9pm. Sonia wasn't aware, so Gregory had to look for distractions as Sonia wanted to go eat. It was only 8.20pm and the restaurant was ten minutes away. Gregory grabbed Sonia as they left the department store and cuddled into her, kissing her on the lips. Sonia smiled as she wasn't expecting this and she kissed him back.

He then said, "Let's just walk a little as I would like to look at the Christmas lights." Sonia was surprised at this because Gregory normally wouldn't pay any notice to the lights and Sonia loved the build up to Christmas. They walked down Oxford Street and looked at the lights. As they turned onto Regent Street, the lights were white shaped angels all the way along the street. Sonia was in awe as she walked holding Gregory's hand.

Sonia stopped Gregory and turned towards him, pressing her body against his, and looked into his eyes. She then kissed him on the lips and said, "I love you."

Gregory felt really special just then and he kissed her back and said, "I love you too." He then said, after looking at his watch, "Shall we go eat?"

Sonia replied, "Where?"

He said, "Follow me."

Sonia walked with Gregory as he took to walking a little quicker than they had been. Sonia said, "Where are we going?"

Gregory said, "I know a place around here somewhere, I walked past it the other day while doing an errand for work."

Sonia said, "Okay." They walked for another five minutes and Gregory opened the door. Sonia said, "This looks nice." She was relieved that she had washed her hair the night before and taken the time to touch up her makeup. She walked in as Gregory held the door. Waiting inside was a hostess greeting Sonia as she asked for the reservation name. Sonia just turned and looked at Gregory as he followed behind.

Gregory replied, "Fitzpatrick."

The lady then said, "Very good, your table is ready. Your waiter is Tom and he will be looking after you this evening."

Tom walked up to Sonia and asked for her coat, then he asked for Gregory's, hanging them both on a coat hanger and putting them in the cloakroom. He then said, "Please follow me." Sonia, while standing, had grabbed her tights from outside her dress and pulled them up just before she followed. She walked behind Tom and was seated in a chair positioned with a view into the kitchen area. Sonia liked this as it was alive with activity. Gregory pulled out his own chair and sat as Tom took Sonia's table napkin and placed it in her hands. Gregory sat and took his napkin and placed it on his lap. Tom asked if there were any allergies that the chef needed to be aware of before cooking.

Sonia said, "Yes, I am coeliac."

Tom replied, "That's fine, I will give you the gluten-free menu." Tom left the table and retrieved the menus. He handed Sonia her menu and walked to Gregory to hand him his. After this, he asked if they would like to order a drink or see the wine list.

Sonia said, "Yes please, can we see the wine list?" Gregory sat quietly observing the atmosphere and Sonia as he watched her glow in the dim ambient light. Tom returned to the table and handed the drinks menu to Sonia and said he would return shortly. As Tom left the table, Sonia leaned forward and said to Gregory, "This is a nice surprise."

Gregory said, "Yes, it's a nice place." Sonia handed Gregory the menu to choose a bottle of wine. Gregory took the menu from Sonia and said, "You look very beautiful tonight. I love the red dress." Sonia smiled and adjusted herself in her chair.

Tom returned with water and began to pour a glass for Sonia and then for Gregory. While doing this, he asked Gregory if he had decided on anything.

Gregory said, "Yes. Can we have the sauvignon blanc from Chile, please?"

Tom said, "That is one of my favourites."

Sonia said, "That sounds like a nice wine."

Tom smiled and left the table to go to the bar. He stood at the bar area and requested the wine from the bartender and proceeded to get a bucket with ice. He walked to the table with the wine and the hostess positioned the bucket stand and bucket of ice between Sonia and Gregory. Tom held the bottle for them both to see the label and asked, "Who would like to sample?"

Gregory said, "Sonia, please."

Sonia repositioned herself in her chair and waited for Tom as he took his corkscrew from his right-hand side jacket pocket. He removed the foil and pierced the cork, turned in a clockwise motion and pulled it from the bottle. He poured a sample taste for Sonia as she watched him do this with precision. She said, "That is very nice," after she took a drink. Tom poured some more into Sonia's glass after she placed it back on the table and then poured Gregory's glass. Once finished, he positioned the bottle in the bucket and placed the table towel on the stand. He said he would return to take their order.

Gregory took a mouthful and swallowed. He said, "That goes down easy."

Sonia smiled and said, "We might be ordering a second."

Gregory smiled. He then asked Sonia, "What would you like to eat?"

Sonia looked at the menu and said, "I would like the fillet steak with peppercorn sauce, green vegetables and mashed potatoes. Oh, and spinach."

Gregory said, "I'll get the same." Tom returned and they both placed their orders and relaxed some more. Sonia began to feel sad, emotional and upset. She had realised how much she was in love with Gregory but felt emotional because she wished she had met him years ago and not in her late thirties. Gregory noticed that she had gone quiet and asked if she was okay. Sonia sat and nodded her head as she drank from her wine glass. As Gregory looked at her he said, "I love you." Sonia swallowed as a teardrop emerged from her eye and ran down the right side of her face. Gregory asked, "What's wrong, are you not happy here?"

Sonia nodded and said, "Yes I am, but I'm just emotional."

Gregory began to feel uncomfortable as he could see that Sonia was getting worse with emotion as several other people in the restaurant began to notice. To Gregory, it felt like people were thinking that he was an asshole breaking up with his partner. He reached forward to hold Sonia's hand and she jumped up from her chair, placed her napkin on it and walked towards the toilets. Gregory took a drink from his glass and sat looking around at the décor.

Gregory began to feel very irritable as Sonia was gone from the table for nearly fifteen minutes. The waiters began to take the food to the table and Sonia emerged, walking towards them. She took her napkin and plonked into her chair.

Gregory said, "The food looks very nice," as the waiters left the table. Sonia agreed. Gregory lifted his knife and fork and began to cut his steak. Sonia took a sip from her wine and sat quietly staring at the plate of food in front of her. She then proceeded to take her cutlery and taste the potatoes.

She said, "The potatoes are lovely, try them."

Gregory said, "Yes, I have already, the food is great."

Tom walked over and asked if everything was okay.

Sonia and Gregory at the same time said, "Yes."

Tom said, "If you need anything, please ask. Enjoy your evening." He walked to another table.

Gregory asked Sonia if she was okay. Sonia said that she was just very emotional and didn't know why, but she knew. Gregory continued to eat and so did Sonia.

Gregory said, "Can't wait until next week, Edinburgh."

Sonia said, "Me too."

They spoke about their trip and what they would like to do, feeling pretty good and happy with the evening. They finished their main courses and Gregory decided upon the cheesecake for dessert. Sonia decided to have the pavlova. They never ordered a second bottle of wine but agreed to have a latte each with their dessert.

Sonia was feeling very tired and emotional, trying her best not to burst into tears. She was really happy with the evening but found it hard to remain within the happiness. This feeling made her anxious and not in control. She felt vulnerable and didn't know how to react. In a way, she felt uncomfortable in her own skin. She loved the attention that she was getting from Gregory but kept thinking the worst.

She was thinking that once he found out about Andrew, they would break up. The dessert arrived at the table and Sonia picked up her spoon and scooped a small amount of pavlova with cream and offered it to Gregory to try. Gregory leaned forward and Sonia placed the spoon in his mouth. Gregory closed his lips on the spoon and slowly retreated back into his chair. He sat a while, allowing the pavlova and cream melt in his mouth, and then he swallowed.

He said to Sonia, "That's really good, would you like to try mine?"

Sonia replied, "Yes."

Gregory lifted his plate and positioned it beside Sonia's so that she could take what she desired. She took her spoon and scooped some cheesecake off the top, away from the biscuit base. She placed it beside her dessert and handed back Gregory's plate so that he could eat. The coffee arrived just as Gregory put his plate on the table and they both tried their own.

Sonia immediately said, "I chose the right one," without tasting Gregory's, but he disagreed once he had some of his. They both laughed and continued to eat. Sonia said to Gregory, "I have really enjoyed tonight. It was a very nice surprise and I am sorry for being emotional earlier. I look forward to Edinburgh. One week to go."

Gregory picked up his coffee and said, "Cheers to that."

Sonia smiled, lifted her coffee and said, "Cheers." They both took a sip, looking into each other's eyes. Sonia placed her cup down, sat back into her chair and just stared at Gregory. Gregory noticed this as he was placing a large spoonful of cheesecake into his mouth.

He continued and chewed quickly, then said, "What?" Sonia just sat smiling. Gregory continued to eat until he had the last piece of cheesecake on his plate. Sonia had scooped another piece of her dessert and placed it in her mouth.

Once finished, she placed the spoon on the plate and said, "I'm stuffed, I can't eat the rest." Gregory looked at what was left and decided not to eat any more. He was also full. He made a gesture to Tom to have the bill.

Tom went to the bar area and requested the bill, returning to the table with a card machine. Gregory had already removed his debit card from his wallet and was waiting. He offered the card to Tom and Tom entered the amount and handed the machine to Gregory. It gave the option to add a service charge with a 'yes' or 'no' button. Gregory selected 'no' and entered his pin number. He opened his wallet, took out a £10 note and handed it to Tom and said, "I would rather give a tip to you."

Tom took the £10 note and said, "Thank you, sir. I will get your coats."

Sonia and Gregory stood up from the table and Tom helped Sonia to put on her coat, then assisted Gregory. Once they had both buttoned up their coats, they were escorted to the door and thanked for their custom. Sonia and Gregory embraced each other outside and kissed.

Sonia said, "Thank you for the wonderful night, sorry I was emotional but I have my period."

Gregory said, smiling, "Don't worry, I just looked like an asshole."

Sonia said, "Why?"

Gregory replied, "I'd say several thought I was breaking up with you or being a male chauvinist plonker."

Sonia laughed and started to walk with Gregory towards the Tube station. While walking, Gregory said that he really liked the Christmas displays. Sonia was surprised as Gregory didn't much like Christmas. Sonia loved Christmas and the whole experience surrounding it. As they walked, they stopped a few times to look at the window displays. Some had Christmas themes and others had new stock arrivals. Gregory was more interested in the items for sale than the Christmas themes. However, Sonia had to stop and take lots of pictures while Gregory stood waiting in the cold. He could never understand why Sonia would have to take a picture of everything. He remained quiet standing in the cold; he felt it was best as she had already been emotional in the restaurant. Sonia took one picture and realised that the flash hadn't worked so she fiddled around with the settings while Gregory stood watching her. Eventually she managed to get the flash to work and she took some more pictures. Once Sonia was finished, she threw her phone into her handbag and they walked to the Tube station. They got their trains and Sonia closed her eyes on and off during the journey. She had cramps in her stomach, which didn't help. She was also very tired and had a headache.

Once they arrived at Gregory's, Sonia went straight to the bedroom and began to get ready for bed. She brushed her teeth and lay in bed, pulling the duvet over with her dress on. Gregory entered the room with two glasses of water and Sonia asked for a tee-shirt. Gregory placed the water on the bedside table and grabbed a tee-shirt from his wardrobe. He threw it gently towards Sonia and it landed in front of her face as she was wrapped in the duvet. Sonia sat up and reached behind her to unzip her dress and pulled it over her head. She placed her hands inside the tee-shirt, pulled it over her head and threw her dress onto the chair. Gregory had already undressed to just a tee-shirt and he went to the bathroom.

Once he had finished, he jumped into bed and switched off the light. He leaned over to kiss Sonia and held his position until she responded. She lifted her head and kissed his lips. He lay his head down beside hers and asked how she was feeling. Sonia replied that her cramps were bad and that she needed to sleep.

Gregory said, "Turn onto your side and I'll cuddle into you." Sonia turned after kissing him again on the lips and Gregory positioned himself with his left arm under her and his right hand resting on her belly. His face was up against her head and her hair was tickling him. He asked her to move her hair over her shoulder and Sonia did this. They both fell asleep shortly. During the night Gregory woke, feeling his arm numb as the blood flow was reduced. He pulled his arm free and turned over on his side, facing the bedroom door. Sonia felt him move and she adjusted herself to cuddle into him. They slept until 11.30am the next morning. Sonia woke first and reached for her phone beside her on the bedside table. She opened the phone by entering her pin and the bright light woke Gregory.

He said, "What time is it?" in a croaky voice.

Sonia replied, "11.33am."

Gregory grunted and closed his eyes. Sonia continued on her phone and switched off aeroplane mode. Shortly after, her phone sounded ping several times as she received text messages. This made Gregory turn onto his back while saying, "Can you mute it, please?"

Sonia just muted her phone as he mentioned it and continued to view her messages. She had received some pictures from her father. Her dad would send her texts most days and sometimes pictures. Sonia would also return pictures that she had taken. She had also received a text from Andrew. He said in the text message: *Hi Irish, I was thinking about you and the nice time we had together, we must do it again.* Sonia moved onto the next text she had received. It was from a guy she had met at a work function. His name was Philip. Philip had text her the following message: *Hello Sonia, it's Philip here, we met at the company function last month. I would like to meet you for a coffee or a drink if you are up for it?* Sonia remembered Philip. He was a very nice guy. He was in sales, from what she remembered of the conversation they had had, and he was good-looking. Sonia continued on her phone, checking through emails, deleting the ones she didn't want.

She was content doing this but the bright light was annoying for Gregory. He opened his eyes and turned over to face her. Sonia immediately closed her phone cover. She placed her phone beside her and leaned towards him for a kiss. They kissed. Gregory asked how she was feeling and Sonia said that she felt the same. He jumped out of bed and went to the bathroom. Sonia opened her phone and closed the apps properly, then left her phone on the bedside table. Gregory returned and asked if she would like to use the shower first. Sonia told him to go ahead. Gregory showered and Sonia after. They got dressed and went to the kitchen. They both decided on porridge so Gregory placed a pot on the gas hob and added the porridge with milk. He cooked it slowly while Sonia sat on the kitchen stool, talking. She was excited about Edinburgh and Gregory asked about Thailand.

He said, "Can we look at Thailand this morning?"

Sonia took her phone and started to look at dates. They decided on the month of March the following year. Sonia looked up flights and Gregory agreed with everything that she said. Sonia was getting giddy and was feeling much better. Gregory had finished making the porridge so he prepared one bowl and placed it in front of her. He also took the honey from the cupboard and a spoon. He placed both beside her bowl and then prepared his own. Once he had filled his bowl, he washed the pot and the utensil in the sink. He then sat beside Sonia and kissed her on the lips.

He said, "Enjoy."

Sonia said, "You too."

They both took a spoonful and sat looking out of the dining room bi-folding glass doors. It was raining and the birds were feeding from the bird feeder. Sonia continued looking at places to visit in Thailand on her phone. She found a beautiful hotel on the outskirts of Chiang Mai. There was a swimming pool and spa area and it was surrounded by trees. They both liked this hotel but Sonia continued to check out the alternatives while Gregory ate his porridge. The other hotels were nice but this one was the one they both agreed on. Gregory finished his porridge and washed his bowl and spoon.

He then said, "I'll get my laptop and we can look with a larger screen."

Sonia said, "Good idea."

He left the kitchen and removed his laptop from his study area. He took the power cable and plugged it in under the countertop, switched it on and entered his password. He then slid it towards Sonia and said, "There you go."

Sonia took it in her hands and positioned it so that she could type. She opened the web browser and typed Thailand hotels. She found a hotel but got sidetracked looking at things to do while in Chiang Mai. Sonia continued to eat as she browsed the internet, listening to the birds singing outside. They had both agreed that they would travel to Thailand but would need to agree on the hotel.

Gregory left the kitchen to go to the bathroom. Sonia picked up her phone while he was gone and another text was received from Philip. It read, *Hi Sonia, I have been invited to a music event with VIP passes and I was wondering if you would like to join me?* Sonia loved music so she replied straight away. *Hi Philip, when is the event?* Philip replied, *Wednesday evening, 7pm.* Sonia replied, *I'd love to go.* Philip sent his last text that morning: *Great, I will text you tomorrow with the details.* Sonia said, *Thank you.*

Just as she had sent her text, Gregory walked in and he felt his stomach turn. He asked Sonia if everything was okay and if she had found flights. Sonia said that she was still looking and mentioned having a cup of coffee.

Gregory laughed and said, "Ah, so I'll make the coffee."

Sonia smiled and said, "You know I love you."

Gregory filled the kettle, switched it on, grabbed two mugs from the cupboard and added coffee to both. He opened the fridge door and took out the milk. As he opened the milk, he said to Sonia, "I would like to do a cooking class in Thailand. I love the food so much I would like to learn how to cook it."

Sonia smiled and said, "Yes, that's a great idea. I would love that." She continued to search for flights and Gregory prepared the coffee. He handed Sonia her mug and she said, "Thank you."

Gregory said, "I'm becoming your biatch."

Sonia said, "Funny," as she sipped her coffee. She then said, "I'm not feeling great and my cramps are sore. I will need to rest a bit more before I leave."

Gregory said, "Let's book the holiday and then watch a movie. I'll get a blanket and if you fall asleep, that's no problem."

Sonia agreed and continued to search on the internet. It took about forty-five minutes as Sonia compared two airlines. She picked one eventually due to the longer stopover in Beijing. Sonia wanted to not rush through the airport but rather relax and take it all in. Gregory also agreed so they booked the flights. Gregory handed Sonia his credit card and requested that she booked the flights and the hotel. Sonia said to Gregory that she would pay half and they both agreed. Sonia booked the holiday and she got very excited. She got off her stool and hugged Gregory while he was sitting on his.

They kissed and Gregory said, "I'll get a blanket. I'd love another coffee," as he walked out of the kitchen. Sonia made one as he returned, switching on the television. They both agreed on a movie to watch. It took a while for them both to decide on one. Sonia walked over with two mugs of coffee and they cuddled into each other. Gregory selected the movie and they both watched, enjoying each other's company. Once the movie had ended, Sonia lifted her head off Gregory's shoulder and kissed him on the cheek. She then pulled the blanket off herself and made her way to the toilet. As she was walking, she noticed that it was getting dark outside and it looked very cold. Gregory also got up, folded the blanket and placed it on the couch. He tidied up the cushions and proceeded to the kitchen with their mugs. He washed both in the sink and as he was drying them, Sonia walked in behind him. She wrapped her arms around him from behind and snuggled her head against his back. Gregory stopped drying and stood still as he enjoyed the embrace. Sonia lifted her head and said that she needed to go home and sleep. Sonia moved away and stood watching as Gregory placed the mugs back in the cupboard. As he was doing this, he said that he would walk her to the Tube station while hanging up the dishcloth on the oven door handle. Sonia acknowledged and went to the hallway to get her coat and shoes. She already had her handbag. She was not feeling too good as her cramps had continued all day. Gregory followed behind her, grabbing his coat from the hallway cupboard and putting on his slip-on trainers. Sonia grabbed him as he was standing upright and she held him tightly. She kissed him on his lips and Gregory held her also as he straightened himself. He switched off the light on the landing and left the hall lights and kitchen lights on. While he was switching on the alarm, Sonia opened the front door and they both walked outside. Gregory closed the door and locked the lower lock.

Gregory followed Sonia onto the pavement and they walked, holding each other. Sonia said that she would miss him and that she looked forward to Friday. Gregory also said that he would miss Sonia for the week but looked forward to Edinburgh. They arrived onto the Main Street and Sonia pushed the button on the traffic light. Both stood quietly, feeling the cold. Sonia looked in both directions as the lights turned red and she walked first onto the road. Gregory was a little slower as Sonia pulled away. He followed behind until Sonia stopped and waited.

Laughing to herself, she said, "Come on, old man." Gregory ignored her comment and walked up beside her. She took his right hand and they walked to the entrance of the Tube station. Sonia kissed Gregory, hugged him and said, "I'll see you Friday."

Gregory said, "Yes, text me when you're home."

Sonia replied, "Will do," as she walked through the turnstile and disappeared on the escalator, descending as she went underground.

Gregory began walking back home but decided to get a bar of chocolate on his way. He dropped into the corner shop and bought himself a Bounty bar. He put it in his pocket until he got home as he wanted to have a cup of tea with it. Once home, he relaxed with his bar and a cup of tea while watching the television. He just relaxed for the evening until Sonia text to say she was home. He then retired to bed and slept for the night.

Sonia returned home and ran a bath. She soaked for an hour or so and then prepared for bed. She placed her clothes out for work the next morning and searched through the internet looking at clothes to buy. She didn't find anything that she liked so she went to sleep.

The next morning, Sonia woke to her alarm and went to work. She felt good and refreshed as she had slept well. Sonia sent a text to Gregory: *Good morning, hope you have a great day.* Gregory replied, *You too, miss you.* Sonia sent, *Me too.* She continued her work as it was very busy that morning.

It was 11.25am when she received a text from Philip: H*i Sonia, can we meet at Covent Garden Tube Station at 7pm Wednesday evening?* Sonia read the message but couldn't reply straight away as she was with a client. She was excited because she didn't know who they were seeing that night and she loved Covent Garden. It was 12.45pm when she replied as she was checking out of work for lunch. She replied, *Hi Philip, yes that's great, I am looking forward.* Philip replied, *Don't eat as we can grab something beforehand.* Sonia replied, *Okay, noted.* Sonia went to the local coffee shop and ordered her caffe latte with cinnamon and a gluten-free sandwich. She sat and drank her latte, looking up venues in Covent Garden for the Wednesday night on her search engine. She couldn't find any for music. This was intriguing as she then knew it was a private gig.

She text Gregory, *I'll be going out with work Wednesday night, have you any plans for the week?* Gregory replied, *I was just thinking about you. Nah, I'll take it easy before the weekend.* Sonia replied, *Can't wait for Friday.* Gregory replied, *Me too, miss you.* Sonia replied, *I miss you too.* Gregory then sent a message: *I'll call you later once home, pretty busy and driving most of the day.* Sonia said, *No worries, chat later.* She also sent a big red love heart. Gregory replied with the same love heart.

Sonia took a bite from her sandwich and decided to text Philip. *Hi Philip, can you let me know the dress requirements for Wednesday?* Philip replied, *Casual is good, anything comfortable. I have booked a table for 7.15pm.* Sonia replied, *Oh great,* as she was surprised by this. Philip replied, *Nothing special. See you Wednesday.* Sonia replied, *Yes you will, looking forward.*

Sonia placed her phone on the table, picked up her sandwich and took a big bite. As she moved the sandwich away from her mouth, mayonnaise dropped onto her dress. She quickly placed the sandwich back on the plate and took the napkin, wiping her dress. It didn't remove the whole amount but smudged it in slightly. She put the napkin on the table and continued to eat, but first licked the side of the sandwich so that she didn't mess herself again. The rest of the day for Sonia passed well with no issues. She finished work and got home at 9.30pm and went straight to bed. Tuesday was also a long day for Sonia. Gregory also had two busy days, but they managed to chat each evening and text periodically during the days.

14

The venue

It was Wednesday morning and Sonia had the day off. She woke early as her body clock was programmed to waking at 6am. She sent her usual text to Gregory: *Good morning XxX.* Gregory also replied, *Good Morning X,* when he awoke for work, as usual. Then they always asked each other if they slept okay and then went to work. Gregory had work that day but Sonia remained in bed until 11am, sleeping on and off. She was restless as she was thinking about the night ahead and wondering what she would wear. She tried to sleep but images of all her dresses with things that she had to do, kept going through her mind. She sat up in her bed, switched on her tablet and took her mobile phone from the bedside table. She checked her mobile phone and there were no messages, so she put it down and opened the apps on her tablet. She scanned through the latest news and then lay down again as she felt tired. Sonia slept for another hour and then got up to go to the bathroom.

Once in the bathroom, she switched on the hot water tap for a bath. She waited for the water to get warm before placing the plug into the plug hole and adding some bath salts. The bath plug was loose and left sitting on the bath behind the taps as she had broken the connecting chain a month prior. The bath was filling with water as she plucked her eyebrows, looking into the mirror over the sink. Sonia had to wipe the condensation from the mirror several times as she struggled to make her eyebrows look similar in alignment. Sonia liked her bath to be very hot. She checked her legs with her fingertips and realised that she had small hairs visible, therefore she decided to shave them also. She reached for her shaving oil and began to rub it into her legs. She started shaving her right leg, placing her foot on the side of the bath, and rinsed the blade under the sink tap as she proceeded onto the left leg. Once finished, she cleaned the razor in the sink. She then brushed her hair before rinsing it with the shower head over the bath, with the water adjusted to a cooler temperature. After rinsing, she placed the shower head on top of the taps and squeezed her hair through her hands to get the excess water out. Sonia applied a conditioning shampoo and left it in her hair for twenty-five minutes wrapped in a towel. As she was preparing for the night ahead, Sonia began to feel guilty. She began to feel the physical pain in her stomach again, with the combined feeling of being frustrated. She felt unworthy and hateful towards herself, enhancing the internal feeling of pain within, becoming more physical and uncomfortable. The feeling of heaviness on her shoulders became more apparent as she felt sick. She felt the urge to call Philip and cancel the evening but then felt that it would make him get mad and she didn't want that either. Sonia didn't like to let someone down and she didn't want Philip to think less of her.

An image of Gregory would appear in her mind from time to time and this would make her feel worse as she didn't want to upset him. She told herself that she would go to the event, not drink more than two drinks, and that she would leave early so that she would have plenty of time to pack the next day. She started to feel better as she planned the evening in her mind. She still felt anxious and confused but continued to focus on the night ahead. She went to her room after switching off the bath taps. She looked at her dresses hanging in the wardrobe. She decided to wear a black dress with a lace overlay design across the shoulders, down the sleeves and below the hem. She hung the dress on the outside of her wardrobe and went back to the bathroom. She left the towel that was wrapped around her on the sink and climbed into the water slowly. The bath water was near the outlet hole so as she entered the bath water drained out, making a clunking noise. The water was very hot but Sonia enjoyed the sensation as her body became red. She positioned herself so that her head was just above the water level, with her feet resting on both sides of the taps. Sonia lay there in silence and closed her eyes.

She had fallen asleep and woke as the water felt cold on her body. She was surprised that she had fallen asleep and this concerned her. She thought to herself that if her head had gone under the water, she would have woken anyway. Sonia stood up in the bath, drew the shower curtain closed and pulled the plug out to allow the water to drain. She switched the electric shower on, removed the towel from around her head and washed her hair. Once finished, she climbed out of the bath and dried herself. The bathroom floor was pretty wet as some water had splashed out around the bath while she showered, the walls had a film of condensation sitting on the paint, and both the ceiling and walls had drips of water. Sonia grabbed the towel from the sink and gently rubbed her body until she felt it was dry, then dropped her towel on the floor. She moved the towel around as she stood on it with both feet, soaking up the excess water before throwing it into the wash basket. She walked into her bedroom, wrapped a towel around her head and took her dressing gown from behind her chair and put it on. She then climbed onto her bed and checked her mobile again. There were no messages.

She text Gregory. *How's your day going?* Gregory was driving so he didn't see the message until later that morning. Once he stopped for fuel, he text Sonia. *Busy driving all over the place. How is yours?* Sonia replied, *Just had a bath and relaxing.* Gregory said, *That's good, enjoy. I'll chat later, I'm on my way to an appointment.* Sonia replied, *Okay.*

She placed the phone back on the bed and got up to fetch her hairdryer. It was located under the mattress in the bed drawers. Sonia's bed had two drawers. One she used for all her electrical gadgets and the other for her underwear. She unwrapped the towel, rubbed it vigorously on her head dropping the towel on the floor. She switched on her hairdryer and proceeded to dry her hair. Standing in her dressing gown thinking about the night ahead. She started to feel excited but also reminded herself about the week before with Andrew. She wanted to get home by midnight as she was up for work early the next morning and also she had to pack her bag for the trip to Edinburgh. Sonia also had a bundle of clothes to wash in her clothes basket and on the floor around it.

She placed the hairdryer down to apply some hair oil and then brushed it to help remove the tangled ends. After brushing, she continued to dry it some more and then jumped back on her bed to relax. As she lay on her bed, she noticed that her feet had dry skin so she felt them with her hands and decided to scrub them with her foot scrub stone. She walked into the bathroom, reached for the scrubbing stone on her shelf and sat on the toilet. She sat scrubbing around the heel of her left foot and then the heel of her right foot. Once finished, she applied some skin cream and proceeded to apply some to her legs also.

It was nearly 1pm and Sonia felt hungry. She hadn't had any breakfast and she thought about what she was going to eat. Sonia wasn't very organised and didn't have much food in as she ate out most of the time. She decided to order a pizza from the local takeaway. Walking to the bedroom, she took her tablet and opened the app for a takeaway. She decided on a gluten-free nine-inch pizza with chicken and hot spices. She also ordered a lemonade drink. She continued on the app, paid with her debit card and selected that they call her mobile once they arrive. Sonia placed the tablet down and closed her eyes as she climbed onto her bed again.

As she lay for a few minutes, her phone chirped. It was a message from Philip. Sonia took her phone and opened the app. It read: *Hey Sonia, looking forward to seeing you tonight. I'll see you at Covent Garden for 7pm?* ☺ Sonia replied, *Yes, I will be there for 7, can't wait.* Sonia felt excited and then wondered what Gregory was doing. She text Gregory. *I miss you.* Gregory replied, *Miss you too.* Straight after texting he called her phone.

Sonia answered. "Hiya."

Gregory said, "How is your day going, resting? Are you looking forward to your night out?"

Sonia went quiet and then replied, "Yes. I am still tired but looking forward to tonight. I won't be drinking as I am up early tomorrow morning." Gregory got the sick feeling again in his stomach and he was wondering why this was happening as he talked to Sonia.

He said, "I'm looking forward to seeing you on Friday."

Sonia said, "Me too."

Just as she said this her phone beeped, indicating another incoming call. She said to Gregory that she would chat later and they finished the call. She answered and the pizza delivery man said that he was at her front door. Sonia jumped up from her bed, tied her gown tighter and proceeded to the hall door. She opened it and the delivery man handed her the pizza with his motorbike helmet on. He said, "Enjoy your food." Sonia just closed the door and walked to her bedroom. She sat back on her bed after closing her bedroom door and opened the pizza box. Her phone chirped again. It was Gregory. "I'll call you later as I have to drive again. Love you."

Sonia replied, "Okay, love you too." She took a slice of pizza and sat eating on her bed, leaning on the pillows against the wall. As she was eating she looked at the time and decided to put on a wash of her dark clothes because she had time before going out. She knew the dryer would take over an hour to dry the clothes. She continued to eat and selected some music to listen to as her mind drifted. She thought about Philip and also about what she would eat later that evening. She didn't want to eat too much while in his company as it was her first time out with Philip. She was curious as to where they were going to eat. She took her tablet and searched restaurants in the area. There were plenty to choose from, so she started to search for and look at new dresses again.

Once she had finished eating, Sonia took the pizza box, grabbed her laundry basket, squeezed the clothes from the floor into it, took a washing tablet and made her way to the kitchen. She dropped the pizza box on the floor and opened the washing machine door. She pushed as many of her dark clothes into the machine as she could and threw in the washing tablet. She selected a thirty-degree wash and pressed the start button. The machine began to fill with water and Sonia picked up the pizza box and placed it in the kitchen bin after pressing the foot pedal to open the lid. She removed her foot, allowing the lid to slam closed. Sonia opened the fridge door and looked at what was there. She had some cheese that had gone mouldy, some butter and some milk. There was a carton of orange juice that she took out and she looked at the use-by date. She was happy because it had one day left. She closed the door and fetched a glass from the cupboard. She poured what was left in the glass and placed the carton on the counter while she drank the juice. Once finished, she washed the glass and left it standing upside down on the drainer. She then walked to the bin, pressed the bin pedal and waited for the lid to open, then threw the carton in. She then opened the fridge door and took the cheese out. She looked at the wrapper and saw the mould, then opened the bin lid and threw it in. The rubbish bin was nearly full, but Sonia decided to leave emptying the filled bag until another time. The thought of having to carry the bag to the front of the house and place it in the wheelie bin while in her dressing gown put her off.

She walked to her bedroom and sat again on her bed. While sitting, Sonia decided to wear her single diamond stone necklace with her black dress. She also decided on her red leather handbag. This meant that she had to empty what she needed from her black bag. Sonia took both bags and emptied the contents onto her bed. It was a mess of receipts, used chewing gum wrappers, lipsticks and tissues, and there was a pair of knickers and panty liners that had all types of contents stuck to them. There was also an assortment of pens and, in one bag, a banana that had gone completely brown and had leaked onto her bag as the skin had split open. Sonia took a baby wipe from her bathroom and cleaned the inside of her black bag, removing the banana that had soaked into the bag lining. After she sorted out what she wanted for the night ahead, she refilled her handbags. Her bed had a lot of dirt and loose particles on that she just brushed off onto the floor. Sonia threw the pair of knickers onto the floor for washing and put a clean pair in her red bag. She also put two new panty liners in her bag. She had just finished her period and from time to time she had slight spotting.

She began to feel nervous about meeting Philip because he wasn't aware that she was dating Gregory. They had never discussed if they had partners. Sonia looked at her phone and saw that it was 3.10pm and she decided to sleep for an hour. She was still feeling tired as her mind would never stop thinking. She was worried that Gregory would call later that evening when she would be in the company of Philip. She knew that she wouldn't be able to answer because he would suspect that she was with another guy and then the night she had spent with Andrew would become an issue also. Sonia decided to call Gregory herself at 6.30pm so that he wouldn't call her later that evening.

As she was thinking to herself, Philip text. *I'm leaving work now so that I'll be on time. See you at 7pm.*

Sonia thought to herself, *God, I know, 7pm.*

She replied to his text, *Yes, I'll be there on time.* Philip replied with ☺ *x* and Sonia sent *X* back to him. She felt strange sending him a kiss but felt intrigued also as he had sent one to her. Philip planned to finish work early and get home to shower and change his clothes before meeting Sonia. She turned her phone onto aeroplane mode and plugged it in to charge, leaving it on the floor beside the plug adapter. She pulled the pillows away from behind her, leaving one so that she could lay her head down. She had a slight headache and felt tired. As she lay with her eyes closed she felt herself drift into sleep.

Sonia went into a deep sleep and woke at 5.35pm in a panic as she hadn't realised that she would sleep for so long and she hadn't set an alarm. She was feeling very heavy within herself until she noticed the time on the phone display as she moved her head to the edge of the bed to look. She said aloud, "Shite," and pulled the covers away from herself, feeling disorientated. She was feeling very hot and it was dark in her room. She switched the lights on and moved swiftly to the bathroom. She passed her fingers through her hair and gave it a shake about, allowing it to settle naturally. She then took her makeup and began to apply foundation. Once she had finished blending it in, she added eyeliner and mascara. To finish, she decided on her bright red lipstick that had a wet gel look. She put the lipstick in her handbag as she entered the bedroom and removed her dressing gown. She opened the bed drawer and selected a matching red pair of knickers and bra. She dressed herself as she stood facing the mirror and adjusted her breasts while admiring herself. Sonia felt better as she was more awake and she was nearly ready. She took the black dress from the hanger, put it over her head and reached behind to pull the zip up. The zip glided easily as it was a new dress. She took her red high-heeled shoes from behind the chair, blew hard to remove the dust particles and brushed over them quickly with her hands. She put her feet into them and stood, again admiring herself in the mirror. She grabbed her scarf and tied it around her neck and took her coat from behind the door. She buttoned her coat, looking down at each button as she moved from the bottom to the top. Once done, she looked at herself again and took her perfume from her black bag, squirted some, moved her head into the vapour and then placed the perfume in her red handbag. She checked her bag for her wallet and grabbed her phone and charger from the floor. Sonia was ready but felt nervous and a little sick again in her stomach. She was also excited about the evening because she didn't know where she was going or which music event it was. She opened her bedroom door, switched off the lights, locked it and walked through the corridor towards the hall door.

The street lights illuminated the hallway through the glass panel above the front door. The light was dim but Sonia could manage to see her way to the front door. She opened the door and closed it behind her. She pulled her phone and text Gregory by accident: *I'm on my way.* As she sent it, she realised her mistake and panicked. She held her phone in her hand, looking at the screen, awaiting a reply from Gregory as she walked. Gregory replied, *I think that wasn't for me?* Sonia replied, *No, it was for Lauren.* Gregory replied, *Ah okay, enjoy your evening.* Sonia sent the text to Philip. *I'm on my way.* Philip replied, *Great, me too!*

Sonia entered the Tube station and made her way to Covent Garden. On the way there, she felt that she needed to call Gregory once she got to the exit of the station, before Philip would arrive. She didn't want Gregory calling her when she would be in Philip's company, especially when they would be sitting in the restaurant. Sonia arrived and passed through the turnstiles after offering her Oyster card to the reader, and walked onto the street. She looked left and right to see if Philip was there but was relieved that he wasn't. The time was 6.43pm. Sonia walked to the side street where it was less congested with people and noise. She took her phone and called Gregory. She stood in the cold as the phone prepared to call with a beep, then the ring tone began. It rang a few times but there was no answer. Sonia stood looking at her phone and decided to text, *I just called you.*

Gregory was at home but had placed his phone on the kitchen countertop while he refilled the bird feeders in his garden. He couldn't hear the phone as he had closed the dining room door to keep the warmth inside. Once he had finished, he walked back inside and washed his hands in the kitchen sink. He noticed his phone LED indication light for received messages was flashing. He reached for his phone after drying his hands and read the message from Sonia. He thought to himself, *Wow, of all the times you call me and I don't answer.* He called Sonia back. It was 6.53pm.

The phone rang twice and Sonia answered in a rushed voice, "Hiya, I'm just going into the event. I wanted to say have a lovely evening and I'll call tomorrow." Gregory felt sick again while Sonia was speaking. He also felt the cold sensation on his left side again, down his left arm.

Gregory replied, "Okay, have a lovely evening and chat tomorrow. Bye." He hung up the phone as he felt very strange and wondered why Sonia had to rush to her event. It was meant to be a get-together for work colleagues.

Sonia got annoyed that Gregory hung up the phone quickly as she didn't get a chance to say good night. She was also aware that Philip could be around the corner waiting. It was 6.59pm. She turned her phone to silent and threw it into her handbag while she walked around the corner. Philip was standing looking at his phone just beside the entrance to a shop. Sonia walked up to him and he noticed her as she was about to say hello. Philip smiled and said that she looked very nice and he proceeded to give her a hug. Sonia smiled and said thank you as they embraced. Sonia then asked where they were going as soon as they stood apart.

Philip said, "We need to walk just up the street a hundred metres."

Sonia said, "Great."

Philip asked Sonia if she was okay. He noticed that she was elsewhere in thought. Sonia said that she was good and excited. They walked together, talking about the start time for the event and saying that they would need to be at the venue fifteen minutes prior. Philip said that it would begin at 8.30pm. Sonia felt at ease as she knew she didn't have to rush her food. They arrived at the restaurant and Sonia noticed that it was established in 1917. She was very impressed with the décor while she looked around. Philip was escorted to a table and Sonia followed, to be seated by the host. Their coats were taken to be hung up. A bottle of champagne was sitting in a silver bucket, awaiting their arrival.

Sonia smiled at Philip and said, "You have been busy."

Philip nodded and smiled as he took his table napkin to place on his lap. Sonia also placed hers. The waiter opened the bottle of champagne and poured their glasses. Philip took his glass and said, "Here's to a lovely evening."

Sonia said, "I agree." Sonia took a sip from her glass as Philip passed a comment.

He said, "Sonia, you look beautiful in that dress, very nice." He raised his glass to her and drank again.

Sonia said, "Oh, thank you." She took another sip from her glass, blushing.

The menus were handed to them both and Sonia noticed the fillet steak. She decided not to have a starter but to just have a main course. Philip also decided on the fillet steak. They ordered and sat talking. They talked about work, current news, the world and also relationships. Sonia had already finished her glass of champagne and Philip did shortly after her. Sonia began to get uncomfortable with the conversation as Philip asked about her last relationship and why it had ended. The waiter walked over and began filling her glass just as the question was asked. She was relieved but knew she had to answer. Their glasses were replenished by the waiter as the steaks arrived. The plates were positioned in front of both of them, with the vegetables and potatoes also.

Sonia looked at Philip and said, "I don't really want to talk about that right now."

Philip said, "Okay, that's fine, no problem. Enjoy your food."

Sonia took her steak knife and fork and cut a slice of meat. She opened her mouth and placed it on her tongue. It was moist and very tender as she chewed. It was a succulent steak. As she chewed, she thought about Gregory and she felt sick in her stomach.

Philip asked her, "What do you think of the food?"

Sonia swallowed and said, "It's very nice." Sonia took another mouthful of champagne and so did Philip.

He looked into her eyes and said, "The venue you will like; it's a private gig with about fifteen people only."

Sonia smiled and said, "That will be very intimate."

Philip smiled and said, "Yes, it will."

He continued eating his food and Sonia too. They talked about their love for music and attending events. Both had a similar interest and Sonia liked this. Sonia loved music and attending events of any kind. They finished their food and the waiter poured another glass each, taking the empty bottle away. Sonia could feel she was more relaxed. In fact, she was feeling light-headed as the alcohol made an impact on her. She was happy and was enjoying the company of Philip. They decided to not have a dessert and make their way to the venue. It was about a fifteen-minute walk from the restaurant. The time was 8.05pm. Philip paid the bill and their coats were brought to the table by the hostess. Sonia thanked Philip for a lovely meal and they made their way out.

As they walked together towards the venue, Sonia tripped a little and managed to regain her balance. Philip took her arm and said, "I will hold you," as he laughed. Sonia felt excited as she was feeling a little drunk. She laughed aloud and allowed him to stay beside her. She talked about the area and how much she would enjoy going to the markets on the weekend. Philip also enjoyed attending the markets and coffee shops. They arrived at the venue. Philip pressed the intercom entry panel button and the door was released from inside. Philip pushed the door open and allowed Sonia inside before closing it. Once inside, a girl was standing behind a small counter, requesting his name. He gave his name and she marked the paperwork and told him to go to the second floor.

Gregory looked at Sonia and said, "Shall we?"

Sonia smiled and walked ahead of Philip. They reached the second floor and Philip walked over to the bar as Sonia sat down at a table. Philip ordered a bottle of white wine. He paid and brought the wine over to Sonia with two glasses. He sat down and placed the wine and glasses on the table. The wine had a twist cap, therefore he opened it easily. He poured the wine after Sonia had inspected that her glass was clean. She always checked for lipstick marks before using a glass.

He raised his glass and said, "Great company and great night so far."

Sonia agreed as she smiled and said, "Yes, to that."

They both took a large mouthful and agreed that the wine was very good. Sonia took her phone from her bag and checked for any messages. There were none. She was relieved and placed the phone back into her bag.

Philip said, "Are you expecting a call?"

Sonia said "No, just checking if work have contacted me."

Philip said, "Ah okay."

As they sat talking, a girl walked into the room and said, "We are ready if everyone would like to make their way to the front room."

Sonia stood and Philip did too as he grabbed the wine bottle and both glasses. They followed the rest of the group to the room and sat down towards the back. Sonia placed her glass on the floor and began to remove her coat. The room was very small so she struggled. Philip reached over after placing the glasses and the bottle on the floor. He pulled her coat down from her shoulders and Sonia wiggled it off, smiling. Philip also smiled and once she was sitting again, he reached for her glass and handed it to her.

Taking a drink, Sonia said, "Thank you. It's hot in here."

Philip also removed his coat and placed it on his lap. The room had about twenty chairs facing the front of the building. The front wall had two sash windows with closed shutters. The lighting was dimmed and there were two candles positioned on a table in the front centre beside the microphone stand. There were three guitars positioned beside one another, sitting on their own stands. The room had several paintings mounted on the picture rails displayed around the walls. There was a man sitting at a table with a music mixer control set up, doing some last-minute sound checks. Philip picked up his glass from the floor and also the bottle.

He said to Sonia, "Would you like me to fill your glass?"

Sonia smiled and held her glass to be filled. She said, "Yes please."

Philip opened the wine bottle and poured some into her glass. He also filled his own, placed the bottle cap back on and put the bottle on the floor under his chair. He turned to face Sonia as she said cheers. He raised his glass and said cheers also.

Philip didn't look Sonia in the eye, so she said quickly before he took a mouthful, "Wait, you didn't look me in the eyes when you said cheers."

Philip was surprised and asked, "Why would one need to do that?" with a smile on his face.

Sonia said, "It will affect you sexually if you don't."

Philip said, "Oh, well then, we can't have that." He raised his glass and said, "Cheers," looking straight into Sonia's eyes.

There was a slight pause between them both as they made eye contact. Sonia felt a little uncomfortable but excited and she took a drink from her glass as she continued to look at him. Philip got embarrassed and Sonia noticed as his face went red.

He immediately said, "God, it's hot in here."

Sonia poked him as he was looking straight ahead and said, laughing to herself, "Shy, are we?"

Philip turned to face her and said, "Maybe, you do look stunning tonight."

Sonia replied, "Thank you," as she took another drink.

It was 8.37pm and the singer walked into the room. The host also followed and took the microphone. She thanked everyone for attending and asked for mobile phones to be put on silent.

She spoke about the singer and mentioned how many records she had sold and her next events that had been scheduled for the coming months. The audience clapped with joy and excitement as the host finished and welcomed their guest.

The singer introduced herself, took a guitar and adjusted the shoulder strap as she strummed it while talking. She tuned it slightly and then said, "I'll start with this one, 'Love Me Like You Do.'"

Sonia sat up in her chair to watch as the atmosphere became electric. Philip also adjusted himself to get a better view. The sound was intoxicating as they could feel the vibration seeping through the solid wooden chairs from the floor. They could hear every note from the guitar and the singer's voice was crisp. Philip took another drink from his glass as Sonia took out her phone and began to record. The bright light from the flash came on permanently and Sonia slammed the phone onto her lap, facing downwards, as she selected the settings to remove the flash. Philip took another drink from his glass as he felt embarrassed. Sonia fiddled a little and managed to change the settings to record. She lifted her phone and began to record again as she looked at Philip and smiled. She managed to capture the last few words of the song before stopping the recording and taking a drink from her glass.

Sonia leaned over to Philip's left ear and said, "Wow, this is great, thank you."

Philip turned to Sonia, leaned to her right ear and said, "You are very welcome." He then kissed Sonia on the cheek and moved back to facing towards the singer.

Sonia froze but felt excited and her body became very hot, as though her blood was on fire. She could feel a tingly feeling all over her body as she became aroused. She took another drink from her glass and looked at Philip as he was watching the singer sing her second song. Sonia was thinking that she would go home after the event and not encourage Philip to try and kiss her again. She drank again from her glass and Philip noticed it was nearly empty. He bent down and reached for the bottle, opened the cap and filled her glass. He also replenished his.

He said to her, "Shall I order another at the break?"

Sonia said, "Yes," without thinking.

The singer sang many songs before the break, which lasted thirty minutes. Sonia excused herself and went to the bathroom. Philip also went to the gents' toilet and he ordered another bottle of wine on his way. He collected it on the way back. Sonia was gone for quite some time as Philip sat waiting. Sonia didn't feel great as she got dizzy and felt drunk while she was in the toilet. She made herself sick by sticking her fingers down her throat, then wiped her face with a baby wipe and touched up her makeup before returning to the room. Philip stood up and allowed Sonia to squeeze past him as she was sitting in the corner.

He said, "Are you okay?"

Sonia said, "Yes, the bathroom was busy." She reached for her glass and drank some more wine. Philip also took his glass and held it.

The interval had finished and the singer returned to begin again. She took another guitar from its stand and said, "This one is called 'Burn'."

Sonia began to feel uplifted and excited as she loved this song. She drank some more, then took some pictures and also took a selfie with Philip. Philip put his arm around Sonia when she decided to take the selfie and she moved her body closer as she placed her head next to his. She also took a picture as they faced one another. Sonia moved her body back over to her own seat and placed her phone into her handbag. Philip noticed that Sonia had an eyelash sitting at the edge of her eye and he offered to take it away. Sonia moved her head closer and Philip carefully extracted the hair with precision.

Sonia smiled and lifted her glass. "Here's to a great night and company."

Philip raised his and said, "Cheers," as he smiled and looked into her eyes again.

Sonia felt excited and hot. She felt her body getting aroused and she wanted to kiss Philip. Philip sensed that Sonia liked him and he took a drink from his glass. He picked up the near-empty bottle, opened the cap and poured the contents into each of their glasses equally. He then put the cap on and placed it under his seat. He then said, "I really like this wine."

Sonia agreed by nodding her head as she listened to the song being sung by the singer. The time had passed quickly and it was 10.45pm. The singer announced that the next song would be her last and the group applauded. She sang 'Falling For You'. Sonia began to feel emotional as she listened to this song. She thought about Gregory and she wished that he was there with her rather than Philip. Philip noticed that Sonia was crying and he placed his hand on her leg. Sonia wiped her face with both hands but left his hand on her leg. She began to get more emotional, so Philip moved closer to her and put his left arm around her. Sonia leaned her head onto his shoulder. They both sat listening to the song. Once the song had finished and the singer had thanked everyone for coming, she left quickly. Sonia also got up from her chair and squeezed past Philip, making her way to the bathroom. Philip remained in the room and watched everyone disperse. He continued to finish his glass of wine. He waited for Sonia to return.

Sonia arrived back and stood to Philip's right-hand side. She said, "That was really good. I enjoyed the evening and loved the song selection."

Philip stood and said, "We can make our way to the bar if you like."

Sonia replied, "Yes, that sounds good." Philip took his coat from behind him, bent over and grabbed the wine bottle and moved to the side to allow Sonia to get her things. Sonia took her handbag and her wine glass and shuffled her coat free from the back of the chair. She walked beside Philip and he said, "Ready?"

She replied, "Yes, I'll follow you."

Philip walked through the double door and entered the bar off the corridor. He noticed a table with one chair that was free so he made his way there. He said to Sonia, "You sit and I'll find something," as he placed the bottle and his glass on the table. Sonia also placed her glass beside his. She put her coat around the chair and sat quietly scanning around the room to find a chair. Philip returned some minutes later with a stool. He laughed and said, "I guess this will do."

Sonia smiled and said, "At least we will be the same height now."

Philip was five feet eleven inches in height and Sonia five feet seven inches. Philip placed the stool on the floor and sat while manoeuvring it closer to Sonia to get a better position in front of her. When he felt comfortable, Sonia placed her hand on his leg and asked, "Would you like some more wine?"

Philip said, "Yes." She poured the remainder of the wine into both glasses. Taking the empty bottle, Sonia walked to the bar and ordered another. She returned to the table, opened the bottle and poured him some more. She also filled her own glass. Philip asked Sonia, "Could you eat something, are you hungry?"

Sonia laughed and said, "Yes, I am."

He then said, "There is a Spanish restaurant around the corner, we could get some tapas."

Sonia said, "Yes, that would be nice."

They continued to drink the wine and decided to leave and have some food as they were both hungry again. They arranged to meet at the main entrance door as they both needed the toilet before leaving. It was 11.25pm as Sonia looked at her mobile phone while in the bathroom. There were no texts from Gregory so she was relieved. She applied her red lipstick before making her way to the entrance. Philip was standing at the main entrance door with his coat and gloves on. Sonia walked down the final steps as Philip opened the door.

Sonia walked past and said, "Thank you," to the girl behind the desk.

The girl replied, "You're welcome, have a lovely evening and safe journey home."

Philip also said, "Thank you," as he allowed the door to close behind him. Sonia stood facing Philip as he exited the building and Philip walked up to her. He embraced her with a hug and said, "Great company," as they both lost their footing and regained their balance, laughing. Sonia was feeling tipsy and Philip wasn't far behind. Philip pointed down the street and said, "This way," as he held Sonia. They both stepped together as they made their way down the pathway. Sonia was watching her footing as she was in high heels. Philip was laughing as Sonia would lift her legs without bending them as if she was marching. He decided to mimic her and she laughed but got paranoid and felt he was mocking her. She got a little defensive but Philip stopped and said, "It must be hard walking in them." Sonia agreed with a nod. Philip stopped at the road junction and faced Sonia.

He kissed her on the lips and Sonia wasn't expecting this. It was totally unexpected as she didn't feel that they had much chemistry during the evening. Sonia said straight after, "I need to pee again."

Philip laughed at her response and said, "Okay, the restaurant is just there."

They walked together until they reached the entrance door. The inside was full and the atmosphere was exciting. The kitchen was open plan so that the patrons could see the preparation area. Philip opened the door and entered first. Sonia followed as Philip said, "Toilets are that way. I'll find a seat."

Sonia walked towards the toilet as Philip requested seats. The guy at the door said that they only had stools at the kitchen area. Philip agreed and he was pointed in the direction. Philip walked to the stools and sat down. He was handed menus.

Sonia returned with a smile and said, "Busy place."

Philip looked around and said, "Yes, it is." He looked at the wine menu and selected a white wine.

Sonia said, "Are you trying to get me drunk?"

Philip smiled and said, "Maybe."

Sonia smiled back and said, "Be careful what you wish for."

Philip said, "Always," with a cheeky smile. He called over the waiter with a hand gesture and pointed at the menu. He said, "Can we have this one, please?" The waiter acknowledged and walked away. Philip said, "I'm hungry."

Sonia said, "Me too. Can't believe I'm eating again."

The waiter arrived with the wine, opened the bottle and poured two glasses. Sonia took a sip and looked at Philip. Philip took a sip and said, "Give it a few minutes to settle."

Sonia placed her glass back on the counter. She then proceeded to look at the menu. Sonia felt a little strange being told what to do, but she listened and waited a few minutes. She was feeling dizzy as the alcohol was taking effect on her body. She found it difficult to focus on the menu, so she looked at Philip and said, "Have we waited long enough?"

Philip turned his head and faced Sonia. He smiled and said, "Try it now."

Sonia reached for her glass and positioned it in front of Philip. Slurring her words, she said, "Cheers."

Philip also raised his glass and said, "Cheers," looking into Sonia's eyes. Philip realised that she was getting drunk so he got the attention of the waiter and requested some still water. Sonia sat staring into the kitchen as the cooks prepared the food. Philip said, "What do you think of the wine?"

Sonia replied as Philip was drinking from his glass, "It's fine. I really like it." She drank some more.

The waiter arrived with the water and Philip asked Sonia, "What would you like to eat?"

Sonia looked at the menu and said, "You order and I'll pick from what you get."

Philip took his menu and requested the tortilla Española, sherry-glazed chorizo and chickpeas and patatas bravas. Sonia was happy with the order because she loved spicy food and potatoes. Philip poured Sonia a glass of water and he also poured himself one. Sonia continued to drink from her wine but Philip drank some water.

He turned to Sonia and said, "I'm so hungry again."

Sonia poked his stomach and said, "Need to watch the six pack."

Philip reacted as he jumped back on his stool and laughed. He jokingly said, "Maybe you will get to see it."

Sonia smiled and said, "Maybe I will," as she drank some more.

The food arrived with the waiter to the counter area and was placed in front of Sonia and Philip. The waiter then wiped two additional plates with a cloth and placed them in front of them both. He said, "Is there anything else that I can get you?"

Sonia said, "No thank you." Philip acknowledged with a nod.

Sonia took her knife and fork and scooped some spicy potato. As she put it into her mouth, she could taste the hot flavours. She chewed and swallowed quickly and reached for her glass of water. She drank some and faced Philip, smiling as she said, "That's hot."

Philip smiled back and said, "I'll try it."

Sonia watched Philip take his fork. He took a small amount and chewed. He also reached for his water and drank some. They both laughed and took their wine and celebrated the hot dish. Sonia was feeling really energetic and excited. She leaned over to Philip, kissed him on the left cheek and said, "Thank you for a wonderful night, I needed this."

Philip said, "It's not over yet," as he smiled and ate some of the chorizo with chickpeas. Sonia was giddy and she teased Philip about his hair, which was parted to the side. Sonia reached and messed it up a little with her right hand as Philip sat, not impressed. He remained stiff sitting on his stool as she did this but laughed as he was not expecting it at all. He reacted by poking his finger at her belly. Sonia jumped back on her stool, nearly falling off. Philip managed to grab her arm to stabilise her.

She returned the poke back to his belly and said, "Yep, six pack no more," laughing to herself.

Philip said, "Ah yeah, we will see," as he drank some more wine. Philip enjoyed the banter and he said to Sonia as they began to eat some more, "Would you like to come back to my place?"

Sonia felt shy when he said this and she replied, "I don't know."

Philip replied, "I don't bite."

Sonia then agreed by saying, "Okay, but just as friends."

Philip agreed. They continued to eat some more and eventually finished the wine. Sonia excused herself and went to the bathroom. Philip called the waiter over and he paid the bill. He put his coat and scarf on and awaited Sonia's return. Sonia had already been gone about twenty minutes. She was trying to touch up her makeup. She was feeling drunk and full of energy. She returned to Philip in front of the kitchen area and put her coat on.

Philip smiled and said, "You fix up nicely."

Sonia poked him again in the stomach and continued to button her coat. She was feeling excited. Philip walked to the door and opened it. Sonia followed. As she walked through the door, she decided not to go back to Philip's place.

She said, "I think I will go home."

Philip said, "It's 1.15am and there will be no Tubes now."

Sonia took her phone out of her handbag and said, "Oh shite," after she looked at the time.

Philip smiled and said, "Look, come back, nothing will happen."

Sonia said, "Okay."

Philip took her arm and they walked down the street. Sonia was feeling the effects of the fresh air and the alcohol as she stumbled a few times, laughing aloud as Philip grabbed hold of her tightly. He also felt a little drunk but focussed on the walk home. It wasn't long before they arrived at his front door. He lived in an apartment in central London. He opened the main entrance door with his key and walked to the lift.

Sonia was impressed with the marble floors and décor. She said, "Very posh," as they walked into the lift and Philip pressed button '4'. Philip released Sonia as they stood facing one another. Sonia said, "God, it's hot in here," as she unbuttoned her coat.

Philip said, "Yes, it is."

Sonia grabbed Philip's coat with both hands and pulled him closer to her. She kissed him on the lips and let him go. Philip grabbed her back and placed his left hand behind her head as they kissed more. Sonia began to get excited as she gasped for air. Philip had lipstick smudged on his face as they stood back when the lift doors opened. Sonia laughed but said nothing. As they walked down the corridor, Sonia followed and gently tapped Philip on his bottom. Philip turned and said, "Cheeky." Sonia laughed and did it again as Philip was opening the door to his apartment.

Philip stepped in and held the door open as Sonia walked past. He closed the door and asked Sonia for her coat. Sonia was already unbuttoning her coat and was pulling it off herself as she was struggling with the heat. The apartment was very warm.

Philip took her coat with his right hand, leaned in and kissed her on the lips. Sonia asked to use the bathroom. Philip pointed to a set of double doors and said, "Go through the doors, first left."

Sonia walked down the hall and through the doors. Her high-heeled shoes echoed loudly. The apartment had marble floors also. Philip entered the living room and opened another bottle of white wine. He poured two glasses and waited for Sonia to return. Sonia entered the room holding her handbag in her left hand and her shoes in her right. She smiled when she saw the glasses of wine.

Philip said, "Just a night cap."

Sonia said, "Perfect."

Philip sat on the black leather couch and Sonia sat beside him. He took the two wine glasses and handed one to Sonia. They both raised their glasses, looked into one another's eyes and said, "Cheers." Sonia and Philip continued to drink from their glasses as they looked into each other's eyes. Sonia placed her glass on the living room table and she moved closer to Philip. Philip placed his glass on the table and slowly moved his head towards hers. Sonia acknowledged by moving towards his. They kissed. Philip adjusted himself on the couch and placed his left hand on her bare leg. They embraced in a kiss as he slid his hand along her leg under her dress. He opened his hand so that his thumb caressed over the top of her leg. Sonia groaned as he placed his right hand on her right breast. Sonia reached for the front of Philip's trousers and felt for the zip. She eventually found it and began to unzip it. Philip felt excited and moved his body closer to hers. Sonia reached inside his fly with her fingers and gently caressed him. She could only use her fingers like this, so she opened his trouser button and unbuckled his belt. Philip moved his left hand over Sonia's underwear and felt towards the heat. Sonia groaned again as she felt his gentle touch make her more aroused. Philip stood up and pulled Sonia up into his arms. Sonia stood as they kissed. Philip reached behind her and unzipped her dress. Sonia dropped Philip's trousers as she slid them off his hips.

Sonia asked, "Do you have a condom?"

Philip said, "I'll get one now." He took Sonia's hand and walked her to the bedroom. Her dress was loose as she walked. Philip walked into the en-suite and Sonia took her dress off, getting into the bed with her underwear on. Philip walked back into the bedroom with a condom still in its wrapper. He said, "I have one."

Sonia said, "Great."

Philip pulled the sheets back and climbed on top of Sonia. He positioned his legs both sides of hers as he leaned, resting on his elbows. He kissed her and said, "You have a great body."

Sonia said, "Thank you." She grabbed his belly and said, "A bit of work required here." Philip jumped back slightly and laughed. He kissed her again and she embraced him. She reached down and grabbed his manhood. Philip froze as she did this while Sonia bit his lip. Philip took his right hand and pulled her bra down from over her right breast. He then kissed her nipple. Sonia thrust her body up towards his, pressing against his penis. He licked around her areola and continued under her breast. He grabbed it with his right hand and pinched her nipple. Sonia gasped again and she reached down with her right hand, placing her fingers under his boxer shorts, grasping his penis.

She said in his ear, "I want you." Philip pulled back, kneeled upright and placed both hands each side of Sonia's underwear, slowly pulling them down as she arched her back, lifting her bottom off the bed. Sonia said, "Can you turn the light off?"

Philip said, "I will." He continued to remove her underwear. He got them clear from her feet as he stood at the end of the bed. Sonia sat up and removed her bra. Philip said, "Very nice." He then dropped his boxer shorts, revealing his erect penis.

Sonia said, "Wow, you're big," with excitement.

Philip took the condom from the bed and proceeded to remove the wrapper. He held the condom between his fingers and carefully put it on. He looked at Sonia as she lay watching him. Philip climbed back onto the bed and Sonia pulled him towards her to kiss again. They embraced, kissing, as Sonia opened her legs, allowing Philip to move his body between them. As they kissed, Philip pressed his penis against her and Sonia groaned. He moved his head to her right breast and kissed her nipple.

Sonia got very aroused and told him, "Fuck me." Philip lifted his head and smiled. He took his penis and leaned back as he positioned himself to insert it inside her. He spat on his right hand and rubbed his saliva on the condom. He took his penis in his right hand and positioned the head at the entrance of her vagina. He moved gently and pushed it slowly inside. Sonia went, "Oh," arching her head back as he moved the shaft inside halfway. He pulled it out to allow the moisture to build. Sonia moved her pelvis as he did this. She said, "You're so big." Philip pushed himself in further as Sonia groaned again, leaning her head to her right. She turned her head to the left-hand side while he was inside her as she arched her back, gasping for air. The temperature in the room felt so much hotter to her. Her body was in spasm as he inserted himself all the way.

Sonia felt herself get very aroused as Philip said, "God, you are wet." He gently manoeuvred in and out slowly as Sonia continuously adjusted her body. She was feeling hot all over. Her face was becoming very red and Philip noticed this.

She lifted her head and said to Philip, "It feels like you're in my belly." Her chest was showing red blotches in places. Philip began to pick up the pace as Sonia got more and more aroused. She grabbed the bed sheet on both sides of her and started to make a sound each time he thrusted inside her. Her lips began to feel dry and her mouth also. She began to feel a tingly sensation throughout her body as she lay, limp. It was an intense feeling. It was bliss.

Sonia pushed Philip back and said, "Wait." She pulled herself off him and positioned herself on her hands and knees. Philip moved up behind her as Sonia reached back with her hand and guided him inside her. He penetrated hard and Sonia gasped. She leaned her head onto the bed sideways, facing to the left. Philip grabbed both sides of her hips and continued repetition. Sonia couldn't feel her body anymore, she could just feel the intense internal feeling. Philip pulled out and then entered her again. He slipped off the condom without Sonia knowing and inserted himself inside her.

He said, "Oh my God, you are wet." Sonia reacted to him and moved her body with him as he penetrated faster. Philip gasped and said, "I'm going to cum." Sonia pushed back against him with her body and Philip pushed her away as he pulled out. He came all over the left side of her bottom and Sonia felt it.

She jumped forward and said, "Where is the condom?"

Philip said, "I just pulled it off."

Sonia said, "You didn't cum inside me, did you?"

Philip said, "No," as he jumped off the bed to fetch a towel from the bathroom. He said on his way, "I'll get something to wipe it off." Sonia remained in the same position until he returned. She was annoyed about what he had done and was agitated because she could feel something running out of her vagina. She placed her fingers on her vagina and felt the fluid as it exited. It was very little but she knew that it wasn't hers as she smelled her fingers. She questioned Philip as she wiped her leg and bottom with the towel.

She said, "Were you inside me without a condom?" Philip denied it. She wasn't sure so she continued to dry herself and lay back on the bed. She then said, "Wow, that was amazing."

Philip felt exhausted and was feeling really sleepy. Sonia was wide awake now and wanted more. It wasn't long before Philip fell asleep. Sonia lay looking at the ceiling with the lights still on. She was still aroused and felt very horny. Philip was out cold, fast asleep, but Sonia lay thinking. She could still feel some fluid between her legs and this worried her. She got out of bed and put on her knickers. She went to the bathroom and examined herself to look closer at the fluid. Sonia became worried as she had no contraception and didn't want to fall pregnant. She had worked out the days that she could have intercourse with Gregory according to her menstrual cycle. This wasn't a good day to take a risk. She decided to get the morning-after pill later that morning from a pharmacy. She was frustrated and wanted to leave the apartment but knew she couldn't get home without calling a taxi.

She walked back into the bedroom and Philip was awake. He said, "Are you okay?"

Sonia said, "No. There is semen inside me."

Philip said, "Did the condom burst?"

Sonia said, "I hope not."

Philip then said, "We will sort it out in the morning. I take it you don't have birth control?"

Sonia replied, "No, I don't."

Philip said, "Let's not panic."

Sonia said, "Easy for you to say."

Philip then said, "I came on your back."

Sonia then shrugged her shoulders and got into bed. Philip turned and faced Sonia as she lay on her back with her head facing him, pulling the duvet over herself. She said, "I can't complain though, my body feels amazing."

Philip smiled and said, "I'm horny again if you're up to it?"

Sonia nodded her head and said, "Hell yeah."

Philip jumped out of the bed and retrieved another condom from the bathroom. He walked back and handed it to Sonia and said, "Here, you put it on."

Sonia reached and took it from him. She placed it between her teeth and ripped the wrapper open. She pulled the condom out and said, "Come closer." Philip wasn't erect so Sonia moved her body closer to his. She took his penis in her right hand and caressed it. "Ah, it's waking up," she said as she began to place her lips over the head. She continued to caress with her hand as she licked it. Philip became erect in seconds and Sonia positioned the condom over the head of the penis, holding the tip of the condom to prevent air filling it as she unravelled it down his shaft. Philip pulled her towards him when she finished and he kissed her. Sonia embraced him and touched herself under her underwear.

Philip said, "Take them off." Sonia stood up and pulled her knickers down. Philip stood beside her and bent her over on the bed as he inserted himself inside her.

Sonia gasped and said, "Go easy, I'm very sensitive."

Philip penetrated hard as he grasped her hips with both hands. He thrusted inside her as deep as he could go with great intensity. Sonia tried to pull away as he pulled her closer. She was grabbing the pillows and covering her face as she gasped for air. Sonia screamed as she orgasmed. It was instant and she had no indication that it was going to happen. The feeling of Philip inside her was too much and her body was on fire. Philip continued to penetrate hard until he also ejaculated and he withdrew. Sonia dropped her body onto the bed and exhaled with relief as her body was still tingling inside. Philip removed the condom, with his semen visible, and he showed her before going to the bathroom to dispose of it. Sonia was too tired to register it as she lay on her back. Philip returned and cuddled up to her, switching off the light. Sonia pulled the covers over them both and she cuddled into Philip. They both fell asleep.

Sonia woke to the sound of Philip's alarm clock the next morning. She felt really hungover and very hot. Her mouth was dry and she had pushed the bedclothes off herself during the night. Philip turned to face her after he reached to switch off the alarm clock sitting on his bedside table under the lamp. He said, "Good morning," with a croaky voice.

He stared at Sonia as she said, "Good morning," back to him. He noticed that Sonia had eye makeup rubbed into her face. She turned onto her right side, closed her eyes and said, "Ten more minutes. I need water."

Philip said, "Okay," as he got out of bed and went to the kitchen. From there he fetched some water after he drank some himself. He felt dizzy as he stood drinking. He took the water to Sonia and said that he was going to shower first to let her rest. Sonia looked with one eye at the glass of water when Philip placed it on her bedside table. She had to take a minute or two to calculate the logistics of lifting her head, reaching for the glass and drinking it. This she did with speed so that she could lay her head back down again. She could hear Philip in the bathroom showering when she panicked about her mobile. She didn't know where she had left her handbag and phone. She thought about Gregory. It was 7.15am and she would normally be awake at 6am. She climbed out of the bed and struggled to walk to the end of the bed as she used her hand to balance herself, touching the mattress from time to time. She sat at the end of the bed and sighed as she felt dizzy. She looked around the room. There was minimum lighting, but there was light shining through from under the bathroom door. She could see her bag on the floor beside the curtains. The curtains were a heavy material, dark brown in colour to match the dark brown doors and skirting boards. The carpet was cream with a high pile that felt so soft to walk on. Sonia crawled over towards her bag and knelt down to feel for her bag strap. She managed to grab her bag and pulled it towards her as she lay back against the bed with a sigh.

As she was sitting up opening her bag, one of her shoes was tangled in the bag strap. She unzipped her bag and felt around to find her phone. Once she located it, she pulled it out and checked the battery life. There was half battery life left, which surprised her, but she hadn't used her phone at all the night before. Sonia opened the app and text Gregory: *Good morning, I miss you.* She threw her phone back into the bag and sat quietly on the floor, thinking about what she had to do next. She had to find her clothes and have a shower. She also remembered that she had to wear the same dress to work. She had no hairdryer so she couldn't wash her hair, and she had just over an hour to get ready and be at work. It was 7.30am. Philip emerged from the bathroom, clean shaven and showered. As he opened the bathroom door and entered the room, the light was so bright that Sonia covered her face. Sonia had her back to the bathroom and the light was making her head feel sore.

Sonia said, "I might call in sick to work, I don't think I could manage today."

Philip said, "I also don't feel great, I am very dizzy. That was a mission to shower as the heat made me worse." He also contemplated calling in sick.

Sonia asked, "Do you have any painkillers?"

Philip said, "Yes, I'll get you some."

He walked out of the bedroom and into the kitchen, reached above the extractor fan and opened the kitchen cupboard door. This is where he kept all his medication and plasters etc. He reached for the painkillers, closed the cupboard door and walked back to Sonia. He stood above her in the bedroom with a towel wrapped around him and handed her the box containing the painkillers. Sonia took a moment to acknowledge that he was there beside her so she laughed to herself. She said, "God, I feel like a mangled badger."

Philip noticed that she hadn't any water so he took her empty glass and refilled it in the kitchen and returned it to her. On his way back, he felt very dizzy so he handed the glass to her and lay on the bed. Sonia opened the box, took out the tablet strip and popped two out. She put them in her mouth and drank some water. She turned to face Philip while sitting on the floor and said, "That's a good idea." She pulled herself up with great effort and lay on the bed beside him.

Philip reached over with his right hand and touched Sonia on her leg. He said, "It was a great night."

Sonia looked towards him as she also lay on her back and said, "Yes it was, but I can't remember everything."

Philip said, "Me neither." Philip lay on the bed with his towel wrapped around him and Sonia lay naked. The room was very hot as the heating was on. They both fell asleep again. It was 8.45am when Philip woke and looked at the alarm clock. He woke to the sound of the bin men collecting the containers outside the restaurant across the road from his apartment. He turned to Sonia in a panic and said, "Sonia, it's 8.45."

Sonia opened her eyes, lifted her head and said, "I feel worse."

Philip replied, "Okay, maybe call in sick." Sonia pulled herself to sit up and threw her legs over the side of the bed. She wiggled herself down along the bed and dropped to the floor in a sitting position again. She reached into her bag and grabbed her phone. When she opened her phone, she noticed a message from Gregory: *Good morning. I'm in London this morning, can you meet for a coffee later?* Sonia read the message and opened the phone app. She scrolled down her contact list and selected her work office number. She pressed call and the phone rang once, twice and then a woman answered. She answered with the usual message and asked how she could help.

Sonia spoke with a croaky voice and said, "Hello, can I have the HR department?"

The woman replied, "Yes, certainly, I will transfer you now." The call went silent and then there was a beep. A male voice answered.

"HR department, Tom speaking, can I help?" Sonia said her name and told the man that she wasn't feeling well and that she wouldn't make it to work. The man repeated her name and said, "That's fine, thank you for letting us know. I hope you feel better soon."

Sonia said, "Thank you," and hung up the call. She then opened the app with Gregory's message and typed, *Hiya. I'm really busy today with meetings and clients, I won't make it, but I can't wait for tomorrow.* She sent the message and put her phone back in her bag. She sat leaning against the bed with her eyes closed and she thought about the night before. She remembered that Philip had removed the condom and she felt nauseous in her stomach. She knew that she had to go and get the morning-after pill just as a precaution. Philip got out of the bed as Sonia was sitting and he made his way into the living room. She could hear him make a phone call to his office and he also cancelled his day. She felt more at ease to know that she didn't have to rush because she wasn't feeling well at all. In fact, she felt like she had a temperature and was feeling totally exhausted, with no energy. Her head was also starting to feel heavy. The painkillers had had little or no effect. She pulled herself up into a standing position and took her knickers off the floor. She pulled them on and climbed into the bed. Sonia was not feeling well. Philip returned and saw her lying on her back, so he lay beside her.

They both lay there and Sonia said, "Do you remember taking off the condom?"

Philip said, "No, I don't." But he did remember.

He lay quiet as Sonia then said, "I'll have to get the morning-after pill, will you come with me?"

Philip said, "Yes, I'll go with you."

Sonia said, "I need to sleep some more."

Philip said, "I will too."

They both dozed off again for a few hours. It was 1.23pm when Sonia woke up. Philip was still asleep as she faced his direction. She felt a little better but was sweating as she had this very heavy strange feeling throughout her body. She reached over and pressed Philip's nose.

He opened his eyes and stared at Sonia for a moment before saying, "What time is it?"

Sonia said, "The clock says 1.25. I still don't feel good."

Philip said, "I feel a lot better. I'm hungry now."

Sonia replied, "I couldn't eat. I need to get to the pharmacy. I'll go have a shower if that's okay?"

Philip said, "Yes, be my guest, there are towels on the rail." Sonia climbed out of the bed and walked to the bathroom. As she walked, she tripped over her handbag shoulder strap and fell on the floor. Philip laughed out loud but Sonia wasn't impressed. She got back up and walked into the bathroom, closing and locking the door. Sonia stood in her knickers with both hands each side of the sink, holding herself straight while she looked at herself in the mirror. Her face looked greyish in colour and she had makeup rubbed around her eyes. Her hair was matted and she felt terrible. Her whole body was aching with a heaviness around her head. She thought about the night before with Philip and wondered what would happen. She was worried as she remembered that she had felt fluids coming out of her vagina and wondered if he had removed the condom towards the end of the sex. She felt used again and had a sick feeling in her stomach. She wanted to leave but knew she wasn't capable of going outside for some time until she felt better. The thought of walking in the bright sunlight was enough for her to take her time. She turned towards the shower and took her knickers off. The shower was an open-style shower with a drain on the floor. Sonia turned the shower knob and stood back to feel the temperature. The water felt right so she stood under the shower head. She just stood, feeling the water on her head and body while trying to relax. The thoughts continued through her mind as she felt anxious. She took the shower gel from the shelf and began to wash herself. She felt sick in waves as she washed. Her mind was thinking all kinds of scenarios including Philip and how she was going to leave later that day. She thought about the morning-after pill, where she would buy it and how it would make her stomach sick. Gregory also flashed through her mind and a feeling of sadness overwhelmed her. She felt ashamed and used again by Philip because she knew he didn't want a relationship. It was just about the sex for him and she felt ashamed that she had got drunk again and couldn't control her sexual urge. She was feeling worse as she began to shampoo her hair. She began to think about life and what her purpose was. She thought about her age and the fact that she had nothing to her name but the clothes on her back and a few items in her flat. She began to make herself feel miserable and worthless. The feeling of having sex again with another guy just made things worse for her. She began to think about Gregory and how he would leave her if he found out.

She felt dizzy as she washed the shampoo into her hair. She finished rinsing the shampoo out and switched off the shower. She looked around the room as she stood still to find the towel rail. It was above the toilet, wall mounted. She walked over and reached for two towels. The towels were very soft and large. She wrapped one towel around her head, securing her long hair, and the other around her body. She walked to the mirror and wiped the condensation off to see how she looked. She still looked grey in colour and she felt sick. She stood for a few moments, staring at herself with a blank mind. Bending over and taking her knickers off the floor, she unlocked the door and walked into the bedroom. Philip was gone from the room. She could hear some movement and voices from another room. The voices were from the television.

She walked into the kitchen to see Philip making a fry-up. He had the news on the television as he was focussing on the task of making breakfast. Sonia walked over to the kitchen stools and sat quietly. She just observed him from behind. He didn't hear her enter and sit behind him. Sonia sat looking at the nice apartment and wished she had a home of her own. Philip turned to look at the television and jumped when he noticed Sonia sitting behind him.

He said, "God, you shocked me."

Sonia smiled and said, "I've been watching you cook."

He asked if she would like a coffee and Sonia said yes. He pointed to the coffee maker and said, "Help yourself, take whichever flavour you fancy and put it in the machine, then push the button." Sonia looked over at the machine and got off her stool. She selected a cappuccino from the selection Philip had in a carton and placed it in the machine. She put a mug under the spout and pressed the touch-screen button. The machine began to make noise and shortly after, the fluid began to run from the spout into her mug. Philip turned as he was presenting the food onto plates and said, "There is a chocolate shaker in the cupboard above if you like that?"

Sonia said, "Oh yes," as she opened the cupboard door. She saw the metal shaker and took it down. Once the machine had finished, she used the shaker to add chocolate to her cappuccino. She then asked, "Which flavour would you like?"

Philip said, "I'll have the same."

Sonia made Philip a cappuccino while he arranged the table. Sonia was still feeling sick and wasn't sure if she could drink the cappuccino, but the smell was enticing her. She walked over to the kitchen table and placed a mug in front of Philip as he had already sat down.

While Sonia sat next to him, he said, "Oh, would you like some orange juice?"

Sonia smiled and said, "Oh God, no."

Philip replied, "Okay." He jumped up, opened the fridge door and took the cartoon out. He opened the cupboard above the sink and took a glass. He poured himself a glass of orange juice while telling Sonia to start eating without him. Sonia took her knife and fork and selected some bacon, a sausage and two eggs. Her stomach turned when she looked at the food on her plate. She remembered that she needed to be ready for the next morning to go to Edinburgh. It was going to be an early morning start and she needed to be feeling better. She cut her egg and it was runny. She pierced the sausage with her fork and cut a piece with her knife, dipping it into the egg. She took a small bite and placed the fork, with the remainder of the sausage still attached, on her plate. She chewed and struggled as she was feeling nauseous. Philip had sat down beside her and he noticed her struggle to eat.

He said, "Are you okay? You look not too good."

Sonia replied after she swallowed. "Really? Thanks. I don't feel great, probably the wine."

Philip said, "I feel okay now, just tired."

Sonia said, "Check you out."

Philip smiled as he placed food on his plate. He continued to eat as Sonia excused herself from the table, saying that she couldn't eat. She walked back into the bedroom and sorted out her clothes. She put back on her knickers, bra and dress as she struggled with the feeling of weakness. He body felt drained and she sat again on the bed, holding her head. Her forehead was sweaty and her tummy felt sick. She leaned down and grabbed her bag, lifting it onto the bed beside her. She opened the handbag and grabbed her makeup bag. She got up from the bed and made her way to the bathroom. There she applied makeup and used the toilet. When she used the toilet, she noticed a slight amount of blood on the tissue when she wiped herself. She just thought that it was because she had just finished her period a few days prior. She washed her hands and opened the bathroom door. Philip was in the bedroom dressing himself.

Sonia said, "I feel awful."

Philip turned to face her and said, "I feel okay. Do you normally suffer from hangovers?"

Sonia replied, "No I don't, that's why I am concerned. I might have caught something."

Philip reached for the painkillers and said, "Take these with you today," as he handed them to her.

Sonia said, "Thank you," as she threw them into her bag. She then said, "Where is the closest pharmacy from here?"

Philip replied, "Just around the corner. Give me five minutes and I'll go with you."

Sonia said, "Okay," as she sat down on the bed again. She reached for her phone as Philip was tying his shoelaces. She text Gregory, *How is your day going?* Gregory replied, *I'm in London and missing you.* Sonia felt terrible when she read this but replied, *I miss you too*, making herself feel worse with guilt.

Philip noticed her looking worse, therefore he asked, "Is everything okay?"

Sonia said, "Yes, I'm the same as I was ten minutes ago."

Philip replied, "Okay," in a sarcastic manner. He stood up and said, "I'm ready, I'll get the coats."

Sonia replied, "Thank you," as she placed her phone back in her bag.

Philip walked out of the room and re-entered with both coats and scarfs. He handed Sonia hers and said, "Is there anything I can do?"

Sonia said, "It's all good."

Philip said, "Okay," as he finished putting his scarf and coat on. He walked to the front door as Sonia followed. He opened the door, allowing Sonia to pass as he closed it behind him. Sonia stood in the corridor as Philip locked the door. They both walked beside each other to the lift. Sonia felt weak and her body began to sweat again. She knew the lift, being in a confined space with the heat, would challenge her. The lift doors opened and she entered. She remained silent as she concentrated on herself, just breathing. Philip pushed the ground floor button and the lift doors closed. He looked at Sonia as she remained in silence. It only took a few seconds before the lift door opened again. Sonia pushed past Philip to exit and stood in the hallway, placing her hand on the wall.

She said, "I have never felt this way before, I need to lie down."

Philip said, "Maybe you need to go straight home."

Sonia said, "Pharmacy first," as she could feel that he wanted her to go. Philip walked to the main entrance door and opened it by pressing the egress button. The door released as he pushed it open. Sonia followed.

He said, "The pharmacy is just around the corner, this way," as he continued in that direction. Sonia felt the distance between them as Philip walked; there was an awkwardness between them. She felt sick again and wanted to leave him as quickly as possible.

They entered the pharmacy and Philip walked down one of the aisles as Sonia approached the pharmacist. He noticed that they spoke for a few minutes before the pharmacist entered the back of the shop. She returned with a box and placed it in a bag after scanning it at the cash register. Sonia paid with her card and placed the bag in her handbag. She turned to look where Philip was and walked towards him. Philip was looking at the latest electric razors.

Sonia walked to him and said, "Let's go." Philip acknowledged and followed Sonia as she left the shop. She walked into another shop on the corner and bought two bottles of water. She handed one to Philip and opened the pharmacy bag. She took the box out and released the single tablet, placing it into her mouth. She opened the bottle of water and took a large mouthful, tilting her head back as she swallowed. She drank some more. Philip just stood watching.

When she placed the lid back on her bottle, he said, "Well, I hope this relaxes you a bit."

Sonia replied, "I'll let you know in a few weeks." Philip remained quiet during this awkward moment. Sonia said, "Okay, I'll go home. Thank you for last night." She hugged Philip and he hugged her back. Sonia walked down the pathway towards the Tube station. Philip walked back to his apartment. Sonia clutched her handbag with her left hand as it rested on her shoulder. She felt very weak and her stomach wasn't feeling well at all. Sonia returned home and decided to go straight to bed. She text Gregory, *I will be busy until later today. I hope you are good and having a great day, chat later XxX.* She turned her phone onto aeroplane mode after setting her alarm clock for 6pm. Sonia undressed, threw her clothes on the floor and put on her pyjamas. She climbed into bed and fell asleep quite quickly.

Gregory received the text while in London and replied, *Hey, good to hear from you. No worries, chat later X.* He felt very strange again but was busy between appointments with clients. Gregory just wanted the day to finish so that he could unwind and pack his bag for the trip the following day. Gregory finished his appointments at 4.30pm and he began to make his way back home.

Sonia had woken after her alarm clock sounded but remained in bed, checking her mobile phone for messages and news. She saw the text from Gregory but didn't reply. She decided to leave replying until later that evening. She got out of bed and felt much better but was still very heavy around her head. She went to the bathroom and turned on the hot water for a bath. She placed the plug in the plug hole, turned on the hot water tap and added bath salts. She left the bathroom and picked her clothes off the floor and placed them in the washing basket. She sat on her bed and looked at the floor.

Sonia began thinking about the night before with Philip. She couldn't believe that he took off the condom. This concerned her because she didn't know Philip's sexual history, and there was the fact that she had to take the morning-after pill. She felt completely empty and wasn't too excited to see Gregory. She just wanted to be alone. She knew that she had to pack her bags so she got off the bed and opened her underwear drawer. She selected some underwear and placed it on the bed. She opened her wardrobe and selected three dresses. She placed them on the bed also. She pulled her suitcase out from the wardrobe and placed it on the floor. Opening the zips, she remembered the intensity of the intimacy with Philip the night before. She remembered how it felt so numb inside but exciting. She then realised that Philip hadn't text her to check that she was okay. She felt used by Philip as she realised that he didn't care, and her energy was low. She thought about Gregory and decided to text him. *Hiya, how was your day?* Sonia threw her phone on the bed as she continued to pack. Gregory received the text but he was driving and had to wait until he was parked to reply. Sonia started to feel anxious and disappointed with herself for sleeping with Philip.

She walked into the bathroom and switched off the hot water as the bath water was overflowing through the overfill outlet. She felt the water with the tips of her fingers and it was very hot. She knew she had to release some water before entering as the bath would overflow onto the bathroom floor if she got in. She went into her room and took a wire coat hanger from the wardrobe. She unravelled and straightened it, then walked into the bathroom and hooked the bath plug with it. Pulling gently, she could feel the resistance as she pulled against the water pressure. The plug lifted and she could hear the water empty. She moved the plug away from the plug hole as she sat on the side of the bath. Sonia watched the swirl of water as it drained. She felt a little dizzy with the heat in the bathroom. She placed the plug close to the plug hole and allowed the downforce suction to pull it into position, sealing the remainder of the water in the bath. Sonia removed her pyjamas and slowly climbed into the water. She positioned herself in a lying position and laid her head against the wall, closing her eyes.

While Sonia was in the bath, Gregory replied to her text: *Hi, why don't you come and stay at mine tonight then we can leave together tomorrow?* Gregory locked his car and walked into his house. He switched off the alarm and walked up to his bedroom. There he grabbed his suitcase from behind the chair and opened it. He grabbed some boxer shorts from his wardrobe shelf and pulled out some jeans. He took three tee-shirts and some socks. He folded his clothes and placed them in the suitcase. He took another pair of jeans and located his belt. He placed these over the back of the chair and took a shirt from a hanger. He threw this over his jeans. He placed a pair of boxer shorts on the chair and put his red trainers and a pair of socks in front of the chair on the floor. He walked into the bathroom and took his razor, shaving cream, shampoo, toothbrush and toothpaste. He threw them into his case and closed it over. Gregory undressed from his suit and walked into the bathroom for a shower. He was feeling excited to meet up with Sonia and he was looking forward to going to Edinburgh. While he was showering, he remembered to check-in for the flights. Gregory had booked the flights with his credit card and the confirmation emails were sent to his inbox. His finished his shower and wrapped a towel around himself after he dried himself off. He entered his room and took his mobile from his jacket pocket. He noticed that there was no reply from Sonia and he wondered what she was doing. He placed his towel on the radiator and put his dressing gown on. He opened his emails and downloaded the app for the airline. Once downloaded, he entered the flight number and completed the check-in process. He selected seats and confirmed.

He put his phone down and walked to the kitchen to prepare a sandwich. He opened the fridge door and took the butter and beetroot and closed the door. He took two slices of bread from the freezer and placed them in the toaster. He took a plate from the cupboard and a knife from the drawer. As he waited for the toaster to finish, he thought that it was strange that he hadn't heard from Sonia for the majority of the day and also the night before. He was curious to hear about her night out. While he was thinking about her, he felt the sick feeling again in his stomach and the cool feeling down his left arm. He thought to himself, *I wonder what this very strange feeling when I think of her is.* The toast popped up and Gregory plucked the slices out one by one and placed them on the plate. He opened the butter wrapper and sliced a strip, placing it between the two slices of toast to melt. He opened the fridge door and returned the butter. He opened the beetroot jar and took a fork from the drawer. He pulled the slices of toast apart and spread the butter with the knife. He took the fork and picked out some beetroot, placing it on the toast. He placed the other slice of toast on top of the other and pressed down. He washed the knife and fork and put the beetroot back in the fridge. He ate the sandwich and washed the plate, dried it and put it back in the cupboard. He walked into the sitting room and turned on the television. It was 7.10pm and he was feeling tired.

Sonia decided to finish in the bath. She reached and pulled the plug, placing it behind the taps. She stood and switched on the electric shower to rinse off. Once finished, she reached for her towel and began to dry herself, then stepped onto the floor mat. Sonia placed her towel on the sink and began to inspect herself. She had noticed that she was a little sore, with a slight redness around her vulva. She thought to herself that it was due to the sex the night before and walked into the bedroom. She bent over and opened the bed drawer, taking a fresh pair of knickers and putting them on. She walked over to the mirror and checked her chest, gently touching with her fingers for anything out of the ordinary. She stood for a moment and looked at herself in the mirror. She felt herself become distant and empty. She thought about her life and wondered if she would ever have children.

She turned her head and noticed her phone message indication LED was flashing. She took her phone and opened the app to see Gregory's message. She replied after a few minutes as she felt nervous about seeing him. She text, *Okay, I will get dressed and make my way over.* Gregory replied, *Great. What time?* Sonia replied, *8.30ish.* Gregory text, *See you then, look forward.* Sonia threw her phone onto her bed and began to get dressed. She zipped up her suitcase once she had finished packing and put her coat on. As she opened her door, she remembered to take her phone charger. She closed the door and walked to the opposite side of her bed and unplugged the charger from the adapter. When she bent over to take the charger, she felt dizzy again. She sat on her bed to compose herself. She stood and walked to the door, grabbed her suitcase and wheeled it to the main entrance door. She checked for post while in the hallway and opened the door. Once outside she walked to the pathway, turning towards the Tube station. She was feeling apprehensive about seeing Gregory because she was feeling sick and knew that he would be asking about her night out. She decided to tell him that she left early and went home because she wasn't feeling well.

She entered the Tube station and stopped at the barrier to find her Oyster card. Once she found it, she offered it to the barrier reader and the double gate opened to allow her to pull her suitcase through. She reached the escalator and put her suitcase in front of her as she held the handle. While descending on the escalator, she felt dizzy again so she placed her right hand on the rail. She felt her head go heavy and her body go light and weak, and her stomach felt sick again. As she disembarked from the escalator, she stumbled as she lifted her suitcase to position behind her. She began pulling it as it had wheels. She walked to the platform and checked the display. It said three minutes for the next Tube. Sonia sat on the platform seats as she waited. She took her phone from her pocket and connected to the Wi-Fi. She text Gregory, *I'm not feeling too good.* Gregory received the text while sitting in the sitting room watching TV. He replied, *What's wrong?* Sonia replied, *Feeing really dizzy and weak.* Gregory replied, *I'll meet you at the Tube station, what's your ETA?* Sonia replied, *40 mins.* Gregory said, *I'll be there.*

Gregory walked up to his bedroom and placed his dressing gown on the bathroom door hook. He took his clothes that he had prepared for the morning and got dressed. He walked back downstairs and grabbed his jacket. He opened the front door after switching on the alarm and walked to the Tube station. On the way to meet her he thought about Sonia and he wondered why she wasn't feeling well. His first thought was that she had a hangover. He waited at the Tube entrance while he scanned through the news app on his mobile. It wasn't long to wait before Sonia appeared at the top of the escalator and walked to the barrier, placing her card down while pulling her suitcase. Gregory walked towards her and held his arms out for a hug. Sonia just walked up to him and stood still while he hugged her and kissed her on the cheek. He felt that it was strange since they hadn't seen each other in a few days.

He commented by saying, "Great start to the weekend break."

Sonia replied, "I'm not feeling too good."

Gregory said, "Hangover, maybe?"

Sonia gave him a dirty look as she stopped walking beside him. She said, "Hopefully you're not going to quiz me about last night."

Gregory said, "Nope, no intention." But he was curious. He followed behind Sonia as she dragged her suitcase. He smiled to himself because he had asked if he could take it for her and she had just ignored his question. The walk back to Gregory's was very intense because Gregory could feel that Sonia wasn't feeling good. She was struggling, so he said, "Once inside you should go to bed and get some rest."

Sonia nodded in agreement as she stood at the front door while Gregory opened the door with the key. He switched off the alarm and Sonia stormed past him with her suitcase and began walking up the stairs. He just said to himself, "Okay," as he took his coat off and walked into the sitting room. He turned on the television and started to watch a documentary. About an hour had passed when Sonia walked in wearing one of his tee-shirts and her knickers. She sat beside him and grabbed the blanket as she covered herself.She said, "I'm so cold, my body is shivering from inside."

Gregory looked at her and said, "Maybe you got a cold."

Sonia said, "This feels terrible. My whole body feels so weak and I just have no energy to do anything."

Gregory said, "Can I get you anything?"

Sonia said, "A hug would be nice." He leaned towards her and she remained rigid.

He said, "How can I hug you like that?" Sonia put her arm around him and they held each other for a few moments. Gregory noticed that she was sweating; the tee-shirt that she was wearing felt damp down her back. He said, "You are sweating."

Sonia said, "I told you already, I'm not feeling well."

He said, "Okay," as he got off the couch and opened the medicine cupboard. He took some paracetamol from the packet and poured a glass of water. He walked back to Sonia and said, "Here, take these."

Sonia looked at him and said, "What is it?"

He said, "Paracetamol."

Sonia reached for them. He dropped the two tablets into her hand and she took the glass, threw the tablets into her mouth and drank some water. She handed him back the glass as he stood watching. He walked back to the kitchen and rinsed the glass out. Sonia took the remote control while he washed and dried the glass. She began flicking through the channels on the television. It was 9.30pm and a movie was just starting on the movie channel.

Sonia called Gregory and said, "A movie is starting, come watch." Gregory placed the glass back into the cupboard and he sat beside her. Sonia was wrapped up in the blanket and Gregory pulled at it to get her to share. Sonia flicked some from her right side and Gregory pulled it over himself. Sonia cuddled into him as they watched the movie and fell asleep. Gregory could feel the heat coming off Sonia. She was sweating; he could see her face was showing signs of moisture on her nose, cheeks and forehead. He wondered if she had caught the flu.

The movie finished and Gregory spoke to Sonia. He said, "Time for bed." Sonia groaned and Gregory pulled the blanket off her. Sonia got up quickly and felt dizzy again with the cold air circulating her body. She sat back down. Gregory said, "You look green."

Sonia looked at him and said, "Really? Thanks," as she made her way up to the bedroom. Gregory tidied up the sitting room, folded the blanket and switched off the kitchen lights after he got two glasses of water to take to the bedroom. He switched on the alarm with the night setting and walked up the stairs. As he was walking up the stairs, he wondered if the weekend would get any better, thinking about Sonia and her mood due to her being unwell. He switched off the landing light and entered the bedroom to find Sonia was already fast asleep. He checked his mobile phone and set the alarm for 6am. He took off his clothes and placed them back on the chair with his trainers in front on the floor. After climbing into bed, he switched off the lights. As soon as he got under the duvet, he could feel the heat from Sonia. She was sweating again. He kissed her on the forehead and turned to face the door. He took some time to fall asleep as his mind was constantly thinking about the last few weeks of their relationship. He eventually dozed off to sleep.

15

The weekend break

GREGORY WOKE THE FOLLOWING MORNING TO THE SOUND OF his alarm clock on his mobile phone. He reached over and grabbed his phone, switching off the alarm. He placed the phone back on the side table and turned to cuddle into Sonia. As soon as he did this, he felt that she was soaking wet with sweat. He pulled back from her and said, "You are soaking wet."

Sonia groaned and said with a croaky voice, "Yes, I know, I feel weak and cold."

Gregory said, "I think we should forget about the trip, you need to rest." Just as he was about to finish the sentence, Sonia was on her feet, standing at the side of the bed.

She said, "I will shower first," as she made her way to the bathroom.

Gregory waved his hand in the direction of the bathroom and said, "After you."

He lay in bed for a few minutes after Sonia closed the bathroom door. He looked at his phone and it displayed 6.15am. He waited until Sonia had finished and he entered the bathroom when she opened the door. The bathroom was a mist of condensation so Gregory decided not to shave that morning. He jumped into the shower and washed himself quickly. When he had finished, he entered the bedroom, drying himself while walking. Sonia was sitting on the chair on top of his jeans, blow drying her hair. The room sounded like a jet engine. He looked at Sonia and could see that she was struggling to cope with the heat of the hairdryer as she held it to her head. He walked to the chair and pulled at his jeans from under her. Sonia shrugged herself off as he pulled them from under her, pulling a face of dissatisfaction. Gregory grabbed a clean pair of boxer shorts from the wardrobe and put them on. He pulled his jeans on and started to loop his belt through the belt loops when Sonia finished drying her hair.

He said, "I see you brought your jet with you."

Sonia just replied with, "Haw haw," as she looked at herself in the mirror. She stood in her dress with a slight wobble as she corrected her stance. She was still feeling dizzy. Sonia took her makeup bag out of her handbag and started to add foundation. As she was doing this, Gregory walked up behind her and embraced her from behind. Sonia closed her eyes and dropped her hands to hold his around her stomach. She said, "I was waiting for a hug."

Gregory said, "I tried several times before and got no reply so I stepped back."

Sonia said, "Whatever," as she grabbed his hands tightly.

Gregory pulled away and said, "Okay, we need to move it."

Sonia continued with her makeup and Gregory finished getting dressed. He took the wet towels from the bathroom and off the floor surrounding Sonia. He made his way downstairs to the utility room. He threw them into the washing machine and closed the door. He switched on the hallway light and the front door porch light. He also turned on the television. He wanted to leave them on while away to give the impression that someone was home. Sonia finished her makeup and walked down the stairs to Gregory. She had her coat and handbag in her hands.

She said, "Could you take my suitcase down, please?"

Gregory ran past her up the stairs, saying, "No worries." He entered the room, grabbed his suitcase, zipped it up, and grabbed Sonia's. He walked with both suitcases down the stairs, being careful not to mark the wall. Sonia was putting her scarf and coat on. Gregory placed the suitcases on the hallway floor and ran back upstairs for his phone. He took it from the bedside table and walked down to fetch his coat.

He had started to put it on when Sonia said, "I'm hungry but don't know if I can eat."

Gregory said, "I'm starving."

Sonia replied, "What's new?" He finished buttoning up his coat and switched the alarm on as Sonia stared at the floor. He opened the door and waited for Sonia to walk out, crashing her bag against the door frame as she pulled it.

Gregory sighed and said, "Happy you're going to repaint the door when we return."

Sonia just walked to the footpath, where she waited for him to lock the five-lever lock. As soon as Gregory walked alongside Sonia, she said, "Maybe you could show some more attention towards me as I'm not feeling great." Gregory just walked behind her after she said this. He felt strange inside again and wondered to himself quietly if they should go at all. Sonia realised he was quiet and said, "Are you okay?"

Gregory said, "Yes, just thinking if I have everything." They continued walking to the Tube station. It was busy already with people travelling to work. Sonia and Gregory reached the platform and Gregory continued to walk to the end of the platform, where it was less congested. Sonia followed him but was feeling very weak. As soon as he stopped to wait for the train, Sonia stood next to him, leaning on him. He knew she wasn't well at all but there were no signs of coughing or a runny nose. He started to wonder what it was that she had caught but the train arrived, and he changed his thoughts to getting in the carriage. Gregory let Sonia on first and he followed as she dragged her suitcase over the door ledge instead of lifting it. She stood at the partition glass and leaned against it, holding her suitcase. Gregory stood beside her and held the rail above him. Sonia remained quiet as she struggled with the heat and congestion with the other passengers. Gregory took his phone from his pocket and glanced at the time. It was 6.45am. They needed to change at Stockwell to get the Victoria Line to Green Park, and change once more to the Piccadilly Line to Heathrow Airport. Gregory realised that he had lost the excitement for the trip as he felt Sonia wouldn't be up to much sightseeing. He had been looking forward to the tour they had booked for Mary King's Close. He thought that he shouldn't get excited because they probably wouldn't make it.

They arrived at Stockwell station and Sonia got off first as she was next to the door. She continued to pull her suitcase as other passengers tried to get past her, nearly tripping over her bag as it trailed behind her. Gregory carried his and followed several people behind her. Sonia was on a mission to get to the airport and she was oblivious to anything else going on around her. When she reached the Stockwell platform for the Victoria Line, she turned around to see where Gregory was. She managed to see him as he squeezed by some other passengers to find he couldn't get beside her. She waved and took her earphones out of her handbag. She placed the two earpieces in each ear and fiddled with her phone while selecting music. As she was doing this, a train pulled up and the doors opened. The crowd pushed forward as Sonia lifted her bag on. Gregory also managed to get on board just as the doors closed. The carriage was completely full, with arms everywhere reaching for whatever handrail was available for support while the train moved between stops. It was a relief when the doors opened at each station because a rush of cooler air swept into the carriage, giving some small amount of relief. Gregory was right at the door so he could feel the benefit most. Sonia, however, was on the other side of the carriage, pinned up against the opposite door. She was really feeling sick at this stage and focussed on her music as she held the handrail. Gregory caught a glimpse of her when some people departed at a station and he noticed that she was pale in complexion. She looked like she was going to faint. She was very focussed on looking at the floor while listening to her music. Gregory looked at the map above him and noted that they had two stops to go before Green Park. They had just left Pimlico Station. He caught Sonia's attention and he lifted his hand, showing two fingers to indicate two stops to go. Sonia nodded as she continued to look at the floor.

They reached their stop and the doors opened. Gregory pulled his bag off with him as others followed behind in a rush. Sonia had to squeeze past those who were remaining on the train, dragging her suitcase off. Gregory reached for her bag as he was on the platform waiting but she ignored his gesture and yanked it off, crashing it onto the platform as she made her way to the platform seats. There she sat with her bag alongside her.

Gregory followed and said, "That wasn't very nice." Sonia remained quiet. Gregory stood in front of her as she sat looking at him. He said, "Look, if you're not up to going that's fine, I'd rather you felt better."

Sonia said, "I like travelling, so let's go," as she stood up and began to walk over to the other platform. Just as she started to walk, another train arrived at the platform and they could both hear the doors opening from behind them. Sonia walked faster to reach the new platform before the other passengers disembarked. Sonia walked to the far end to get on the last carriage as the train pulled up. There were plenty of seats on this train as they both watched each carriage go past before the train stopped. Sonia climbed on first as the doors opened and Gregory followed. Sonia sat at the glass partition and Gregory stood with both suitcases. Sonia sat and placed her earphones back into her ears as she closed her eyes. Gregory counted the stops on the map displayed above the door as the train continued on its journey. Approximately forty minutes passed and he tapped Sonia on the shoulder. She opened her eyes with a grumpy-looking face.

He said, "Next stop."

Sonia closed her eyes again. The train pulled up to the platform and Gregory poked Sonia on her arm. She opened her eyes as he was pulling the suitcases towards the door. The door opened and Sonia got up and followed behind him. He placed both suitcases on the platform and Sonia stood next to him.

He said, "Okay, let's go," with relief that they were at the airport. Sonia followed Gregory as he made his way inside the terminal building via the escalators. He could hear every so often Sonia's suitcase crashing off something. She was not in any mood to be pulling a suitcase behind her. They reached the terminal building check-in area and queued to check in for their airline. Sonia decided to walk over to a seat and leave Gregory standing on his own, moving both bags as the queue reduced. The queue reduced down to two people in front of him and he tried several times to gain Sonia's attention to get her to come over as she had to show her passport at the check-in desk. Sonia was resting with her eyes closed.

He said to the person behind him, "Sorry, I have to get my partner over there, can I leave my bags for a moment?"

The person said, "Yes, I will look after them."

Gregory moved swiftly, without running, towards Sonia. Just before he reached her, she opened her eyes and he said, "Come on," giving a hand gesture as he turned back. Sonia was in a right hump now and Gregory was showing signs that he was getting fed up and needed to eat as his energy was running low. They checked in and both walked towards the security area to reach the departures lounge. Sonia walked through the barrier after scanning her boarding card on Gregory's phone while staring at the camera. She passed the phone to Gregory and he also followed her to the security checking area. Sonia took her bag from her shoulder and placed it in a bin. She took her coat and scarf off and also placed them beside her bag. She looked at Gregory as he was beside her, emptying his pockets and placing his belongings in the bin to be X-rayed. Sonia walked through the metal detector when prompted to do so by the security man standing on the opposite side. Gregory followed behind to hear a beep. The man requested that he raise his arms, so Gregory did and he was scanned with a metal detector. Another man requested that he place his hands forward with the palms upwards as he swabbed them. He placed the swab in a machine as Gregory watched. A green banner appeared on the screen and he was told to proceed. Sonia was standing at the baggage escalator waiting for her bin to arrive. Gregory walked up to her and placed his hand on her back as he kissed her right cheek. Sonia smiled and looked at him.

She said, "I need some water but I don't even know if it will stay down."

Gregory said, "You have very strange symptoms."

Sonia sighed as she watched her bin roll towards her after being x-rayed. She took the bin and walked to a counter area to put her coat back on. She put her scarf into her bag and took her phone from her pocket. Gregory took his bin and walked to the spare counter area beside Sonia as she stood waiting for him.

Gregory said, "I could eat something now."

Sonia replied, "What's new?" as she walked towards the shopping area. Gregory followed when he had sorted himself out to find Sonia looking at makeup. He thought to himself, *Nothing wrong with her now.* But as soon as he stood beside her, she said, "I need to buy foundation as it's much cheaper here." She found the one she used and proceeded to the checkout. Gregory just followed as he looked at all the items for sale. He couldn't believe the number of different tones available. This kept him amused while Sonia paid. Once done, she put the foundation in her handbag and said, "Okay, I'm good."

Gregory said, "Food," as he walked towards the restaurant area of the terminal. Sonia followed but wasn't hungry at all. Gregory stood at the entrance to a restaurant and waited to be seated.

A girl walked up to him and said, "Two?"

Gregory said, "Yes."

She took two menus and said, "This way." Gregory and Sonia walked behind her to a table. She placed the menus down on the table and said, "I will be back to take your order when you are ready."

Gregory said, "Thank you," as he took his coat off and placed it on the back of the chair. Sonia sat on the long bench with cushions. She took the menu and glanced over it. Gregory said, "Oh, porridge with mixed nuts and honey. A latte too."

Sonia looked at him and said, "I'll just have water."

Gregory said, "Okay."

Sonia took her phone out and checked through her apps while they waited for service. The girl returned and Gregory ordered. Sonia just asked for still water. The girl entered the order on her handheld device and said, "Thank you, I will be back shortly with your order." The girl left the table and Sonia said, "I will be better later once I've slept on the plane."

Gregory said, "That's good, the flight is one hour and forty minutes." Just as he said this, a waiter came with his latte and a still water for Sonia. Sonia reached into her handbag and took the paracetamol packet out. She took two tablets from the foil wrapper, popping them into her palm, and opened the bottle of water. She poured her glass full and placed the tablets in her mouth. She drank the water, throwing her head back quickly. Gregory took a sip from his latte as he watched her and thought to himself, *I have never seen Sonia take painkillers so much before.*

Sonia looked at him and said, "What's wrong?"

Gregory said, "I was just thinking that I have never seen you this sick and taking so many painkillers before."

Sonia replied, "I have never felt this way before."

Gregory then said, "Maybe get a blood test."

Sonia reacted by standing up and walking out of the restaurant towards the toilets. Gregory thought, *Righty-ho,* as he took a drink from his coffee. Shortly after, the waitress came with his porridge and said, "Enjoy your food," as she placed it in front of him. Gregory took his spoon and cleaned it with the table napkin. He then opened the miniature honey jar and poured the honey into the bowl. He stirred it well. He took a spoonful just as Sonia returned.

She said, "I'm sorry for being cranky; I just feel so depleted."

Gregory swallowed and said, "That's okay, I understand."

Sonia replied instantly, "You don't understand, how could you?"

Gregory took another spoonful and continued to eat. Sonia sat with her phone as she flicked through her apps. Gregory thought to himself, *God, what am I doing?* He continued to eat and drink his latte as Sonia sat in a mood across from him. He looked at his watch and said to her, "We have twenty minutes before the gate will be on the screen, do you want to get anything?"

Sonia looked at him and said, "Nope."

Gregory said, "No worries, I'll get the bill." As he said this, he reached for his phone from his coat pocket behind him. He opened the phone by entering his passcode and opened an app. It wasn't long before he smiled. He had received a message from a girl he knew. She had sent him a picture joke.

Sonia immediately perked up and said, "What's so funny?"

Gregory said, "Nothing."

Sonia replied, "Who sent you a text?"

Gregory said, "A girl I know, why?"

As soon as he mentioned another girl, Sonia got annoyed. She said, "Is this someone you like?"

Gregory said, "She is a friend, that's all."

Sonia said, "Why is she texting you?" Gregory realised that Sonia was feeling vulnerable and jealous. She said, "Fine, I have many male friends too."

Gregory was surprised with her reply, so he said, "What's this about? I feel a little uncomfortable right now."

Sonia said, "Why are you giving girls your number? Is she an ex-girlfriend?"

Gregory said, "Enough, Sonia. I'll get the bill. This is a great start to a weekend I was really looking forward to, spending it with you, just the two of us. Does that not mean anything?"

Sonia replied, "Whatever," as she pulled her coat from behind her and put it on. The waitress came over and Gregory paid with his debit card. He stood up and put his coat on as Sonia walked out towards the shopping area.

Gregory followed and said, "I'm going to the toilet," as he walked past. Sonia could feel that he was annoyed. Gregory went to the toilet and thought to himself as he was washing his hands, *Why is Sonia so insecure right now?*

As soon as he walked out of the toilet, Sonia was waiting in the corridor for him. She embraced him in a hug and said, "I'm sorry, I am just very tired."

They kissed and Gregory said, "Can we just have a nice weekend together?"

Sonia said, "Yes," as she kissed him on the lips again. They both walked to the shopping area, holding hands. They walked to a seating area and both sat while Gregory watched the departures screen to find out their departure gate and Sonia rested her head on his shoulder, closing her eyes. Gregory was concerned about Sonia but he was afraid to say anything more after her sudden charge to the toilet but then he decided to tell her to get a blood test. It wasn't long before gate number twelve showed on the screen.

Gregory touched Sonia on the nose with his right hand and said, "Gate twelve." Sonia opened her eyes and lifted her head off his shoulder. Gregory stood looking at Sonia as she climbed off her seat. She was a little slower than usual. Sonia looked white again and drained in appearance. Gregory wondered again what it was that she had caught. He didn't feel any symptoms himself as she complained about feeling light-headed and sore all over. Gregory took her hand and walked slowly with her towards the gate. After some time walking, they arrived at the gate to pass through passport control and boarding pass checks. They both sat again in the waiting area before boarding. Gregory decided to look up Sonia's symptoms on his phone but he couldn't find anything other than the flu. He put it down to this and closed his phone. They boarded the aeroplane and sat in row fourteen, in the emergency escape seats. Sonia sat at the window seat and Gregory in the middle. Sonia fastened her seat belt and leaned against the window to sleep. Gregory was surprised as she didn't say anything, she just fell asleep within a few minutes. He knew that this wasn't normal but Sonia was struggling to keep her eyes open. She slept for the whole flight duration and Gregory did also for at least thirty minutes. Sonia woke when the air hostess announced that the flight would be landing in approximately ten minutes. Gregory turned and looked at Sonia when she moved and opened her eyes.

She smiled and said, "Wow, that was a deep sleep."

Gregory said, "Yes, you passed out."

Sonia took his right hand in her left as she sat quietly while the aeroplane landed. It took a few minutes for the aircraft to be driven to the arrival gate. Once the 'fasten seat belt' sign was disengaged, the person beside Gregory released his belt with haste and stood up to open the overhead locker, pulling his bag out. Gregory also stood and stretched. Sonia stayed sitting until she saw people begin to depart the aircraft. Gregory remained standing until the queue moved. He turned to Sonia when it was ready to depart and took her hand to help her stand. Sonia followed Gregory as the other passengers let her out in front of them.

Sonia said, "Thank you," to the elderly gentleman. She walked behind Gregory and departed down the stairs. Once on the runway, Sonia tapped Gregory on the shoulder. He turned and Sonia kissed him on the lips and said, "Welcome to Edinburgh."

Gregory took both her hands and he kissed her lips softly, saying, "Welcome yourself," as he laughed. He said, "Full of beans now, are we?" as he walked into the arrivals corridor. Sonia smiled as she followed. She was feeling a lot better but still clammy feeling uncomfortable.

As they walked down the corridor towards the escalators, Sonia said, "I need the loo," as she saw the sign for the ladies' toilet.

Gregory said, "Me too." They both entered the toilet area. Gregory finished and walked out first while he waited in the corridor for her. He was there for about ten minutes before Sonia surfaced. She looked very pale when she walked up to Gregory and he said, "You don't look good."

Sonia gave him a dirty look and replied, "Thanks," as she walked past him down the corridor towards the security doors to the arrivals hall. Gregory just walked behind as he thought to himself, *Here we go again.* Sonia stopped as she passed the baggage area and waited for Gregory. He walked up to her and stood beside her. She said, "That wasn't a very nice thing to say."

Gregory said, "Sorry."

She took his right hand as she moved closer to him and she leaned her head on his shoulder. She said, "I do love you."

Gregory turned his head and kissed the top of hers. He said, "I love you too."

The sounder activated and the beacon flashed as the baggage conveyor started. Gregory moved closer to the edge as more people arrived and queued around the conveyor. Sonia stood behind him, checking her mobile for messages. As she was searching through her phone, Gregory took his suitcase off the conveyor.

Sonia said, "There is a cocktail bar in the hotel," as she searched through the internet.

Gregory replied, "I could do with a few after this morning."

Sonia replied, "What do you mean, after this morning?"

Gregory said, "Well, the mood hasn't been jolly, has it?"

Sonia looked at him with a glare as he smiled at her. Sonia said, "Well, wait until you're sick with the man flu and we will see who is chirpy, won't we, darling?"

Gregory smiled and said, "Man flu. Funny, aren't we?"

Sonia smiled and said, "It's the truth, though."

Gregory noticed Sonia's suitcase slide down the ramp and onto the conveyor. It distracted him as he didn't want to be involved in the conversation any longer. Sonia noticed this and continued to look on her phone. He pulled the suitcase off the conveyor and positioned it beside Sonia while erecting the handle. Sonia closed her apps and put her phone into her handbag as Gregory pulled his handle out and began walking towards the exit security doors. Sonia followed, watching Gregory from behind. She knew that the morning had played a toll on him and that she needed to win him over again. Gregory walked through the glass partition doors as they swung open, detecting his movement. Sonia walked behind in single file.

As they exited the security doors, Sonia noticed a shop. She said, "I have to go here for a moment." Gregory stopped and took her suitcase while Sonia entered the shop. She appeared a few minutes later with a bag.

Gregory asked, "What did you buy?"

Sonia said, "Nothing," as she unzipped the front pocket of her suitcase and stuffed the object inside. Gregory started to walk again as Sonia stood up straight. She followed him to the front of the terminal. There was a taxi rank so Gregory walked to the counter and asked to be taken to the hotel. He showed the postcode on an email on his phone and the lady typed in his contact details. He agreed to pay cash to the driver.

Once booked, a gentleman walked over with a ticket and said, "This way, please." He took Sonia's suitcase and pulled it behind him as Gregory and Sonia followed.

Sonia said to Gregory, "I'm looking forward to a drink now."

Gregory said, "You haven't eaten all day."

Sonia said, "A brandy and port."

Gregory said, "Is your stomach sick?"

Sonia smiled and replied, "I can't eat anything and this will kill everything."Gregory just remained quiet. They reached the taxi and the man opened the boot. He placed Sonia's suitcase in and took Gregory's from him, placing it beside Sonia's. Sonia had opened the left-hand side rear door and climbed inside.

Gregory followed as the taxi man got into the driver's seat. Gregory leaned forward with his phone and showed the driver the hotel website with its postcode. The driver said, "Ah yes, I know where it is." He fastened his seat belt and put the car into gear. As the car began to move, Sonia leaned onto Gregory's left shoulder. She placed her head against the side of his face and turned, facing him for a kiss. Gregory turned slightly, kissing Sonia on the lips. She then rested her head on his shoulder and closed her eyes.

The taxi man then asked where they were from.

Gregory said, "Ireland."

The taxi man said, "Are you here on holidays?"

Gregory said, "Just for the weekend." The taxi man nodded and continued driving. It wasn't long before they reached the hotel. Gregory shoved Sonia with his shoulder and she woke. He said, "I hope you haven't drooled on me?" Sonia lifted her head and wiped her mouth, looking at his shoulder. Gregory opened his door as the taxi man got out of the car and opened Sonia's door, and then walked to the boot and opened it, removing the suitcases. Gregory stood beside the taxi man and asked, "How much do I owe you?"

The taxi man said, "Twenty-two, please."

Gregory took twenty-five from his wallet and paid the man. He said, "Keep the change."

The taxi man closed the boot and said, "Thank you, have a great time." He walked to the driver's door and started the car. Sonia and Gregory walked to the hotel entrance door, which opened automatically. She walked into the foyer and Gregory followed.

As soon as Sonia reached the reception counter, she noticed the cocktail bar. She pointed to it as Gregory walked up beside her. She said, "I'll go have a look at the menu." Gregory was left standing as the receptionist requested his name. He checked into the room and made his way over to Sonia. Sonia said, "I have taken the liberty of ordering you a drink. Please sit and rest your tired feet." Gregory smiled and sat beside her. He was curious as to what drink she had ordered him. Several minutes later, a waiter appeared with two drinks, one a 'Godfather', which Sonia pointed to Gregory's side, and the other called the 'Sneaky Pete'.

Gregory looked at Sonia and said, after the waiter had gone, "That one suits you to a T."

Sonia looked at Gregory with a dirty look and said, "What do you mean?"

He replied, "Nothing, don't worry. Cheers!"

As he held up his glass, Sonia reached for hers and said, "Cheers, here's to a great weekend."

Gregory said, "I agree," as he sipped his drink.

Sonia said, "Ugh, mine is strong. I might order the brandy and port."

Gregory said, "I like that," after he drank some more of his.

Sonia got up and went to the bar. She spoke to the barman, ordering the brandy and port, and he poured the drink for her. She paid the bill and returned to the table. She said, "You have this one too," as she pushed her first order beside Gregory's Godfather glass.

Gregory took the Sneaky Pete and drank some. He said, "Yep, that's different." Sonia smiled as she sipped her brandy and port. They both sat quietly looking at the bar surroundings. They were the only two in the bar so it was peaceful. Gregory said, "Let's go to the room and unpack."

Sonia said, "Okay, we can go out for a walk after the drinks." Gregory was relieved as he had thought that Sonia would be in bed for the whole weekend.

He said, "Cheers to that," as he raised his glass in Sonia's direction.

Sonia raised her glass and said, "Cheers," as she sipped some more.

"Righty-ho," said Gregory as he got off the seat with his two glasses. Sonia stood also. Gregory knocked back the Godfather in one go and said, "Ahh, can't carry two glasses and pull a bag."

Sonia said, "Check you out," as she followed him to the lift. Gregory pushed the lift button as they both stood looking at each other. Sonia said, "What?"

Gregory said, "What yourself?" The lift door opened and Sonia walked in first. She dragged her suitcase behind and Gregory had to wait for her to stand it up straight. The lift wasn't too big. He entered, pulling his case right beside his feet. He pushed the button for floor four and the doors closed. Sonia sipped her drink and leaned forward towards Gregory for a kiss. She made a fish face as she curled her lips. Gregory looked and said, "I ain't kissing that." Sonia straightened her face and waited. Gregory kissed her lips quickly and took a drink from his glass.

Sonia said, "Not very romantic, are you?" Gregory was just about to speak when the doors opened. He walked out and Sonia followed. He paced up the corridor with his bag behind him, checking the door numbers. Sonia followed and waited as Gregory opened the door with the card key. It was room 413. Sonia said, "Nice room," as she walked in behind Gregory.

He walked to the bed near the window and said, "I'll be on this side."

Sonia said, "Fine."

Gregory left his bag standing and climbed onto the bed. Sonia placed her drink on the bedside table and pulled the coloured cushions from behind Gregory. She also pulled the bed design sheet off the base of the bed. "They are disgusting, never washed," she said as she lay beside Gregory. "Where's my pillows?" she said as she peered into Gregory's eyes.

Gregory pointed above the wardrobe and said, "Up there," with a smile.

Sonia looked in that direction and said, "Thanks," as she saw two more pillows wrapped in plastic. "I guess I will have the clean ones, so…" She jumped off the bed and reached for them. Gregory watched as he sipped his drink. Sonia pulled off the protective wrappers and threw them into the bin. She climbed onto the end of the bed and crawled, holding her two pillows, and stacked them against the headboard. The headboard was leather with a dark timber surround. She leaned against the pillows and reached for her drink as she made a sound as if she was making an effort.

Gregory said, "Exercise would be good this weekend," looking in her direction.

Sonia turned towards him and said, "Feck right off," as she drank some more. "I'm feeling better already." She sat comfortably, looking at the décor of the room. Sonia turned towards Gregory and said, "Let's go out."

Gregory replied, "Okay, let's go," as he got off the bed and faced her. "Well?" he said as she didn't move. Sonia took another sip and got off the bed. They both walked to the door and Sonia pushed Gregory against it. She snuggled in towards his body and smiled as she kissed his lips.

She said, "I love you."

Gregory kissed her back and said, "I love you too. Let's go," as he pulled the key card from the slot. They both walked hand in hand as the door slammed closed behind them. Sonia pushed the lift button and they both kissed again. The lift doors opened and they entered. Gregory said, "I would love to get into this lift with strangers and purposely face the wrong way."

Sonia laughed aloud and said, "That would be intense, weirdo," as she poked him in the stomach. Sonia was feeling much better after having had the brandy and port drink but she was still feeling weak. Her complexion was dull and she was trying her best to be more upbeat.

They decided to walk to Edinburgh Castle but Sonia could feel that her legs were getting tired already and they hadn't left the hotel yet. She was starting to sweat down her back, under her arms, in her groin area and behind her knees. As they arrived onto the street, Gregory got excited as he could see the castle in the distance. Sonia could hear the excitement in his voice so she just listened and continued walking. She had a headache and was feeling a pain that was beginning in her legs and buttocks area.

She said to Gregory, "I need to sit for a few minutes and use the bathroom."

Gregory turned his head and looked at Sonia before saying, "You look a little green again."

Sonia replied, "Thanks, like Princess Fiona going back to her castle. I don't feel great, sorry."

Gregory said, "We can stop at the first café if you like? I could get a coffee."

Sonia said, "Okay, I am sweating and my throat doesn't feel great."

Gregory replied, "Yes, I can hear your voice has changed. Definitely a Princess Fiona going on there," as he laughed.

Sonia just looked at him with disgust and continued walking. It wasn't long before they reached a row of shops. There was a coffee shop that looked very busy so Sonia said, "It would be nice to feel the heat," as she was also feeling the cold, damp weather. Gregory opened the door and let Sonia walk inside first. She scanned the seating area and pointed to a free table. Gregory walked over as Sonia located the toilet. He sat and looked at the menu board attached to the wall. There was a selection of cakes and the cheesecake appealed to him. He knew that Sonia wouldn't allow him to have it but he continued to think about having one anyway. Sonia was gone for about fifteen minutes and Gregory started to become worried about her.

The waitress walked over and asked if he would like to order. Just as he was about to say that he was waiting on Sonia, she walked up behind her. Gregory requested a latte and Sonia stood looking distant with her hand on the back of the chair. She said, "I would like the energy booster, please."

Gregory said, "Oh, and the cheesecake." Sonia looked at him but said nothing.

The girl asked Sonia if she would like anything else and Sonia said, "No thank you." The girl walked behind the counter area in the café and Sonia sat down. She said to Gregory, "The sweat is dripping off me and I'm afraid that it will show through my clothes."

Smiling, Gregory replied, "As long as you don't smell, we are all okay," but when he noticed Sonia wasn't impressed, he said quickly, "We can go back to the room if you don't feel up to it?" Sonia sat quietly as she wiped her forehead with the white paper napkin that was wrapped around the cutlery. Gregory watched and said, "I hope I don't get that."

Sonia said, "I don't know if it's the flu or a bug I caught." Gregory adjusted himself in his chair as the latte and energy booster were placed on the table. The girl walked back behind the counter and brought the cheesecake. Gregory sat and observed the cheesecake before taking his fork. He asked Sonia if she would like some but she refused. She sipped some of her drink through the straw provided. Gregory drank some coffee and sliced a piece from the pointed end of his cheesecake. He placed it into his mouth and sat back as he allowed it to melt around his tongue.

He swallowed and said, "Wow, that's good."

Sonia said, "I am happy for you. This is cooling me down a bit," as she played with the straw stirring her drink.

Gregory said, "Good," as he scooped some more cheesecake onto his fork. Sonia reached into her bag and popped two painkillers from the wrapper and placed them into her mouth. She drank some more and swallowed. Gregory watched as he ate. Sonia took her phone and opened her browser. She looked up at the castle and said that there was a tour that took approximately two hours and that it might be good to learn about the history. Gregory agreed.

She said after that, "I will probably need to rest a while before we go out later tonight." Gregory agreed as he finished the cheesecake. He wiped his mouth with the napkin and drank some latte. Sonia said, "Okay, I am ready when you are."

Gregory stood and said, "Let's go." Sonia took her wallet from her bag and walked to the counter. She requested the bill and the girl printed the receipt. Sonia paid and they both left.

Sonia said, "It's the first time that I am happy being in the cold air."

Gregory said, as he wrapped his scarf around his neck, "Hopefully the tablets will regulate your body temperature."

Sonia walked alongside him as she adjusted her handbag on her shoulder. They walked for another ten minutes along the Royal Mile, the high street connecting to the castle. The street had many landmarks such as Palace of Holyroodhouse, the Scottish Parliament, and St Giles' Cathedral. They also passed the Real Mary King's Close tour that they were doing the following day. Sonia was feeling the strain on her legs as they had to walk up a hill to the castle entrance. Gregory noticed that she was falling behind as she struggled to keep up. Every now and again she would stop to take a moment to rest her legs.

Gregory stood and waited for her to join him. He said, "Are you okay?"

She said, "My legs are really sore and around my bottom."

Gregory said, "That's because you are using muscles you haven't in a while," as he smiled at her. Sonia knew that this wasn't the case and she wondered what was wrong with her. Gregory took her hand and walked alongside her. They remained quiet until they arrived at the entrance. Gregory purchased two adult tickets when they entered the building and Sonia's handbag was searched by security. Sonia excused herself and went to the toilets. Gregory decided that he would use the bathroom also before the tour. They both met in the souvenir shop. Gregory was looking at the postcards when Sonia stood next to him.

She said, "Are you sending a card to someone?"

Gregory replied, "No, just looking at the old pictures. Imagine living back then, the poverty and smell."

Sonia said, "Okay, let's go through and look around." Gregory leaned forward and kissed Sonia on the lips. She said, "Are you sure that was a good idea?"

Gregory said, "Oh shite, I forgot. But I would have already caught it by now."

Sonia smiled as she thought it was nice of him to feel compelled to kiss her. They walked into the entrance hall and Sonia said, "Let's look ourselves, I don't want to be around people." Gregory felt up to it so he just nodded and followed Sonia. They both walked around the castle and the grounds until they felt that they were satisfied.

They left and Gregory decided to hail a taxi as Sonia was not in the best of form after all the walking and standing. She had become very tired and wanted to rest. They decided to return to the hotel and venture out later that evening. Sonia sat in the taxi beside Gregory, leaning on his shoulder. Gregory was starting to become concerned as he had never heard Sonia complain before of not feeling well. As soon as they arrived at the hotel, Gregory paid the fare and they both made their way to the hotel room. The atmosphere was intense as Sonia was a little snappy towards Gregory and she had a tendency to put him down when she wasn't in a good mood. Gregory just remained quiet.

Gregory opened the hotel bedroom door and Sonia followed. She walked into the bathroom and Gregory lay on the bed and switched on the TV. He began to watch a documentary when Sonia came out of the bathroom and lay beside him. She said, "That's too noisy." Gregory sighed and switched off the TV, staring at the ceiling. Sonia slipped her shoes off and climbed under the sheets. Gregory just remained still as she made herself comfortable. He thought to himself, *What will I do if I can't watch TV?* He got off the bed and fetched his mobile phone from his coat pocket. While he was standing retrieving his mobile, Sonia lifted her head and asked him to close the curtains. He took his phone and closed the curtains. The room was very dark and he made his way back to the bed. As soon as he lay down and made himself comfortable, he opened his mobile. Sonia opened her eyes and said, "Really, you're very inconsiderate. That's too bright."

Gregory said, "What am I supposed to do?"

Sonia said, "Go somewhere, I need to sleep." Gregory got annoyed and climbed off the bed. He pulled his coat from the back of the chair and felt his way to the bedroom door. He opened it and let it slam closed as he walked to the lift. He pushed the lift button and exhaled as he was annoyed. The lift door opened and he entered. He pushed the ground floor button and thought to himself, *Where will I go, what will I do?* He decided to go back to the shops.

Sonia text his phone as he was making his way through the hotel lobby: I'm not well and you should be looking after me. Gregory read the text and ignored replying. He thought to himself, *All I have been doing is making sure that you're okay.* He walked with agitation down the street. Shortly after, his mobile rang. He looked at the screen and it was Sonia.

He answered, "Hello," with apprehension.

Sonia said, "Hello, it wasn't nice that after I asked you to close the curtains you used your phone."

Gregory replied, "Oh, so I am to lie in the dark and do nothing while you sleep."

Sonia remained quiet, then said, "I need to rest and you know this."

Gregory said, "Have all the rest you need. Chat later." He hung up the phone. He placed his mobile back into his pocket and continued walking. As he walked another few metres, his phone beeped. He read the message from Sonia: *Enjoy your day. That wasn't nice hanging up on me.* He closed his phone and placed it back in his pocket. He felt emotional and angry but resisted returning a message back to Sonia. He decided to walk it off. He reached the shops on the Royal Mile and he entered some of the tourist shops. He just wandered about and bought nothing. He decided to get a coffee and relax. In the coffee shop, he sat watching people walk past the café window. He thought to himself that he and Sonia shouldn't have come for the weekend. He wondered how long it would take before there was drama of some sort. Several hours passed as Gregory walked around the streets looking at the buildings' architecture. He was feeling the cold through his coat as the sun began to set. It was 4.15pm and he wondered if Sonia was awake or still sleeping. He decided to walk back to the hotel. He was beginning to feel tired himself.

As he walked through the cobble stone street, he received a text from Sonia: *Where are you?* Gregory felt relieved to receive a text from her so he replied, *Walking back.* Sonia replied, *Good, I just woke.* Gregory said, *I will be there in 20 mins.* Sonia said, *Okay.* Gregory placed his phone back in his pocket as his hands were feeling cold holding the phone. He walked towards the hotel and he began to feel sick in his stomach. He was thinking about Sonia and the way her attitude had changed over the last few months. This concerned him as he felt content in the relationship until Sonia started to show her anger and frustrations again. She would always make him feel like it was his fault that she hadn't had children and wasn't married. This wasn't the case as Sonia and Gregory had met after Sonia experienced a breakup after an engagement. Sonia would blame others for her hardship and Gregory was always the one in the firing range. She would never see that it was her behaviour that caused the communication issues within any of her relationships. She would expect the best from everyone but couldn't give the same in return. Gregory thought about the last few weeks and the way that he was feeling. He also acknowledged the way Sonia and her attitude had changed.

He reached the hotel entrance lobby and walked through the foyer to the lift. As he pushed the button for the lift, he felt the cold feeling down his left arm again and a sick feeling in his stomach. He entered the lift and pressed the floor button. As the lift moved, he looked at himself in the reflection of the chrome design plate surrounding the lift. He felt fed up and drained and his reflection mirrored this. The lift doors opened and he walked down the corridor. As he placed the key card on the door lock to the bedroom, he noticed that Sonia had placed the 'do not disturb' sign on the outside handle. He opened the door and the room was dark. He walked in and felt his way along the wall as the door closed behind him. As he passed the bathroom door, he noticed the reflection of Sonia's mobile phone on the ceiling and walls. She finished a text as he walked up to her side and she closed her phone, placing it on the bed beside her.

Gregory said, "How are you feeling?"

Sonia said, "Fine, what did you do?"

Gregory said, "Walked about."

Sonia said, "Okay, I will get up soon."

Gregory walked around the edge of the bed to the other side and he climbed onto the bed. He asked, "Did you sleep?"

Sonia replied, "Not much."

Gregory remained quiet, but he thought to himself, *Why didn't you text me?*

Sonia noticed he was in deep thought, so she asked, "What are you thinking?"

He said, "Nothing."

Sonia said, "Okay, be like that then."

Gregory got off the bed and walked to the bathroom. While urinating, Gregory wondered why Sonia was being so strange. He finished, flushed the toilet and washed his hands, looking at himself in the mirror.

He opened the door and said, "What's going on, Sonia?" The light from the bathroom gave enough light for Gregory to see Sonia.

She lifted her head and said, "Nothing is wrong. Why?"

He replied, "Well, I have been gone hours and you didn't tell me you were awake."

Sonia immediately butted in and said, "I was sleeping on and off."

Gregory said, "Okay."

Sonia then said, "A cuddle would be nice," as she pulled away the covers to invite him under. Gregory saw that she had removed her clothes. He walked over and removed his clothes, climbing in beside her. He took a condom from his wallet as he knew what was going to happen.

Sonia leaned her face on his chest and put her right leg over his as he lay on his back. She said, "Did you miss me?" while she caressed the hairs on his chest with her right hand.

He said, "Yes I did."

Sonia said, "I missed you," as she moved her hand down to touch his penis. Gregory sighed as she did this and she said, "Oh, I guess you have missed me?" Gregory could feel himself becoming aroused as she played with the head of his penis. He took the condom and placed it on his penis. After this, he gently moved his hand between her legs and he touched her with the tips of his fingers. Sonia lifted her leg slightly to allow him to find a better position. He touched her vagina and Sonia jumped back slightly. "I am sensitive," she said as she placed her hand on his and pushed him against her. He pushed his finger inside and she moved her body as she was becoming aroused also. "I want you inside me," Sonia said in his ear. Gregory twisted his body from under her leg, lifting it up onto his shoulder. Sonia said, "What are you doing?" as he rubbed his penis against her vagina.

"Wet, aren't we?" Gregory said as he pushed himself inside her. Sonia placed her hand on his hip, holding him back as she adjusted herself. She reached down and took his penis with her other hand and moved it about until she was satisfied. Once she let go, Gregory pushed himself all the way inside her.

Sonia groaned and said, "God, you have become bigger." Her face and chest area became red as she became more aroused. Gregory held her thigh with her leg alongside his head to help with the penetration. Sonia grabbed the pillows beside her head and placed one on her face as she was making loud noises as he became more forceful. "Fuck me hard," Sonia said as he was picking up momentum, "cum inside me." Gregory was feeling the intense heat from Sonia as she was sweating more than usual. There was sweat between her breasts as he would from time to time grab one and pinch her nipple to arouse her more.

Sonia lifted her head with intensity and Gregory said, "Are you about to cum?" Sonia nodded and Gregory said, "Me too." Sonia leaned forward and grabbed both of his hips, pulling him harder towards her as he penetrated her. He placed his left thumb on her clitoris and gently caressed her. Sonia groaned and let go of Gregory, dropping backwards onto the bed. He bent her body more to the left and he picked up the pace until he also ejaculated. Sonia held him as he dropped his body beside hers and they lay together in each other's sweat. "Wow. You are sweating," Gregory said as he placed his hand between her breasts and ran his fingers down her body.

Sonia said, "I know, I am on fire down there. That was great. My head felt like it was going to explode." Gregory smiled and lay catching his breath. The room heating was also on so that didn't help. Gregory slipped off the condom and flung it onto the floor. Sonia reached over and touched his penis. "It's really wet," she said as she could feel the moisture and the remainder of fluid exiting as she played with him. She released his penis and moved her hand onto his chest and said, "I love you."

Gregory turned his head to his right and said, "I love you too." She cuddled into him and pulled the sheets over them both. Gregory closed his eyes and so did Sonia as she laid her head on his chest. They both fell asleep. Gregory woke about twenty minutes later feeling hot and sweaty. Sonia's body was very hot as she lay pinned against him with her head in the same position. He moved and she also woke, lifting her head.

She said, "Wow, that was a deep sleep," as she looked at him with one eye, moving her body away from his.

He said, "My body is wet with sweat."

Sonia said, "Mine too."

"I'll go have a shower," said Gregory as he climbed out of the bed. He could feel the sweat run down his chest as he stood. He rubbed it with his hand and walked to the bathroom. He switched on the shower and stood under the water. He washed himself and shampooed his hair to return to Sonia. "It's free now," he said while he stood drying himself, bending over to open his suitcase.

Sonia struggled to sit up but she managed after two attempts. Sitting with her legs hanging over the bed, she said, "I'm sore down there."

Gregory smiled and said, "Me too, a little raw."

Sonia looked at him and said, "I'll have a shower." She got up and lost her balance, correcting it as she entered the bathroom, closing the door behind her. Gregory could hear her as she sat on the toilet urinating. She said aloud, "I'm burning as I pee."

Gregory remained quiet as he dressed himself. He heard the shower switch on. When he had finished dressing, he pulled the sheets back off the bed. He noticed that there was a blood stain and a light splatter of blood spots around where Sonia had been lying. He knew that Sonia had her period about two weeks prior so he became concerned. He lay on the bed to the side of the blood stain and stared at the ceiling. As he lay quietly, he heard Sonia's phone vibrate. Her phone was under the pillows. He reached for it and took it, looking at the screen. It showed a message icon. He placed it back under her pillow and lay his head on his.

Sonia came from the bathroom and said, "I just had a pee and it was sore."

Gregory pointed to the bed and said, "Look at the stains."

Sonia looked and said, "I don't have my period."

Gregory said, "It could be a tear."

Sonia said, "Maybe." She bent over and pulled her suitcase towards her. She opened the zips and reached for a pair of knickers. She put one foot at a time into them, bent over, and pulled them up as she stood straight. A towel was wrapped holding her hair as she looked at Gregory. Her chest was still red after the sex. Gregory got up off the bed and he hugged her.

He whispered in her ear, "Want to go again?"

Sonia pushed him away gently and said, "Really?"

He smiled and took her hand, placing it on his groin.

She said, "I see," as she felt his bulge. She grabbed a dress and said, "I'll be ready in a while. Can we go and eat?"

Gregory lay back on the bed after agreeing. Sonia went into the bathroom with her makeup bag and applied makeup.

Gregory lay on the bed and thought to himself, *It's nice when there isn't any drama, how it just flows.* He reached for the remote control and switched on the television.

Sonia stuck her head out the door and said, "Can you put on the music channel?" Gregory flicked through the channels until he found one. He lay listening to the music, thinking about going on the tour the next day. While he was thinking to himself, he felt the cold down his left arm again. As soon as he registered it, Sonia's phone beeped again. He looked around the room to see if the air-conditioning was on or if Sonia had opened a window. The air-conditioning was off and the window was closed. He lifted his head and lifted the pillow.

He said, "Your phone is beeping."

Sonia looked out the door again and said, "I'll look in a minute." She felt a nervous flutter in her heart and a sick sensation in her stomach.

Gregory also felt sick in his stomach. He said, "I feel really weird all of a sudden."

Sonia replied from the bathroom as she was putting mascara on. "What do you mean?" She felt worse and became worried that he would ask questions.

Gregory said, "I had a cold feeling down my left arm and then immediately your phone beeped."

Sonia said, "Wow, that's strange."

He said, "I know, right. It's happening a lot lately, as if something or someone is trying to warn me about something." After he said this, he wondered why he had said it in the first place. The words just came out. He started to think about what he had just said. "Wow, that makes so much sense," he said to himself.

Sonia got worried and thought, *I wonder if he knows about Philip.* She finished her makeup and walked back into the bedroom. "I'm ready now," she said as she took her coat and handbag.

Gregory looked at her and said, "You look nice."

Sonia said, "Thank you."

Gregory jumped up and grabbed his coat also. As he put it on, he asked "Is everything okay with us?"

Sonia felt sick again and said, "Yes, why would you ask?"

Gregory replied, "I honestly don't know but I felt I had to ask. You would tell me if something was up, wouldn't you?"

Sonia replied with a croaky voice. "Of course I would. I can't believe you asked me that." She opened the bedroom door. Gregory followed as Sonia removed the key card from the holder and handed it to him for safekeeping. He pulled her towards him and he kissed her lips.

He said, "I feel raw down below as I walk; let's not walk too far."

Sonia smiled and said, "We can eat here if you like?"

Gregory said, "Yes, good idea." He opened the bedroom door and they both placed their coats on the chair. They left the bedroom and walked to the lift. Sonia pressed the lift button as she turned to look at him.

She moved closer to him and cuddled, looked into his eyes and said, "Kiss me."

Gregory kissed her and Sonia said, "I feel wet again." Gregory smiled as the lift door opened. There was another couple in the lift. Gregory entered first and Sonia stood in front of him while the door closed. Sonia reached and placed her hand on his crotch gently and Gregory jumped back against the wall with shock.

Sonia smiled and looked at him over her shoulder. Winking, she said, "Everything okay?"

Gregory said, "Just lost my balance," with embarrassment as the other couple were listening. He felt hot and sweaty until the lift door opened and they walked out. He walked behind Sonia and felt her bottom, squeezing her left cheek.

Sonia stopped in her tracks and turned with a smile. "Cheeky," she said, smiling as they entered the foyer. They both walked towards the cocktail bar and Sonia said, "I'd like another brandy and port."

Gregory replied, "I'll have the Godfather."

Sonia walked to the bar and ordered the drinks. Gregory requested a table with the waitress as she walked past him.

She said, "I will be back in one moment." Gregory waited patiently as he watched Sonia look at her mobile phone. She turned towards him as she opened the phone app and smiled. The bartender placed one drink onto the bar as the waitress returned to Gregory. "Table for two?" she said.

Gregory replied, "Yes please," as he followed her to a table. He sat and looked around the restaurant. There were only three other guests sitting but it was only 7.45pm. The waitress handed Gregory a menu and she placed another on the table.

She said, "I will return for your order shortly." Gregory nodded his head and began to read the menu. Sonia arrived with the two drinks and she placed the Godfather in front of Gregory.

She said, "Cheers," as she sat down.

Gregory lifted his glass and said, "Cheers," and they both drank looking into each other's eyes. Gregory decided to have the hamburger and Sonia chose the salmon. The waitress came over and took their order. Gregory looked at Sonia and asked, "Who was texting you?"

Sonia took her drink and sipped it. She looked back at him and said, "It was one of the girls."

Gregory said, "Ah okay. Everything okay?"

Sonia said, "Yes." Gregory drank some of his drink and looked around the room at the décor. He felt uncomfortable again with the cold feeling down his arm. He remained silent and Sonia said, "Are you okay? Your energy has changed."

He replied, "Yes. I just felt a dip, I guess I am hungry and a little tired."

Sonia smiled. "I am full of energy after that intense moment upstairs."

Gregory said, "That was intense, you were sweating."

Sonia said, "Thanks. Yes, I know I was." Gregory smiled and drank some more. Sonia felt the pain in her buttocks area again and down her legs. She felt a little wobble of dizziness as she sat looking at the dessert menu that was on the table. Her phone beeped as Gregory was taking a drink from his glass.

He placed his glass on the table and said, "Aren't you going to check your phone?"

Sonia said, "No, it can wait, I am with you." After saying that, Sonia stood and said, "I need the bathroom." She reached and took her handbag from the floor and said, "I can feel wet, I just have to check," as she walked away.

Gregory knew that she was going to check her mobile phone while in the bathroom. He felt sick again and knew something was going on. He drank some more and looked at the other patrons in the restaurant as he enjoyed people-watching. The waitress came with the food and placed it on the table. Gregory sat and waited for Sonia to return. It was a while before she returned. When she did, she smiled and sat down.

"Wow, that looks really nice," she said as she examined her plate and looked at his food.

Gregory said, "Yes, enjoy." Sonia could feel he was a little edgy but she didn't say anything. She took her knife and fork and placed the napkin on her lap.

She asked Gregory, "Do you think that I will ever have children and settle down?" Gregory had just taken a bite from his burger. He chewed it quickly after Sonia had asked the question because she sat looking straight at him.

He took a drink from his glass after he swallowed the food and said, "Sonia, it's never about the right time, but it's about how two people blend and flow together, moving forward in harmony. Lately something has happened between us and I can't put my finger on it. Your attitude has changed and you take out your frustration and anger on me for all the mistakes you have made in your life – you have centred it all on me, I have become your blame."

Sonia replied as she adjusted herself in the chair, "That's not true, I don't blame you." She took a sip from her glass and asked, "Would you drink some red wine?"

Gregory said, "Okay," knowing that she was going to get drunk and bring up the past again. He took another bite from his burger as Sonia caught the attention of the waitress by waving her hand. The waitress came over and Sonia asked for the wine menu.

She said to Gregory, "Please pick a bottle, you always know your wine."

Gregory nodded his head as he chewed. Sonia started to eat some more of her food but she mainly picked at it. Gregory asked, "Is your salmon okay?"

She said, "Yes, it's very nice but I have lost my appetite."

The waitress returned with the menu and she stood as Gregory choose a South African wine. She left the table with the menu to return with a bottle.

Gregory said, "Sonia will taste."

The waitress poured some into her wine glass and Sonia just took a sip this time. She said, "Yes, that's nice." The waitress poured some more into her glass and also into Gregory's. She placed the bottle on the table. Sonia raised her glass and said, "Here's to a better future."

Gregory looked at her and said, "Cheers," drinking some wine.

Sonia began to get tired again. She looked distant sitting across from him. She stared into space for a moment as Gregory finished his burger. She drank some wine as she remained in deep thought. Gregory continued to eat his sweet potato chips, dipping them in his mayonnaise while Sonia drank some wine. She said, "I am looking forward to tomorrow, going on the tour."

Gregory said, "Yes, that will be interesting to hear about the history. Imagine living in that era." Sonia nodded as she drank some more.

She looked at Gregory and said, "I'm finished eating, do you fancy taking the bottle to the room and watching a movie?"

Gregory said, "Good idea."

Sonia raised her hand again and the waitress approached the table. "I would like the bill, please," Sonia said. The waitress walked to the till area and proceeded to print the bill. Sonia reached for her bag and took her wallet out. She pulled her debit card out and waited for the waitress to return to the table with the card machine.

Gregory said, "Thank you for dinner."

Sonia said, "You are welcome. Let's relax now." Gregory took the bottle and his glass and waited for Sonia to pay.

The waitress completed the transaction and said, "Enjoy the rest of your evening," as she walked away. Sonia got off her chair and took her glass also. They made their way to the bedroom.

Sonia said, "I am sorry for asking questions but I am feeling a little down."

Gregory said, "No problem at all."

Sonia then said, "It is a problem." Gregory remained quiet and walked to the bedroom door and opened it. Sonia followed behind him, letting it slam shut. Gregory walked around to his side of the bed and he took the remote control. He switched on the television and selected the movie channel. Sonia said, "I have my tablet, we can watch something on it." Gregory switched off the TV and placed the remote on the bedside table. Sonia opened her suitcase and took out her tablet. She switched it on, entered the password and handed it to Gregory. "Here, you have a look," she said as she walked into the bathroom.

Gregory lay on the bed and searched through the app. He found a movie that was action-packed so he left the movie opened for Sonia to read about or watch the trailer of. Gregory removed his clothes and climbed under the covers. He poured a glass of wine for them both and he positioned Sonia's glass at her bedside. He took a drink from his wine and waited for Sonia to return. He was feeling a little tired himself after all the drama and emotions of the day.

Sonia was in the bathroom and she noticed some blood on the tissue paper after she urinated. She looked at the paper and wondered if she had something wrong. She then thought that it was probably a tear, but then realised she wasn't sore. She wiped again and there wasn't any blood. She washed her hands and removed her makeup. As she was removing her makeup, she remembered that her message app was downloaded onto her tablet. She was worried that Philip would text again that evening because he had text earlier to ask if she was feeling better and to let her know that he had no symptoms. This worried Sonia as she was the only one with the symptoms. Gregory also didn't show any signs of catching what she had. She finished cleaning her face and brushed her teeth.

When she entered the bedroom, her tablet was lying on the duvet and Gregory said, "Take a look at the movie I have chosen, see what you think?"

Sonia sat on the bed and said, "Thank you," as she drank some wine. She opened the tablet again as the screen had timed out and looked at the movie choice. Sonia read the first line and said, "Nah, too much violence." She looked at Gregory and said,

"I'll look."

Gregory said, "Once it's not a girly flick."

Sonia continued to look. Gregory lay with his eyes closed, relaxing. Sonia turned to him and said, "This one looks good, it's an action, a thriller." Gregory reached out for the tablet to read the caption but Sonia had already pressed play and began to lay back to watch.

Gregory said, "Okay, I guess it's this one then."

Sonia smiled and took her glass of wine. "Cheers," she said.

Gregory picked up his and said, "Cheers," as they both drank. Gregory decided to use the bathroom and while he was gone, Sonia deleted her message app from the tablet. He returned soon after and they cuddled beside each other and watched the movie. Sonia was holding the tablet and she passed it to Gregory as her hand was getting tired. As soon as Gregory began to hold it, he continued to watch it while Sonia fell asleep. Gregory finished watching the movie and switched off the tablet with the bedroom lights.

They both slept until 11am the following morning. Gregory woke to use the bathroom and he looked at his phone to see the time. He pushed back Sonia's hair and said good morning.

Sonia opened her eyes and said, "Good morning," with a croaky voice.

Gregory said, "It's after 11."

Sonia said, "Good, I needed the sleep." Gregory then remembered that breakfast finished at 11am. He went to the bathroom. Sonia turned and took her mobile phone from the bedside table. She had placed her phone on aeroplane mode so that it wouldn't beep during the night. As soon as she opened the phone and removed aeroplane mode, her phone beeped several times as messages arrived. She opened the app and the messages were from Philip. She read them quickly. **8.10pm:** *Hi, hope you are okay, I haven't received a message back from you.*

9.16pm: *Hey, is everything okay?* **10.45pm:** *I'm off to bed, good night.* Sonia text back, *Sorry, I had my phone switched off. I am still not 100% and I have no idea what is wrong with me. Very strange to be honest, especially that you haven't got it!* She closed her phone and placed it back on the bedside table.Gregory opened the bathroom door and walked out. Sonia reached out with both arms and said, "Come here and give me a kiss." Gregory walked over and lay beside her as they cuddled. Sonia said, "Climb under and cuddle me properly." Gregory stood as Sonia pulled back the duvet and he climbed under with her. Gregory positioned his head on Sonia's right shoulder and he closed his eyes. Sonia lay on her back and also closed her eyes. They both relaxed in each other's arms. Sonia's phone vibrated on the bedside table next to Gregory. He moved his head and Sonia said, "Probably updates or something."

Gregory lifted his head and looked into her eyes. He said, "I'll go shave and shower."

Sonia said, "Okay," and they kissed each other. Gregory climbed out of the bed and walked into the bathroom, closing the door. Sonia reached for her phone and opened the message app. It was Philip. *I don't know what you mean but I hope you are okay x.* Sonia read the message and decided not to reply. She deleted the thread and placed her phone back on the bedside table. She lay on her back, looking at the ceiling, thinking. *I still don't feel great, my legs and buttocks are still aching. I wonder what it is. A virus maybe?* She continued to question different alternatives and Gregory appeared from the bathroom. "It's all yours," he said as he dried himself, naked in front of her. Sonia got out of the bed and walked to Gregory. She kissed his lips and touched his penis. Gregory pulled her towards him and she pushed away.

"Not now," she said as she walked into the bathroom. She closed the door and Gregory continued to dress himself. He waited for Sonia, lying on the bed. Sonia appeared and said, "I felt dizzy again in the shower. God, I hope this passes soon."

Gregory replied, "It's a weird one."

Sonia continued to dress herself, pulling clothing from her suitcase. Gregory lay with his eyes closed. Sonia started to dry her hair with her hairdryer. The noise was getting to Gregory so he walked to her and said, "I'll meet you in the lobby." Sonia nodded and he walked out of the bedroom. As he entered the corridor, the cleaning staff were two bedrooms away from theirs. He walked past a girl and said, "Hello."

She replied, "Good morning."

He entered the lift as it was already on the floor and pressed the ground floor button. The doors closed and he stood looking at his reflection in the metal surround. He felt sick again and wondered if it was hunger. Soon after, the chilling feeling moved down his right arm. He said, *Hello* in his mind and felt his face become cold. This freaked him out. The door opened. He walked out of the lift onto the ground floor and sat in a seat in the lobby area. He took his phone from his pocket and text Sonia. *I'm in the reception area.* Gregory was very hungry and becoming irritable. He had been sitting in the lobby for twenty minutes when he took his phone and called Sonia. The phone rang out. He looked at the screen and called again. As he was doing this Sonia walked up beside him, oblivious that he was calling her.

He said, "Don't you answer your phone?"

Sonia replied, "Didn't hear it," as she looked and saw a missed call. Then she said, "I was in the lift, there was probably no reception." Gregory stood and they both walked towards the main entrance door. Gregory walked behind Sonia as she pushed the door open. Gregory reached forward and held it as she passed through. She turned when she stood on the pavement and asked, "Where will we eat?"

Gregory looked at her and said, "I have no idea."

Sonia then said, "Did you not look up a place?" as she pulled her phone from her pocket. "I guess my hands have to freeze now," she said as she entered her passcode.

Gregory just walked towards the shops and Sonia followed. He said, "I don't really care where we eat, maybe the place we went to yesterday?"

Sonia closed her phone and said, "Okay." She knew that he was irritable so she took his arm and they walked together. Sonia pulled herself closer to him because she was feeling the cold.

Gregory asked, "How are you feeling this morning?"

Sonia replied, "I'm much better but still don't have an appetite." They reached the café and entered. It was very busy, therefore they had to wait at the door for the next available table. Sonia stood beside Gregory and she started to feel faint with the heat. She walked away towards the toilet without saying anything to Gregory. He remained in line waiting for a table. It was about five minutes that passed and the waitress came over to Gregory and asked him to follow her. He was seated next to a window looking into the back garden. Sonia returned, looking very pale.

Gregory said, "Are you okay?"

Sonia sat with her arms folded and said, "Not great."Gregory took the menu card and began to select what he wanted in his mind. He wasn't in the best of moods. Sonia looked quickly and placed the menu back on the table. She said, "I'll just have a cup of tea." Gregory was just about to answer when a waiter came over.

He asked Sonia, "What can I get you?"

Sonia replied, "Oh, I'll just have an Earl Grey Tea please."

He replied, "Okay, and you, sir?"

Gregory said, "I'll have the Hawaiian pizza with chips and a latte, please." The waiter took the order and left the table.

Sonia looked at Gregory and as she took her coat off, she said, "I'll take two paracetamol."

Gregory said, "Good idea." Sonia took her handbag onto her lap and searched through the items inside. Gregory took his coat off and opened his phone. Sonia found the tablets and placed them on the table, putting her handbag on the floor. Gregory then said, "Oh, they take a picture of us during the tour. You look like a ghost anyways." He smiled.

Sonia wasn't amused. She replied, "Haw haw, very funny."

Gregory suggested that they have a brandy and port again as it helped her the day before. Sonia agreed that she would before the tour. The tour was booked for 3pm so they had time to have a drink and relax. The waiter returned with the tea and latte, placing them on the table with a knife and fork for Gregory. He asked if they were sharing while holding a second set of cutlery.

Sonia said, "No thank you, but I might have some chips."

The waiter placed the cutlery on the table in front of Sonia and said, "Just in case you change your mind," smiling as he walked away.

Gregory said, "You should try to eat some chips."

Sonia said, "I will," as the pizza and chips arrived. She said, "Oh, chunky chips, yum," as Gregory looked at his pizza. It was at least thirteen inches and he was very pleased. Sonia took a chip and placed it on the side plate that was left for her. She said, "I'll wait for it to cool down." Gregory was already slicing up his pizza with the pizza cutter. Sonia took her tablets and poured her tea. She added a small amount of milk and placed the two tablets in her mouth. She reached for her cup and drank some tea. She paused for a moment, holding her tea cup in her right hand, and jerked her neck back, quickly swallowing. She drank some more. "I hate swallowing tablets," she said as she placed the cup back onto the saucer.

Gregory had just shoved a larger amount of pizza into his mouth because the cheese kept stretching. He watched her and just nodded as he chewed. Sonia said, "Hungry, are we?" as she watched him chew. She sat back into her chair and looked at the single chip on her plate. She picked it up and took a bite, slowly chewing and eventually swallowing. She sat for a while to see how she was feeling. Gregory was munching through his pizza when Sonia's phone rang. "Oh, I wonder who that is on a Saturday." She reached for her phone in her pocket and it displayed Philip's name. She silenced the phone and muted the volume, placing her phone back into her handbag. Gregory had his mouth full again, therefore he waited to ask who it was until he had eventually swallowed. Sonia said, "It was a private number so I wasn't going to answer it, I have no idea, probably a sales promotion thing."

Gregory looked at her and felt sick again as he drank some of his latte. He said, "That's weird," as he took another slice of pizza into his hand.

Sonia said, "Do you not get calls?"

Gregory replied, "I do," as he took a mouthful.

Sonia said, "Well, then," as she put the rest of her chip into her mouth, feeling smug. She took another chip from the chip bowl and placed it on her plate. This time, she reached for the mayonnaise sachet and tore it open. She squeezed some onto the chip and the rest onto the plate.

Gregory said, "Feeling better, are we?" Sonia looked at him and ignored him as she took a bite. Gregory said, "Do you want anything better to eat?"

Sonia said, "Maybe the poached eggs." Gregory got off his chair and walked to the waiter. He ordered the pouched eggs and returned to his seat. Sonia said, "Thank you."

Gregory smiled and said, "No worries, you're paying," as he took another slice of pizza. Sonia remained quiet and took another chip, dipping it into her mayonnaise.

She said, "I would like a cuddle later."

Gregory looked and said, "Okay," as he continued to chew.

The poached eggs arrived to the table with gluten-free bread.

Sonia looked at the waiter and asked, "Is the bread gluten-free?"

He replied, "Yes, please enjoy."

Gregory sat feeling smug as Sonia grinded some pepper onto her eggs. She took the cutlery and began to eat. Gregory at this point had two slices left of his pizza and was feeling full. He sat back into his chair and said, "Enjoy," as Sonia placed some food into her mouth. She looked at him and nodded her head while chewing. He took a drink from his now-cold latte and relaxed into his chair. His stomach was full and he couldn't finish the pizza. He excused himself and walked to the toilet. Sonia continued to eat while she thought about why she hadn't been feeling well for so long and the symptoms, which were very strange to her. She remembered that she hadn't replied to Philip, therefore she reached into her bag, looked in the direction of the toilets to make sure Gregory wasn't returning, and opened her phone. She text, *Hi Philip, I have been feeling very sick and nauseous since we were together, no idea what it is. How are you?* She sent the text, switched off the mute and placed her phone back into her bag. She sat thinking and continued to eat some more. It wasn't long until Philip replied. Sonia turned to see if Gregory was returning and as she turned her head, he was standing beside her.

She jumped with surprise and Gregory said, "Am I that scary?"

She wiped her mouth with her napkin and laughed. "No, silly, you caught me by surprise."

Gregory kissed her on the cheek and proceeded to sit down. Sonia's phone beeped a second time as another message arrived. Gregory sat and looked at Sonia. He said, "You're popular." Sonia ignored him and continued to eat. She was cutting the bread with her knife and fork and spreading the yellow of the egg over the bread with the knife just as her phone rang. She placed her knife and fork on the plate with haste and reached for her phone. It was Philip calling. She muted the sound and looked at the display. Gregory said, "Aren't you going to answer?"

Sonia felt anxious and said, "No, it's work, probably looking for weekend workers, they are low on staff to fill the hours.

Gregory replied, "Okay," as he felt the energy a little off. He could feel something wasn't right and he said, "I'll get the bill. I need to go to the shop next door. I'll meet you there." Sonia could feel he was a little off and just agreed as she drank some tea. Gregory stood and grabbed his coat, making his way to pay the bill. He stood at the counter and put his coat and scarf on. The waitress handed him the bill and he took his debit card from his wallet. As he scanned his card over the card machine, he looked at Sonia. She was staring at him. He turned his head back to the machine and saw the 'approved' sign and placed his card back into his wallet. He reached into his pocket and took two pounds in change and handed it to the girl.

She said, "Thank you, have a lovely day."

He replied, "You too," as he walked towards the door.

Sonia knew that Gregory felt something wasn't right and she felt frustrated. She finished her breakfast and poured another cup of tea. As Gregory left the café, she reached for her bag and looked at the messages. They were from Philip. One read, *I'm not great since yesterday.* The second read, *Probably just flu.* Sonia selected Philip's number and she called his phone. He answered after the first ring. "Hey you," Sonia said. "Hey, I think I will get a blood test because this isn't right, I am worried about what happened also."

Philip remained quiet for a moment.

Sonia said, "Hello," as she thought he wasn't there.

Philip replied, "I'm here, just thinking about what you said. Why a blood test?"

Sonia replied, "I want to make sure that everything is okay as I am very tired."

Philip said, "Okay, let me know how that goes. I am just on my way to the supermarket to get supplies."

Sonia said, "Ah okay. Have a nice day."

Philip replied, "You too, take care." He hung up the phone and continued to the supermarket.

Sonia drank some more tea and stood to put on her coat. She bent over and took her bag up onto the chair as she took some chewing gum out. She squeezed one down the wrapper and placed it into her mouth, throwing the packet back into her bag. She threw the bag over her shoulder and proceeded to the door. She pulled the door open with force as it was heavy and walked out onto the footpath, letting it bang closed behind her. She walked towards the shop next door and looked in the doorway to see if she could see Gregory. He wasn't visible, therefore she walked in. She noticed a magazine section and wandered over while scanning for Gregory. He was standing in the gadget section, looking at earphones. He looked up and Sonia waved to signal that she was in the shop. He waved back and continued to read the back of a packet. Sonia picked two women's magazines and walked to the cashier desk. She handed the items to the cashier when Gregory walked up behind her. He placed his right hand on her side and stood next to her. She turned her head and acknowledged him by leaning her head onto his and then proceeded to pay for her items. Once the payment was authorised, she stuffed the magazines into her handbag as she had it perched on the countertop.

Gregory watched and said, "Amazing, the crap women fit into their bags."

Sonia smiled and said, "I have everything in here."

Gregory replied, "I bet you have."

Sonia took it off the counter and said, "Here, feel the weight."

Gregory took it in his right hand and said, "What is in here?"

Sonia said, "Now you can carry it for a bit," as she fixed her scarf around her neck. Gregory placed the handbag closer to her as he extended his arm. Sonia took her bag and placed it on her shoulder.

Gregory said, "Are we ready?"

Sonia said, "Yes," so they walked out onto the footpath. It was 2.25pm so they made their way to the tour venue. They were on the high street so it wasn't far to walk. Gregory was excited because there was a network of hidden streets within the venue, frozen in time since the seventeenth century. He was excited to see and feel what it could have been like to live in that era.

Sonia took Gregory's hand as they walked. She said, "Are you okay?"

Gregory said, "Yes, why?"

Sonia replied, "You seemed a little strange in the café."

Gregory said, "Nah, I'm okay," as he thought that something was weird with the way Sonia had been the last few weeks. They arrived at the entrance of the venue at 2.45pm and Gregory said, "Let's have a look in that shop," as he pointed towards the window.

Sonia said, "Okay," so they walked over and looked at the items on display. Gregory walked to the door and pushed it open as he turned and waited for Sonia. She walked up to him and they kissed as they continued inside. The shop was full of small tourist souvenirs – mugs, hats, tee-shirts, etc. Gregory just walked about looking at all the items. Sonia stood reading what was written on the mugs. Gregory looked at his watch and decided it was time to leave and go inside the venue for the tour.

They both left and entered the venue building. Gregory handed their tickets over and they were shown into the waiting area. There were several others waiting as they entered the room. Gregory and Sonia stood to the back of the group and remained holding each other. Sonia looked into Gregory's eyes and she kissed him on the lips. She said, "Creepy place," as she pulled him closer to her.

Gregory kissed her again and he said, "I love it."

Just as he said this, the tour organiser walked into the room and introduced herself. She said, "I am Linda, I will be escorting you through the buildings. If you have any questions, please don't hesitate to ask. If I can answer I will. So, let's start by going this way, please." She opened the door and walked through. The group followed behind as she began to talk. Gregory and Sonia couldn't hear what she was saying as they were too far behind.

Sonia poked Gregory and said, "Let's get to the front."

Gregory said, "No, I want to feel what it's like down here myself. I want to hang back."

Sonia said, "Okay." They walked from room to room and Gregory felt strange feelings. He could imagine what life would have been like back then. As he was walking, he wondered if the buildings were haunted. Just as he thought this, he could feel the cold down his left arm again. This time it was very obvious to him. He realised that it was a spirit blending with him. He stopped and looked at Sonia.

He said, "I wonder if this place is haunted?"

Sonia smiled and said, "Yeah, it should be, it's really creepy. I wouldn't like to have lived in the seventeenth century – all the sickness, rats… ewwww. I couldn't have lived here; I'd be better suited to the castle." She smiled.

Gregory said, "I feel something; it's like I can feel them."

Sonia stopped them both as they were walking and looked very concerned as she looked at him. "What do you mean? You're creeping me out now."

He said, "I can feel them."

"Who?" Sonia replied as she stood with her arms across her chest, looking at him

Gregory said, "The dead."

Sonia said, "I want to leave now, you are freaking me out now."

Gregory said, "Don't worry, I have been feeling weird sensations for the last few weeks, on and off. It's like they are trying to tell me something."

Sonia started to walk towards the group because they had disappeared through a building ahead. She walked in front of Gregory, remaining quiet, looking at the walls and floor ahead of her. She wondered what Gregory was talking about. Gregory walked behind her, feeling the cold on his left arm. He could also feel a tickly feeling, as though there was a web on his face. He wiped his face several times but the feeling remained there. They caught up on the group and entered another room. As soon as they walked into the room, Gregory felt sick and very weak and wanted to leave the room. Sonia became very worried and they both walked ahead of the group. The tour organiser requested that they wait in the next room and didn't walk ahead.

Sonia stood with Gregory and she asked him, "Are you okay?

Gregory said, "I feel very sick and weak."

Sonia stood back with her arms crossed again and said, "I'm not enjoying this."

Gregory said, "It's nothing to worry about; I am not scared. I want to know more about what it is."

Sonia said, "Maybe go have a tarot card reading or something like that."

Gregory said, "Good idea. Let's look it up after this."

The group began to enter the room that they were in and Sonia cuddled into Gregory. She said, "I am cold and a little worried."

Gregory smiled and kissed her. He said, "The strange thing is that my left arm is freezing cold but it feels warm to the touch."

Sonia slid her hand under the sleeve of his coat and felt his wrist. "Your wrist feels warm." She decided to check his pulse rate. She stood concentrating and then mumbled to herself.

He said, "What?"

She replied, "You're fine."

He said, "I still feel light-headed and have the sick feeling in my stomach."

Sonia said, "I wonder if you are getting the flu thing I have had?"

Gregory said, "I don't feel sick that way."

Sonia said, "Which way?"

He replied, "I don't have symptoms, I just have a feeling of being sick. I can't explain it but it is just like a knowing feeling, it's really weird."

Sonia swallowed and then replied, "I wonder if you are feeling people."

Gregory asked, "What do you mean?"

Sonia said, "Dead people," as she shivered and made a strange *brrr* noise. "I am freaked out now," she said, standing against the wall.

Just as she said this, the tour organiser said, "This is the area in which many people with the plague would have resided, all lying on the floor and dying as there wasn't medicine available."

Sonia grabbed Gregory and said, "Oh my god, I am fucking freaking out now."

Gregory went white in his complexion and Sonia noticed this as she kept looking at him. She could see that his face was changing. He was looking older. The light was dim and the building itself had an eerie feeling to it. Sonia was not happy at all being there. Gregory stopped for a moment and stood quietly as he felt a heaviness come over him. He felt his head expand while his feet felt like they went down through the building and into the ground. He was completely absorbed in this feeling. It was surreal. He felt whole and not alone. Sonia pulled his coat as she looked at him in a frozen state.

She said, "Are you possessed?"

Gregory turned his head and said, "No," as he remained, feeling what was going on. The group began to walk past them both to continue the tour. Gregory walked behind and Sonia followed.

She said, "I feel sick again."

Gregory said, "I feel better now," as they left that area and entered a stairwell. "I feel like whatever that was is gone now."

Sonia sighed and said, "Thank God, you were freaking me out. I won't sleep tonight."

Gregory hugged her and said, "Oh, I'll help you fall asleep, I know just the thing."

Sonia smiled and kissed him and said, "I might have a headache later," as she began to walk up the stairs. Gregory followed behind, watching her taking each step. He wondered what it was trying to tell him, this spirit communication. He was excited and curious also. He wondered why he could always feel them when certain things happened between himself and Sonia. When they reached the landing area, Sonia stopped and turned to wait for Gregory. He could feel the muscles in his legs as he climbed the last few steps. His body was feeling very tired and weak. Sonia noticed that he was struggling and that his face was very dull. She took a bottle of water from her handbag and handed it to him. He opened the bottle top and took a large mouthful. He swallowed and took another drink. He stood for a moment and appeared distant as Sonia watched him.He took another drink and said, "God, I felt faint."

Sonia said, "I know, I could see you were not in the physical."

Gregory said, "I need to sit down." Sonia looked around and there was nowhere to sit. She followed the group, walking with Gregory arm in arm. They entered a room that had a video playing and seating. Gregory said, "Great," as they walked to sit on the bench. Sonia stood as Gregory sat. She told him to drink the rest of the water. He drank the remainder of the bottle and handed it back to her. She placed the blue bottle top back on the bottle and placed it in her handbag. He sat with a distant look on his face as the film played. The lighting shifted several times as the screen changed scenes and the room ambiance felt calm and warm.

Gregory said, "I don't feel the sick feeling anymore; I feel light and more alert." Sonia just looked at him without saying anything and from time to time was distracted by the film. She placed her hand on his head and stood close to him as he leaned on her side. She moved her arm down to his shoulder and rested it there. Gregory closed his eyes for a moment and relaxed. He was feeling very drained. The short film finished and the organiser requested everyone to follow her. She opened a double set of doors and proceeded through to the next room. The group followed. Sonia and Gregory remained seated until the last couple walked towards the doors.

The organiser announced as they were walking, "We will now go back down towards the ground level, no more flights of stairs to climb." Gregory was relieved as he wasn't feeling too energetic. Sonia walked ahead of him and kept turning to look at him. He could see that she was concerned. Gregory took her right hand and he walked with her.

Sonia said, "That was really creepy back there."

Gregory smiled and said, "I know but I enjoyed it." Sonia squeezed his hand and released as they walked. Gregory squeezed hers and smiled. They walked to some stairs and followed the group down three floors. They walked past several rooms and then entered the entrance area. The guide announced that it was the end of the tour and thanked everyone for attending. She pointed towards the souvenir shop, but Sonia pulled Gregory towards the exit doors. Gregory followed with relief as he just wanted to get some fresh air. They both stood on the footpath as Gregory took a moment to breathe in some fresh air. Sonia could see clearly that the colour had begun to reappear on his face.

She said, "Let's go get something small to eat and have a drink, a nice cool drink."

Gregory looked up from the ground and said, "Yes, that's a great idea."

Sonia felt a distance between her and Gregory. He was very quiet in thought. She asked, "What are you thinking?"

Gregory said, "Nothing in particular. I'm just very conscious of my body; I feel lighter and much more alert."

Sonia said, "Great, I'll check that out later," as she walked ahead of him to a café. Gregory smiled as he watched her walk away. Sonia stood at the café door as she held it open. Gregory walked up to her and she said, "After you." Gregory walked in with a smile.

Sonia grabbed his bottom as he walked past her and he jumped, just as the waitress asked him, "A table for two?" Gregory took a moment to reply as he composed himself and said, "Yes please," as he turned and smiled at Sonia. Sonia stood behind with a smug face and acted all innocent. Gregory followed the waitress and sat down. Sonia walked to the table and looked at Gregory.

She said, "You look pale." She walked to the counter area and requested a glass of tap water. Gregory sat looking out the window, thinking about the feeling he had experienced while walking through the building. Sonia came beside him and offered the glass of water. She said, "Drink this."

Gregory said, "Thank you," as he took a large mouthful, gulping it down. He finished the lot and placed the glass on the table as he watched Sonia take her seat and look at the menu.

"I feel like having something sweet, do you?"

Gregory didn't have to think about his answer, he just replied, "Yes," in an instant. He took the menu and looked at the options.

Sonia said, "After this, how about we go back to the room and have a rest?" She smiled as she continued to look at her menu. She went to rub her foot up against Gregory's but failed by kicking him in the shin.

Gregory said, "What was that for?" as he moved his leg.

Sonia replied, "Sorry," as she smiled. She was beginning to feel much better and this was starting to show as she was beginning to get giddy. Gregory, however, was feeling a little exhausted after his experience and he kept going into deep thought. Sonia was feeling a little left out, so she placed her hand on the table with her palm facing upwards. Gregory took a while to react by taking her hand with his. He was sitting in a still posture with vacant expression on his face . Sonia said, "Oh, your hand is cold," as she naturally reacted by starting to feel his pulse on his wrist.

Gregory said, "I am not going to die just yet," as he smiled. Sonia was counting in her head so she just ignored his comment.

The waitress walked over and asked, "What can I get you?"

Sonia said, "I'll have a mocha and gluten-free apple tart and ice-cream," as she pulled her hand away from Gregory's, sitting back upright in her seat. The waitress stood writing on her notepad and looked at Gregory when ready to take his order.

Gregory said, "I will have the latte and cheesecake, please."

Sonia said, "Have something different, you've had that already."

Gregory said, "Ah no, I'll have the cheesecake," staring at the waitress.

The waitress said, "Okay, thank you. Is that all?" with a smile as she looked at them both for confirmation.

Sonia said, "Yes thank you." The waitress walked away and Sonia slid her hand back onto the table with her palm facing upwards. Gregory placed his hand on top and they intertwined their fingers. Sonia said, "I can't wait to have a cuddle later."

Gregory felt excited; he could feel his energy boost a little through his body. He said, "Yes, that would be really nice. It's been a while." Sonia pulled her hand away and said, "Really?" She sat up in her chair and then reached for her handbag.

Gregory said, "You know what I mean, you haven't been well and that's absolutely fine."

Sonia continued to remain quiet and rumble for her phone. She said, "Oh, I can't find my phone," as she continued to panic.

Gregory said, "You put it in your right-hand side coat pocket."

Sonia reached with her right hand and felt her way to the pocket on her coat. She placed her hand inside and said, "Found it," with a smile, as if she had accomplished it all on her own. Gregory just stared at her as she continued to check her phone for messages etc. He sat looking around the café and noticed an elderly woman sitting peacefully on her own, reading a book while drinking some tea. He wondered about her life, the experiences that she had had and why she was on her own. She looked as though she was in her late eighties and he felt a beautiful presence around her. Gregory felt very peaceful within himself as he continued to watch her. Sonia noticed that Gregory was staring across the room as she looked up from her phone. She turned her head and looked around the room. Her first notion was that he was staring at another girl, but she was pleasantly surprised when she realised that it was the woman reading a book.

She turned back and said, "Checking out the talent, are we?" as she chuckled to herself.

Gregory took a moment as he was in a daze. He looked at Sonia and said, "What do you mean?" in a serious manner.

Sonia said, "What's happened to you?"

Gregory said, "I don't know but I feel really floaty and it's kind of nice."

Sonia noticed the waitress walking towards the table and said, "Ah, coffee time." Gregory turned as the waitress appeared to his right as she placed the drinks on the table. She walked to the counter and brought the desserts over.

Gregory said, "Thank you," as the waitress said, "Bon appétit."

Sonia was already sipping her mocha. Sonia stared at Gregory as he placed his napkin on his right leg and took his fork. He looked at Sonia and said, "Enjoy," as he scooped a piece from his cheesecake. Sonia continued to hold her coffee close to her face in both hands as she was liking the feeling of heat on her hands. She just watched Gregory chew as she thought to herself. She was thinking about where to have the blood test.

Sonia was in deep thought when Gregory said, "Are you going to eat?"

Sonia said, "Yes," as she took her spoon. She said to Gregory, "I am going to go and have a blood test. Do you want to get one too?"

Gregory said, "For what?"

Sonia replied, "Oh, because of this sickness – I just want to know my bloods are okay."

Gregory said, "Okay, let's do it."

Sonia was relieved as she scooped some apple tart and ice-cream. She placed it in her mouth and allowed it to melt, tasting the flavours as she swallowed small amounts to make it last longer. They both sat eating their desserts in silence. Gregory finished his first and began to drink his latte when Sonia said, "I can't finish this, would you like it?"

Gregory said, "No thanks, I'm stuffed." Sonia just placed her spoon on the plate and pushed it away from her. She took her mocha and drank some more.

She sighed and said, "I'm tired now. We must get some water on the way back to the room."

Gregory said, "Good idea," as he stood up. Sonia drank some more and placed her mug on the table, pushing her chair back with her feet. She stood and grabbed her handbag then walked towards the cashier counter area. She proceeded to pay while

Gregory took his time putting his coat and scarf on. He stood watching the elderly woman again as she sat quietly reading her book. He thought to himself that she was enjoying her own space and how nice that was to see.

Sonia walked over and grabbed Gregory and said, "Stop fantasising about that woman, I am here," as she smiled and kissed his lips.

Gregory replied, "Really?" as he looked into Sonia's eyes. She had this mischievous look about her as she reached for her coat.

As she was putting on her coat she said, "Water and sleep." Gregory walked towards the door and Sonia followed. As he opened the door, he could hear the waitress say, "Thank you," and he turned to say it back to her. Sonia pushed Gregory out the door as she held on to him. Sonia grabbed him from behind and said, "Wow, look at the moon." It was getting dark and the moon was rising as the night was getting colder. Sonia moved towards Gregory's front and she stood looking into his eyes. She said, "I really love you," as she kissed his lips, closing her eyes. Gregory also closed his and he felt the warmth of her moist lips caress his. She kissed him again and pulled her head back from his.

Gregory felt aroused and said, "I see what you are doing."

Sonia looked at him and smiled. "What am I doing?" she said as she reached down between his legs with haste and gently pressed against his manhood.

Gregory said, "Uhh, cheeky," as Sonia walked away fixing her handbag on her shoulder. She turned her head and looked at him as she continued to walk into the shop next door. Gregory composed himself and walked after her. When he entered, Sonia was already standing at the till, paying for the water. She scanned her card and walked towards Gregory. She handed him both bottles of water and walked out the door. Gregory's hands could feel the icy cold water as he held them. He said, "Ah yeah, let my hands freeze." Sonia was already putting on her gloves and when finished, she took the two bottles and walked ahead. Gregory followed as he could feel his face get very cold. He said to Sonia, "God, it's cold tonight."

Sonia replied, "Yes, you will need to give me plenty of cuddles tonight." Gregory walked alongside Sonia and they held hands as Gregory took one of the bottles of water. They entered the hotel and walked to the lift. The lift door opened as they approached it and several other guests walked out. Sonia walked in first and pressed the button for their floor. She placed the bottle of water on the floor and put both arms around Gregory's shoulders. She kissed him again and they embraced. The lift beeped as it reached their floor and the doors began to open as they moved apart. Sonia reached for her water and Gregory walked out first, making his way to the bedroom door. He pulled out his wallet and took the card, swiping it across the card reader. The lock disengaged and he opened the door. He stood and said, "After you," as Sonia walked past and straight to the bathroom. Gregory walked to the bedroom chair as the door slammed behind him. He unlaced his shoes and took them off. He removed his coat and threw it over the back of the chair. He heard the toilet flush and continued to remove his jeans. He was standing with his jumper and boxer shorts on when Sonia walked out of the bathroom.

She looked and said, "Oh, what a sexy surprise, love the socks." Gregory reached down as he laughed and pulled his socks off each foot with haste. He stood up straight as Sonia walked towards him.

She placed her hand on his crotch and said, "I want you now."

Gregory felt fire rage through his body with excitement. Sonia slid her hand down his front and held him as he said, "God, your hands are cold."

Sonia smiled and said, "That's not stopping you, is it?" as he was becoming more erect. Gregory grabbed Sonia and kissed her as he placed his right hand under her dress until he reached her bra. He gently manoeuvred his fingers to grip the top of it and he pulled it down to release her left breast. Sonia exhaled as he felt her nipple. She squirmed as he pinched it, pushing him away. She pulled her dress over her head and dropped it on the floor. Her left breast was exposed and Gregory grabbed it with his hand, licking her nipple with his tongue. Gregory had also noticed that Sonia had removed her tights and knickers. This excited him so much that he could feel his penis secreting fluids as he was erect, pressed up against his boxer shorts. Sonia grabbed him closer. Sonia pulled his boxer shorts down and told him that she was wet. She got on her knees and placed Gregory into her mouth and caressed him. Gregory was feeling more excited and a lightness came over him. Gregory reached behind Sonia and released her bra. She stood and pulled him to the bed and flung him on his back. Gregory pulled himself onto the bed and Sonia climbed onto him.

Gregory said, "Be careful, I have no condom on."

Sonia replied as she took his penis. "I want to feel you bare inside me, just a little." She placed his penis under her and she began to sit down onto it. Gregory felt his manhood slide inside with no friction and Sonia gasped. She slowly moved her body on top of him and this drove Gregory crazy. He could feel the heat and intensity around his groin so much he felt dizzy.

Sonia continued for a while until Gregory said, "God, I am going to cum."

Sonia pulled herself off and said, "Get a condom." Gregory looked dazed and he looked around the room as if he was disorientated. He got up and walked to his suitcase. He pulled out his wash bag and took a condom. Sonia followed behind and she grabbed his penis, massaging it as Gregory tore open the wrapper. He placed the condom on and turned to face Sonia. She looked into his eyes and leaned on the bed saying, "Fuck me." Gregory positioned himself behind her and he inserted his penis. Sonia sighed and pushed her body against his. Gregory built up his momentum as Sonia dropped her body lower, grabbing the sheets with both hands. She remained still as she enjoyed the intensity and overwhelming feeling inside. She said, "I feel you in my stomach. God, this is so intense." Gregory was in complete bliss as he could feel Sonia and the intensity surrounding them. He was out of body. He could feel the build-up just before he orgasmed and Sonia pushed herself against him again as he did. Sweat was running down his forehead and chest as he stood still inside her. He was very weak and felt floaty, holding both sides of her hips. Sonia could feel that Gregory was distant so she pulled herself away from him and guided him to lie beside her. He was gasping for air as his breathing was heavy.

Sonia placed her hand on his chest and said, "Wow, that was amazing."

Gregory said, "Yes," in a faint croaky voice. Sonia grabbed a bottle of water while she sat up and opened the bottle top. She handed the bottle to Gregory and he lifted his head to drink. He could feel the cold water enter his mouth and run down his throat. He drank some more, handing the bottle back as he rested his head again. Sonia drank plenty and placed the bottle top back.

She said, "You rest, I will run the bath." She kissed his lips and got off the bed and walked to the bathroom. Gregory closed his eyes. Sonia closed the bathroom door behind her as she felt relieved that they had had sex without a condom. The night with Philip remained very much on her mind. She switched the bath plug to seal and turned on the hot water. She stood looking at herself in the mirror and examined her body. She felt relaxed as the bath water produced steam. The mirror began to show condensation, so she sat on the bath side and thought about the tour and the way Gregory had changed. She was concerned and wondered if he was possessed by anything. This made her a little uncomfortable, so she walked out of the bathroom to check on him. Gregory was asleep. He was lying on his front, naked, with his head turned to the left side. Sonia pulled the sheets over him and she kissed his forehead. She walked back into the bathroom and closed the door. The bath was filled to just below the drain hole so she turned on the cold and switched off the hot water. She sat again for a moment and wondered where her life was going. She thought about her age and how she wanted to have a child. She began to get frustrated again as she touched her belly. She switched off the bath water and began to slowly climb in. The water was very hot but that was the way she liked it. Her skin was appearing red as she entered the water and she could feel her heartbeat as she lay down with her head just above the water level. Sonia lay in the water and closed her eyes as she was thinking about her life and work. She didn't take long to fall asleep, which was dangerous but the heat of the water made her sleepy. Over an hour passed before she woke. She was feeling a little cold as the water temperature had dropped.

She climbed out of the bath and took a towel from the towel rack on the wall. She dried herself and wrapped her wet hair in another towel. She unplugged the bath by twisting the mechanism to let the water drain before she showered and washed her hair. She opened the door and walked into the bedroom. Gregory was still asleep so she climbed onto the bed and cuddled into him. He started to move slightly as he opened his eyes. Sonia lay with her face next to his as he had turned facing inwards on the bed. She smiled as he started to function properly but was feeling heavy.

She said, "You had a nice sleep," not letting him know that she too had slept, especially that she had slept in the bath.

Gregory took his arm from under the cover and placed it over her, pulling her closer to him. Sonia shifted her body wrapped in the wet towel beside him.

He said, "Climb under."

Sonia got off the blankets and dropped her towel, climbing in beside him. They cuddled together. Gregory asked what the time was and Sonia said, "I don't know."

Gregory reached for his phone as he turned away and saw that it was 7.25pm. He said, "That was a nice sleep. Do you fancy a drink?"

Sonia said, "Hell yeah." Gregory placed his phone back and they embraced again. Sonia said, "I will go have a shower and wash my hair, then you can have one."He said, "No worries." Sonia kissed him, took her towel off the floor and proceeded to the bathroom again. Gregory sat up in the bed and reached for the remote control. He switched on the television and scrolled down through the channels. He found the Discovery Channel and left it on. There was an engineering programme on that he watched.

While Sonia was washing herself, she noticed a sore on her lower spine area, just above her anus. She touched it a few times and realised it was painful to touch. She finished her shower and wrapped her hair up again. She grabbed her vanity bag and took her miniature mirror from her bag. She bent over and placed it between her legs to try to see the sore. After a few different positions, she managed to see the redness. She took some non-perfumed moisturiser and rubbed it on. She continued to dry herself and wrapped the towel around herself. She was concerned about the sore. She had never had anything like this and was confused as to what it was. She opened the bathroom door and walked into the bedroom. Gregory was sitting up drinking some water when Sonia said, "The bathroom is yours," as she stood right in front of the television.

Gregory replied, "Okay," as he climbed out of the bed and placed the water back on the side table. He walked into the bathroom and noticed that the floor was all wet. He closed the door and jumped into the shower. Gregory wasn't long washing himself and when he had finished, he dried himself and walked into the bedroom naked. Sonia was drying her hair with the hairdryer attached to the upper drawer in the cupboard. She was bent over with her hair down, flicking her hand through it, applying the dryer up and down. Gregory walked over and cuddled her from behind, dropping her towel.Sonia smiled and said, "Cheeky." Gregory caressed her breasts with both hands and then walked away. Sonia said, "You're a tease!" Gregory opened his suitcase and began to get dressed. Sonia finished drying her hair to the best that she could and also opened her suitcase. She pulled a dress, tights and underwear out. Gregory was dressed and already back sitting on the bed, changing the channel back to the Discovery Channel as Sonia had put on a music channel. She pulled on her knickers and tights and walked into the bathroom with her bra as she was putting it on. She proceeded to put on some makeup and brushed her hair with a detangling brush. She wasn't long, which made a change. She slipped into her dress and asked Gregory to zip the back. He sat to the edge of the bed and closed the zip. Sonia turned and faced him.

She said, "I am a little sore after this afternoon."

Gregory said, "Me too!"

Sonia said, "We will have to behave later."

Gregory said, "Maybe."

Sonia smiled and said, "I am looking forward to a drink. I don't feel hungry." Gregory agreed as he wasn't feeling hungry either. Sonia grabbed her handbag and coat and said, "I am ready." Gregory still had to put on his shoes so he switched off the television and Sonia opened the main door to the room. She stood leaned up against it as she waited for Gregory. She had already removed the card from the slot so the power went out as Gregory was lacing up his second shoe. He sighed as it wasn't the first time that Sonia had done this.

Sonia said, "Whoops, sorry," as she fumbled for the card in her bag. Gregory managed to tie the shoelace so he grabbed his coat and walked to her. She was so busy rummaging through her stuff that she didn't realise he was ready and standing beside her. She found the card and placed it back into the slot, then jumped as she noticed him beside her.

Gregory smiled and said, "One day you will not do that." Sonia pulled the card back out and handed it to him.

"You take the card, then," she said. Gregory took the card and placed it into his wallet. On the way to the lift, Gregory spoke to Sonia and they decided to just stay in the hotel and have a drink. This suited both of them. Sonia was feeling a little tired and Gregory was rested but didn't want to overdo it. They entered the reception area from the lift and walked towards the cocktail bar. Sonia pointed to a seating area in the corner and Gregory nodded his head as he followed her. They sat beside each other and Gregory placed his right hand on Sonia's leg as she looked at the bar menu.

"Oh, there are nibbles to order," Sonia said with excitement. She continued to look and read out the nibbles. Gregory just relaxed in the chair and listened. They had mini burgers and chips, and that's what Gregory felt like. Sonia chose the cheese plate but she couldn't eat the biscuits or bread.

She looked at Gregory and said, "What do you want?"

Gregory replied, "The burgers with chips and a Godfather."

Sonia smiled and said, "I'll have the cheese plate and a gin and tonic."

Gregory got off his chair and walked to the bar. He placed the order and was told that it would be brought to his table. He gave his room number and returned to Sonia. Sonia looked at him with surprise and said, "And where are the drinks?"

Gregory said, "They felt that you were underage so you have to produce ID."

Sonia sighed and said, "Are you being serious?"

Gregory said, "Yep."

Sonia grabbed her bag in frustration and walked towards the bar. She placed her bag on the bar stool and took her wallet out. The barman returned and asked, "What can I get you?"

Sonia offered her driving licence and said, "Here is my ID."

The barman stood confused and said, "Sorry ma'am, but I didn't request this."

Sonia turned to face Gregory, holding her ID, and said to the barman, "No problem, thank you." She walked back to Gregory. Gregory was laughing as he sat comfortably in his chair. Sonia walked up to him and said, "Any particular reason why you did that?" in a joking way, placing her driving licence back into her wallet.

Gregory said, "Yes, you looked too relaxed," as he laughed.

Sonia let out an *umm* sound and thought to herself, *We will see.* She sat back down beside him. Gregory lifted his arms for a cuddle but Sonia sat with her two hands clasped together between her legs. She just gave him a serious look and turned her head towards the bar.

Gregory smiled and said, "Ah, baby."

Sonia said, "Don't 'baby' me," as she waited for her drink. Sonia got off the seat and made her way to the toilet. Gregory watched her walk away. He watched how she gracefully moved in her high-heeled shoes as they clacked across the wooden floor. While he sat quietly in his own space, a gentleman approached the piano to his far right. He watched the man take some papers from his bag, place them on the holder and put his bag on the floor beside him. He pulled his stool closer to the piano and he sat for a moment before he lifted the cover to expose the piano keys. Placing both hands in front of him he began to play 'Music of the Night' from

Phantom of the Opera. As he played, Gregory was lifted within himself but he then felt an overwhelming sadness come over him. Gregory began to think about his great-grandmother Winifred and the happy times that they had had together. He thought about all the apple tarts that they had prepared and eaten together with ice-cream. He could feel himself getting emotional as the sensation moved into his heart area. He wished that he could have got to know more about her and her life, but he was too young back then to comprehend everything that was happening. He could only feel grateful to have had such a beautiful grandparent to show him the love that he experienced, even though he was oblivious to feeling with his defensive walls up.

The pianist started to play Pink Floyd's 'Comfortably Numb' as Sonia appeared in the distance. Gregory watched her walk towards him and he felt the sick feeling begin again in his stomach. He could feel the cold feeling down his left arm as Sonia sat beside him. She looked at Gregory and said, "Are you okay?" with concern.

Gregory replied, "Yes, I was just moved by the music; it's beautiful."

Sonia looked at him with surprise and said, "Wow, that's never happened before." Gregory placed his hand on her leg again. Sonia placed her hand on his and said, "I am concerned about you. It's been a really strange day."

Gregory replied, "Something is happening to me and I need to know more."

Sonia said, "Know more about what exactly?" as the barman arrived to the table with their drinks. He placed two coasters on the table and put the drinks down.

He said, "I will bring you food now," as he walked towards the dumbwaiter.

Sonia took her glass and said, "Cheers," looking into Gregory's eyes.

Gregory looked into hers and he felt her emotions. He was aware that she was worried that he would leave her. He said, "Cheers," and took a sip from his drink.

Sonia turned to him and said, "Are we okay?"

This gave Gregory confirmation of what he had felt and he was amazed. He realised that he could read people all through his life but he hadn't made the connection before as he was so flustered with his own personal events that it passed him. The pianist began to play Chopin's 'Spring Waltz' and Gregory felt his presence move over towards the piano to listen to the music. He felt himself being carried by the music as if he was getting lighter. Sonia was feeling the distance between them both so she took another drink from her glass. The food arrived to the table with cutlery, mayonnaise and ketchup. Gregory was aware of everything happening around him, but he focussed on the music.

Sonia looked at Gregory and said, "What's going on?"

Gregory lost his focus on the music and felt himself very present with Sonia. He said, "What do you mean?"

Sonia said, "Well, we are here together and you are more engrossed in the music and the old woman in the coffee shop."

Gregory laughed and said, "What are you talking about?"

Sonia took her knife and sliced a piece of cheese. She turned to him and said, "You are very strange since we got here," putting the piece of cheese into her mouth.

Gregory sat for a moment in silence and he thought to himself, *Do I need this right now?* He replied, "Can we just enjoy the break away?" and took another sip from his glass.

Sonia remained quiet and continued to eat some more cheese. She sat quietly, also staring at the pianist. Sonia felt annoyed that she couldn't relate to her emotions and that she was closing up. She drank some more as she was feeling pressure in her chest area. The heaviness of emotion came over her and tears began to emerge from her eyes. She sat still, staring towards the piano and looking into the emptiness surrounding her. The room became out of focus as her eyes welled up. Sonia got off the seat and walked to the restrooms without saying a word. Gregory knew that she was upset but didn't know why. Sonia pushed the toilet door open and burst into tears as she entered the room. She walked into one of the toilet cubicles and closed the door. There she closed the toilet seat and sat. She felt an overwhelming pressure move upwards towards her throat and she burst into tears. Her body struggled to function correctly as she stiffened up as the shock penetrated her. Still sitting, she continued to wipe the tears from her face as they cascaded down her cheeks. She felt hopeless and wanted her father. She just wanted to be held by her dad. She missed her father because they had had such a beautiful relationship and he had made her feel whole. Sonia sat in silence for a few moments as the emotions dissipated. She sat wiping her eyes and realised that she had forgotten her handbag. She had no makeup. She opened the cubicle door and walked to the mirror. She looked at herself and noticed how drawn she looked and the fact that she had lost weight over the last few days. She wet her fingers and wiped gently under her eyes with toilet paper to remove the eyeliner marks that had run down her cheeks. She was grateful that the bar lighting was dimmed so that nobody would notice that she had been crying.

Gregory was totally fixed on the music while waiting for Sonia to return. Several covers had been played and he was aware that she had been gone for some time. This wasn't new to Gregory, so he left her to her own devices. He knew that she needed her own space. The pianist began to play Queen's 'Bohemian Rhapsody' as Sonia returned from the toilet.

Gregory looked at Sonia as she was sitting down and he said, "Why are you emotional?"

Sonia replied as she took another drink from her glass. "I don't know." But she felt alone. She felt that nobody cared for her. She missed her father and the way that he would place her up on a pedestal. She felt wanted around him but couldn't fill that void with another man in her life. This frustrated Sonia. She took another drink from her glass. She looked at Gregory and said, "You don't have to worry about time. I am getting older and I would love a family and a house." She took another drink from her glass and sat waiting for a reply.

Sonia said, "Right," and drank some more.

Gregory said, "Can we not just enjoy each other's company and you let me make my own decisions and have my own feelings, without you telling me how I am and how I feel?" Sonia took another drink and got up again to go to the restroom. Gregory sighed and took a drink from his glass. He felt that he just wanted to leave the bar and go to the room but he knew this would create an even bigger issue. This was what he felt Sonia was heading towards and he knew that she always felt better in herself after she brought him down from a good feeling. Gregory couldn't understand why this always happened when the attention was on him. He decided to go to the bar and order another round of drinks. He stood at the bar and looked around at the other patrons sitting enjoying each other's company, and thought that it would be nice to be able to do this with Sonia.

The barman came over and asked Gregory, "What would you like, sir?"

Gregory replied, "The same as before, please."

The barman said, "On its way, please sit and I will bring it to you."

Gregory walked back to the table and sat listening to the music. He realised that Sonia was gone for some time yet again so he decided to walk towards the toilets. As he reached the toilet corridor, Sonia walked out. He noticed that she was on her phone as she looked startled as she realised it was him.

Sonia immediately said, "Are you okay?" holding her phone at the side of her bag as she kissed him on the lips.

Gregory realised that all of a sudden, her mood had changed and he felt the sick feeling again in his stomach. He said, "Yes, just going to the toilet. I have ordered another drink for us both."

Sonia said, "Great." As she made her way back to the table she placed her mobile back into her bag, trying to hide it so Gregory wouldn't see. He was very aware that she was on her phone secretly. This concerned him while urinating in the urinal while staring at the plastic mesh guard. He finished and washed his hands as he stood looking at himself in the mirror. He grabbed some of the paper towels positioned on the counter top and dried his hands, throwing the used paper in the bin. He stood for a moment and placed his focus towards his stomach, where he could feel a nervous feeling, a feeling of worry and frustration. He stood looking at himself in the mirror and fixed his hair as he opened the door to enter the bar area. As he walked towards Sonia, he could see that she sat without her phone, holding her glass and listening to the pianist play. As he approached her, she had lipstick on her teeth as she smiled at him. Gregory walked around the table and sat beside her.

He reached for his glass and Sonia said, "Cheers." The round of drinks had already arrived and Sonia had finished her first drink and had therefore started the new one. Gregory was still drinking the first one.

Gregory turned to Sonia and said, "Are you being truthful to me?"

Sonia swallowed and said, "What do you mean?" as she appeared unrelaxed.

He said, "You seem to always go on your phone and hide it, thinking I don't notice."

Sonia replied, "Don't be silly. I love you. I am a little worried where this is going."

Gregory replied, "Okay, it's just that you looked shocked when I bumped into you and you hid your phone from sight."

Sonia sat back in the seat and said, "What is wrong?" in an agitated, stern voice.

Gregory said, "Nothing is wrong. I guess I am tired of the way things always end up this way after a few drinks."

Sonia took another sip from her glass and said, "Let's just enjoy the evening," as she leaned against his shoulder. Gregory placed his arm around her and they sat quietly listening to the music. Sonia held her glass and continued to drink from time to time while Gregory relaxed. Sonia was in deep thought and he could feel that she wasn't herself. From time to time, he could hear her phone vibrate with receiving messages and this concerned him. He decided not to question her about it. He just wanted to relax and keep the peace between them. After all, they were flying back to London the next day.

Gregory took his glass and said, "Shall we get another drink and go to the room and relax, maybe watch a movie?" He finished the drink and placed the glass on the table. He had already had a full glass but Sonia was halfway through her second.

Sonia said, "I'll go get the drinks and pay." Gregory sat while Sonia walked to the bar. As she stood observing the room, the pianist began to play 'Wishing You Were Somehow Here Again' from *Phantom of the Opera*. Sonia could feel herself become emotional as she listened to the music. Each note resonated with her, making her feel pressure in her chest area. She began to feel her eyes well up and a tear ran down the right side of her face. She wiped it quickly so that no one would notice.

The barman walked towards her and asked, "What would you like, madam?" Sonia turned with surprise as she was totally engrossed in the music.

She swallowed and began to speak but her voice was weak, so she cleared her throat and said, "Sorry, I would like the same again," as she smiled. "I will pay also."

The barman said, "Yes, ma'am," as he prepared the drinks. Sonia turned to look at the pianist play the remainder of the song. She could feel a pull on her heart and therefore looked towards Gregory. He was staring at Sonia. She smiled and touched her lips with her right-hand fingers, blowing a kiss gesture to Gregory. He acknowledged by placing his right hand over his heart. Sonia stood feeling alone and she wondered what this was all about. The barman placed the two drinks on the counter and proceeded to enter the total into the card machine. Sonia took her card and placed it into the machine, entering her pin number when prompted. The barman took the receipt once printed, handed her both the card and receipt and said, "Have a lovely evening."

Sonia said, "Thank you, you too," as she took the drinks and walked to Gregory. Gregory stood up and took his drink. Sonia said, "Ready?" as she placed the drinks on the table and placed her card and receipt back in her wallet.

Gregory said, "Thank you." Sonia didn't hear so he repeated himself.

Sonia said, "You're welcome," as she stood with her handbag on her arm and her two glasses. Gregory reached and took his second and they made their way to the lift. Gregory pushed the button with his little finger as he continued to hold the glasses. Sonia placed her arms around Gregory and she kissed him. Gregory kissed her back and the lift door opened. They entered and he pressed the floor button. The doors closed and Sonia looked at him.

She stared and Gregory said, "What?"

Sonia said, "Nothing."

He laughed and said, "It's been a weird evening."

Sonia said, "What do you mean?"

He said, "Ah, it's not important," as the lift doors opened. Sonia walked out first and made her way to the bedroom door. She stood and waited for Gregory to place his drinks on the floor and pull his wallet out of his left-hand side jeans pocket. He took the room card and swiped the lock, opening the door. Sonia pushed the door and entered the room. Gregory placed the card in the slot and the lights turned on. He bent over and picked up his drinks, walked into the room and closed the door behind him. Sonia placed her drinks glasses on her bedside table. She pushed past Gregory to get into the bathroom and she closed the door behind her. Gregory undressed to his boxer shorts and jumped into bed, reaching over to Sonia's side to grab the remote control. He selected the options menu and began to scroll through the movie menu. Sonia walked out of the bathroom just as he started to scroll and she stood looking at the television.

Gregory said, "This one looks good," as he turned to look at Sonia. It was an action movie.

Sonia said, "Oh no, too much violence."

Gregory threw the remote onto the other side of the bed and said, "You look while I use the bathroom."

Sonia replied, "Okay," taking the remote while sitting down on the bed. Gregory closed the bathroom door and began to prepare his toothbrush with toothpaste. He switched on the cold tap and ran his brush under it for a second and placed it in his mouth. As he was brushing, staring at himself in the mirror, he thought about the bar and how Sonia had hid her mobile when they met in the corridor and how her mood had changed so quickly. He knew that she had panicked and that she had a worried look on her face. The feeling he had down his arm and the sick feeling in his stomach was the main concern for Gregory. He wondered what it all meant. Furthermore, he thought about the tour and how he felt internally. He finished brushing his teeth, rinsed his mouth out and washed the toothbrush. He wiped his mouth with the hand towel and used the toilet. Once finished, he washed his hands and stood looking at himself again in the mirror. This time he felt a little dizzy. The light-headedness came over him suddenly as he grabbed the countertop to keep upright. He felt his body sway slightly, as if he had stepped out of his own body. The feeling he had was similar to being very drunk, like the feeling you have if you laid down and you feel as though your body is spinning around. This feeling was like he had stepped out of his own body, as if he was looking at himself. His eyes became slightly blurry and the image of himself in the mirror began to appear older. This freaked him out a little and with the shock, he came back into himself suddenly. The dizziness dissipated and he could feel his legs become very heavy. His head felt very light and the cold feeling down his left arm became very obvious. He knew he wasn't alone. This intrigued him. He wanted to learn more and discover what was happening to him. He looked at himself once more and everything was normal, so he opened the door and entered the bedroom, switching off all the lights from the entrance hallway.

Sonia was already lying under the covers and watching the television. As Gregory walked over to the far side of the bed, he noticed Sonia's mobile phone blue LED light flashing to indicate that a message was received. Sonia was drinking from her glass when Gregory said, "You have a message on your phone."

Sonia turned her head to look at the phone and said, "Ah, probably an email or something." Gregory pulled back the sheets and climbed in beside Sonia. Sonia placed her glass on the side table and cuddled into Gregory. He put his right arm around her and they kissed. Sonia said, "I love you."

Gregory kissed her again and said, "I love you too."

Sonia lay back against her pillows and said, "I have chosen this movie, what do you think?" It was *Bridesmaids*.

Gregory replied, "Okay."

Sonia pressed the okay button on the remote and the movie started. They both cuddled into one another and watched. Sonia reached for her glass and drank some more. Gregory was feeling a little tired so he closed his eyes. It wasn't long until he fell asleep. Sonia noticed that he had fallen asleep nearly halfway through the movie. She continued to watch but her mind was busy thinking about life. She reached for her phone and looked at the messages. A message came from Philip so she read it. *Hi Sonia, would you like to hook up this week?* Sonia was flattered but knew that it would be risky. She didn't reply and closed her phone and placed it on aeroplane mode. Sonia continued to watch the movie and thought about Philip. She had had a lovely evening with Philip but didn't enjoy the sex too much, especially when she felt he was venting his frustration out. She was also concerned with the strange sickness she had. She drank some more and continued to watch the movie, allowing her mind to run free with her own ideas of how she would like to get married and the perfect venue. As she was thinking, she looked at Gregory as the light from the television reflected off his face. She noticed that his forehead was sweating so she pulled back the covers a little. She placed her hand on his forehead and she realised that he had a temperature. He was out cold in a deep sleep. She placed her hand under the cover and onto his chest. It was dripping with sweat. She pulled the covers off herself and Gregory, placed her glass down and went to the bathroom for a towel. She rinsed the hand towel under cold water and wiped his forehead. Gregory opened his eyes and mumbled a few words, then fell back asleep.

Sonia lay back against her pillows and stared at the television. The movie had just finished with the credits. She lay there as she knew that Gregory had caught the virus that she had. She was worried because they were to board a flight the next afternoon and she knew that she wouldn't have been able to the way she felt the first day with the virus. There again, she also had a hangover. She turned onto her side and watched Gregory sleep. The night was long for Gregory as he woke several times, soaking wet with sweat. He got out of bed and entered the bathroom several times to wipe himself down with a towel. As he was doing this, he was feeling very light-headed and nauseous. He woke before Sonia, around 6am, and lay beside her. He didn't have much energy and was very thirsty. He lay there thinking about drinking water but couldn't get focussed to actually move and open the bottle that was on the bedside table near him. He reached and touched Sonia on her side. It took a while for Sonia to register him and she turned around.

She said, "It's very warm in the bed. You are burning up." Gregory just watched her without saying anything. Sonia immediately went into work mode by checking his forehead and pulse. She remained silent as she calculated his heartbeat via his wrist and placed his arm back down, looking at him with a distant glare. She said, "Your pulse is very low, we need to get your temperature down." She jumped off the bed and fetched the paracetamol packet. She dropped two into her hand and grabbed the water beside Gregory. Holding the tablets and water, she faced Gregory and told him to take them. Gregory lifted his head and drank the water after putting the tablets in his mouth. He swallowed and dropped his head back down onto the pillow. Sonia went to the bathroom and fetched a hand towel that she had soaked in cold water and rinsed it. She positioned this on his forehead as he lay quietly. Sonia started to get worried as she was concerned now that Gregory had caught the virus that she had had. His symptoms appeared to be different to hers. She knew that she had to get his temperature down and ensure that he ate something prior to flying back to London. Gregory fell back asleep as Sonia was in the bathroom. She had taken her phone and began to look up the symptoms. She was getting frustrated while checking different sites on her phone and was feeling tired. She walked into the bedroom and climbed under the duvet beside Gregory. She lay looking at him sleeping on his back. She could see the sweat rolling down his forehead, so she took the towel and tapped it gently so as not to wake him. She took her phone and checked her messages. There was one from Philip. *Hey you, I hope you're well. Just checking in on you!* Sonia read the message and deleted it. She wasn't in the mood and was very concerned about Gregory. She continued to scroll through her messages and continued to delete threads. The light was very bright from her phone and Gregory began to move a little. Sonia placed her phone beside her and she continued to wipe his forehead with the towel.

Gregory opened his eyes and Sonia said, "Good morning, how are you feeling?"

Gregory said, "I feel better but very strange. I am sweating buckets."

Sonia said, "I know." Gregory wiped his forehead with his hand and rubbed it on the sheets. Sonia said, "It's 7.15am and if you like, I can go get you some breakfast."

Gregory said, "Okay."

Sonia said, "I will shower and go." She jumped off the bed and entered the bathroom. Gregory just lay quietly as he listened to the sound of the shower. It wasn't long before Sonia had finished and entered the room. She stood blow drying her hair with the hotel hairdryer attached to the drawer. Gregory turned his body to face the wall as he found the noise annoying. Once finished, she got dressed and walked over to him. He was asleep again so she kissed his forehead and left the room, allowing the bedroom door to slam behind her. Gregory jumped but continued to sleep as he was totally exhausted. Sonia made her way down to the breakfast area on the ground floor. Sonia stood in the queue as there were several other guests queuing for a table. As she waited, she was contemplating on what she would like to eat. She decided to look at the fruit section for herself and get porridge for Gregory. The guest service assistant asked Sonia what her room number was. Sonia gave the number and she was escorted to a table.

While walking behind the lady, Sonia asked, "Would it be possible that I take a few plates to our room as my partner isn't feeling well this morning?"

The assistant said, "Please help yourself and if we can help, please ask."

Sonia requested two coffees and walked to the breakfast display area. Sonia requested porridge for two from the woman behind the hot food section while she took a bowl and walked to the fruit area. There she filled her bowl with fruit and took a yogurt. She walked to the table and left the food waiting while she fetched a chocolate croissant for Gregory. The coffee was already sitting on the table and she wondered how she was going to get all the plates and drinks to the room. She walked to the waiter and requested help. He obliged and pulled over a trolley.

"Room 413, please," Sonia said as she and the gentleman placed the items on the trolley. Sonia walked slowly behind the man as he pushed the trolley towards the door, making his way to the lift. The other guests waiting in the queue watched as they passed and Sonia heard one say, "That's an idea." She smiled and felt good about herself. They both entered the lift and Sonia pressed the floor button.

The doors closed and Sonia said, "Thank you so much, I really appreciate this."

The gentleman said, "No problem at all." The lift stopped and the doors opened. Sonia walked ahead and made her way to the bedroom door as the man followed pushing the trolley. Everything banged against each other, making a clanking noise.

Sonia opened the door and held it open until the man pushed the front of the trolley inside. She then walked ahead and drew the curtains back slightly to allow light into the room. The man positioned the trolley beside the table as Sonia took items off it. They both transferred the food and cutlery onto the table. Sonia thanked the man again as he made his way to the bedroom door. He let himself out as Sonia poured herself a coffee. She took a sip as Gregory remained asleep. The coffee was lukewarm but she was happy with her achievement of getting breakfast to the room.

Sonia positioned the food on the table and the cutlery correctly before waking Gregory. She walked over to the bed so she was alongside Gregory and tapped him on the shoulder. He didn't move the first time so she tapped again. Gregory opened his eyes and jumped, with a shocked expression on his face. He lay on his back and looked at Sonia. Sonia said, "I got breakfast," pointing over to the table with a smile on her face. Gregory lifted his head and looked towards the table, but he hadn't fully focussed as his eyes were adjusting to the dimly lit room.

He said, "Okay."

Sonia said, "Good to know you're excited about it." Gregory sighed and looked at Sonia. Sonia walked to the table and sat down. She took her coffee and sipped some more as she watched Gregory lift himself out of the bed. He felt his body get cold very quickly as he stood. His tee-shirt and boxer shorts were damp. He pulled his tee-shirt off and walked to the bathroom. There he dried himself, feeling a little warmer. He placed his towel around him after he removed his boxer shorts and made his way to his suitcase. He placed his tee-shirt and boxer shorts on the floor and sat beside Sonia. Sonia sat and watched as Gregory was in his own world. She got off her chair and pulled the curtains back slightly. Gregory closed his eyes and opened them shortly after with a squint. He wasn't feeling well at all. Sonia adjusted the curtains to allow a little light in, just enough for them both to see the table. Gregory poured himself a coffee and drank some. He sat back in the chair and looked at the porridge. It had a skin already formed on the top as it had been sitting for a while. He didn't feel hungry at all.

Sonia reached for her handbag and took her paracetamol tablets out. She handed him two tablets and said, "Take these to keep your temperature down." Gregory took the tablets and swallowed them with another drink of his coffee. Sonia began to eat her fruit and yogurt mixed together while Gregory sat quietly staring at her. Sonia continued until she was finished and Gregory drank his coffee. He could feel his body starting to sweat again. Sonia placed her bowl back onto the tray and said, "I'll start to pack my clothes." She got off her chair and stood beside Gregory, bending over as she kissed him on the lips. "I hope you will feel better before we fly," Sonia said as she walked to the bathroom and closed the door.

Gregory looked at the croissant and he decided to eat it. He took a bite and he allowed the chocolate to melt in his mouth. He managed to eat as he continued to drink his coffee. Once finished, he pulled the duvet back over the bed and he lay on top of it. The bed on his side was damp from sweating all night. He lay on the bed with the taste of chocolate still in his mouth. He closed his eyes and allowed himself to drift off. It was 9.35am and they had a few hours to kill before making their way to the airport. Sonia entered the bedroom and sat on one of the chairs, scrolling through her mobile phone. She was restless and wanted to go outside and get some fresh air but was also concerned about Gregory. She got off her chair and left the bedroom to go to the reception desk. She decided to order a taxi to bring them to the airport for 12.30pm. Once ordered, she sat in the bar and ordered a cappuccino. Sonia sat for two hours scrolling through her phone, deleting messages and old emails that had accumulated since she purchased the phone. She also checked through her photos and was surprised to see that there was one of Philip and herself at the music venue they went to. She deleted this and also many other photos that she had taken of plates of food etc.

It was 11.30am and she decided to go back to the room and wake Gregory. When she entered the bedroom, Gregory was sitting up in the bed watching television. Sonia walked to the bed and said, "Why didn't you text me that you were up?"

Gregory replied, "I was letting you have your time alone."

Sonia walked closer and kissed him. She felt his forehead and said, "Your temperature is down. How you are feeling?"

Gregory said, "I'm much better. Still sweaty but better." Sonia then told him that she had ordered a taxi for 12.30pm at the reception. Gregory looked at the time on his watch and said, "Better make a move." It was 11.45am. He walked into the bathroom and closed the door. Sonia reached for the remote control and made herself comfortable lying on her side of the bed. She flicked through the channels until she found the music channel. She lay back and closed her eyes, placing the remote by her side. Gregory showered and decided not to shave. He was still feeling weak but relieved that the light-headed feeling was gone. He brushed his teeth and took his toiletry bag with him as he opened the door. As he walked into the bedroom, Cyndi Lauper's 'Girls Just Want To Have Fun' was playing. He noticed Sonia lying with her eyes closed as he pulled the curtains open. Sonia groaned and turned onto her side. Gregory opened his suitcase and placed his boxer shorts and tee-shirt from earlier into his bag with the other used clothes. He decided to wear a white tee-shirt and jeans as he was concerned that he might sweat again. He didn't want to wear a blue shirt that would show the sweat, especially passing through security at the airport. Gregory sat on the bedroom chair beside his suitcase and looked at the television. He was wishing that he was at home and not having to go to the airport.

It was 12.09pm as he looked at his watch. He turned towards Sonia and said, "We will need to get a move on."

Sonia lifted her head and said, "What time is it?"

Gregory said, "12.10pm."

Sonia replied. "Plenty of time."

Gregory looked at the floor and her suitcase. Everything was scattered all over the room. He thought it best to just remain silent. He got off the chair and fetched his mobile phone and the remote control for the television. He switched channels on the television and Sonia moaned. He then sat on the bed and flicked through his apps. He was feeling very tired and was planning on sleeping for the flight. At 12.20pm, he got off the bed and zipped his suitcase closed. He walked into the bathroom and took Sonia's shampoo and conditioner to her suitcase. He called her and said, "Okay, time to move."

Sonia lifted her head again and turned onto her back. She wiped her eyes and began to roll off the bed. When she stood, she said, "I have to brush my teeth." Gregory sat in the chair and waited as he watched Sonia prepare her stuff. Taking her toothbrush and toothpaste, she went into the bathroom and closed the door. Gregory felt a wave of light-headedness again and a sweaty feeling down his chest and back. He could also feel his forehead and hair line get hot. Sonia returned from the bathroom and knelt in front of her suitcase, squashing everything in.

She just piled in her clothes and items and squeezed the lid closed, zipping it shut. "Now I am ready," she said as she stood, proud of herself, putting on her coat. Gregory just observed and took his coat off the back of the chair and buttoned it up. He just wanted to get home. Sonia grabbed her suitcase and pulled it to the bedroom door, which she opened. Gregory followed as he looked back and made sure that they hadn't left anything behind. Once in the corridor, the door slammed behind him.

Sonia was already at the lift, waiting. Gregory stood beside Sonia and she placed both hands on each side of his face, looking into his eyes, and said, "I love your cheeky face," as she squeezed his cheeks and kissed his lips. Gregory just remained numb to the whole experience as he just wanted to be at home in bed. Sonia looked at the time on her phone and said, "Once at the airport you need to take two more tablets." Gregory nodded as they both entered the lift. There were several others standing in it so they had to squeeze in with their bags. Gregory began to sweat again as the lift descended and he felt uncomfortable. He kept wiping his forehead with his hand, sweeping his hair to the left. Sonia was aware that he was sweating as she watched his face become pale in complexion. She thought to herself that she just needed to get him through security at the airport and sitting down to rest as soon as possible.

They entered the hotel lobby area and there was a queue of people checking out. Sonia pointed to the reception seating area and told Gregory to go sit. Sonia stood and glanced through her mobile phone as she waited to be served. It wasn't long and the assistant checked the bill, mentioned that it was all paid in full and printed off a receipt. Sonia took the receipt and walked to Gregory. Gregory at this point had removed his coat and was sitting slumped in the seat. Sonia said, "Ready."

Just as she said this, a taxi driver said, "Sonia." She acknowledged the man as he took her suitcase. Gregory followed behind, pulling his as he held his coat. The taxi was parked right outside the main entrance door. Gregory placed his bag at the rear of the car as the man positioned Sonia's suitcase in the boot. Sonia was already sitting in the rear seat of the taxi, checking her mobile phone.

As Gregory got in, she said, "Do you have the boarding cards ready?" Gregory had forgotten to check in so he did this en route. Sonia sat looking out of the window in silence as they drove through the streets. Gregory finished checking in and he placed his phone in his coat pocket. Sonia took his hand as she cuddled into him. Gregory closed his eyes. He could feel that he was fading and that he just needed to get on the plane to sleep. Sonia was also concerned but said nothing. She reached for her bag and took the paracetamol out. She handed the packet to Gregory but didn't realise he had closed his eyes. She tapped his leg and handed them to him. Gregory placed them in his pocket with his phone. The taxi arrived at the airport terminal and Sonia paid the driver. Gregory got out and waited at the boot to retrieve the suitcases. The driver opened the boot and allowed Gregory to pull them out. Sonia stood and watched. They both said thank you and began walking towards the entrance doors. The doors rotated as people entered the building. Gregory and Sonia stood looking at the departure gate sign as they entered.

Sonia said, "What is the flight number?"

Gregory took his phone and opened the app. "BA2931," he said.

Sonia replied, "Found it; check-in area 21." They both turned and looked for the gate number. Sonia said, "This way," as she pulled her suitcase. Gregory followed, placing his phone back into his pocket. He could feel his body getting clammy as the terminal building was very warm. Sonia walked to the queue for check-in and Gregory stood beside her. He could feel himself getting sweaty as he stood beside the other travellers waiting in line. He was feeling more and more uncomfortable as they got closer to the check-in desk. Sonia said, "I can feel the heat radiating from you." She reached and placed her hand on his forehead. She said, "You're a little hot. Oh, we forgot to get water, and you need to take the tablets."

Gregory nodded and looked towards the check-in desk. There was a family of three and a couple ahead of them. Sonia hugged Gregory and said, "Once this is done we can go through security and find a seat to relax in."

Gregory replied, "Yes, I am looking forward to sleeping on the plane."

Sonia looked up to his eyes and smiled, kissing him on the lips. The family had finished checking in so they moved up the queue, waiting at the red line on the floor to be called. Gregory asked Sonia to take out the passports from her handbag and he took his phone from his pocket, opening the airline app. Just as he did this, Sonia began to walk to the free check-in desk. Gregory walked behind and placed his phone on the counter as Sonia put the passports down. The girl behind the desk asked for the final destination and if they had bags to check in. Sonia said, "London, with two bags." Gregory positioned Sonia's bag on the escalator and the weight showed 11.2kg. The girl printed off a tag and stuck the label on the handle. The bag moved down the escalator and Gregory placed his bag on it. His bag read 9.8kg. He stood waiting until his bag was tagged and Sonia was given the passports and boarding passes.

The girl said, "You need to go to gate 11. Enjoy your flight."

Sonia said, "Thank you," as they both walked away towards the security gate entrance.

Gregory was feeling weak and he needed to take the paracetamol. He said to Sonia, "I need some water."

Sonia replied, "Oh God, yes," as she stopped and looked for a shop. There was a shop at the front of the terminal. She said, "You wait here and I'll get the water." Gregory stood and watched Sonia walk towards the shop. Sonia took one small bottle of water as she knew that they couldn't take it through security. She paid for the water and walked towards Gregory. He was standing looking at the floor with his arms crossed.

Sonia handed him the water and he said, "Thank you." Gregory took two tablets and placed them in his mouth. Sonia watched as he drank some water.

She said, "That will take effect in about thirty minutes." Gregory handed Sonia the water and she drank some too. They walked towards the security area and Sonia placed the empty bottle in the bin. Sonia placed her handbag on the counter area to prepare her items before proceeding. Gregory moved his wallet and watch into his coat pockets. Sonia grabbed her handbag and placed it on her shoulder as they both walked to the boarding pass turnstile. Gregory opened the app and scanned it as he looked at the camera. The barrier opened and he walked through, handing Sonia his phone with her boarding pass highlighted. Sonia also scanned and walked through. They kissed as they walked to the queue for the X-ray area. Sonia placed her handbag and coat into a plastic bin while Gregory waited for a free space. She pushed it forward and the escalator took it to the X-ray. She walked over to the X-ray standing area and walked through. At this point Gregory got his plastic tray and he placed his items in it. He could feel his body sweating as he did this. He turned once he had pushed his tray onto the escalator and walked to the X-ray area. Once he got the all clear to walk, he proceeded through the gate. He was relieved that it didn't beep. Sonia was waiting for her tray to come out the other end so he stood beside her. She placed her arm around him and kissed his cheek. Gregory just watched each tray come down the escalator. It wasn't long before Sonia's tray arrived so she grabbed it and walked to an area to sort herself out. Gregory continued to wait for his as he watched other travellers walk through the security gate. His tray arrived and he removed his coat. He walked over to Sonia and they both left, walking towards the terminal area. Sonia said, "I'd love a coffee."

Gregory replied, "Okay, that sounds good." They both walked through duty-free and made their way to the coffee shop.

Sonia told Gregory to sit and asked, "What would you like?"

Gregory said, "A cappuccino and a muffin." Sonia knew he liked the blueberry muffin so she made her way to the counter area. Gregory found a table with two chairs. He sat and waited as he looked out the window at the aircraft parked. Some were taking on passengers and others were unloading. He was feeling sweaty again but just wanted to be on the aircraft so that he could try to sleep. Sonia walked over with the drinks and she sat opposite him. She placed the tray down and Gregory immediately noticed the blueberry muffin. He said, "Is that for me?"

Sonia replied, "Yes, it's not gluten free."

He said, "What will you have?"

Sonia reached into her handbag and pulled out some biscuits in a wrapper. "I'll have these," she said as she smiled, thinking that she was all marvellous, but Gregory wasn't impressed with how the wrapper looked. It was all tatty and he could only imagine that it had been bouncing around the handbag for some time. He took his blueberry muffin and thanked Sonia. He drank some coffee and sat back in his chair as he watched Sonia examine her biscuits as she took one out of the wrapper. She said, "Yep, that's okay," as she took a bite. Gregory smiled and ate some blueberry muffin. It wasn't long after that the gate number appeared on the TV screen. Gregory had finished his muffin and coffee and Sonia was halfway through her coffee.

Gregory jumped up and said, "Gate eleven," as he took his coat, waiting on Sonia.

Sonia sat and looked at him. "Are you in a hurry?" she said, while pointing at her coffee. Gregory sat back down and watched Sonia take another mouthful. He could feel his body sweating again as he wiped his forehead. Sonia said, "You're still sweating, aren't you?"

Gregory said, "Yes," in an awkward way as he was feeling uncomfortable.

Sonia took another quick drink as she stood up and said, "Right, I'm ready," looking at Gregory. He jumped up and followed Sonia out of the seating area and they both made their way to the gate. Gregory was feeling tired and he could feel his back was sweaty. He noticed that behind his knees, his underarms and his forehead were sweating also.

He said, "I need to get to the bathroom for a minute." Sonia looked at him and agreed as she noticed that he was very pale again. Gregory made his way into the gents' and Sonia waited outside, checking her mobile phone. She noticed a message from Philip and it read, *Hiya, I am feeling a little off today, not sure if I have what you had.* Sonia replied, *I am feeling much better but not 100%.* Just as she sent it, Gregory emerged from the gents' and he noticed that she placed her phone into her pocket quickly. He walked to her and said, "My back is dripping with sweat and I have dried it several times with toilet paper."

Sonia reached and placed her hand on his forehead. He stood still as she said, "You are hot again."

He replied, "Intelligent diagnosis indeed," as he stood back.

Sonia looked at him and said, "When we are on the plane you will be able to take two more tablets to reduce the fever."

Gregory turned towards the gate and started to walk. Sonia followed behind. They both reached the gate and Gregory took a seat after passing security control again. Sonia was just behind him, feeling his frustration. She remembered that she needed to reply to Philip. She was going to ask him what he thought the virus was. Sonia sat beside Gregory. She placed her handbag on her lap and gave Gregory two more tablets. She said, "Here is two pounds for the machine," and she pointed at the vending machine. "Get yourself some water."

Gregory just looked at her as he continued to feel uncomfortable while sweating. The last thing he wanted to do was to go over and get some water. He just wanted to be at home in his bed. Sonia tried to give him the money again but he refused and sat back, closing his eyes, with the tablets in his right hand. Sonia sighed and got off her seat, making her way to the vending machine. She looked and selected D4 and placed the money into the machine. Shortly after, a bottle of water dropped into the collection tray where she reached in to collect it. Gregory opened his eyes when he heard the clunk sound and he was happy that Sonia had gone over to get water. He really wasn't feeling well at all. Sonia sat beside him and dropped the water onto his lap.

Gregory said, "Thank you. I don't feel well at all." Sonia could see that he was grey again in complexion and she remembered how she had felt in Philip's flat. Sonia took Gregory's hand and he sat with his eyes closed after he drank some water and took his tablets. Sonia sat staring at all the other passengers as they began to queue, waiting beside the doors to the staircase that leads to the aircraft. It wasn't long to wait as the announcement came over the PA system letting them know that they were about to start boarding. Gregory opened his eyes and said, "Let's wait for the end of the queue before boarding." Sonia nodded in agreement, so he shut his eyes again. Sonia watched as the other passengers walked through the double doors and she nudged Gregory when the last passengers approached. Sonia stood with her handbag and Gregory got up slowly. Sonia linked her arm with his and they walked together to the stairs. Sonia could feel the heat from Gregory's body. He was sweating from his forehead again so he wiped it quickly with his right hand. They walked down the stairs and through the doors to the airfield, where they walked to the aircraft. They queued again at the aircraft stairs, with Gregory enjoying the cold air around him. Sonia wrapped her scarf around her neck.

Gregory began to climb the stairs first as he had the seat numbers on his mobile. Seat numbers 14A and 14B. He wanted to sit at the window so he could sleep and Sonia was happy enough with this. She had already decided that she would have a glass or two of wine. Gregory took his coat off and placed it in the overhead locker as Sonia was removing hers. He accidently banged Sonia on the head with his elbow and she said, "Ouch."

Gregory said, "Sorry," as he climbed into his seat.

Sonia followed, holding her head. She sat annoyed and Gregory could sense this. She said, "I can't believe you did that."

Gregory again said, "Sorry," but she kept going on about it. He closed his eyes and relaxed into his seat, leaning his head against the aircraft window. It wasn't long before he fell asleep. Sonia looked at him several times and spoke but there was no reaction from him so she left him alone. She took her earphones from her handbag and placed them in her ears, attaching the connection to her mobile phone. Once she had selected some music, she sat waiting for the aeroplane to taxi to the runway. Sonia was anxious to order a glass of wine. She couldn't stop thinking about the illness and what it was. Many thoughts passed through her mind until she felt a shudder from the aircraft. Shortly after, it started to move backwards. She was relieved that they were beginning their journey back home. She looked at Gregory asleep and glanced out of the window. She wondered what life was all about. She was feeling a little down in herself and wanted to just feel that life was going in her direction. She decided that she would try and improve her life focussing on her relationship and career. She wanted a family so badly that she was beginning to feel agitated again. She decided that she would book to get both their bloods checked as soon as she returned to London. This gave Sonia something to think about and plan. She felt a little better but also wanted a glass of white wine.

Just as she looked out of the window, the low-pitched sounder beeped throughout the aircraft and shortly after the aeroplane moved onto the runway. The aircraft stopped for a moment as the engines roared. Sonia looked at Gregory and he didn't flinch. The aircraft began to pick up momentum as it raced down the runway to lift off. Sonia felt her body press down as the aircraft began to ascend. She closed her eyes and leaned back into her seat. Gregory began to wake up, feeling all sweaty. He moved his head as it was feeling stiff due to the position that he was in. He adjusted his head and remained with his eyes closed. He sat up straight and took a moment to compose himself before opening his eyes. Just as he opened his eyes, the seat belt sign was switched off. Several passengers began to move from their seats to make their way to the toilets. Gregory watched as he was still in a daze. He turned and looked at Sonia with her eyes closed. He could hear the music screeching from her headphones. He placed his right hand on her leg and she opened her eyes with surprise, pulling the ear phone from her left ear.

"Oh, you're awake," Sonia said. "Yes, I feel worse, I need some water," Gregory said in a croaky voice. Sonia placed her hand on his and remained quiet. She was sad that he was feeling this way. She knew that he was struggling as she remembered her journey back to her flat after staying with Philip. She remembered that she didn't feel great either, with her mind just wanting to sleep as she had no energy. She knew that he was finding it difficult and was grateful that he didn't take out his frustration on her. Gregory just endured the feeling and remained calm. Sonia took the earphones out of her ears and she switched off the music on her phone.

She said, "Do you feel hungry?"

Gregory said, "No, I just want some water and to try to rest a bit more." He was feeling sweaty again; his back felt wet. Sonia squeezed his hand and looked towards the front of the plane as the air hostesses began to serve food and drinks. She noticed that his hand felt clammy. Gregory closed his eyes and leaned against the window surround again. Sonia sat and looked at the airline instruction sticker on the seat in front of her. She was finding it difficult to focus on, so she looked around the aircraft at all the people and what they were doing. Some were asleep, playing games, listening to music on their phone or watching a movie. The man beside Sonia was fast asleep with his mouth open. Sonia found this to be gross so she just ignored him. It wasn't long to wait until the air hostesses arrived beside Sonia. She ordered a still water for Gregory and two white wines for herself. She took her wallet from her handbag and scanned her debit card to pay.

Opening her table in front of her, she thought that she wouldn't wake Gregory. She placed the drinks on the table as she slid her handbag back onto the floor. She twisted a wine bottle open and poured the contents into the plastic cup provided. She screwed the bottle closed and placed the bottle back on the tray. Taking a sip from the cup, she allowed the taste to surround her mouth before she swallowed. She sat in a subdued way, looking at everyone in front of her on the plane. Sonia nudged Gregory and handed him his water bottle and plastic cup. Gregory opened his eyes and reached for them both.

He placed the plastic cup on his table and opened the water. As he poured it, he said, "Thank you. I am so looking forward to getting into bed."

Sonia raised her cup and said, "Cheers," as she drank, then looked at the man beside her with his mouth open. Gregory drank his water and placed the bottle and cup on Sonia's table, putting his in the upright position. He leaned against the window again and closed his eyes. Sonia was feeling strange again. There was a feeling of emptiness and she also felt lonely. Even though Gregory was beside her, she felt alone. This was a constant battle that Sonia would feel from time to time. It was a deep, immersed feeling that would make her feel lost within herself. There was a sensation of giving up on everything; an overwhelming feeling not to bother anymore. She could feel herself heavy in the seat as she drank some more. This caused internal frustration as she could feel her lack of confidence. She looked out the window to distract herself to try and avoid this sensation. She began to worry that she would be alone, that Gregory would leave her again and that she was getting too old to have children. This made her get upset again so she drank some more. It didn't take her long to drink the first small bottle of wine, so she poured the second into the clean plastic cup. She placed the earphones back into her ears and she played her playlist. She just wanted a distraction from her thoughts as she was feeling deflated. She sat listening to her music while taking sips from her wine.

The pilot announced over the PA system that there was fifteen minutes before landing. Sonia was surprised. She thought to herself, *Where did the time go?* She drank some more. Gregory was still asleep beside her. The air hostess passed collecting rubbish, so Sonia took the last mouthful of her wine and hand all the packaging to the girl. She closed her seat table and felt more relaxed and ready to get home. She was concerned for Gregory and felt that he would need to take the following day off work. The aircraft landed heavily, therefore Gregory lifted his head with shock. Sonia smiled and grabbed his hand.

Gregory sat up in his seat and mumbled, "Have we landed?"

Sonia said, "Yes, we are here. You slept for the whole flight."

Gregory sat quietly, waking up. He felt very groggy. Sonia handed him the water she had minded for him from her lap. He said, "Thank you," as he opened it and drank from the bottle. He was feeling very dehydrated and hot. He continued to drink the whole contents of the bottle, then placed the cap back on the bottle and handed it back to Sonia empty. Sonia took it in her hand without thinking. She then realised it was empty and said, "That's cheeky."

Gregory smiled and adjusted himself. His chest and back felt wet with sweat and he could feel it between his legs also. He was concerned about getting off the aircraft and getting home. He said to Sonia, "I feel soaking wet all over."

Sonia replied, "We will go straight to the toilet and you can sort yourself out." Gregory at this stage had his hand under his top, feeling how his chest was perspiring with sweat. He could feel the intensity of his heartbeat pounding. This was worrying him. He remained quiet and waited for the aircraft to come to a stop.

The seat belt sign was disengaged by the pilot and Gregory said to Sonia, "Let's wait a bit." Sonia just looked at him as she wanted to get off the plane. She could see that he was very uncomfortable and worried. The man beside Sonia stood up and opened the overhead locker, pulling his suitcase out. Sonia and Gregory remained seated until most people had left the aircraft.

Sonia said, "Okay, let's move," as she stood up. Gregory also stood, looking down at his seat, noticing that there was a wet mark left behind. He felt his jeans and they were damp. Sonia reached into the overhead locker to take her coat. Gregory put his on as soon as possible to hide his rear end from sight as he walked up the aisle behind Sonia. He was feeling very dizzy. Sonia was feeling quite good after the two bottles of wine. She thanked the air hostesses as she disembarked down the stairs. Gregory followed behind. When she reached the base of the stairs on the concrete, she said, "We will both go together and get a full blood test. I will organise it tomorrow." Gregory remained silent as he just wanted to get home. Sonia said, "Would you like me to come back to your place with you tonight?"

Gregory said, "Yes." Sonia had offered without thinking but realised that he wanted company. She also didn't want to be alone that evening.

She said, "Once back at yours, I will make something to eat and you will get straight into bed." Gregory agreed and walked beside her to the terminal building. They entered through the double doors and walked towards the baggage reclaim. Once they arrived at the baggage reclaim, Gregory continued towards the gents' toilets. Sonia also walked to the ladies', where there was a queue. She turned off aeroplane mode on her mobile and a text message was received. It was Philip. The message read, *Hiya. Do you want to meet during the week?* Sonia closed the app and placed the phone back into her coat pocket. She wasn't in the mood to reply to Philip and she was also worried about Gregory.

Gregory walked out of the gents' toilet and took a position between the other passengers waiting for the bags to appear on the baggage conveyor. Sonia walked out of the ladies' some ten minutes later. She walked up beside him and placed her arm around his back, cuddling into him. Gregory stood still while she kissed his head.

She looked into his eyes and said, "We need to get a few items in a shop before we get to your place."

Gregory agreed. He nodded and said, "Yes, we need milk."

Sonia replied, "Some chocolate and wine would also be nice."

Gregory just remained quiet as he wasn't in the mood for drinking. He just wanted to sleep. Sonia's suitcase appeared onto the conveyor belt and she watched it move slowly towards her. As soon as it arrived, Gregory reached for it and took it off the belt, standing it up straight in front of her. Sonia grabbed the handle and released the rail to allow her to pull it behind her. As soon as she completed this, she continued to look for Gregory's suitcase. Sonia spotted Gregory's suitcase and she got excited by grabbing his arm, gently pulling at it with a smile. "Here it comes, yay." Gregory was looking out the window at this point and turned his head to look. Once it arrived, he pulled it off the belt and they started to walk towards the exit. Sonia took the lead and Gregory followed. He was amused at how she managed to bump her case on every wall or door while passing through.

It wasn't long before they arrived at the Tube station platform. The train sign showed that the next train was in two minutes, therefore Sonia cuddled into Gregory. The platform was above ground and open to the elements and therefore it was very cold. Gregory was happy that his body could cool down. Sonia complained of how cold it was just as the train pulled up onto the platform. The doors opened and they both entered. Gregory lifted his suitcase while Sonia dragged hers on, bumping it over the step to board. Gregory just looked behind him as he heard the thump noise. She stood beside him with a smile and held the handrail. Gregory just stared at her.

Sonia moved closer to him and said, "I think you should call in sick tomorrow." Gregory agreed as he wasn't feeling too good. She said, "I am on nights so we don't have to get up early." This was a relief for Gregory. She also said, "I will book blood tests in the morning." Gregory also agreed by nodding his head as he didn't want to have this conversation on the Tube. Sonia turned and watched the train arrive at the next station. She went into her own world, thinking about where they would go to have blood tests. She was also thinking about Philip's text earlier and that she had to reply.

The train continued between each stop until they arrived at their station and changed platforms. Sonia got off first, dragging her suitcase behind her, making her way to the next platform. Gregory followed, carrying his. He was a few people behind her but eventually caught up to her. She stood at the yellow line awaiting their next train. Gregory stood behind her as there were already other passengers standing in line. At this stage, Gregory was sweating down his back again and he could feel his chest was also wet. He wiped his forehead quickly, fixing his fringe to the left. The train pulled up and Sonia pushed on first, dragging her bag. She never waited for the passengers to get off and Gregory noticed the frustration of one woman who wasn't amused. Gregory waited his turn and climbed on board. He was standing on the opposite side of the carriage to Sonia but they both made eye contact.

The carriage was full and very hot. At each stop, the passengers reduced in number and therefore the temperature also dropped. Gregory just wanted to get home. He was pretty fed up at this stage. Sonia walked over to him at the second to last stop. She said, "You have gone pale again." Gregory just looked at her with no response. Sonia knew that he wasn't happy. The train pulled up to their platform and Sonia jumped off, pulling her bag behind her with a clump. Gregory carried his suitcase off the train, placed it onto the platform and extended the handle so that he could pull it behind him. Sonia had already walked to the escalator and stepped on to ascend to the ground level. Gregory took his time as he let the other passengers leave the platform to exit. When he reached ground level, Sonia was standing on the entrance side of the barriers, waiting. He walked to the barrier and offered his card to the reader. As he walked through the barrier, Sonia said, "Let's go to the shop to get some snacks." Gregory agreed and walked behind Sonia as she took off out onto the footpath, dragging her suitcase behind her.

Gregory followed and entered the shop. He couldn't see Sonia when he entered so he stood at the doorway. Sonia appeared from one of the aisles, holding several items under her arm as she pulled her suitcase to Gregory. She left it beside him and said, "Just have to get milk and we can go."

Gregory said, "Okay, I'll wait here with the suitcases." Sonia just walked away, focussed on what she needed to do. Gregory stood watching people enter and leave the shop as he felt the heat from the heater positioned above the main entrance door. He just wanted to get home and go to sleep. Sonia walked towards him with a bag so Gregory turned both suitcases and walked out the door. Sonia followed and Gregory offered to take the bag.

Sonia said, "It's only up the road, I'll manage." Gregory said nothing and just followed behind, navigating around lighting and parking poles and the odd uneven surface for the suitcases to travel over. Sonia walked to the front door and waited for Gregory to organise and lift both suitcases from the path over the step to the front door. He placed both in the porch and took his keys from his pocket.

Opening the door, he said, "I'm just going to go to bed," switching off the alarm.

Sonia replied, "Do you not want food? I have just bought something light and it will be ready in no time."

Gregory said, "I'll go up and lie down."

Sonia said, "Okay," as she took her suitcase from Gregory. He walked up the stairs after taking off his shoes, carrying his suitcase.

He said, "I'll come down for your suitcase."

Sonia said, "I'll leave it here," as she walked into the kitchen, switching on the light. She placed the bag of groceries on the countertop and switched on the kettle. She unpacked the bag, placed the milk in the fridge and began to prepare some food. It didn't take long to cook in the frying pan as she helped herself to a bottle of white wine. Drinking while stirring the food, she was thinking about what it would be like if they both lived together. She switched off the gas burner and left the food to simmer in the pan. She took another drink before leaving to make her way up to see Gregory. As she entered the hallway, she noticed that he had forgotten to collect her suitcase and take it upstairs. She grabbed the handle and dragged it up the stairs step by step.

She entered the bedroom and Gregory was fast asleep. All the lights were left on and she noticed he was wearing a hooded top. She placed her suitcase beside the chair and left the bedroom, switching off the light. On her way down to the kitchen she remembered about the text from Philip. Sitting in the kitchen on a stool, Sonia took her mobile from her coat pocket and began to check her phone. She stopped for a moment, lifting her head and just glancing around the room while thinking about the text from Philip. She decided not to reply back and began to think about Gregory in bed, sleeping. She placed her phone on the countertop and took a drink from her wine while sitting looking out the window, holding the glass. She reminisced on the memories they had together and she wondered why she wasn't married and with children. She looked around Gregory's home and thought to herself, *Why aren't we living together?* Sonia drank some more wine and topped up her glass. She got off the stool and opened the cupboard to take a plate. She got some cutlery from the drawer and scooped some food from the pan onto her plate. She left some for Gregory in case he woke up. Sonia walked to the dining room table, holding her plate and glass in both hands. She sat for a moment, taking another drink from her glass. She felt lonely while looking at her reflection in the glass door. She took some food onto her fork with her right hand and placed it into her mouth. As she did this, she knew that she wasn't in the mood for eating. She chewed and continued to think about what life would be like being married and if she had a child of her own. She drank some more and felt frustrated because the breakup flashed in her mind. She remembered the time Gregory finished the relationship with her. She knew that things between them weren't good but was willing to stick with him. He walked away and this really affected her. She never got over the heartbreak. She drank some more and wondered how he was doing. She sipped from her glass and placed it back on the table and made her way to Gregory. On her way up the stairs she decided that first thing in the morning, she would book an appointment for them both to get their bloods checked. She thought that maybe they were run down. She entered the room and Gregory was in the same position. As her eyes adjusted, she noticed that he was sweating again. She walked over and sat on the bed beside him. As her weight adjusted the mattress, Gregory opened his eyes.

He lay dazed and Sonia said, "Oh, you're awake."

Gregory said, "How long have you been here?"

Sonia said, "A little while. I was watching you sleep." He took his hand out from under the cover and reached out towards her. Sonia took his hand in hers.

He said, "What time is it?"

Sonia said, "About 8.15. I don't have my phone."

Gregory replied, "I'll get up for a while. I am hot."Sonia said, "I have cooked food." Gregory began to move towards the side of the bed, pushing the duvet off him. He wiped his forehead with his hand while he sat at the edge of the bed. He was feeling dizzy. Sonia sat beside him on the edge of the bed. She leaned her head against his and said, "I miss cuddles." Gregory placed his arm around her and he kissed her head. Sonia leaned closer and held him tightly. They remained embraced for a few minutes until Gregory announced that he had to pee. Sonia got up and said, "Go then," walking out the door and making her way back downstairs. Gregory walked into the bathroom, switching on the light. He looked at himself in the mirror and removed his pullover. His tee-shirt was damp so he removed this also. He could feel the cold air surround his body and this made him shiver as he used the toilet. He flushed the toilet and washed his hands, then he grabbed a towel and dried his body. Keeping the, towel around his shoulders, he walked into the bedroom to fetch a clean dry top from his wardrobe, using the light from the bathroom to see what he was doing. As he put on his tee-shirt, he could hear that Sonia had switched on the television. He grabbed a jumper with tracksuit bottoms and put these on too. He switched off the bathroom light and took the towel with him downstairs. He walked into the kitchen to smell the food cooked by Sonia earlier. He could smell the garlic and spice sauce that she used. He opened the door to the utility room and threw the towel into the washing machine. He closed the utility door and walked back into the dining area as Sonia was flicking through the channels.

He asked, "What are we watching?" Sonia ignored him as she took a drink from her glass. She had her food positioned beside her on the couch.

She said, "There is food in the pan, just heat it." Gregory decided not to say anything as he could feel the tension. He walked to the kitchen and grabbed a bowl from the cupboard. He scooped some food from the pan and placed it into the bowl. He opened the microwave door, put it in and switched it on for three minutes, then watched the bowl spin around in front of him. Sonia glanced over and said, "I see you're more interested in watching the microwave than me."

Gregory looked up to the ceiling and thought to himself, *God, here we go again.* The microwave beeped as the timer finished and he took the bowl out, being careful not to burn himself. The food was piping hot. He placed the bowl down quickly onto the countertop as he took a table cloth from the cupboard. Sonia found a movie and she said, "This movie is starting now; do you want to watch it?"

Gregory replied, "Yes, coming." She turned up the volume as he made his way over to her, holding the bowl with the tea towel. Gregory sat beside Sonia and he began to eat very small amounts as the food was hot. Sonia began to get agitated as he was eating because she could hear his fork touch his teeth and he would release air from his mouth as he allowed the food to cool. Sonia got off the couch and sat on the chair next to the lamp. Gregory just looked at her as she began to focus on the television. He continued to eat and every so often Sonia would turn her head to look at him. He knew that she was annoyed but he continued to eat.

It wasn't long after he finished that Sonia said, "About time."

Gregory laughed and said, "Really?" Sonia sighed as she drank some wine. He then said, "Do I not get any more cuddles?" Sonia took another drink from her glass and Gregory made his way to the kitchen. He turned on the hot water tap and began to wash his bowl and cutlery. He dried them with a dish cloth and placed them back into the cupboard and drawer. He continued to watch the television as Sonia had raised the volume so that she couldn't hear him cleaning up. This suited Gregory because he could also continue to enjoy the movie.

He called Sonia. "Do you want some more wine?"

This got her attention as she said "Yes, please," and raised her glass, looking in his direction. Gregory took the remainder of the bottle to her and he poured, refilling her glass. Sonia got up and kissed him, then she climbed back onto the couch. She tapped the couch with her hand and said, "Are you sitting?" Gregory was still standing holding the bottle of wine.

He said, "In a minute," as he walked past her to the kitchen. He took a bottle of whiskey and poured himself a glass. Sonia looked over her shoulder and it made her happy that he was joining her for a drink. She reached over and pulled the blanket over herself and waited for Gregory to join her.

As he sat, Sonia said, "This is what I like," placing some of the blanket on his legs. He said, "Cheers," and Sonia clanked her glass against his saying, "Cheers," as she took a drink. They both sat comfortably on the couch watching the television. Sonia rewound the movie and played it again. It wasn't long after the movie had started that Sonia fell asleep. She managed to hold her glass steady while sleeping even though there wasn't much wine left in her glass. Gregory continued to sip his whiskey while he watched the movie until the end. As soon as it finished, he took the blanket off himself and gently pulled it off Sonia. As soon as he began doing this, Sonia opened her eyes and said, "I enjoyed that movie." She drank the remainder of her wine and got up off the couch. As she did this, she said while standing, "Oh, I feel dizzy." Gregory continued to tidy the room after he switched off the television. Sonia walked to the kitchen and rinsed her glass, leaving it upside down on the draining tray. Gregory also washed his while Sonia made her way to the bedroom. Gregory poured two glasses of water into fresh, clean glasses and he made his way upstairs, switching on the alarm and turning off the lights behind him.

As he reached the stairs, Sonia appeared on the landing. "I forgot water," she said, noticing that Gregory had two glasses. She said, "Ah, thank you," while she waited for him to reach the top. There she kissed him on the lips and took a glass from him. Gregory just followed her into the room, switching off the landing lights. Sonia had climbed into bed and was on her phone as he entered. She said, "Just turning off my alarm for tomorrow."

Gregory replied, "Yes, I have to do the same." He entered the bathroom and closed the door. Sonia scrolled through her apps while Gregory was brushing his teeth. As Gregory opened the door, she quickly closed her apps and entered Google. There she began to type 'Blood tests near me'. Gregory said, "I will set my alarm for 8am so that I can call in sick." Sonia agreed by nodding her head. She continued to search for a surgery near them. She found one that was in London but wasn't near them.

She said, "I have found a place to get our bloods checked. I will call them in the morning and book us both in." Gregory was undressing while Sonia was talking.

Gregory said, "Okay, is it a full medical exam?"

Sonia looked and said, "They have different options. Would you like a full medical?"

Gregory said, "Nah, just the bloods," as he was getting under the duvet.

Sonia placed her phone by her side and she cuddled into him. Gregory pulled his arm up and Sonia moved to allow him to place it under her. He pulled her closer to his body and she shuffled to get comfortable. As they looked at each other, Sonia said, "I love you."

Gregory looked into her eyes and he said, "I love you too." They both kissed and Sonia squeezed herself against his body as she exhaled. Gregory closed his eyes while lying on his back, enjoying the embrace. He could feel that Sonia was getting very hot around her chest area as he could feel the energy on his right-hand side. She placed her right hand on his chest and began to play with his chest hair. She gently ran her fingers through the hairs while touching his skin. Every so often, she would gently scrape with her nail when she would feel a black head. Gregory opened his mouth and said, "Grooming time, is it?"

Sonia laughed with a, "Haw haw," placing her hand flat on his chest. She lay looking at his face and said, "I like this."

Gregory said, "Like what?"

Sonia replied, "Feeling safe with you; you make me feel safe." Gregory turned his head facing into her and they looked into one another's eyes. Sonia pulled her left hand from under her pillow and placed her hands on each side of his face. She moved her lips closer to his and allowed hers to touch his softly, gently kissing. Gregory closed his eyes and he felt the moist, warm sensation as she parted, exhaling her breath. He opened his eyes and Sonia smiled, staring into his.

She said, "I am falling in love with you again. It's like each time we meet I fall in love with you."

Gregory remained quiet as he looked into her eyes. He could tell that she was waiting for a reply. He said, "We need to book the Thailand trip." Sonia sighed and pulled herself away from him. She lay on her back and stared at the ceiling. Gregory said, "What's wrong?"

Sonia said, "Nothing," as she felt for her mobile phone on the bed. Gregory turned his body in her direction, clenching his pillow with his right arm under his head. Sonia continued on her phone as he remained looking at her.

He said, "Do I not get any more cuddles?" Sonia ignored his comment and continued to scan the internet looking at new boots. He said, "You have gone funny."

Sonia looked at him and said, "I was enjoying feeling you and I told you something personal, and then you mention Thailand; it's like you don't care."

Gregory swallowed and thought to himself, *Here we go.* He replied, "Sonia, I love you too, I was just mentioning booking Thailand. Do we need to do this before we sleep again?"

Sonia said, "Do what again?"

Gregory said, "This, what is happening, drama."

Sonia placed her phone down and turned to Gregory. "Kiss me and make me feel it."

Gregory wasn't in the mood as he felt the frustration from Sonia and now he knew that he had to kiss her or have an issue all night. He lifted himself up off his pillow and stretched over to her. He hovered over her face while looking into her eyes. Sonia had a sad face, so he licked the top of her nose and around her nostrils. Sonia quickly pushed him away, turning her head to her right side, bursting out, "Ewwwww." Gregory rolled off the bed onto the floor as he couldn't contain the laughter.

Sonia wasn't finding this funny at all. She jumped from the bed and walked to the bathroom. Gregory climbed back onto the bed as he rubbed his eyes dry. Sonia closed the door and he could hear her wash her face. Several minutes passed and Sonia emerged from the bathroom as Gregory was looking at his mobile. She switched off the light and said, while making her way to the bed and climbing in, "That was disgusting, I can still smell your whiskey garlic breath."

Gregory laughed and reached towards her, saying in a baby voice, "Cuddles, give us a cuddle," curling up his face, trying to look cute.

Sonia looked at him and said, "You need help," as she fixed the duvet around her. Gregory lay back and looked at the ceiling. They both lay in silence for about five minutes until Sonia said, "A cuddle would be nice." Gregory was falling asleep at this stage so her words registered but his body was slowly unwinding. He turned his head and looked in her direction as the bedside table lamp was still on. "Come here then," he said.

Sonia grunted, "Why do I always have to?" Gregory sighed and moved towards her. They embraced and remained there until both of them fell asleep.

The next morning, Gregory woke at just after 6am. He turned away from Sonia and looked at his phone. He closed his eyes and fell back asleep. Sonia noticed that he moved away from her so she cuddled back into him. He was in the foetal position, so she cuddled into his back. They both fell asleep again until Gregory's alarm sounded at 8am. Sonia pulled herself away from him and she lay on her back. Gregory took his phone and switched off the alarm. He opened his phone and called his boss. There was no answer so he left a message: "Hi Paul, it's Gregory. I am sorry but I have picked up some virus and have been sick for the holiday break away. I won't make work today." He hung up the call and placed the phone back. He cuddled into Sonia, squeezing his right arm under her body. Sonia shuffled to allow him to do this. He placed his left hand under her tee-shirt and placed it on her right breast as he cuddled into her. She placed her hand on his and they both remained sleeping. They both slept until after 11am. Sonia woke as she needed to use the toilet. She took Gregory's hand and slowly moved out of the bed. Gregory woke and turned over onto his back. Sonia walked to the bathroom and closed the door. Gregory opened his eyes and remained on his back. He waited for Sonia to come back into the bedroom.

She opened the door and he said, "A coffee would be lovely."

Sonia said, "Really, am I your slave?" Gregory smiled as she climbed in beside him. He could feel that her body was bare and that she had removed her underwear. Sonia climbed on top of him and she lay there.

Gregory said, "What are you doing?"

Sonia reached under her and grabbed his penis, saying, "What do you think I am doing?" Gregory jumped with shock as he wasn't expecting this but he enjoyed it. He grabbed her bottom with both his hands and squeezed it, pushing her down on him. Sonia smiled and said, "Ermmmm, are we excited?" Gregory smiled and Sonia kissed him. She jumped up, sitting on top of him and said, "You are sick so maybe we shouldn't."

Gregory said, "I feel great." Sonia got off and walked naked to the bedroom door, exiting to the landing. Gregory said, "Hello?" but there was no reply.

Sonia went down to the hallway and switched off the alarm, entering the kitchen. She was feeling the cold but continued to fill and boil the kettle. She stood shivering and then walked to the couch to take the blanket. She waited for the kettle and prepared two mugs of coffee. Fixing the blanket over her shoulders and leaving it to hang, she took the two mugs, making her way up the stairs. Sonia managed to spill some several times but used her right foot to rub it into the carpet. She entered the bedroom and Gregory was asleep again. She placed the two mugs on her side of the bed and jumped on top of Gregory. He got the shock of his life, pushing Sonia onto the floor with haste. Sonia hit the floor with a wallop and she remained there as she hit her head as she fell backwards.

Gregory sat up quickly and said, "Why did you do that?" Sonia remained, holding her head. He realised that she had hurt herself so he rushed over to her. He lifted her up and pulled back the duvet. Sonia pushed him away and she walked into the bathroom. Gregory also got up and he walked around the bed to fetch his coffee. He said out loud so Sonia could hear, "Thank you for the coffee." There was no reply. He sat up in the bed and waited for Sonia to return as he drank his coffee. She came back into the room and he said, "Thank you for the coffee."

Sonia said, "Okay," as she took hers and also sat in the bed.

Gregory asked, "Are you okay?"

Sonia said, "I hit my head off the skirting board."

Gregory laughed and said, "You scared the shite out of me. I was in a deep sleep."

Sonia drank her coffee and she said, "Sorry."

Gregory replied, "Don't be sorry." They both sat in silence as they enjoyed drinking. Gregory then said, "We must look at Thailand today since we are together."

Sonia looked at him and said, "Yes, that would be nice." She took her mobile and opened Google to get the clinic's telephone number. She called the number and spoke to the receptionist. She managed to get a cancelled appointment for the same evening, so she booked them both for 5.45pm. Gregory sighed as he just wanted to relax for the day. He wasn't in the mood to go out later that evening. Sonia felt all smug after the call and she said, "All sorted. I am amazing," as she drank the last of her coffee. Gregory remained quiet. "Now to sort out Thailand," Sonia piped up as she walked back onto the landing, naked. This time she forgot the blanket that she had brought up from the couch. Halfway down the stairs, she remembered as she felt the chill on her body. She walked back into the room and took the blanket from the floor beside Gregory.

He quickly jumped up and grabbed her, pulling her back on top of him in the bed. He covered her under the duvet and said, "Stay here for a little bit." Sonia relaxed and they both cuddled into one another.

Sonia said, "What would you like for breakfast?"

Gregory replied, "Porridge and toast."

Sonia said, "Okay, I will go to the kitchen." She pulled herself away from him and grabbed her tee-shirt from the bathroom. She placed it on and threw the blanket over herself. She walked down to the kitchen with her mobile phone. Gregory also got up out of the bed and he entered the bathroom. While organising the breakfast, Sonia began to think about Thailand and how nice it would be to feel the sun. She was also feeling good about her relationship with Gregory. She took her phone and typed in the search engine on her phone, 'Thailand holidays'. Several items appeared just as Gregory entered.

He said, "I am feeling much better today." He noticed that Sonia had no underwear on as he walked up beside her. He said as he placed his hand on her bottom, "I love the new you." Sonia smiled and they kissed. Sonia showed him her phone with the Thailand pictures. He said, "Let's try to book something today."

Sonia got excited and said, "That would be great, something to look forward to." Gregory boiled the kettle again while Sonia continued with the porridge. He made two mugs of coffee after rinsing out the mugs he had carried down from the bedroom while Sonia made the porridge. She preferred to prepare it in a pot rather than the microwave oven. She stood over the pot, stirring it, while looking at her phone for places to see in Thailand. Gregory took some bread from the freezer and placed it into the toaster. He stood and watched Sonia, half-naked, looking at her phone. He was beginning to feel a little aroused but knew that Sonia wasn't in the best of form, so he remained watching the toast. Sonia continued to stir the porridge until she felt it was right for her. She poured two bowls and placed the pot into the sink, turning off the gas hob. She filled the pot with water from the kettle and squirted some washing-up liquid in also.

Gregory said, "Wow, you are becoming domesticated."

Sonia replied, "What do you mean?"

Gregory knew to tread carefully. He said, "Thank you for helping, that's all."

Sonia took two bowls and spoons from the drawer and she made her way to the dining area. Gregory's toast popped up so he took the butter from the fridge and buttered it. Sonia sat scooping a little bit of porridge each time onto her spoon and placing it into her mouth. Gregory walked over and sat beside her. He placed his hand on her leg and said, "It's dangerous you being like this."

Sonia replied, "Like what?" in a slight mood.

Gregory said, "Half naked." Sonia relaxed a little and smiled. She was expecting him to say something else.

She opened her legs and said, "Do you like your porridge?"

Gregory looked and said, "I have lost my appetite all of a sudden, my mind has just been distracted."

Sonia said, "Really?" as she closed her legs and continued to eat hers.

Gregory felt a hot sensation over his body as he continued to eat. He said, "What hotels have you found?"

Sonia replied, "I'm looking around Chiang Mai."

Gregory said, "I will look in a little bit with the laptop." Sonia found a cooking course and places to see while there. She was getting really excited as she continued to look. Gregory finished his porridge and stood beside Sonia, kissing her on the forehead before making his way to the kitchen.

Sonia said, "A coffee would be nice," as she held her mug up. Gregory turned back and took her mug with his. He placed his bowl in the sink and refilled the kettle, switching it on. Sonia said, "You haven't eaten your toast."

Gregory replied, "I don't feel up to it."

She said, "I thought you said that you were feeling much better?"

He said, "Yes I was, but my body is still strange."

Sonia remained quiet and scrolled through hotels in Chiang Mai. She managed to find a hotel with a spa so she saved this and continued to look. Gregory made coffee for them both after he washed the pot and cutlery. Sonia walked over with her bowl and she placed it beside him on the countertop. She said, "Thank you," as she took her coffee with her, walking to the couch. Sitting down, she could feel the cold on her bottom as the leather touched her skin. She adjusted the blanket and wrapped it tightly around her body. Gregory walked over after drying up and putting the pot, bowls and cutlery away. He grabbed his laptop off the dining room table with the power lead and placed it beside Sonia. Once he had plugged it in, he sat beside her and switched on the laptop, entering his passcode.

Sonia sat holding her mug with both hands. She said, "It is cold this morning."

Gregory put down the laptop and he switched on the heating via the thermostat on the wall. He said, "It will be warmer in about thirty minutes or so," as he sat back down beside her. He opened Google and began to search for holidays in Chiang Mai. Between them both, they managed to find a flight and a hotel for December, over the Christmas break. Sonia was really excited and Gregory decided to book it. He paid via his credit card while Sonia went to the bathroom. When Sonia returned, he said, "I have booked it. You had better get your swimming outfit ready."

Sonia was shocked and said, "Yeah right." Gregory turned his laptop to face her and it stated 'confirmed' at the top of the page. Sonia said, "Oh my God, I am so excited!" as she jumped up and down. "We are going to Thailand."

Gregory laughed and said, "Yes, we are."

Sonia grabbed him and kissed his lips. She said, "I will pay my end, let me know how much."

Gregory said, "No worries," as they hugged.

Sonia then said, "I need to have a rest. Shall we go upstairs and rest a little?" Gregory agreed and they both went back up to the bedroom. Sonia went straight to the bathroom and Gregory jumped under the covers. The bed was still warm so he cuddled into the duvet. Sonia was so excited and happy that she just smiled at herself in the mirror as she looked at herself while washing her hands. She felt that she was appreciated and happy that she had something planned with Gregory as she was worried that she was going to lose him. She feared that he would find out about her affairs and that he would dump her. This feeling was electric and Sonia was feeling alive again. She removed her tee-shirt and washed her face. She brushed her teeth and opened the door. She stood leaning against the door architrave and said, "Do you want this?" as she gestured towards her body, waving her hand.

Gregory looked up from his phone and said, "Oh yes," as Sonia walked over, all sexy, with a smile. She reached the edge of the bed.

"How would you like me?" she said as Gregory pulled off his boxer shorts under the duvet. Sonia grabbed his tee-shirt and pulled it off as he was throwing his boxers onto the floor. She threw his tee-shirt in the same direction. She pulled the duvet off him and sat over his groin area. She said, "I am so wet already," as she took his penis and placed it inside her. "Slowly," she said as Gregory got excited and tried to enter fully, lifting his body towards hers. Sonia took control and she leaned forward, holding both his hands as they clasped fingers. "I can really feel you, but you need to get a condom."

Gregory said, "Oh fuck, I forgot," as he pulled away. Sonia moved herself to his side as Gregory walked to the wardrobe. He took a condom, ripped open the wrapper with his teeth and placed it on as he watched Sonia touch herself.

She said, "God, I am so wet."

Gregory said, "Turn around and bend over." Sonia did this and Gregory put saliva on his hand and rubbed the condom. He positioned himself behind her and she guided him inside her. Sonia felt as though his penis had entered her stomach. She could feel the heat and the amazing sensation all over her body. She was so aroused that her chest began to get very hot. Gregory just remained fully inside her and Sonia could feel the pulsation of his penis.

She said, "You are getting bigger," as she dropped her head on the bed, looking to the right side. Gregory pulled himself out slowly and re-entered just as the tip of his penis was visible. Sonia said, "God, I can really feel you." Gregory started to build up momentum, slowly ensuring that he entered fully each time, pulling her body towards him. Sonia felt an overwhelming feeling come over her as he leaned forward and grabbed both her breasts with his hands. He pinched her nipples and Sonia gasped while he thrusted inside her. Her face was becoming very red as she was feeling the intensity all over. Gregory continued to hold her breasts while he pressed his body against hers, so that his penis was fully inside her. Sonia said, "Fuck me hard." Gregory got really excited when she said this so he grabbed her hips and he thrusted hard. Sonia grabbed the bed sheets and scrunched them in her hands as she gasped for air.

Gregory could feel the build-up within his penis and he said, "I am going to cum."

Sonia said, "Cum inside me." Gregory lost control as the sensation in his body was electric. He thrusted harder and faster as the sweat ran down his chest. Sonia was moaning as she felt her body go numb but the feeling was intense between her legs. "Oh God," she said as Gregory came. He leaned over as he exhaled, fighting for air. Sonia dropped her body onto the bed as Gregory removed himself. "Wow," he said as he looked at the full condom. Sonia turned and looked.

She said, "That's a lot," as Gregory slipped the condom off. She then said, "I am so horny." Gregory looked at the glasses from the night before to see if there was water. Sonia's glass had some left, so he reached over and downed the remainder. Sonia said, "I need some too."

Gregory stood up and he said, "I feel dizzy," as he made his way to the kitchen. He filled two fresh glasses and made his way back. When he entered, Sonia was under the duvet. He handed her the glass and he drank from his while Sonia did from hers.

"Wow," she said. "That was amazing." Gregory jumped back into the bed and they both cuddled. Gregory didn't take long to fall asleep again and Sonia eventually did too.

Sonia woke to the noise of someone knocking on the front door. She turned towards the bedroom door and listened. Taking her phone, she noticed that it was 1.43pm. She climbed out of bed and made her way to the landing. There was no more noise so she returned to Gregory. He was still asleep. Sonia sat on the edge of the bed and she said, "Gregory," in a soft voice. There was no movement so she poked his shoulder. This woke him.

He opened his eyes and said, "What time is it?" as he stretched. Sonia placed her hand on his chest and said, "It's after 1.30." Gregory replied, "Oh okay, I'll get up," as he lay there. Sonia got off the bed and said that she would have a shower. Gregory said, "Okay, I will rest another bit," as he closed his eyes while Sonia entered the bathroom.

Sonia stood looking at herself in the mirror and imagined living with Gregory. She was feeling good and not worrying for a change. She checked her face in the mirror, gently touching it with her fingertips. She was looking for any new lines. Nothing stood out so she removed her tee-shirt and switched on the shower. As the water got hot, Sonia climbed under the shower head, leaning her head back to feel the water over her face. She stood for a few minutes enjoying the sensation while thinking about the check-up. She was confident that it was just a virus and that they would both boost their immune systems by getting the correct vitamins or supplements after the results. Sonia washed her hair as she stood again, allowing the water to penetrate the top of her head. She found allowing the hot water to run down her back very relaxing. The bathroom was filled with condensation as Sonia enjoyed having the water very hot. She switched off the shower and reached for her towel, which was sitting on the sink. She dried herself before leaving the shower and stood wiping the mirror with her hand after she had wrapped the towel around herself. She felt lighter as she looked at herself in the mirror. Her forehead was sweating as she wrapped another towel around her head to keep her hair up. She could feel her body sweating under the damp towel as she opened the door to enter the bedroom. Gregory was already up, getting his clothes out of his wardrobe. Sonia walked over to him as the condensation followed her out the door.

Gregory said, "I see we have a steam room."

Sonia looked back over her shoulder and smiled. She kissed him on the lips and said, "It's free for you." Gregory walked over and entered the bathroom to find the floor soaking wet. He took the floor towel and dragged it with his foot to dry up the excess water. Sonia turned on the television and selected the music channel. Gregory closed the bathroom door and attempted to shave. He wiped the mirror several times to try to see his face but it kept fogging up. He gave up in the end and just showered. Sonia liked the rough rugged look anyway, so he wasn't concerned that he wasn't shaven. He finished and dried himself, taking all the towels with him. He walked into the bedroom as Sonia was drying her hair with her portable hairdryer. As he walked into the bedroom, he could feel the heat from the hairdryer as his nose began to dry up inside. He took Sonia's towels that she had disposed of onto the floor and he continued to the utility room. There, he threw the towels into the washing machine and selected a hot wash. He walked into the kitchen and filled the kettle. Taking two mugs, he prepared a coffee for them both. He could still hear the hairdryer as it wasn't quiet at all. As the kettle was boiling, he walked back up to the bedroom to get dressed.

Sonia said as he walked into the room, stopping the hairdryer, "Ohhh, you are naked. Are you hungry?"

Gregory replied, "Yes, I am."

Sonia said, "We can go to the pizza restaurant near the clinic." Gregory agreed as Sonia switched back on the hairdryer, continuing to shape her hair. He took a pair of jeans and a tee-shirt from his wardrobe. He then took some boxers and socks and put them on. He sat on the bed after putting on his jeans and pulled his tee-shirt over his head. Sonia had finished drying her hair so she walked over and pushed him back onto the bed. There she kissed him as she lay on him. Gregory took his hand and moved her hair from covering her face as he tucked it around her ear. Sonia kissed his lips and pulled herself back off him. Gregory groaned as he struggled to get himself back up off the bed. Sonia said, "Old man," as she walked out of the bedroom to go to the kitchen.

Gregory got off the bed and he took his jumper, putting it on as he left the bedroom. Sonia poured herself a coffee that Gregory had left beside the kettle and walked to the couch. Gregory walked in as she was just about to sit and he said, "Thanks for the coffee."

Sonia acknowledged this and said, "You're welcome," as she sat down. Gregory poured his cup and walked to the dining room window as he watched the birds eat from the bird feeder. It was dull outside with cloud overcast. He remembered that he left the heating on. The rooms were nice and snug so he walked over and switched off the heating from the thermostat.

Sonia sat staring at the floor while drinking her coffee. Gregory sat beside her and she said, "Do you think that I will have children?"

Gregory said, "Yes, why wouldn't you?"

Sonia drank some coffee and then said, "When?"

Gregory replied, "Do you want children?"

Sonia said, "Yes, I do."

Gregory replied, "After Christmas, lets have this conversation again." Sonia sighed with frustration and agreed. Gregory asked, "What time do we need to leave?"

Sonia said, "Four o'clock." Gregory looked at his watch and it was 2.45pm. Sonia leaned into him. He placed his arm around her and they both sat drinking their coffee. Sonia said, "When I have finished this coffee, I want to check my emails etc."

Gregory said, "You can use my laptop if it is easier." Sonia got off the couch and reached for the laptop sitting on the dining room table. She handed it to Gregory to open it and enter his password. He did this and Sonia sat at the dining room table accessing her email account. She left the kitchen and went back up to the bedroom to fetch her mobile phone. Gregory placed his mug in the kitchen sink and he took the bird food from the cupboard. As he opened the dining room door to the garden, Sonia walked into the kitchen.

She said, "Oh, don't let the heat out." Gregory looked and just closed the door behind him. He filled the bird feeders and stood in the garden, enjoying the damp cold feeling around his body. He noticed the light rain as it reflected from the light in the dining room. It was beginning to get darker. He opened the door and looked at the clock in the kitchen. It was 3.25pm and Sonia was sitting working on the laptop. He entered and closed the door, locking it behind him. Sonia felt the cold rush in.

She said, "God, it is cold out there."

Gregory said, "Yes it is, and it's starting to rain."

Sonia sighed and said, "I just washed my hair."

Gregory continued to the kitchen where he cleaned up. He washed his hands, changed his damp socks for dry ones and put his trainers on. He called Sonia as it was nearly 4pm. Sonia was still on the laptop so he had to remind her twice to get ready. She closed the laptop lid and made her way to the bedroom to fetch her handbag. She walked into the bathroom and started to put on her makeup. Gregory pottered around the kitchen and utility room, hanging up the wet towels to dry on the airing stand. He took his coat off the rail in the hallway and stood waiting for Sonia. He waited another ten minutes while sitting on the stairs, looking at apps on his mobile phone. Sonia walked down the stairs and she asked for her coat. Gregory stood and reached for it, giving it to her. Sonia put it on and stood at the front door while Gregory switched on the alarm. She then remembered that she should take her suitcase as she wouldn't be returning back to his place after the appointment.

She said, "I need my suitcase, would you mind getting it?" Gregory turned off the alarm and walked up to the bedroom to get her suitcase. It wasn't closed shut, with several items lying on the floor and on top. Gregory opened the case and he stuffed everything inside, pressing it shut and zipping it closed. He grabbed the suitcase and carried it down to Sonia. He placed it on the floor and pulled out the handle for her. Sonia said, "Thank you," as she turned to face the front door. Gregory switched on the alarm and Sonia opened the hall door. Locking the door behind them, they left and walked hand in hand towards the Tube station. They had to travel to London Bridge Station, therefore they only had one Tube to catch.

They both stood on the platform staring at the advertisements on the opposite wall. Gregory looked at the train timetable display and it said, 'Stand back, train approaching'. He walked to the yellow line and stood, watching in the direction of the incoming train. Sonia pulled her bag and herself closer to Gregory as the train pulled up. They both entered the carriage after letting some passengers off. Sonia sat on the end seat, pulling her bag against her legs. Gregory sat looking around at all the other passengers. Sonia closed her eyes and relaxed. Gregory then counted the number of stops, looking at the displayed route map. He then sat and watched at each stop who got off and on the train. They reached their stop, so Gregory nudged Sonia. She opened her eyes in a daze and pulled her suitcase to follow Gregory as he was already standing to get off, facing the door. Sonia stood behind and grabbed him for support as the train came to a stop. The doors opened so Gregory walked onto the platform, turning to watch Sonia depart the train. She just dragged her suitcase with a wallop as it plonked onto the platform.

Gregory smiled and said, "Love the determination."

Sonia replied, "Haw haw," as she pulled her bag while it was struggling to stay on two wheels. They reached the stairs to the platform so Gregory carried her suitcase to the ground floor entrance area. He then placed it on the footpath and Sonia began to pull it behind her.

Gregory stopped and faced Sonia. "I want to get a coffee and something small to eat before I get prodded with needles." Sonia agreed as she looked around. She pointed at a coffee shop and they both walked towards it. Gregory walked ahead as he listened to Sonia's suitcase click clack along the lines in the pavement as she followed behind. Gregory wasn't looking forward to the examination, but he was curious what the results would be. Gregory reached the main entrance door and he opened it and held it for Sonia to pass through. She pulled her suitcase inside and stood at an empty table.

"What do you want?" she said while letting go of the suitcase handle.

Gregory looked at the display board above the teller area and said, "I'll have a cappuccino and blueberry muffin."

Sonia replied, "Nothing changes," as she smiled, walking to the counter area. Gregory sat down and opened his coat. He looked over towards Sonia as she was paying for the drinks and food. He took his phone from his pocket and looked at an email that he had just received. It was from the airline, confirming the booking. He closed his phone and placed it back into his pocket as Sonia arrived at the table with a tray. She placed it on the table and walked to the counter to get some napkins and stirring sticks. Gregory placed the cups on the table with the food plates. He removed the tray and placed it on the table beside them. Sonia sat down and said, "I got a gluten-free chocolate," as she smiled. Gregory looked at his muffin and he took a chunk from it with his fingers, placing it into his mouth. Sonia opened the wrapper on her bar of chocolate while Gregory took a mouthful of his drink.

Sonia asked him, "How is your muffin?"

Gregory replied, "It's good."

Sonia then said, "You're welcome."

Gregory just sighed as he continued to eat. He thought to himself, *Why does she need praise for everything that she does?* He continued to remain silent while he ate. Sonia also continued to eat slowly as she looked at her mobile phone. She opened an app for things to do in Thailand. Gregory finished his muffin and continued drinking his cappuccino.

It was 5.35pm so Sonia said, "We should make our way to the clinic." Gregory started to fasten the buttons on his coat as Sonia stood fixing hers. She stood waiting as Gregory got off his seat. Sonia pulled her suitcase and struggled to open the door. Gregory reached past her and pushed it open. Sonia pulled her bag over his trainers and continued out the door. Gregory just sighed as he followed. Sonia turned down the street and watched the numbers on the doors.

"Here we are," she said as they reached number eight.

She pushed the intercom button and the receptionist answered, "Hello, how can I help you?"

Sonia replied, "It's Sonia and Gregory for the 5.45 appointment." There was silence and then the door began to buzz. Sonia pushed the door open and Gregory followed her inside. They walked up the hallway and followed the reception sign pointing to the left. Sonia pushed the door open and walked in, letting the door close on Gregory. She walked to the counter and the girl handed them both a clipboard to fill in and sign. They both sat in the waiting area filling in the forms. There were two other people in the waiting room sitting in their own thoughts, just observing Sonia and Gregory. Gregory looked around the room a few times as he felt uncomfortable. He filled in the form with the help of his mobile phone as he couldn't remember his doctor's surgery's contact details. Sonia also had to use her mobile for reference numbers. They filled the forms in and Sonia took them to the reception desk.

She was told by the receptionist, "It won't be long to wait."

Sonia said, "Thank you," as she walked back to Gregory and sat down. She said to Gregory, whispering, "Are you nervous?"

Gregory looked at her and said, "Nooo."

Sonia smiled and said, "Liar," as she laughed to herself. Gregory's name was called from a door to the opposite side of the reception. He stood and said, "Yes," as he made his way to the doctor.

The doctor introduced himself as he shook Gregory's hand. "I am Dr Rogers." Gregory followed him into the room and the doctor asked him to sit. "So you are here for a full blood test?" the doctor announced as Gregory sat.

Gregory replied, "Yes." The doctor asked him to remove his coat and jumper and to pull up his sleeve. Gregory took off his coat and the doctor hung it on the back of the door.

Gregory placed his jumper on his lap as the doctor placed the tourniquet rubber band around his arm to increase the blood pressure.

He tapped the veins and said, "You have some nice healthy veins," as he prepared the needle. He wiped the area with an alcohol wipe and then said, "There will be a little prick." He inserted the hollow needle into the vein and they both watched the blood begin to fill the collection tube. The doctor switched several collection tubes and then removed the needle, placing a cotton ball over the area. He asked Gregory to apply pressure while he pulled some tape to hold the cotton in place. Once finished he said, "That's all done, we will be in touch in the next week with the results." Gregory put on his jumper and stood while the doctor handed him his coat. The doctor opened the door and asked Gregory to send in Sonia. Gregory walked out into the reception while putting on his coat.

He walked to Sonia and said, "Your turn, enjoy."

Sonia got off her seat and walked to the doctor's room. She knocked on the door as it was closed. The doctor acknowledged, saying, "Come in, please." Sonia opened the door and the doctor was still writing on the collection tubes. He said, "Please sit, I won't be long." Sonia sat on the chair, looking around the room to make sure it was well sterilised. The doctor walked over to her, removing his rubber gloves and throwing them into the bin. "I am Doctor Rogers, pleased to meet you," he said as he held his hand out to shake hers.

Sonia held his and said, "I am Sonia." The doctor asked her to remove her coat so she did. He performed the same ritual that he did with Gregory and Sonia left the room after she asked when the tests would be available. The doctor told her about a week, but that she could call after three days. Sonia thanked the doctor and left the room for the reception. There she stood while the girl printed off the invoice.

"This will be £58.00, please, for you both," she said. Sonia took her card from her wallet and paid the bill. She took the receipt and walked to Gregory.

Gregory said, "Thank you, that was a wonderful experience, we should do this again sometime."

Sonia smirked and said, "You don't have to be a smart arse about it," as she walked to the door, pulling her suitcase. Gregory buttoned his coat and followed her. She stood outside and waited as Gregory took his time. He walked out of the door, closing it behind him, and approached Sonia. Sonia said, "Okay let's get some food and have an early night."

Gregory said, "Where is the pizza place?"

Sonia pulled her phone out of her pocket, opened her map and said, "Down that street," as she pointed. Gregory walked in that direction alongside Sonia. She said, "I am curious about the results of the test."

Gregory replied, "Well, we can't do anything until the results, so no point worrying about it now."

Sonia said, "Okay," as she walked with him. They reached the restaurant. Sonia excused herself while Gregory waited to be seated. Sonia made her way to the toilet. Gregory was seated by the waiter and was handed two menus. Sonia returned shortly while Gregory was hanging his coat on the back of his seat. Sonia also placed her coat on top of his. She sat down and said, "I am still wet after this morning."

Gregory smiled and said, "That's nice," as he sat back in his seat, all smug. Sonia sat and took the menu. She wanted the Padana pizza with a gluten-free base. Gregory also wanted the same but with a normal base. The waitress came to their table and took their order. Sonia requested a large glass of white wine and Gregory also the same. Sonia sat forward and reached for Gregory's hand.

She said, "I am so looking forward to Thailand with you."

Gregory replied, "I am also looking forward to it."

Sonia looked into his eyes and said, "I love you very much."

Gregory was just about to reply when the waitress arrived with the two glasses of wine. She placed them on the table and walked away. Sonia lifted her glass and said, "Cheers to the future."

Gregory lifted his glass and clinked it against hers. "Cheers to that." They both drank some and sat back into their seats. Gregory said, "It's okay."

Sonia curled up her face and said, "Nah, I don't like it," and called over the waitress. Gregory sat in his chair thinking, *Please don't make a show.* Sonia spoke to the waitress and said that neither of them liked the wine and could they try another? The waitress looked annoyed but agreed to get another fresh bottle of the same white wine. Sonia took another drink from her glass while she waited. The girl returned with two fresh glasses of white Chardonnay wine. She took the other glasses away. Sonia took a drink from hers as Gregory watched. "Yep, that's better," she said as she sat feeling happy with herself. Gregory also took a drink from his and agreed with Sonia. The waitress brought over the two pizzas and asked if they required anything else. Sonia said, "Can I have some more garlic and spices, please?"

The waitress said, "Sure," as she walked to the counter to get the garlic oil and spicy oil cruets. She placed them both on the table and Sonia began to pour them both on top of her pizza.

"Oh, I love garlic."

Gregory replied with a mumbled, "Glad I won't be kissing you tonight."

Sonia said, "What was that?"

Gregory said, "It's really tasty," as he continued to chew, not repeating what he said first. They both continued to eat and discuss their week ahead. Gregory knew that he would have to catch up after calling in sick. Sonia wasn't worried about her job; she just knew that she was up very early the next morning.

They both finished their food and Gregory got the bill. They put on their coats and walked outside. Sonia decided to call a taxi while Gregory had the journey back on the Tube. They parted with a kiss and a hug as Sonia climbed into the taxi with her suitcase. Gregory waved at Sonia as the car pulled away and Sonia reciprocated. He walked to the Tube station and thought about what he had to prepare for his work the following day.

16

The results

A week had passed, with Gregory returning to work and Sonia having a busy schedule doing overtime to save money for the Christmas holiday break. They kept in touch via phone calls and messaging. Sonia received an email from the clinic letting her know that she had to book an appointment to receive them. This concerned her so she called the clinic to speak to the receptionist. Over the telephone call, the receptionist had informed Sonia that it was normal procedure for the doctor to give the results in person. Sonia knew otherwise as she was in the medical profession, therefore she thought that something had been discovered. Over several days, Sonia became more worried because Gregory would eventually ask if any results had been received. She built up the courage during a telephone conversation and decided to tell him that they both had to visit the clinic for the results.

It was Thursday. Gregory was very relaxed and excited to see Sonia as they had arranged to meet on the Friday evening. Sonia said during a telephone conversation, "I received an email requesting us both to attend to receive the results of the blood tests."

Gregory remained quiet as he was in deep thought.

"Hello?" said Sonia.

"Yes, I am here," replied Gregory. "They must have found something that they need us to attend for."

Sonia said, "Yes," and remained quiet.

Gregory asked, "Do you know what it could be?"

Sonia was agitated and said, "I have no idea, have you?"

Gregory then cleared his throat and said, "I hope it's nothing serious, I am kind of worried now."

Sonia replied, "I am too."

Gregory then said, "I am looking forward to seeing you tomorrow night. When are we to attend the clinic?"

Sonia said, "We can go on Saturday afternoon if you like?"

Gregory said, "Yes, let's get the answer as I am worried now."

Sonia agreed and said, "I will call them tomorrow and arrange the appointment."

Gregory replied, "Okay, that's good. What shall we do on Friday evening?"

Sonia said, "Let's do something light, maybe the cinema and some food. I can stay at yours and we can travel together on Saturday, if that's okay with you?"

Gregory said, "Yes, absolutely, that would be nice."

They finished the phone call and Sonia felt really sick in her stomach. Gregory also felt the cold feeling around himself again. He hadn't felt it for some time so he was intrigued to feel it again. He wanted to know why he was feeling this sensation again. Sonia began to search for different conditions that can be detected via blood tests. She began to Google all sorts of medical problems, making herself feel not good at all. She was worried and then wondered if Gregory had something that he hadn't told her about. Sonia decided to have a bath to try to relax as she was feeling really anxious to get the results of the test. It was after 10pm and she needed to settle before going to bed as she wouldn't be able to sleep for worrying. She walked into her bathroom and turned on the hot water tap to fill the bath. Sitting on the edge of the bath, Sonia thought about the results of the blood test. She was concerned because both Gregory and herself had had a flare-up of some sort and she didn't know what it was. She walked into the bedroom to fetch her phone. She wanted to check her messages as she hadn't contacted anyone over the last few days. She was feeling very agitated about the whole week once she was contacted by the clinic.

The bath was nearly full so she felt the water with her fingers. It was very hot so she added some cold water. Opening an app, she played some music on her phone. She positioned herself slowly into the bath as her body adjusted to the intense heat. Once in, she laid her head against a towel folded against the wall and the edge of the bath. Sonia closed her eyes and relaxed, listening to the music. Several times, Gregory appeared in her thoughts. She was worried about his reaction once they got the results. She was in fear of losing him and knew that there was nothing that she could do to change anything. She was feeling sick again in her stomach and hungry at the same time. Sonia wanted to eat but wasn't in a rush to make anything as there was no food in her flat. She decided to get a takeaway. She looked at her phone at the options for ordering food. No matter what she looked at, nothing satisfied her appetite. She remembered that she had some gluten-free biscuits in her handbag. She decided that this would be enough with a cup of tea. She placed her phone back onto the floor and listened to the music. It didn't take long until Sonia managed to fall asleep again in the bath. She woke when a text interrupted the music with the chirp sound.

She opened her eyes and reached for her phone. It was 10.50pm and the text was from Gregory. It read, *I miss you and can't wait to see you tomorrow XxX.* Sonia replied immediately, *Me too. I fell asleep and your text woke me. I'm in the bath.* Gregory read the message and he was concerned. *You must be exhausted from work?* Sonia replied, *Yes, I have done many hours overtime this week. My legs, feet and back are killing me.* Gregory then said, *Make sure you get to bed soon Xx.* Sonia replied, *Love you, sleep well XX.* Gregory replied, *You too XxX.* Sonia got up from lying down and she bent over to pull the plug. Just after doing so, she felt very dizzy. She sat on the edge of the bath and watched the water drain for a few minutes while she regained her strength. She then climbed out and wrapped a towel around herself. Wiping the mirror, she noticed that her eyes were showing signs of black rings again. She knew that she was over-tired and stressed. She felt better that Gregory had text her but was cold and hungry while standing in the bathroom. It was a cold damp evening outside and the heating went off at 9.30pm. Sonia got dressed for bed and switched off all the lights except for the lamp beside her bed. She left the towels on the bathroom floor for when she was going to do the washing. She checked that her phone alarm was set for 6am and switched on aeroplane mode.

She lay back and stared at the ceiling and decided on what she was going to wear the next day because she was going to see Gregory after work. Sonia switched off the table light and wrapped herself up in the duvet to sleep. Sonia twisted and turned all night, waking at different times as she thought about getting the results. It was 4.55am the last time she looked at her phone clock before waking to the alarm. She opened her eyes and lay on her back for a moment, knowing that if she lay there much longer she would fall back asleep. Slowly dragging herself out of bed, she stood a little dazed then made her way to the bathroom. She switched on the bathroom light and closed her eyes as she sat on the toilet. Her eyes felt dry and the left eye started to become watery. She rubbed her left eye several times but it continued to weep. Once finished on the toilet, Sonia flushed it and proceeded to wash her hands. She felt exhausted but hadn't planned to shower this morning. She washed her face and brushed her hair. Sonia constantly thought about the doctor's appointment and this was beginning to annoy her. She couldn't stop her mind from thinking about it even though she tried to distract herself with other thoughts. Her main concern was how Gregory was going to react, but the fact that she didn't know the result made it more frustrating. She couldn't prepare for her own reaction. She kept telling herself that it could be anything and maybe was nothing serious. Sonia continued to dress herself and prepare her makeup.

Standing at the mirror applying her foundation, she decided to text Gregory. She walked into the bedroom while rubbing the foundation in and grabbed her mobile off the floor beside her bed. She switched off aeroplane mode, opened the app and text Gregory. *Hey, looking forward to seeing you later. Don't forget the surgery appointment on Saturday. X.* She threw her phone onto the tangled duvet and continued to apply her makeup in the bathroom. While doing so, she heard her phone ping. Sonia finished her makeup a while later and proceeded to put her shoes on. She grabbed her coat, handbag and phone off the bed. Putting her coat on, she opened her phone app and read the message, *Hiya. Yes me too. No worries, haven't forgotten, worried. X.*

Sonia felt worse after reading the message and finished buttoning up her coat. She opened her door to the hallway and closed it behind her, making her way out through the main entrance door to the street. It was very cold outside. She could feel the chill on her lower legs and feet immediately as she began to walk to work. With her phone in her hand, she opened her messages and decided to text Philip. *Hi Philip, I have had a blood test and I am called back today for the results, is there anything that I should be aware of?* She sent the message after a few seconds deliberating in her mind. She placed the phone in her pocket and opened her handbag to fetch her gloves. It took a while to get both out as she stood still, feeling the cold even more. Donning her gloves, she began to think about Thailand and how wonderful it would be to feel the heat from the sun. She began to walk again and her phone pinged. She pulled her phone out of her pocket and opened the app. It was a text from Philip. *Hi Sonia, I have no idea what you mean?* Sonia took her glove off and held it in her left hand with the phone while she typed. *Hi Philip, I am just worried and concerned about the results.* Philip replied, *I don't have AIDS if that's what you are asking.* Sonia replied, *Oh okay, good to know. I hope you are well.* The phone remained quiet for some time so Sonia placed it back into her pocket and put her glove back on. She was nearly at the coffee shop where she always ordered a coffee. This time she had to stand in the queue as she forgot to order via her app. She stood waiting behind two others in front when her phone pinged again. She took the phone out and opened the app with her glove in her teeth as she had pulled it off to read the message. It was from Philip. It read, *Hi Sonia. Let's meet soon. X.*

As she read this, the girl behind the counter said, "Next." Sonia was still looking at her phone and the girl repeated herself. "Next, please."

Sonia looked up and said, "Oh, I'll have a latte please, medium." The girl entered the product into the till and Sonia presented her card when the amount showed on the reader display. Once it was authorised, the girl said, "Thank you," and Sonia continued to the end of the counter to wait for her coffee.

Sonia text Philip back. *Yes, that will be nice. X.* She felt more relieved that she had someone to meet up with if everything went wrong with the results on Saturday. Sonia stirred her latte after adding a sugar to it while standing at the counter area. She was feeling warm again and ready to face the cold as she took a sip from the cup. She put on her gloves while leaving the cup standing on the countertop. Walking to the door, she took another sip. Another person was entering the shop so he held the door open for her while she stepped out onto the footpath. Sonia said, "Oh, thank you," while the man held the door. She continued to walk to work, sipping her coffee and looking at the other people making their way to wherever they needed to go. She felt much better after texting Philip. It was like a relief, a weight lifted off her. She started to think that it was something to do with their diets. Maybe it was going to be a warning of some sort to make a change to their diets or something like that.

Sonia entered her work main entrance door and she clocked in using her identity card on the foyer reader. She was greeted by the security man with a nod as she walked towards the back of the building to her changing area. Sonia was still feeling tired and her left eye continued to weep even though she was in the heated building. She continued with her work for the day and got herself ready to meet Gregory once she finished at 8.30pm. It was a long day but she felt relieved as she had three days off.

She hadn't had any time to text Gregory, so she did while changing back into her casual clothes while standing at her locker. *Hiya, where are we meeting?* Gregory took some time to reply but he eventually did. *I am in the café across from your work.* Sonia was pleasantly surprised and excited to see him. She sprayed herself with her perfume and added some lipstick to smarten her appearance. Once finished, she put her coat, scarf and gloves on. She had finished work at last and she was so relieved to be leaving. Once she had clocked out, she walked onto the footpath and headed in the direction of the café. She crossed the road and tried to see Gregory through the window covered in condensation as she approached the door. He was sitting right at the window with a mug raised in his hand, as if he was saluting her. Sonia smiled and made a gesture while saying, "Where is mine?" even though he couldn't hear her. Gregory smiled and took a drink, knowing that Sonia was watching.

She opened the door and entered, walking straight towards him, saying, "Yeah yeah yeah, what about me?" Gregory got off his stool and raised his arms to give her a hug. Sonia walked into his arms and she embraced him, pulling him closer to her. She said, "I missed this." Gregory just remained quiet and they parted looking at each other.

Gregory said, "Are you hungry?"

Sonia said, "Yes I am. I'd like a Thai."

Gregory replied, "Shall we go to the place we went to last time?"

Sonia agreed while Gregory put his coat, scarf and gloves on. She had decided not to have a coffee before eating. She knew it might upset her tummy. They both made their way out of the café and in the direction of the restaurant. Gregory took Sonia's hand as they walked. Sonia felt good, therefore she leaned into him and they both kissed. As they walked, Sonia asked Gregory, "I was thinking so much about Thailand all day, are you excited? I have to buy so many things."

Gregory replied, "Yes, I am excited," as he thought to himself, *What do you need to buy?* He decided not to ask the question as he knew that Sonia would get frustrated.

Sonia said, "You don't seem to be too excited with your reaction." Gregory just looked at her and continued to walk. They eventually reached the restaurant and waited to be seated. It wasn't too busy, which was a relief being a Friday evening. They sat and deliberated on what they were going to order. They decided on sharing so they both ordered different dishes. Sonia wasn't herself at all. She was on edge and tired. Gregory was on great form. Sonia ordered a bottle of white wine for them both. Once the wine had arrived at the table, Sonia perked up a little. She talked about how excited she was about having a massage in Thailand. Gregory also liked the idea of a spa day, just a day where they could both relax and do nothing. The food arrived and they both continued to talk about different excursions they could do while on holiday. Gregory was excited about renting out a motorbike. He really wanted to travel to places off the tourist map. Sonia was excited but worried about this idea. She hadn't experienced being on the back of a motorbike before but Gregory was an experienced rider.

They finished the bottle of wine and also their meal. Gregory said, "Shall we go to a bar and have a drink instead of staying here?"

Sonia smiled and said, "Yes, that's a great idea." She jumped off her chair with haste and pulled her handbag off the floor, rooting for her wallet. As soon as she stood, the waiter noticed, therefore she gestured for the bill by waving her right hand in the air as though she was writing. Gregory smiled while he put on his coat.

The waiter arrived with the card machine and bill. He said, "Did you enjoy?"

Sonia said, "Yes, it was very nice." Gregory just nodded as he put on his hat and started with his gloves. Sonia handed her card to the waiter and he entered it into the machine with the amount. Sonia covered the keyboard and entered her pin code. She stood back as the waiter watched the machine. Nothing happened for a minute of two then the paper began to print.

He said, "This happens on weekends," as he handed Sonia back her card. "Have a nice evening."

Sonia said, "Thank you, you too." She looked at Gregory, standing ready to go. She said, "I have to pee," as she dropped her wallet into her bag and walked towards the toilet. Gregory just sat back in his seat while waiting for Sonia. Sonia used the toilet, washed her hands and used the paper hand towels to dry her hands. She was feeling really happy. She felt light and excited about the holiday. There was a connection between herself and Gregory that felt so loving, a feeling that she wanted to be with him for the rest of her life and that she couldn't imagine her life without him. She had forgotten about the doctor's appointment the next day as she threw the paper towel into the bin. She stood and gave her hair a shake to add volume before leaving the bathroom. The wine had kicked in and Sonia was feeling on top of the world.

As she walked towards Gregory, Sonia had to focus on each step as she was feeling very conscious that the alcohol had made her a little light-headed. Gregory got off his chair while Sonia put her scarf on. He took her handbag and he held it until she was finished getting ready. Sonia smiled and walked towards the door, leaving Gregory with her handbag. Gregory walked after her and said when he reached her at the door, "Really?" as he handed it back to her. Sonia smiled and placed it over her right arm. Gregory opened the door and the waiter wished them well. Gregory and Sonia walked hand in hand as they looked at the clear sky with the full moon gleaming down. It was a dry, crisp night with a very cold temperature of about minus three degrees.

Sonia said, "Oh, a brandy would be nice to heat up the bones," grabbing onto Gregory's arm as they walked. Sonia stopped and looked at the moon. "Isn't that lovely?" she said as she looked up into the sky.

Gregory replied, "Yes, it's amazing," as he started to walk again, feeling the cold.

Sonia said, "Wait for me," as Gregory stopped and she caught up. She kissed him on the lips and walked on. Gregory followed until they were again beside one another. Sonia looked ahead and said, "Let's check out that pub," pointing down a street. They entered the bar called The Harp. Sonia was so pleased with herself for finding it; after all, they were both Irish. The bar itself wasn't Irish. It was a nice narrow pub with beer mats posted on the wall. Sonia ordered a brandy and Gregory also decided to have one. They both stood as the bar was lively. Sonia and Gregory both removed their coats and Gregory paid for the drinks. They drank, toasting the future. Sonia continued to look for a bar stool while she was talking to Gregory. A gentleman realised what she was doing and he offered his. Sonia didn't have to think twice about taking it. She immediately placed her coat on it, then took Gregory's and placed his over hers. She then pulled it into the position she wanted and sat down, taking a drink from her glass.

Gregory stood beside her and he said, "Why don't you move into mine after Christmas?" Sonia had her glass to her mouth when he said this. She was just about to take a drink when she felt emotional. In fact, the shock made her cry. The tears streamed down her face. She lowered the glass and looked at Gregory.

Her voice was broken when she replied. "Are you serious?"

Gregory smiled and said, "Yes."

Sonia got off her stool and she grabbed him for a cuddle. She broke down crying with joy as soon as she was embraced within his arms. Holding her glass, she could only press her right hand against his back. Gregory whispered in her ear, "I do love you." Sonia snuggled closer to him as she sniffed. Pulling away, she had makeup running down her face. She wiped her eyes gently, but Gregory had to say, "You will need to go to the bathroom to fix that up." Sonia smiled as she continued to wipe the tears off her face. She sat back down and took a drink. Gregory raised his glass and said, "Here is to the future."

Sonia raised hers and touched his glass. "Yes. Here is to us." She drank a full mouthful.

Gregory then said, "You go fix yourself up and I'll order another one."

Sonia replied, "Am I that bad?"

Gregory replied, "No, not too bad, but you would know that you were crying." Sonia then got off her stool and downed the last of the brandy, handing Gregory her empty glass. She walked away as he took it, watching her disappear into the crowd. Gregory stood at the bar waiting his turn to order again, finishing his brandy. The barman served several other patrons before Gregory. He ordered the same again and paid the bill. Sonia returned from the bathroom and sat on her stool. Gregory handed her the brandy and said, "Are you okay now?"

Sonia smiled and said, "Yes, but why do you ask me now?"

Gregory said, "When is the right time?" Sonia just stared at him. She was feeling very emotional and just took a drink from her glass. She took her attention away from Gregory by looking outside the pub window. There were many people standing smoking, laughing and drinking. She also looked around the bar. One wall had beer mats from all over the world stuck on it. She looked at these for a while, guessing the countries that they were from.

Gregory also looked over and said, "Ah, look, the old Guinness beer mat," as he pointed to the top right ceiling area. Sonia focussed in that direction but couldn't see it. Gregory said, "Do you see the red and orange one on the top left? Count five over to the left." Sonia still couldn't see it so Gregory squeezed his way past the other patrons to make his way over to show her. Sonia sat and watched as Gregory reached the wall. He then stood making sure that she was looking in his direction and pointed up. Sonia looked up and nodded with a smile. Gregory then made his way to the toilet. He placed his empty glass on a table on the way to the stairs.

Once he had gone, Sonia reached for her mobile phone. She just wanted to have a distraction as there were several men standing around her. She opened her phone with the code and noticed a message. It was from Philip. It read, *I am free Tuesday if you are. X.* Sonia closed the message and decided not to reply. She looked up and noticed that a guy was standing, trying to get her attention. Sonia looked back at her phone and he said, "Can I get you a drink?"

Sonia looked at him and said, "No thank you," looking back at her phone. Gregory just arrived back at this moment and Sonia kissed him. He could feel that something wasn't right as he stood back from her.

He said, "Are you okay?"

Sonia said, "Yes, all is good. What do you want to drink?"

Gregory said, "Same again, one for the road."

Sonia reached for her wallet inside her handbag and took her bank card. She said, "Can you get it, please?" Gregory took the card and said, "Okay," as he knew something didn't feel right when he got back from the toilet. He thought that it was to do with her on her mobile. Sonia opened her phone again and noticed the reminder for the appointment for 3pm the next day. She felt sick again in her stomach because Gregory had just asked her to move in with him and she always waited for something to go wrong after something good happened in her life. Gregory returned with two drinks and her debit card. He gave her the card first and then the glass.

Sonia said, "Thank you. We will have the results tomorrow."

Gregory sighed. "Oh shite, yes, I totally forgot, what time?"

Sonia replied, "3pm."

Gregory said, "Well, at least we can have a lie-in," lifting his glass for a toast. Sonia lifted hers and they touched glasses before drinking. He then said, "After this, we should make our way back to mine. Well, 'ours' in a few months." Sonia took another drink from her glass. They became quieter as the alcohol was making them both feel drunk. Sonia was sipping hers while Gregory had finished his. He said, "Okay, let's go." Sonia wasn't amused as she still had some of her drink left. She drank a mouthful and held the glass on her lap with her handbag. He then said, "I'll go to the toilet and then we can go." Sonia nodded. Gregory walked to the toilet as Sonia sat looking around. There were less patrons in the bar at this time so she glanced around at all the décor as she took another drink. She also needed the bathroom but decided to wait for Gregory to return so that he could mind the coats she was sitting on.

Gregory returned and Sonia said, "I have to go," as she jumped off the stool, nearly falling over. She laughed to herself as she gained balance, making her way to the stairs. Gregory realised how drunk she had become and knew that the fresh air would make her worse. This he didn't look forward to. Sonia was missing for about twenty minutes when Gregory became concerned. He took the coats and walked to the toilets. Standing outside the ladies', he knocked on the door shouting, "Sonia, Sonia."

There was no answer but another woman appeared to use the bathroom. She asked Gregory, "Are you okay?" with a concerned look on her face.

He said, "My girlfriend Sonia has been in there for over twenty minutes."

The woman agreed to take a look for him. She opened the door and noticed one cubicle was closed. The woman called, "Sonia," but there was no answer. She knocked on the door and she heard a mumble. The woman continued to talk aloud until Sonia acknowledged and answered. It took about ten minutes for Sonia to open the cubicle door and speak to the woman.

She washed her hands and stumbled to the door. When Sonia opened the bathroom door, Gregory was standing waiting.

She looked at him and said, "Ah, the bearer of the coats has arrived." Gregory handed her her coat and she struggled to put it on, so he helped. As soon as she had finished buttoning her coat, he handed her scarf and hat over. She put both on quickly and said, "Gloves, please," with a cheeky laugh.

Gregory replied, "In your handbag."

Sonia laughed and said, "I know," as she opened it and took them out.

As soon as she was finished Gregory said, "After you," as he pointed towards the stairs. Just as he said this, the other woman came out of the ladies'. He said, "Thank you so much."

She smiled and said, "You take care of her."

He said, "I will," as she passed them both, walking up the stairs. Sonia followed taking one step at a time, holding the handrail. Gregory was beginning to get frustrated while talking her through each movement needed to reach the ground floor area. He looked at his watch and noticed that it was 12.15am. He then remembered that it was Friday and the tubes were twenty-four-hour. This was a relief to him. They walked to the main entrance door and Gregory opened it for her. As she walked out onto the pavement, Sonia wrapped her scarf over her face.

She mumbled, "It's freezing out here." Gregory also felt the chill and he grabbed her arm to balance her while they walked to the Tube station. They needed to walk to Leicester Square. Sonia struggled with her handbag so Gregory took it. He was also feeling a little tipsy so he could only imagine how it had affected Sonia. They continued to walk to the Tube station in silence as it was very cold. It was a relief to enter the underground to feel the heat on their bodies. This also made Sonia feel sleepy. They both arrived at Gregory's house just after 1am. Sonia went straight up to the bedroom and changed into one of Gregory's tee-shirts while Gregory fetched water. When Gregory got up to the bedroom with the water, Sonia was fast asleep. He switched off the lights, leaving a glass of water beside her on the bedside table. Using the bathroom, Gregory undressed so as not to make any noise. He washed his face and brushed his teeth. Once finished, he walked slowly to the bed, climbing under the duvet. He lay on his back for a few minutes while listening to Sonia's heavy breathing with a slight snoring sound. He thought to himself, *Ah, great*. He turned over and faced towards the door to try to sleep. It didn't take him long to drop off into a deep sleep.

The following morning Sonia woke thirsty. She turned her head to check if there was water beside her. The thought of lifting her head was too much to contend with. She looked for a while, building up the momentum to move and reach for the glass and drink some. Her head was pounding while steady on the pillow, so she didn't want to move it. It took a few minutes of convincing herself to get up and drink some. Wanting the toilet also made things a little more difficult for her. She eventually moved into position to drink the water, waking Gregory as her movements were not subtle but bouncy as she took the water in her right hand. Sonia drank the whole glass in one go with a gasp at the end.

Gregory said, "Ah, Death has warmed up."

Sonia looked at him and said, "Haw haw," as she dropped gently back onto her pillow, holding her forehead with her hand. The water didn't make any difference to her feeling thirsty, she just wanted more, but the sensation of wanting to go to the toilet frustrated her even more. It was a delicate situation that she was in, clenching her muscles tightly to stop herself peeing while feeling the pounding headache. She turned her head towards Gregory and said, "Can you take the toilet over to me?" She was laughing aloud but making the situation worse for her.

Gregory replied, "I need to pee too," as he sat up in the bed.

Sonia raised her body and said, "Don't you dare go now!" as

Gregory climbed out from under the covers. Sonia jumped up with haste, pushed past him at the bathroom door and dropped herself on the toilet as Gregory watched her lean back while closing her eyes.

He laughed and said, "Nice." Sonia didn't care as she felt the relief but was feeling really dizzy. Gregory decided to use the landing toilet. Sonia finished, flushed the toilet and washed her hands while also throwing water on her face. Her head was pounding so much that she was squinting to find her way back to the bed. Gregory returned with a fresh glass of water and two painkillers. Sonia was lying on her back when he said, "Take these." Sonia opened one eye and sat up to take the tablets.

She said, "God, I am dying. I feel like a mangled badger."

Gregory laughed and said, "You look like one. Very sexy look you have going on there." Sonia handed the empty glass back and lay back on her pillow. Looking at his watch Gregory said, "It's 11.45. I'll wake you at 1.45." Sonia nodded as she cuddled into her pillow. Gregory put on a tracksuit hooded top and some tracksuit bottoms. He went downstairs and made himself a coffee. He wasn't feeling too bad, just tired and hungry. He decided to make a fry-up for himself. Taking bacon rashers from the fridge with eggs and sausages he began to cook. While allowing the food to cook, he filled the kettle and turned it on. Standing over the frying pan, he was in deep thought about his life and what he wanted to do next. He was very content with Sonia and he looked forward to the holiday away. He continued to dish up his breakfast and poured his mug of coffee. He walked over to the couch and switched on the television. He flicked through the channels to find an engineering programme. He then realised that he had forgotten bread and butter.

While opening the fridge door, Sonia walked into the kitchen. She wasn't looking too well at all. Gregory asked if she would like some breakfast and her reply was, "God, no."

Gregory buttered two slices of bread while Sonia sat on a stool watching. He made his way to the couch and she followed. He said, "How is your head feeling?"

Sonia replied, "The throbbing has gone down but I can't sleep." She got up off the couch and fetched a glass of water, then returned and sat beside Gregory. She watched the television for a while with him eating beside her.

She reached for the remote and Gregory said, "Ah," as he chewed.

Sonia groaned and said, "This is boring."

Gregory replied, "Better than watching real-life crap, you can learn from this." Sonia got off the couch and went back up to the bedroom. She was feeling cold, tired and not too well. Gregory continued to eat his breakfast and watch the programme. Sonia managed to sleep for a while longer. Gregory tidied up and went for a shower in the bedroom en-suite. Sonia woke to the sound of the shower as she lay looking at the ceiling. She was feeling much better and a little hungry. She sat up in the bed and looked for her handbag in the room. She got up and took some gluten-free biscuits from her handbag and started to eat one. Gregory entered the bedroom from the shower and was surprised to see Sonia sitting up eating.

Sonia watched as he got dressed and said, "I will shower shortly."

Gregory replied, "I will get you some fresh towels in a minute." He finished dressing himself and he went to the airing cupboard on the landing to fetch some towels. He handed two towels to Sonia and kissed her on the lips. Sonia was still munching on her biscuit. Gregory said, "Don't you want toast or something? There is gluten-free bread in the freezer."

Sonia replied, "Oh, I didn't know that." She continued to eat her biscuit and then went for a shower. Gregory went back downstairs and allowed Sonia to get ready. He relaxed on the couch with another mug of coffee. It was about an hour that passed before Sonia appeared dressed and ready. She opened the freezer door and took two slices of gluten-free bread. Standing over the toaster, she said, "Gregory, were you serious about what you said last night?"

Gregory replied, "Yes, I was." Sonia continued to butter her toast and eat it standing at the counter. Gregory walked over and hugged her from behind. Sonia continued to eat and he kissed her on the left cheek. He looked at his watch and said, "We have thirty minutes to make a move." Sonia sighed as she wasn't feeling excited about getting on the Tube. Gregory left to go and brush his teeth. Sonia cleaned up her mess and followed him upstairs. She climbed back onto the bed and closed her eyes. Gregory also lay beside her. They were both very tired but knew not to fall asleep. Gregory just relaxed with his eyes open while Sonia cuddled into him. He looked at his watch and he said, "In ten minutes we have to leave."

Sonia said, "Okay," as she lay against him. He wasn't looking forward to the travel either but was curious about the results.

He looked again and said, "Okay, time to go now." Sonia opened her eyes and slowly sat up. She took a moment siting on the edge of the bed before putting on her shoes.

Gregory said, "You can come back here after and rest." Sonia was happy to hear this as she wasn't sure what they were doing after the appointment. They both went downstairs and put their coats on etc. Gregory switched on the alarm and Sonia opened the front door. He locked it behind them and they walked to the Tube station. It was about ten degrees with the sun shining. Sonia was feeling much better but very hungry. Gregory was feeling good but a little tired.

They arrived at London Bridge and walked to the clinic. Sonia entered first and walked to the receptionist, who was on the phone. Gregory followed behind and stood beside her. The receptionist finished her call and said, "How can I help?"

Sonia replied, "Sonia and Gregory for 3pm." It was 2.55pm so they were five minutes early. The receptionist requested that they sit in the waiting area to be called. Sonia walked to a seat and Gregory went for a magazine on the rack. Sonia looked at the other people waiting. There was another couple and a mother with a child. Gregory walked over with a *National Geographic* magazine about the Egyptians. He sat quietly flicking through it as Sonia glanced from time to time. She reached over and took his hand. She was feeling very nervous and Gregory could see that she was very quiet. There was a television on the wall opposite with the news showing. Sonia was switching between looking at the television and the magazine that Gregory was reading. A doctor walked into the reception, stood with a piece of paper calling out another patient's name. Sonia felt herself relax a little as she thought that it was their turn. The time was 3.04pm so she was anxious. She just wanted to know the answer and get out as she was still hungry and hungover.

Doctor Rogers walked into the reception and said, "Hello, Sonia and Gregory. Please come into my room." Sonia took her hand away from Gregory's and followed the doctor. Gregory placed the magazine back on the rack and he entered the room as Sonia was sitting down. The doctor said, "Well, I hope that you are feeling better, Gregory."

Gregory replied, "Yes, doctor, I am much better. Not one hundred percent, but better."The doctor said, "Okay, I will get straight to it. You both have the herpes simplex virus." He paused as Sonia gasped and looked at Gregory as if it was his fault.

Gregory sat with his mouth open and then said, "How, and what is it?"

The doctor replied, "Sonia is the host. I am sorry to say, but you contracted it from Sonia."

Gregory looked at Sonia and she sat back in her seat, not impressed. She remained quiet and Gregory then asked, "Is this a permanent virus or do we need to take medication?"

The doctor replied, "Unfortunately it is permanent. The first episode is often more severe and may be associated with fever, muscle pains, swollen lymph nodes and headaches. Over time, episodes of the active disease decrease in frequency and severity. Treatments with antiviral medication can lessen the severity of symptomatic episodes. Both types 1 and 2 are highly contagious and can be passed easily from one person to another by direct contact orally Type 1 and Genital Type 2. Genital herpes is usually transmitted by having sex with an infected person. Even if someone with genital herpes doesn't have any symptoms, it's possible for them to pass the condition on to a sexual partner."

Gregory was shocked but asked, "I don't sleep around and Sonia has been my only partner on and off, so how can this happen?" As soon as he said this, he realised that she had had other partners and then he questioned himself. *I wonder if she knew she had this already?*

The doctor said, "It's all explained on this leaflet, which I will give you both." The doctor could feel the tension in the room as he handed the leaflets to them.

Gregory then asked, "What do I do now?"

The doctor replied, "Read the leaflet, and if you have any questions please call me here in the clinic." With this, he stood and walked to the door to show them both out. Sonia followed Gregory into the reception area. Gregory thanked the doctor and Sonia just remained quiet.

They both walked outside and Gregory turned to her and said, "Did you know you had this?"

She replied, "No I didn't. I am in shock."

He then said, "Well, you are the host so I got it from you."

Sonia replied with frustration, "That's not a nice thing to say."

Gregory grunted as they walked down the road. He looked at the leaflet and folded it, putting it in his pocket to read later that evening. Sonia just followed behind, feeling pretty deflated and hungry. She was worried now about what would happen to them both. Gregory stopped on the footpath and said, "I need a coffee and something to eat."

Sonia replied, "I feel sick."

Gregory immediately hugged Sonia. She was relieved that he did this; it gave her some hope that all wasn't finished between them.

She said, "I am really sorry, I have had no idea and I don't know how I got this."

Gregory replied, "You need to look at who you were with after we broke up and back track."

Sonia said, "Okay, but I haven't been with many."

Gregory replied, "It only takes one."

Sonia pulled away from him and said, "I need a coffee."

Gregory walked towards a coffee shop. Sonia walked beside him on her phone, checking symptoms via her search engine. Gregory just looked and said, "Don't worry about it, we will have to just monitor ourselves and try to prevent flare-ups." Sonia agreed as she put her phone away. He could see the concern on her face but it didn't stop him from thinking about who or how many guys Sonia had been with.

Sonia could see that he was thinking so she said, "What are you thinking?"Gregory replied, "I am thinking about what I will eat." Sonia knew that it wasn't this but remained quiet. They reached a coffee shop and entered. Sonia looked at the sandwiches and selected a gluten-free one. Gregory picked a ham and cheese roll. They stood to be served and Sonia asked for a cappuccino. Gregory also requested the same. Gregory paid and they both sat down at a table. They both opened their sandwiches and started to eat. Gregory sat quietly looking around the room while Sonia just picked at her food. She drank some coffee but struggled with the sandwich.

Gregory said, "We will work this out."

Sonia replied, "It's not reversible, so how can we?"

Gregory said, "We still have to live."

Sonia replied, "This will affect natural childbirth." Gregory swallowed deeply as he wasn't expecting this answer. Sonia continued to say that if she was to fall pregnant, she couldn't have the baby naturally.

Gregory took a drink from his coffee and remained quiet but then said, "I will read the leaflet later tonight. Maybe we can get a takeaway and just stay in."

Sonia replied, "Well, I don't really feel like doing anything."

Gregory agreed by saying, "Okay," and continued to eat. Sonia drank her coffee. While doing so she could only think that it was Philip who had the virus, but then Andrew flashed into her mind and she began to worry. She wondered how she would find out, but was it important? Then she questioned if they knew that they had it and had passed it on knowingly. This frustrated her and made her stomach feel even sicker.

Gregory finished his sandwich and said, "Do you want anything else to eat?" as he watched Sonia take small bites from her sandwich.

"No thank you," she said as she looked into his eyes.

Gregory then got up off his seat and said, "I'm going to have a blueberry muffin."

Sonia said, "Okay," as he walked to the counter area. She sat looking out the window and thought about the nights she had gone out and ended up in guys' pads. She was making herself feel worse. Gregory returned with a blueberry muffin and a gluten-free cake for Sonia on a tray. Sonia looked with surprise and said, "Oh, thank you," as she took another drink of her cappuccino. Gregory sat and realised that her cappuccino was nearly finished and that his was cold, therefore he got up again and ordered fresh drinks. He returned with the drinks and they both ate the cakes.

Gregory said to Sonia, "We can get some food or snacks on the way home." Sonia just agreed and they left the café, making their way back to Gregory's house. They walked to the Tube station holding hands but remained in silence. The Tube ride was no different. Sonia was frustrated and annoyed as she could feel the distance between them both. Gregory was still in shock with the news but remained quiet instead of venting his opinion regarding the situation. He could see that it had impacted Sonia also, so he decided to keep his opinion to himself rather than rock the boat. He wanted to read the leaflet and understand the virus before discussing it with Sonia. They both reached the final Tube destination and made their way to the street. Sonia wanted chocolate and some crisps to eat as a snack. She wasn't in the mood for anything else. She suggested they went to the shop and Gregory agreed. While walking through the aisles in the shop, Gregory said, "Can we order a pizza tonight?" Sonia liked the idea so she agreed. They both grabbed items as they walked around the shop before paying. As Gregory finished scanning the last item, Sonia pressed the finish and pay button and she offered her debit card before Gregory could. They had no plastic bag, so Sonia opened her handbag and packed it full with the items that she could fit in. Gregory carried the milk and bread as they exited the shop.

As they walked along the pavement towards Gregory's house, Sonia said, "I am really upset with the results and I can only imagine that you are too. I have no idea how or when I got this. I was shocked when the doctor said I was the host. In my profession, I know about these sexually transmitted infections and I have been careful."

Gregory listened and said, "I will read the leaflet, but I am shocked that you got it, of all people, and now me." Sonia felt terrible when he said this. It really made her heart flutter with a pressure around her chest area. She felt sick in her stomach and just wanted to be alone.

Gregory opened the front door to the house and Sonia said, "I need the toilet," as she walked up the stairs to the bedroom. Gregory carried her handbag and the items he was carrying into the kitchen. Sonia locked the bathroom door and she sat on the toilet, crying. She felt so deflated and worthless. She felt that Gregory was blaming her for the virus and she couldn't stop crying. Her nose was running and makeup was all over her face. Gregory switched on the heating and the television. He scanned through the channels to see what movies were on later that evening. He realised that Sonia hadn't returned so he went up to the bedroom. There he could hear Sonia sniffling.

He asked, "Sonia, are you okay?"

Sonia took a moment to reply. She replied, "I am okay."

Gregory replied, "Your voice doesn't sound like you are okay. Can I come in?"

Sonia said, "Wait a minute," as she stood and washed her face in the sink. Using the face towel, she wiped her face dry. Sonia opened the door and Gregory stood looking at her. He noticed that her eyes were bloodshot and that she was down in herself. He walked in and held her in his arms. Sonia grabbed him tightly and started to cry on his shoulder.

Gregory said, "Sonia, please don't cry. It's okay, we will get through this like we have all the situations and problems in our lives. If you look back at any situation in the past, you have always come out the other side, right?"

Sonia said, "Yes," but remained tightly wrapped around him. He knew that she was fragile so he said, "How about a cup of tea and we can relax on the couch and watch a movie, order in a pizza and have a glass of wine?"

Sonia pulled away slightly to look into his eyes and she kissed him on the lips. "I love you and I can't imagine you not in my life," Sonia said as she cleared her throat several times, with tears streaming down her face.

Gregory took his hand and rubbed a tear away with his finger and said, "I love you too." They kissed passionately and held each other tightly. Gregory pulled away and said, "Let's go downstairs. I'll make you a cup of tea. Maybe take one of my tracksuits so you can be comfortable." Sonia agreed and Gregory stepped out of the bathroom, making his way to the kitchen. He thought to himself, *What is going on right now? A test of some sort, maybe?* as he walked down the stairs. He switched on the kettle after checking the water level and waited for it to boil. He stood staring at it as it boiled, thinking about how Sonia got the virus. He knew nothing about what she had done while they were apart; he didn't really want to know. The whole situation had him dumbfounded.

He pulled two mugs from the cupboard and two tea bags from the packet. Pouring the water over the tea bags, he heard Sonia make her way down the stairs. She walked into the kitchen and Gregory said, "Just in time," as he handed her the mug with the tea bag inside. "You can take the tea bag out yourself and add milk to your liking."

Sonia took the mug and said, "Thank you," as she stood in his tracksuit. It was a little too big for her but she looked quite sexy in it.

Gregory said, "The hooded look suits you." Sonia smiled and opened the fridge door. Her eyes were swollen slightly from crying and a little bloodshot. She poured her milk into the mug and walked to the sink, placing the carton on the counter.

She turned to Gregory and said, "The milk is here," as she scooped the tea bag out with her fingers and dropped it into the sink. Gregory walked over and took the tea bag out of the sink and placed it in the bin with his own. He decided not to say anything but in his mind he thought, *That will stain the sink.* After he poured the milk into his mug and placed the carton back in the fridge, Sonia was already flicking through channels on the television. She found a comedy that had already started and she left it on. Gregory sat beside her on the couch. It didn't take him long to decide to go to his coat pocket and fetch the leaflet. He returned and sat beside Sonia.

Sonia looked and became frustrated again as he was reading it. She continued to watch the movie but noticed how engrossed Gregory was reading the leaflet. She continued to drink her tea but was getting more and more anxious. She got off the couch and returned up to the bedroom, taking her handbag. While lying on the bed, she took her mobile phone and opened the app to read her messages. She looked at the message from Philip and decided to reply. *Hi Philip, I would love to meet Tuesday evening.* She paused a moment before sending, then sent it as she wasn't feeling happy in the situation that she was in. She continued to read through emails received and old texts, deleting them. A text appeared on the screen as she was checking through emails. It was a reply from Philip. *Great, I will ping you Monday evening to arrange.* Sonia deleted the thread and continued on her phone. Gregory continued to watch the movie until the end and Sonia fell asleep while lying under the duvet. Gregory decided to walk up to her and see what she was doing. When he walked into the room, Sonia was under the duvet with her face barely showing. He knelt down and positioned his face close to the duvet where her head was hidden.

He spoke quietly and said, "Sonia." There was no movement so he repeated himself. Sonia moved slightly, adjusting her body to make herself more comfortable. He repeated himself again and said, "Sonia, wakey wakey." Sonia opened her eyes and looked confused.

She spoke and said, "I was in a lucid dream; it was so real."

Gregory folded his arms on the bed and positioned his chin on them. He said, "Tell me about it."

Sonia groaned as she stretched. "I will tell you later," she said as she pulled the duvet off herself and climbed out of the bed.

Gregory just watched her walk unsteady to the bathroom. He stood up and walked to the kitchen and switched on the kettle. Sonia appeared as he was looking in the fridge to see what he could eat. She said, "Shall we order a pizza?"

Gregory replied, "Yes, let's do just that." Sonia took her phone out of the tracksuit pants and looked up the pizza menu for the delivery outlet nearby. She decided on a gluten-free base with hot chilli toppings. Gregory decided on a Hawaiian. Sonia opened his drinks cupboard and checked out the wine selection that Gregory had built up from previous Christmas presents and found a nice bottle of white.

"Shall we have this one?" she said, holding the bottle facing Gregory.

He replied, "Why not?" Gregory called the pizza restaurant and ordered the pizzas. He was told it would take forty-five minutes. Sonia started to open the bottle of wine. Her phone beeped while she was opening the wine.

Gregory finished the telephone conversation and walked over to Sonia. He said, "It will take forty-five minutes."

Sonia kissed him as she opened the cupboard and took two wine glasses. She asked, "Will I pour you a glass now?"

Gregory said, "Yes please." He left the kitchen to use the downstairs toilet.

Sonia pulled her phone out of her pocket and checked it. It was a text from Philip: *Hi Sonia, do you fancy the theatre for Tuesday evening?* Sonia replied quickly, *Oh, that sounds great. X.* She closed the app and switched her phone onto silent mode, putting it back into her pocket. Gregory returned from the toilet and he felt sick in his stomach as he walked over to Sonia. She stood still as she held his wine glass. He took the glass and kissed her.

After taking a sip of the wine he said, "I have that strange sick feeling in my stomach again."

Sonia said, "Oh, really?" as she took a drink from her glass, looking at him.

Gregory walked to the couch, saying, "I haven't had it in a while and now it's back." He was thinking to himself, *I wonder what it is warning me about* as he sat down.

Sonia followed and said, "What do you mean?"

Gregory replied, "Nothing, don't worry about it."

Flicking through the television channels, Sonia chose a documentary about the canals in the UK. Gregory said, "This could be interesting."

She replied, "I know, that's why I put it on," with a smile. Gregory sighed and took a drink from his glass just as the doorbell rang. He placed his glass on the floor and walked to the front door. Sonia took a drink from her glass and waited as she listened to Gregory speaking at the door with the delivery man. She heard the door close and Gregory walking towards the kitchen. Sonia jumped up with excitement and walked to the counter where Gregory placed the pizza boxes. Sonia opened one and looked. "Oh, that's your one," she said, as she grabbed her own and walked to the couch. Gregory followed with his after he had grabbed some kitchen towel for them both. Sitting down, they both took a slice of their own pizza and started to eat. Gregory handed Sonia a piece of kitchen towel and she left it on her lap. The atmosphere was much better between them since Sonia had gone for a sleep. Gregory, however, was still feeling the sick sensation in his stomach and this was beginning to annoy him.

Sonia said, "Oh, mine is good, try it."

Gregory said, "No thanks, I am good. Have a slice of mine." Sonia immediately took a slice and left it in her box to try later. Gregory was shocked with her reaction as his pizza wasn't gluten free as he continued to eat. While he watched the television, he thought to himself, *What is this strange feeling in my stomach?*

Shortly after, he felt the cold feeling down his left arm again. This was the side that Sonia was sitting on, so he asked, "Do you feel a breeze?"

Sonia looked away from the television and said, "No, why?" as she looked at him, holding the food in her mouth without chewing.

"Ah, I just feel a cold feeling down my arm again."

Sonia moved away slightly to her left as she said, "You are giving me the heebie jeebies."

Gregory smiled as he shoved another slice of pizza into his mouth, taking a bite and placing the leftovers back onto the edge of his box. Sonia chewed her food and took another drink from her glass of wine. Gregory could feel the cool sensation around his mouth while eating and a cobweb feeling on his face. This intrigued him but he decided not to tell Sonia as it would freak her out. He sat quietly watching the television while this happened and remained still. Sonia noticed that he had stopped eating and she turned her head to look at him as she also paused. Shuffling in the position that she was in to make herself more comfortable, she said, "Gregory, you are freaking me out now, what is going on?"

Gregory turned his head and said, "Ah, I was just taking a minute to let the food digest," as he took the remainder of the slice to eat off his box.

Sonia went, "Phew," as she exhaled. Gregory continued to eat but he was aware of a sensation down his front. It felt like a slight pressure pushing towards him around the chest area and then a movement from his groin to his throat. He couldn't explain the feeling because he had never felt anything like this before. He just sat, curious, as he finished his pizza. Taking a drink from his wine, he noticed that the sensation dissipated so he wondered why. Sonia could see that Gregory was in his own world so she finished what she could eat, leaving some of her own pizza and also the slice that she took from Gregory. She placed her pizza box on the floor and snuggled into him, pulling the blanket over them both. She leaned over and took her wine glass off the floor. Gregory handed his pizza box to her and she placed it onto hers. They both kissed and Sonia handed Gregory the television remote in her way of saying 'change the programme'. Gregory took the remote and started to flick through the channels. Sonia would open her mouth and say, "Oh, that one," but Gregory would continue to switch channels. Sonia sat quietly until Gregory stopped at a movie. Sonia read the synopsis and then agreed by saying, "Okay, as long as it's not too violent." Gregory pulled the blanket off him and he took the pizza boxes to the kitchen, leaving them on the counter while making his way to the toilet. Sonia took a drink from her wine while looking out the dining room window. She then took her phone out of her pocket to check her messages. Philip had sent a message: *Theatre booked. X.* Sonia read this with excitement because she didn't know where they were going but hadn't got time to reply as she heard Gregory open the toilet door. She quickly placed the phone back into her pocket and pulled the blanket over her.

Gregory switched off the main lights as he passed through the kitchen, switching on the table lamps. As he did this, Sonia said, "Oh, it would be perfect if we had a fire lit." Gregory pulled the blanket up and sat down, placing it over his lap. Sonia cuddled into him and he pressed play. They both continued to drink the remainder of the wine during the movie. Once the movie was finished, Gregory and Sonia both tidied up the kitchen and they made their way to the bedroom after Gregory switched on the alarm system. They both felt very tired due to the build-up prior to the doctor's appointment.

Sonia walked into the bathroom as Gregory stripped down to his boxer shorts and changed his tee-shirt. He jumped under the duvet as he waited for Sonia to finish in the bathroom. The bed sheets were cold so he rubbed his feet together to try and generate heat. As soon as the bathroom door opened, he jumped up and moved swiftly to use it. Sonia was surprised at the speed at which he charged past her, requesting a kiss before he closed the door. Gregory was bursting to use the toilet so he sighed and kissed her quickly, closing the door. Sonia took off the tracksuit and placed it over the chair in the bedroom. She climbed under the duvet and felt the cold as she made herself comfortable, tightly wrapping herself inside, making sure there was no room for her heat to escape. Gregory opened the bathroom door switched off the light running over to the bed and jumped in, without realising that he had to switch of the bedroom and landing lights. Sonia laughed as he got back out and rushed around the room switching them off. Climbing under the duvet, he cuddled into Sonia, placing his left hand on her back. Sonia jumped while pushing him away from her. He laughed and lay still, trying to heat up. Sonia pulled the duvet around her face as she watched Gregory lie still, facing the ceiling. After a few minutes had passed, Sonia hunched over and cuddled into him. They lay quietly with their eyes closed. Sonia eventually said goodnight and kissed Gregory on the cheek. Gregory turned his head and they kissed, moving back into the same position, cuddling each other. They both fell asleep after Sonia moved away and curled up, smothered in the duvet, while Gregory lay on his back with his head to his left.

They both slept through the night, waking to the sound of a truck beeping its horn outside the house. Gregory got up and looked out the window. There was a truck trying to pass a badly parked car. The driver was sitting in the cab pressing the horn to get the attention of the owner as he couldn't reverse back down to the road. The commotion lasted about thirty minutes but Gregory and Sonia were wide awake. It was 8.45am.

Sonia looked at Gregory and said, "I will leave early and get my flat cleaned and washing done and rest before tomorrow." Gregory lay quietly as Sonia convinced herself of the chores she had to do. Gregory knew that she wouldn't do it all so he remained quiet. Sonia jumped out of the bed and took the tracksuit top as she walked out the door. "Do you want coffee?" she said, making her way to the stairs.

Gregory shouted, "Yes please," making sure that she heard him. Sonia stood in the kitchen while the kettle was boiling, feeling the cold air surround her body and folding her arms tightly. As she stood, she thought about her flat and all the sorting out that she had to do that day. The kettle clicked as it reached boiling point so she opened the cupboard and reached for two mugs. She prepared two coffees and walked towards the bedroom. No matter how careful she tried to be, she spilled one on the kitchen floor and on the stairs. She gave Gregory the mug that had coffee down the side when she entered the bedroom. He sat up as she walked in. Sonia walked to her side and placed the mug on the bedside table before getting under the duvet.

"Brr," she said as she shivered, wrapping the duvet around her. She didn't move for a few minutes while Gregory sipped from his mug, looking at her. Sonia looked back at him and smiled, saying, "You can get the coffee the next morning." Gregory laughed and drank some more. Sonia sat up also and took her mug. She said, "I will leave around 11am and get my flat sorted." Gregory agreed as he had things to do also. Sonia felt that he agreed a little too quickly for her liking and she felt unwanted because he didn't beg her to stay longer. She drank some coffee, staring at the reflection of Gregory in the television hung on the wall opposite them.

Gregory said, "When are you going to take your car home? It's been outside for a while." Sonia looked at him as she was holding the mug against her lips, feeling the warmth. She wasn't happy and she really felt as if he was pushing her away. This wasn't his intention, but Sonia was feeling rejected. She began to think it was because of the virus and that this was his way to slowly break up. Sonia placed her mug on the bedside table and made her way to the bathroom. Gregory watched as she pulled her panties down over her buttocks while walking as they had slipped up slightly. She switched on the light and closed the door. Gregory just continued to drink his coffee, sitting in silence. Sonia finished in the bathroom and she opened the door.

As soon as she entered, she said, "What are you going to do today?"

Gregory sat for a minute and answered, "I will clean the house and my car and relax."

Sonia climbed under the duvet. She then asked, "Are you okay with us?"

Gregory turned his head and said, "Why would you ask this?"

Sonia took her coffee and drank some before answering. "I just feel unwanted."

Gregory sighed and said, "I have no idea how you would feel this. What has happened to trigger this reaction?"

Sonia just said, "Don't worry about it, it's just me."

Gregory just nodded and said, "I am the same as any other day, no change on my side."

Sonia said, "Okay, forget I said it."

Gregory finished his coffee and said, "Do you want to shower first?"

Sonia replied, "You go." Gregory jumped up and walked to the bathroom. Sonia reached across to his side, holding her coffee while grabbing the remote control for the television. She pressed channel 15 for the music. Gregory continued to shower while Sonia sat watching music videos. When Gregory had finished and entered the room, Sonia continued to sit quietly, watching the television. Gregory got dressed and he gestured to take her mug. Sonia handed it to him as he kissed her on the lips before taking his own mug too and making his way downstairs. Sonia grabbed Gregory's pillow, scrunching it up while lying on it, continuing to watch the television. Gregory washed the mugs and he walked to the utility room to put on a clothes wash. Sonia closed her eyes and fell back asleep while Gregory continued to sort out the kitchen, fill the bird feeders in the back garden and take the washing out of the machine to hang up. He noticed that Sonia didn't emerge so he walked up the stairs to check on her. As he walked into the bedroom she was fast asleep.

He sat on the bed and whispered, "It's 10.33." Sonia jumped, lifting her head as she wiped her mouth. Gregory said again, "It's 10.33, you must have fallen asleep again."

Sonia opened her eyes fully and said, "I'm so tired."

Gregory replied, "I've cleaned the house."

Sonia just grunted and adjusted herself as she lay on her back. "I'll get up in a minute," she said as he was watching her. Gregory cuddled against her as they both kissed. Sonia moved and said, "God, I am hot under here." She moved to the edge of the bed and climbed out, walking to the bathroom. Gregory lay watching the television as he could hear the shower switch on. Sonia surfaced some time later with her hair wrapped in a towel. She said to Gregory, "I will go shortly and we can meet Friday as I have lots to do this week in work between shifts." Gregory agreed as Sonia started to dry her hair with the towel. Gregory asked if she would like some breakfast and Sonia said, "Porridge, please."

Gregory made his way to the kitchen. Sonia took her handbag and switched on her mobile phone. As it switched on, the battery signal showed three percent and the phone beeped. She rummaged in her bag and pulled out the charging cable and plug. She plugged it in while she continued to get dressed. Her phone beeped several times as she continued to dry her hair as much as she could with the towel. Opening her phone app, she looked at the messages. Philip had sent her a message: *Tuesday 18.45, dinner and show after X.* Sonia felt excited so she text back, *I can't wait Xx.* Gregory was making the porridge in the kitchen when he felt a cold breeze around him and he shivered. He wondered what Sonia was doing as he looked towards the kitchen door. Sonia left her phone charging as she put on her clothes and walked down to Gregory, flicking her hair several times while walking down the stairs.

As she walked into the kitchen, Gregory asked, "What were you doing just now?"

Sonia went numb for a moment and answered, "Nothing, why? I was drying my hair and getting dressed."

Gregory replied, "I just felt funny again, that's all." Sonia opened the fridge door with her back to him feeling creeped out. She took the milk and closed the door. As she turned, she walked up behind him as he was placing the porridge from the pot into two bowls. She cuddled into him and leaned her face on his back. Gregory stood still as she did this and his stomach felt sick but he didn't say anything. Sonia kissed his back and moved away to switch on the kettle. Gregory placed the pot in the sink and took both bowls to the dining room table. Sonia took two mugs and made coffee while she asked Gregory what his plans for the week were.

Gregory just said, "I will work and catch up on my paperwork." Sonia was thinking at that moment about going to the theatre with Philip. She was looking forward to it but didn't know which show they were going to. Sonia poured the coffee and left the milk on the counter in the event of having another one after. Gregory walked to the cupboard and took the honey out. Sonia walked past Gregory, making sure not to spill the coffee. Gregory felt sick again in his stomach and he wondered what was happening as he stood still for a moment.

Sonia noticed him standing still and asked, "Are you okay?"

Gregory said, "Yes, just a weird sensation again."

Sonia sat down and opened the honey while watching him. As she scooped some honey out with her spoon, she asked, "What do you think it is?" knowing that he might be picking up on her thoughts.

He said, "I don't know but it's when we are close together."

Sonia said, "Right, thanks, that makes me feel a whole lot better."

Gregory replied, "You asked." Sonia placed her spoon with the honey into her porridge and stirred it. She sat quietly stirring as Gregory sat on the opposite side of the table. He said, "Thank you for the coffee." Sonia looked at him for a brief moment and replied, "You're welcome." He drank some coffee and stuck his spoon into the honey.

Sonia said, "You freak me out when you go all funny, you were never like this before."

Gregory replied, "I have no idea what's going on but my system is picking up stuff and it doesn't feel right." Sonia scooped some porridge onto her spoon and placed it in her mouth. She chewed a little and placed the spoon into the bowl.

"I've lost my appetite," she said as she looked at him. Gregory continued to eat his as Sonia drank her coffee. He could feel that there was a tension in the room and he knew that his system was acknowledging it. Sonia was feeling sick because she was starting to feel guilty that she had made plans with Philip behind Gregory's back. She became worried that he might find out. Sonia got off her chair and went to the downstairs toilet. Gregory continued to eat his porridge until he was finished. He was very aware that Sonia was very uncomfortable so he decided to find out why. Sonia returned and asked if he wanted a fresh coffee.

Gregory said, "I would love one."

"What is wrong with you?" Sonia said as she walked to the kettle. "I feel uncomfortable when you go weird."

Gregory sat back in his chair and thought for a moment. He said, "Nothing has changed between us so don't worry." Sonia was happy to hear this. She made the coffee and realised that it was 11.45am.

"I must go soon," she said as she walked towards Gregory.

He said "Okay," as she placed the mug in front of him. He said "Thank you," while looking into her eyes. Sonia sat and smiled, lifting her mug to her lips. Gregory also took a drink. Shortly after drinking her coffee, Sonia placed her mug in the sink and went up to the bedroom to get her phone and handbag. She grabbed her coat at the bottom of the stairs and walked into the kitchen while Gregory was washing up. She stood as he dried the pot with a kitchen towel and placed it back into the cupboard.

Gregory and Sonia hugged and he said, "I will walk with you to the station."

Sonia said, "That would be nice," as she wrapped her scarf around her neck. Gregory fetched his coat while Sonia stood in the hallway. He switched on the alarm and they both left to walk to the Tube station. Sonia took Gregory's hand and said, "I will miss you. Looking forward to Friday."

Gregory stopped and kissed her. He said, "Me too." They walked hand in hand to the Tube station entrance. They embraced, kissed and Sonia walked into the station as Gregory watched her descend on the escalator. He crossed the road and walked back towards his house. On the way he decided to go into the shop and buy a Bounty chocolate bar. He felt lighter for some reason but he couldn't figure this out. Paying for the chocolate, he felt a rush of energy from his stomach to his throat area. This was very strange for him as he was trying to concentrate on buying the chocolate while having these sensations. He paid and walked out of the shop and turned up his street in the direction towards his house.

Once inside, he switched on the kettle and made himself a mug of tea. Standing in the kitchen, holding his mug, he felt a cold breeze around his nose and a web feeling on his face. He placed his hand over his nose and he could still feel the cold around his nostrils. He knew that this wasn't a draft in the room but something else. He said, "Is there someone here?" He stood still to feel as much as possible. He felt a pressure on his chest and he got dizzy. Gregory walked to the couch and sat down. He drank some tea and took the chocolate out of his coat pocket. Sitting with his coat open, he could feel a breeze around him. It was like a whirlwind. Gregory sat for a few minutes until he felt nothing. He switched on the television and opened the wrapper of the chocolate bar. While eating it, he noticed that the room felt a little strange. It felt as though he wasn't actually in the room but looking through it. Gregory took a bite of the chocolate and he started to feel better after eating. He switched the channels and found a building programme to watch. Sonia text Gregory later that afternoon to say that she had arrived home safely and that she missed him. Gregory replied back saying that he missed her. Later that evening, Gregory text Sonia to say that he was going to bed and he wished her a good night. Sonia replied with the same message, wishing him a good night's sleep.

17

The truth

THE FOLLOWING MORNING, SONIA TEXT GREGORY, *Good morning XxX*. He woke and replied the same. They text each other throughout the day and spoke to each other before retiring to sleep. Tuesday morning arrived and Sonia was excited. She wore a nice dress to work. She had prepared herself on Monday evening by relaxing in the bath. She was very excited about the theatre but had had no messages from Philip since the Sunday morning. The day passed quickly as Sonia was very busy with a client all day. She was pretty exhausted from being on her feet all day but looked forward to the night out. She got off work early and checked her phone at her locker. There was a text from Philip: *I will meet you at Piccadilly Circus Tube Station 18.45 X*. Sonia had forty-five minutes to get fixed up and make her way to the Tube station. She had to walk to Baker Street Tube station and travel three stops. She finished her makeup and got into her dress, out of her work clothes. On her way to the Tube station Sonia text Gregory as he had also sent a few messages throughout the day: *Hiya, crazy day with client, couldn't text. Love you X*. She continued to walk while texting Philip. *On my way, see ya soon X*. It was 6.30pm when she walked through the entrance to the Tube station. On her way, while sitting on the train, she couldn't contain herself with the excitement of going to the theatre; it was more the excitement of not knowing what they were going to see. The train was quite busy so Sonia had to stand holding the handrail. She was also starting to sweat a little which concerned her as she didn't want to have a wet stain under her arms when she took off her coat. She only had a few stops but this frustrated her and she counted each stop until she disembarked. Walking along the platform she removed her coat and held it over her arm with her handbag. She stepped onto the escalator and as she was ascending, her mobile beeped. Fidgeting with one hand she managed to open her mobile app and read the messages. There was one each from Gregory and Philip. Gregory wrote, *I missed you all day, hope you are okay and ready to relax. X*. Sonia text back, *Yes, on my way home but will grab a bite to eat first. Miss you too, will text later Xx*. She then read the text from Philip. It read: *Hiya, I am here! Just outside the entrance X*. Sonia smiled and placed her phone back into her pocket as she reached the top of the escalator. Walking through the barrier, she noticed Philip standing beside the newspaper stand. She walked up and he greeted her with a hug and a kiss.

Sonia stood for a moment and exhaled, saying, "What a mission, I am so hot!"

Philip laughed and said, "Yes, you are," as they started to walk towards the street. Sonia could feel the intense cold hit her body but this was what she needed to cool down. Shortly after, she struggled to don her coat but Philip took her handbag to free her arms. She smiled, wrapping her scarf around her neck. Philip said, "I have picked an Italian. I hope you are okay with this?"

Sonia replied, "Absolutely," as she buttoned up her coat. They walked for a few minutes, talking about the Christmas lights and how beautiful this time of the year is. Sonia also discussed the stress families go through just for one day and the debt some acquire to buy presents.

Philip changed the subject by saying, "We are here now," pulling open the door. Sonia followed behind him as he stood for assistance to get a table. The restaurant was busy with an ambience of chatter and a banging of cutlery. Sonia wanted a table that would be in a quiet area but Philip had already agreed a table with the waitress. He began to take off his jacket as Sonia placed her handbag on her seat. Philip sat watching Sonia remove her coat and he said, "I like your dress, very smart and sexy."

Sonia blushed and said, "Thank you." She sat in her chair, placing her handbag on the floor beside her feet. The waitress placed the menus on the table and instructed them both about the specials, and asked if they knew what they would like to drink. Sonia could hear her phone beep as the waitress took the drinks order from Philip. He ordered a bottle of white wine. Sonia also requested still water. She knew that the text was from Gregory but she didn't want to grab her phone as it be rude and Philip would ask who it was. This frustrated Sonia a little as she became a little bothered. She eventually excused herself and grabbed her phone from her coat with her handbag, making her way to the toilet. While standing inside the ladies', she opened up the app and read the message: *What are you going to eat? I am making some chicken. Pretty tired. How are you? X.* Sonia replied, *Just getting some pizza and I will have an early night, I am exhausted too. X.* She placed her phone into her handbag and used the toilet. After, she washed her hands and touched up her lipstick. She walked back to the table and Philip was sitting with his wine. Sonia noticed that he had started without her, so she said, "Hey, you started without me."

Philip smiled and said, "Cheers," as he lifted his glass and looked into Sonia's eyes.

Sonia smiled and said, "Cheers," as she blushed. She took a sip and said, "Oh, that's nice and refreshing."

Philip said, "Yes, it's a light, refreshing wine."

Sonia took another drink. Sonia asked, "Where are we going after? The suspense is killing me."

Philip smiled and took a drink from his wine. He was about to say when the waitress appeared. "Can I take your orders, please?" Philip took his menu and gestured to Sonia to proceed with her order.

Sonia looked at the menu and pointed. "I will have the spaghetti carbonara with gluten-free spaghetti, please."

The waitress took the order and asked, "Do you have any other allergies?"

Sonia shook her head and said, "No."

The waitress turned to Philip and asked for his order. Philip sat up and said, "I will have the sirloin, medium well, with skinny chips, please." The waitress acknowledged and asked if there was anything else that they would like.

Sonia and Gregory both said, "No thank you," at the same time. They laughed and said, "Cheers," taking another drink.

Sonia then said, "So where are we going?" as she sat back into her chair. Philip reached into his coat and pulled out some paper. He reached over to Sonia and she took the paper from him.

He said, "Open it." Sonia smiled and started to open the paper and noticed immediately the word 'Phantom'.

She then said, without opening the paper completely, "Phantom of the Opera."

Philip smiled and said, "Yes, I have booked front row tickets."

Sonia said, "Oh my God, I am so excited." She lifted her glass and said, "Here is to a great night."

Philip lifted his glass and said, "Yes, to a great night."

They both drank some more and Philip filled both glasses with wine. Sonia opened the tickets and read the information. Shortly after, the main course arrived and they both began to eat. Sonia could hear her phone beep again a few times while she was eating. Philip also noticed the beeping sound and he commented on it.

"Are you being missed?"

Sonia blushed and said, "It's probably work looking for me to do a shift." She turned her spaghetti with a fork on a spoon before placing it into her mouth. Sonia felt uncomfortable as she continued to eat, remaining quiet. Philip noticed that her demeanour had changed and she was acting strange.

He asked, "How is your dinner?"

Sonia placed her fork down and said, "It's really tasty. How is yours?"

Philip said, "It's cooked to perfection and I am loving the sauce – peppercorn."

Sonia replied, "That's good."

They continued to eat and Philip noticed that the time was passing quickly. He said, "We will need to make a move in about twenty minutes as we have to walk over."

Sonia nodded and continued to eat. Philip finished his dinner and excused himself, making his way to the toilet. Sonia took this opportunity to check her phone messages. She opened the app with speed and read the first text from Gregory: *Hey, I am going to go to bed shortly, wishing you a lovely evening. X.* Sonia then read the second: *Hello.* Then the third message: *Are you okay?* She also noticed that he had called her phone. Sonia text back, *I am fine, I was out of service. I am also going to bed now. Love you XxX.* She placed her phone back into her pocket and sat taking a drink as she had lost her appetite to finish her meal.

Philip returned and asked if she was ready to leave. Sonia looked up and said, "Yes, I am ready," preparing to stand up. Philip took his coat and he made his way to pay the bill, leaving Sonia to put her coat on. She walked over to him as he had just paid and was putting his wallet back into his front trouser pocket. Sonia said, "Thank you," and Philip said, "You are very welcome. Let's go and have some fun."

Sonia smiled and followed him outside. Sonia grabbed Philip's arm and they both walked down the street. Philip commented, "That's a nice perfume."

Sonia replied, "Oh, I bought this a few weeks ago, thank you." It was bitterly cold that evening and Philip could feel that the cold was affecting his speech, more so the movement of his jaws. Sonia wrapped her scarf over her mouth to keep her face warm.

Philip mumbled, "God, it's freezing tonight." Sonia agreed. They reached the venue and Philip pulled open the glass doors. Sonia followed behind. Philip showed his tickets while the security checked Sonia's handbag at the entrance door. Once inside, Philip asked, "How about a drink in the bar?" Sonia quickly agreed but said that she needed the bathroom.

They both walked up the stairs towards the bar and Sonia turned off to the right to the bathroom while Philip made his way to the queue. Standing waiting, Philip decided to order a bottle of white wine so that they would be guaranteed to have a drink during the interval and not have to queue again. As Philip was ordering, Sonia entered the bar area, waiting at the back wall beside a small shelf to position their drinks. She looked around the room for seats but they were all taken. Philip walked over with a bucket containing the bottle of wine and two glasses. Sonia took the glasses from him as he placed the bucket on the shelf. She then positioned the glasses on the shelf and Philip started to pour the wine. Sonia stood and watched, mentioning how organised he was. He then explained why he bought the bucket. Smiling, Sonia raised her glass and said, "Good plan for the interval."

Philip raised his and said, "Here's to a good night."

Sonia smiled and drank some. Philip also took a sip while he looked around the room. Philip looked at Sonia and said, "I like your dress." Sonia got embarrassed and she drank some more. It didn't take her long to finish the glass, so Philip refilled hers. He said, "Someone is thirsty."

Sonia smiled and replied, "It's a nice wine." Philip agreed just as the public address speaker announced that there was ten minutes before the start of the show. Sonia and Gregory drank their drinks and left the wine and bucket on the shelf. They both walked into the auditorium and Sonia followed Philip as he made his way to their seats. Sonia took her time descending the stairs in her high-heeled shoes. Philip stood and waited for Sonia at the edge of the row, allowing her to enter first and take her seat. They were positioned in the centre of the stage on the ground floor row. Sonia was overwhelmed by the auditorium and the sound of the orchestra practising with their instruments before the show started. Sonia placed her coat on her lap and so did Philip. The lights dimmed as the show began.

Sonia enjoyed the whole experience up to the half-time interval. She turned to Philip and said, "This is brilliant. I am really enjoying it."

Philip smiled and said, "Drink?" Sonia got up from her seat and walked to the bar with Philip. As they entered the bar, their bucket with wine was waiting with two fresh glasses sitting on the shelf. Sonia was happy because there were two stools also for them to sit on. Sonia sat while Philip poured the wine. They both sat talking about the show while drinking. It wasn't long again before Sonia had finished her glass. Philip was very surprised as he filled her glass again.

Sonia said, "I seem to be drinking fast this evening."

Philip laughed and said, "Yes, you seem to like this one."

Sonia replied, "It's going down like water." She excused herself as she needed to go to the toilet. Philip refilled his own glass and he continued to sip his wine while reading the caption under a picture hanging on the wall. Sonia was gone for some time and the announcement to take their seats came over the speakers again. Philip continued to wait until Sonia appeared. She said, "There was a queue, sorry."

Philip said, "Let's go to our seats." He knocked back his wine and Sonia also finished her glass before they walked back to their seats. Just as they sat, the lights dimmed again and the show started. Sonia felt a bit dizzy but she was feeling good. Sonia continued to watch in awe as the show stimulated her imagination. Philip had seen it before, but he didn't tell Sonia. The show ended and they both attended the bar to finish their drinks. Unfortunately the bar was closed so they made their way out of the building with the other patrons. Sonia exited first so she stood to the side and waited for Philip as he was behind her. Once together, Philip noticed a pub across the road with lights flashing inside.

He said, "That looks like a happening place, shall we investigate?"

Sonia looked and said, "Yes, let's have a drink." They waited for a gap in the traffic and quickly crossed the road. Sonia opened her bag and took her phone out to switch it on before entering the bar. Her phone vibrated several times as she put it back into her handbag. Philip pulled open the door and Sonia walked inside, where music was blaring. Philip followed and they both looked around at many people dancing and singing.

Sonia smiled as they approached the bar. Philip shouted for the drinks menu and the barman handed one to him. Both Sonia and Philip found it difficult to see the menu due to the flashing lights and reduced lighting. Philip decided on a whiskey and Sonia chose a brandy and port, mixed. Philip was surprised with Sonia's selection but he ordered it anyway. Sonia started to dance while she was waiting for her drink. Philip remained leaning on the bar while he watched the barman prepare the drinks. Philip paid for the drinks with his card and he turned to face Sonia as she was dancing.

Philip smiled and handed her the brandy and port. He said, "That's a strong one."

Sonia smiled and said, "Thank you. It's great for getting rid of an upset stomach or fighting a cold."

Philip replied, "Cheers to that," as he laughed, not believing her. Sonia took a sip and placed her glass on the bar. She started to dance again, moving her upper body in the same upright position. She grabbed Philip's hands and swung him left and right but he was a little uncomfortable. Sonia released herself and danced in a seductive way. Philip watched as he took a drink from his whiskey.

The song finished and Sonia took another sip from her drink, saying, "I needed that little dance." Philip smiled and he gave her a hug. Sonia stood still and enjoyed the embrace. The music got more upbeat so Sonia started to dance again. Philip knocked back his whiskey and he ordered another.

He asked Sonia, "What would you like?"

Sonia replied, shouting, "I'll have a brandy, please." Philip looked at his watch. It was 10.45pm and he thought to himself, *This won't be a long night*, knowing that Sonia would be drunk very soon.

Sonia took a sip from her glass and she excused herself to go to the bathroom. This time she left her handbag with Philip and she completely forgot to check her mobile phone. Sonia eventually found the toilet sign pointing down the stairs to the basement. She felt herself wobble a little as she stumbled in her high heels. As she descended the stairs, she grabbed onto the handrail to support herself. Making her way into the bathroom, another girl passed her in the narrow corridor. Sonia pushed open the door to find a very small toilet with a mirror and two cubicles. She looked at herself in the mirror and shook her hair a little. She was feeling a little drunk at this stage. She used the toilet and washed her hands. The alcohol was starting to take effect on her mobility, so she placed her left wrist under the cold tap for a moment to cool her system and settle herself. As she did this, she guessed that it was around 11pm so she knew that she needed to have an excuse for why she didn't reply to Gregory's text. She removed her wrist and rubbed it with her right hand.

Walking out of the toilet, she walked up the stairs slowly as she felt the strain on her legs, feeling tired until she reached the ground floor. Walking through the double doors back into the bar, the music became much louder. She was pleasantly surprised as the bar was very full now as she squeezed past the other patrons to reach Philip. Philip was holding her handbag while taking a drink from his glass. Sonia smiled and said in a raised voice, "Oh, that look suits you."

Philip smiled and shouted back, "Really, do you think so?" as he did a little twirl holding her handbag. Sonia laughed as she took a drink from her glass. Philip raised his glass and they just clanked glasses, looking into each other's eyes. It was getting very congested and people had started to shove and nudge Sonia from behind as they were dancing. This annoyed Sonia as she kept turning and looking at the culprits.

Philip said, "Switch with me." Sonia and Philip switched positions and Sonia was much more relaxed. He turned to the bartender and ordered two Jägerbombs.

Sonia didn't hear what he ordered so she shouted, "What did you order?"

Philip smiled and said, "Wait."

Sonia poked him and said, "Are you trying to get me drunk?"

Philip smiled and said, "Maybe," as he turned to face the bar, watching the barman prepare the drinks. Both drinks were positioned on the bar with a can of Red Bull.

Sonia looked and said, "Really?" Philip didn't hear her as he paid and poured the Red Bull into both glasses. He placed the can on the counter and handed Sonia her drink.

"Down the hatch in one go?" he said, looking into her eyes. Sonia went straight ahead and knocked it back without waiting on Philip. Philip said, "Wow," and he followed suit, knocking his back. Sonia slammed her glass on the counter and sighed with a facial expression. She danced and Philip placed his glass down, starting to move a little to the music. Still feeling very self-conscious, he would reach for his drink to distract himself and stop dancing. Sonia, on the other hand, was starting to get into the rhythm of the music and would from time to time pull Philip over closer to her body. This aroused Philip as he enjoyed the flirting. Sonia was drinking quickly and Philip realised that her glass was nearly empty. He asked if she wanted another brandy by gesturing, putting his hand to his mouth and pointing to her glass. Sonia looked and nodded, accepting. Philip turned and walked to the gents' toilet, leaving Sonia dancing on her own. Philip finished in the toilet and stood at the bar, watching Sonia dancing on her own. He ordered the drinks and continued to watch Sonia as he was feeling more relaxed as the alcohol was starting to affect his system. The barman placed the two drinks on the counter in front of him and he scanned his debit card to pay.

Sonia was in her own world dancing. Philip walked over and nudged her, placing her drink into her hand. Sonia stopped dancing and grabbed Philip's arm, kissing him on the cheek and saying thank you into his ear in a very seductive way. Philip pulled her closer to him and he kissed her on the lips. Sonia felt faint as the alcohol was affecting her mobility. Philip realised so he held her upright as she was starting to sway a little.

He said into her ear, "It's time that we go now."

Sonia wasn't happy so she slurred her words, "Oh no, we don't," as she grinned. Philip grabbed his coat from the hook under the counter and he put it on as quickly as possible, releasing his hands off Sonia. Watching her every move, he wrapped his scarf around his neck and zipped his coat up. Sonia grabbed her drink and downed the remainder. Philip took her coat and handbag, trying to get her attention to put it on.

He shouted, "Let's try another bar on the way, one a bit quieter." Sonia nodded and took her coat. He was relieved that she agreed as he thought it was going to be a long night trying to convince her. The bar was very full, with the music creating a vibration with the thumping sound of the bass. Sonia continued to wiggle as she attempted to button her coat. Philip tried to assist but she turned away. He tapped her on the shoulder and pointed to the door as he walked away. Sonia waved and smiled at him. He opened the door and was greeted by the bouncers. He just thought to himself, *Please don't make a show on your way out*, looking back to see if Sonia was following. Sonia had disappeared into the crowd so Philip had to return to try to find her. As Philip moved through the other patrons who were standing and dancing, he thought that she may have gone to the ladies, so he waited at the top of the stairs. He waited for several minutes to no avail. He asked the waitress to check the toilet while he waited. Philip got distracted listening to the music. The waitress came up the stairs and surprised him as she touched his arm. She said, "Your friend is in the toilet being sick."

Philip raised his eyes to the ceiling and said, "Okay, thank you," as he looked down the stairs, wondering what to do next.

"I will take her a glass of water," said the waitress as she disappeared behind the bar. Philip just remained in the corridor above the stairs, looking at the pictures on the wall. He was also tipsy but getting very tired. The waitress smiled at him as she entered the corridor and walked down the stairs.

Philip just waved uncomfortably and said, "Thank you," but she didn't hear him. He decided to get himself another drink as he knew that it would be a while before Sonia would surface. Standing at the bar, he shouted towards the barman, "JD and coke, please." The barman acknowledged and continued to serve another before attending to Philip's drink. He stood at the bar and opened his coat, removing his scarf as the barman placed his drink on the counter. Philip reached for his wallet and scanned his debit card, thanking the barman. He returned the card into his wallet and placed it back into his front left pocket. Standing, Philip took a drink, watching the other revellers dance and have fun. He thought about Sonia so he moved to the stairs to see if she had resurfaced. There was no sign of her so he continued to drink in the corridor, knocking it back. The waitress walked out of the ladies with two other girls and she made her way to Philip.

She said, "Okay, she is standing now at the mirror fixing her makeup, but very drunk. She will need some help to walk."

Philip said, "Okay, I will go down to the door and wait." The waitress walked with him and she took Sonia out to the corridor. Philip gently grabbed Sonia's arm, assisting her to the stairs and up to the ground floor. It was a slow affair as several others waited at the top to get to the toilets. They reached the top, where the waitress opened the door and let them walk towards the exit door. Philip thanked the waitress as they walked out onto the footpath. There was a queue of people standing waiting to get into the venue as the bouncers controlled the movements of those leaving and entering.

Philip stopped Sonia and began to fasten her coat as she slurred, "Em, funny you are dressing me and not taking off my clothes."

Philip smiled and said, "Making sure that you are warm, Sonia." Sonia swayed a few times as Philip corrected her using the weight of his own body as he struggled to fasten the buttons. Once finished, he placed his arm around her as they walked towards his place. Sonia remained very quiet for the whole journey as she concentrated on walking. Philip had to talk to her the whole way as she was feeling extremely tired and didn't want to walk. They reached his apartment and he got her into the lift as quickly as possible. Standing in the lift, Sonia was feeling very dizzy and hot. She began to pull at the buttons on her coat, trying to unfasten them, but couldn't. The lift door opened and Philip walked ahead to open the flat door. Sonia walked with her hand gliding along the wall to balance herself. She entered and slammed the door behind her, not intentionally but unaware of her coordination. Philip walked her to the bedroom and he removed her shoes, allowing her to lie on the bed. He left her while he got some water for them both. As soon as he returned, Sonia was fast asleep. He placed the glasses of water down and he opened her coat buttons, removing her coat with difficulty. He rolled her over and pulled the duvet back, rolling her under, covering her while still in her dress. Philip switched off the hallway lights and he climbed in beside her wearing only boxer shorts. He turned off the light and fell asleep.

Later that morning, Sonia woke all hot and bothered in her dress. She removed her dress and tried drinking some water before falling asleep again. Philip was out cold for the night so he didn't feel Sonia move. Philip's alarm on his phone activated at 7.30am and they both slept through it because he left it inside his coat pocket. It was 2.22pm when Philip woke, looking at his watch. He jumped out of the bed, rushing to find his phone.

Sonia lifted her head while she groaned. Philip said, "It's after half two."

Sonia lifted her head and said, "What? You are joking," as she felt dizzy. Sonia peeled back the duvet to look for her handbag and coat. She asked Philip, "Please pass over my handbag and coat." Philip grabbed them both with one hand while he was calling his office. Sonia knew that she was in trouble but couldn't get motivated to do anything. Her head felt like it was going to explode. She reached into her coat and pulled out her phone. Trying to switch it on, she realised that the battery was drained. She opened her handbag and pulled out the adapter and cord to plug it in. She was getting very frustrated now as she realised that not only would her work be looking for her, but also Gregory. Plugging in her phone, she watched as the battery symbol appeared with the charging indicator. She sat on the floor holding the phone and leaning against the wall. It took several minutes after trying from time to time to switch it on. The phone shone brightly as it went through the sequence of switching on. Sonia was very impatient at this stage. Her phone began to ping several times, then stop and continue to ping. Philip said, "Oh, someone is looking for you," as his call was answered. He told his work that he slept it out due to a power cut and to book him out for a day's leave, apologising.

Sonia opened her app to several calls and messages from Gregory. She felt deflated and worried about what she could say once she could speak to him. Her hangover wasn't helping as she couldn't focus. She decided to call her work and let them know that she slept through her alarm clock. After the call with her work, Sonia once again read through the texts and saw the number of missed calls from Gregory. She replied, *I forgot to charge my phone after work yesterday and went straight to bed, sorry, love you! Really busy in work so I will call you later. Miss you! XxX.*

Sonia took a moment before sending just as Philip walked back into the room saying that he was sorted while climbing back into bed, sighing. Sonia sent her message and also lay back on the bed. She was feeling annoyed with herself and asked, "Nothing happened last night, right?"

Philip looked at her and said, "Nothing, I just put you to bed in your dress." Sonia felt relieved and remembered taking off her clothes during the night when she felt hot. She closed her eyes and started to drift into a sleep. Philip also fell asleep.

Gregory was in work when he received the text, reading it immediately. He was very surprised that Sonia didn't call him, so he called her work to speak to her. The call was answered by one of her work colleagues.

"Hello, Lucy here, can I help?"

Gregory said, "Hi Lucy, it's Gregory. Is Sonia there please?"

Lucy remained quiet for a moment and then said, "Sonia never made it to work today, I have no idea where she is," feeling very uncomfortable.

Gregory said, "Oh okay, I forgot that she was off today." Playing it down. He said goodbye and finished the call. Standing in his work office, Gregory felt sick again. He was surprised that she said that she was busy in work. He knew that Sonia was off until Saturday so he decided to text her: *How about meeting up Thursday evening for a meal in London, I will come to you Xx*. He stood looking at his phone, waiting for a reply, but nothing arrived so he grabbed his coat and made his way to an appointment. He knew that something wasn't right because the sick feeling in his stomach and his thoughts were consuming him.

Sonia remained asleep until 4.45pm and she reached around the bed for her phone, which was beside her leg. She opened the app and noticed a text from Gregory. She replied, *Hiya, I would love that. Love you XxX*, texting with one eye open, feeling her pounding head. She sent the text and looked over at Philip. He was out cold with his mouth wide open, breathing as if it was his last breath. Sonia decided to refill her water in the kitchen so she struggled to motivate herself to get up. Just as she sat on the edge of the bed, Philip opened his eyes and said in a croaky voice, "How are you feeling now?"

Sonia looked and said, "I am wrecked."

Philip said, "You were out of your face last night."

Sonia sighed and said, "Thanks, that makes me feel better," as she walked to the kitchen, asking, "Do you want water?"

Philip said, "Yes please." She grabbed his glass too and walked into the kitchen in her underwear.

Gregory arrived at his appointment early so he decided to text Sonia again: *How is your day going so far?* Sonia's phone buzzed as it vibrated on the side table near Philip. He called her and said, "Your phone is buzzing." Sonia had just finished filling the glasses so she began to walk back into the bedroom. She handed Philip his glass and walked to the other side of the bed, taking her phone. Placing the glass on the bedside table, Sonia opened her phone and looked at the message, taking in a breath. She text back, *Very busy and stressful today XxX.* Gregory received the text just as he entered the reception of the building where his appointment was. He felt completely deflated as he then knew that something was not right and he could only imagine that she was with another guy. He felt weak and was in no form to meet for a sales appointment. He stood at the reception, totally confused and with a blank mind. The receptionist asked, "Good afternoon, can I help?" Gregory stood looking at her, not computing what she had asked. He opened his folder, looking for his paperwork to find the person that he was to meet. He felt very embarrassed as he couldn't function. The receptionist remained focussed on him, waiting for the information so that she could assist. Gregory dropped some paperwork onto the floor as he shuffled through his stuff. Bending down, he saw the appointment at the top of one of the sheets.

He stood up and looked into the receptionist's eyes and said, "Mr James Knight, please."

The receptionist asked, "Is he expecting you?"

Gregory said, "Yes he is," as he tidied up his paperwork. He was asked to wait in the seating area across from the reception. Gregory sat and looked at his phone again. He decided not to contact Sonia again for the day as he was feeling very disconnected with himself. Gregory was relieved when the appointment was finished and he decided to go straight home and chill out for the remainder of the day.

Sonia and Philip decided to get up. Sonia didn't shower as she was feeling very annoyed and frustrated with the whole situation. She couldn't relax at all. Her head was pounding and she felt so tired and hungry. Philip also wasn't feeling too good but wanted to eat.

He asked, "Shall we go to a café for food?"

Sonia replied, "Sure, but I may not be able to eat."

Philip laughed and said, "Okay, let's go!"

Sonia took a while to get her things together while getting dressed. Philip opened his wardrobe and dressed in jeans, a tee-shirt and jumper. Sonia struggled to close the clasps on her high heels, so Philip walked over and kneeled on the floor, assisting while Sonia lay back on the bed. She was feeling so tired that she had no energy and no will to do anything.

Philip closed the clasps and said, "Okay, that's it, done!" Sonia lifted her body and felt dizzy. She stood up and walked over to grab her coat and handbag, which were left on the floor. Philip put his coat on and he stood waiting for Sonia at the entrance door. Sonia walked over, putting her gloves on as he opened the door. "I know a nice place around the corner."

Sonia replied, "Okay," as she stumbled out of the door with a wobble.

Philip noticed that she was struggling, so he took her arm as they approached the lift. Pressing the lift button, Philip looked into Sonia's eyes and said, "I enjoyed last night."

Sonia smiled and said, "I can't remember it," feeling embarrassed. All she could think about was Gregory, hoping that everything was okay between them. As both herself and Philip walked onto the footpath outside his apartment, Sonia said, "I'm sorry but I am going to go home now." She adjusted her scarf while standing looking at Philip.

Philip said, "Okay, are you sure?"

Sonia nodded and said, "I feel really bad, very weak, and need to sleep."

Philip said, "Okay," as he gave her a hug.

Sonia said, "I will text when I get home."

Philip said, "No worries," as Sonia thanked him for a lovely evening. They parted and Sonia walked towards the Tube station, feeling the intensity of the cold air against her face. She walked very much deep in thought, pondering about the night out with the guilt and shame that was starting to annoy her. She was very worried about her work and the fact that Gregory had text so many times and also called. She knew that she was going to be questioned by him. It was just after 5.30pm and it was already dark as she entered the Tube station. She could feel the heat as she scanned her Oyster card as she walked through the barrier. Descending the escalator, the cold air blew her hair all over her face as she stood still. She travelled on the train and walked back to her flat, just wanting to get back into bed and sleep. Just as she opened her front door, her phone rang. She pulled it out of her pocket and was relieved that it was Philip.

She answered, "Hey, is everything okay?"

Philip said, "Yes, just checking you got home okay?"

Sonia said, "Aww, that's very kind of you. Yes, I am home just now, opening the hall door."

Philip then said, "Rest well, I will call you later."

Sonia said, "Thank you again for a wonderful evening."

Philip laughed and said, "Pity you can't remember it." Sonia remained quiet and Philip said, "I am only joking."

Sonia then said, "Enjoy your food. Bye."

Philip said, "I will. Bye."

Sonia hung up and opened her flat entrance door. Placing her handbag on the floor, she dropped her gloves, coat and scarf on the chair. She unzipped her dress, dropping it on the floor while putting on a tee-shirt. Removing her bra, she climbed under the duvet, wrapping herself up to get warm. It didn't take long for her to fall asleep.Later that evening, around 8.15pm, Gregory decided to text Sonia. *Hope the day at work passed quickly for you X.* Sonia heard her phone buzz in her pocket and opened her eyes. Her room was dark and she felt hungry. She climbed out of her bed and felt around until she found her coat pocket. Pulling her phone out, she opened the app and read the message. She felt sick again as she read it. She noticed the time and replied, *Just finishing up now, I will go home and have a bath. How was your day? XxX.* She sent the text and switched on the bedroom light. Gregory read the message and replied, *That's great. I miss you X*, feeling angry that she continued to lie. Sonia received the message and she also replied, *I miss you too XxX.* She wanted to call him but was afraid that he would quiz her. Gregory also wanted to call her and find out the truth, but he preferred to see her in person and get the answers. After all, they were meeting the next evening. He decided to watch some television before going to bed. Once in bed he didn't sleep as his mind was continuously going through the texts and previous months' events between them both. Sonia had a bath and didn't eat as she wasn't feeling well at all. She slept very well.

The following morning, Sonia walked into her work. While changing in the locker room area, she continued with the same story telling her work colleagues that she had slept through the alarm clock. Lucy wasn't on the same shift that day so she couldn't tell Sonia that Gregory called. There was no note left either as Lucy was very busy and had got sidetracked with the demands of the day before. Sonia sent Gregory a text: *Good morning, looking forward to tonight XxX*. Gregory replied: *Good morning, me too, very much X*. Sonia continued with her day and finished work early as she had a training day. Gregory finished his day early too so that he could meet her. He had made his way to her work and he waited outside to greet her. Gregory text Sonia, *I am outside the main entrance door X*. Sonia read the message as she was buttoning up her coat. She didn't text back and walked to the entrance door feeling very anxious and tense. She passed the security guard and said, "Good night," pushing the glass door open.

As she exited the building, she saw Gregory standing beside a lamp post. She smiled and he gestured with a wave. Sonia walked up to him and they hugged each other. Sonia asked, "How was your day?" as they walked up the street.

Gregory said, "Same auld day, usual crap."

Sonia replied, "Okay."

Gregory asked, "How was yours?"

Sonia looked at him and said, "You are a little funny, everything okay?"

Gregory said, "Yes, why?" Sonia remained quiet and walked alongside him. Gregory then said, "We can go to the restaurant that we were in before, the one around the corner."

Sonia just agreed as it was bitterly cold and she was feeling very tired and hungry. They both walked in silence until they entered the restaurant.

After being seated and while reading the menu, Gregory asked, "So where were you Tuesday night?"

Sonia swallowed as she wasn't expecting this question. She paused for a moment and said, "I was working and went home. Why this question?"

Gregory replied, "Well, I called your work and I was told you never made it in yesterday."

Sonia felt very uncomfortable and adjusted herself in her chair. She said, "I slept through the alarm clock."

Gregory took a moment while looking at the menu. He then asked, "You text me that you were at work and very busy twice yesterday – that's a little odd, don't you think? Why lie to me?"

Sonia excused herself and went to the toilet. Gregory sat and realised that she was lying and that there was someone else. He felt gutted and angry. He just wanted to leave but he wanted to know the truth. Sonia returned and sat.

She said, "I went out with a friend and got very drunk. I slept through the alarm clock."

Gregory then asked, "Who with?"

Sonia gasped and said, "Philip, a friend."

Gregory then felt very sick and said, "Did you sleep with him?"

Sonia replied, "No."

Gregory then asked, "Were you with him before?"

Sonia replied, "Yes, why is this important? We just went out."

Gregory said, "What's going on Sonia? You go out with another guy, you lie to me and I wouldn't know, only I called your work yesterday."

Sonia said, "Nothing is going on."

Gregory then said, "Where did you sleep Tuesday night?"

Sonia went very quiet and Gregory asked again, "Where?"

Sonia said, "In his apartment."

Gregory took his coat and started to put it on.

Sonia looked at him and said, "Where are you going? Please talk to me."

Gregory said, "I am done now. God knows what you have been up to, and now I know where the virus has come from. I don't know you anymore." He said, "Take care of yourself" as he walked out the door.

Feeling angry and disgusted with the circumstances, Gregory felt extremely emotional and useless. He walked towards the Tube station, wanting to go back to Sonia, but he knew he had to let her go. He knew that he couldn't continue to look over his shoulder if he continued in a relationship with her. He made his way home and climbed into his bed to sleep.

Sonia burst into tears, taking her coat and making her way to the toilet. She sat on the toilet and cried, pulling the toilet paper from the dispenser, blowing her nose. She spent some time there until another patron walked into the toilet area. Sonia wiped her nose and eyes and walked back into the restaurant, making her way past all the tables and opening the main entrance door. She walked with tears rolling down her face, thinking about Gregory. All she wanted to do was to call him but she knew that she couldn't. The shame and guilt became more apparent as she felt herself crumble from inside. She felt disappointed because she realised that she did care for Gregory more than she thought. The guilt of still living in other people's expectations and not knowing what she should do, caused a build-up of anger from within. The anger that she didn't set boundaries and work on herself for what needed to be changed, resulting in the feeling of shame making her reconnect with herself. This led to the bitterness and sadness making her hold judgements on others and herself, showing her where she needed to heal. This discomfort highlighted the area that she needed to pay attention to, allowing her the opportunity to change. To do something different that she would not typically do.

18

The realisation

Sonia realised that once she slept with another, regardless of the time spent together, she downloaded their issues via an emotional energy connection on top of her own current issues, making things deeper to solve. She was so consumed with her thoughts that her physical body, energy body and mind body weren't working in harmony for her internal organs to function correctly. Her conscious mind was monitoring the body in real time but connecting to the subconscious mind for help in analysing a situation or situations, to make the impact less on the body from past experiences. While she was in the company of another, she naturally blended in energy, therefore constantly adjusted depending on the time spent in that person's or those people's company. She would adjust constantly depending on the experience she was having at that very moment, creating feelings and sensations and resulting in her actions.

Her blending became deeper once she had a sexual experience with another. She would become more relaxed and let her defence mechanisms down, resulting in becoming vulnerable to her feelings and emotions, enabling them to trigger past feelings, bringing them raw to the surface at times. This would normally happen after the sexual encounter or as it was happening. Guilt, shame, feelings of non-worthiness, anger and frustration would form, resulting in the mind taking control once again. Sonia wouldn't deal with the issues, therefore she would suppress them into an energy form, creating an area of turmoil. She would amplify these thoughts, creating an energy and feeling that would be focussed anywhere within her body, physically causing a feeling of discomfort. Sonia's emotions were so intense that with the aid of her mind, she could manifest physical pain. These memories created feelings that she had suppressed, which became emotions that had logged within her subconscious mind. They became posted on her energetic body, harming the physical body via the energy transformation.

Over time, Sonia realised that the subconscious mind monitors past information we retrieve and digest with regards to the past experiences we have experienced from birth to the age of seven. During this time period, she had learnt to build defence mechanisms and developed patterns from her parents, minders, teachers, etc. At this early age she was not taught how to process her own feelings that she had experienced and why she felt the way she did. Unfortunately she learnt to place a barrier, a defence mechanism, so that she could function to the best of her knowledge to move forward, protecting herself. Unfortunately this defence mechanism was normally anger and frustration for her.

She discovered that we just hold memories, past feelings, emotion and pain related to a particular issue, to resurface every time we have a similar experience until we deal with it. Each time similar events occurred in Sonia's life these became more intense and this resulted in her showing physical signs. Her skin would become inflamed or she would develop characteristics such as picking at herself. She would constantly look for distractions when she didn't feel comfortable. Surrounding herself with people became an issue unless she had a glass of wine or some sort of alcoholic beverage to consume. Sonia now had the time to focus on herself.

After some time, Sonia discovered the subtle difference between being true to herself and discovering the essence of her true identity without confining her soul. She realised that tomorrow's plans can change without warning, that her future has a way of failing at any time, maybe from making the wrong decision or simply by the influence of others. Love doesn't mean becoming dependent on another but having the understanding that love comes from within. The company of another doesn't mean security. She began to process that she was born alone and that we pass to spirit alone. She began to accept her defeats with her head held high and her eyes wide open, trusting her inner intuition with an instinct of knowing; that material possessions are not promises to keep her; kisses are not contracts to contain her. She became independent to realise that she had everything that she needed every morning that she raised her head from the pillow, that she would grow with the seeds she planted and nourish her own soul, becoming the true being that she is.

Sonia began to discover her self-worth, knowing that she really is strong and she would learn and learn each day regardless of the struggles she would endeavour to overcome in this life. With every goodbye, she would learn.

She would find her true identity.

 Matador

For exclusive discounts on Matador titles,
sign up to our occasional newsletter at
troubador.co.uk/bookshop